Belinda Seaward

Belinda Seaward is British and teaches at a boys' school in Devon. She has spent time on a coffee plantation in Zambia, in the Middle East and in London, where she was a news journalist on the *Daily Mail* and the *Sunday Times*. Belinda has also raised two young Arab horses. *Hotel Juliet* is her second novel.

Praise for *Hotel Juliet:*

'Africa and aviation, red dust and wide, white skies . . . this romance will soon dispel the blues . . . A thrillingly observant writer and crafter of highly sensual prose, Seaward employs the language and lore of the skies to considerable metaphorical effect . . . its richly descriptive escapism is seductive' *Daily Mail*

'*Hotel Juliet* is a breathtaking work and a deeply moving elegy to the transitory nature of family life' *Scotland on Sunday*

'A gripping evocation of love and passion amid the wild African landscape' *Sainsbury's Magazine*

'This poignant epic is a real page-turner . . . a mesmerising, well-crafted novel' *Birmingham Evening Mail*

'A beautifully crafted tale of love and tragedy that traverses time and continents in the telling . . . Seaward's language is thoughtful and compelling and the story captivates from beginning to end. A wonderful love story' *Daily Mercury* (Australia)

Also by Belinda Seaward
The Avalanche

Hotel Juliet

BELINDA SEAWARD

JOHN MURRAY

First published in Great Britain in 2008 by John Murray (Publishers)
An Hachette Livre UK company

First published in paperback in 2008

3

A CIP catalogue record for this title is available from the British Library

ISBN 978-0-7195-2450-9

Typeset in Aldus by Servis Filmsetting Ltd, Manchester

Printed and bound by Clays Ltd, St Ives plc

John Murray policy is to use papers that are natural, renewable and recyclable products and made from wood grown in sustainable forests. The logging and manufacturing processes are expected to conform to the environmental regulations of the country of origin.

John Murray (Publishers)
338 Euston Road
London NW1 3BH

www.johnmurray.co.uk

Dedicated to the life of Steve Bowra, with love

1

IF YOU ARE LOST

If you are really lost and have no idea of your position, this is the time to take a firm hold of yourself and make up your mind that you are not going to be in a hurry to get down, but that you are going to fly round in the hope of finding an aerodrome up to the last safe half-hour of your fuel.

Zambia, 1972

They removed his left leg in the morning. By the evening he was awake and at first felt no pain because they had given him morphine. His right arm was pierced by the line that fed blood into his vein and the first thing he saw was the transfusion pouch hanging engorged above his head like a dark ripe fruit.

A nurse came and gave him water. She was young with a long face and large liquid eyes. She wore her cap far back on her head, showing her braided hairline divided into minute sections on her bluish scalp. 'Drink,' she commanded in her soft African accent.

He couldn't speak. The rim of the cup felt thick against his lips. His throat was drier than he had ever known. The nurse watched him steadily as he tried to drink.

'More.' He took a sip and handed her the cup. She checked his pulse, holding his eyes, her expression intense as if she had lost something precious.

He slept. When he woke there was a doctor by his bed and the same nurse with the same vehement look in her eyes. The doctor, a tall man in his late thirties with a clean-shaven head and palms the colour of balsa wood, nodded briefly before turning the sheet. A bridge had been placed over the mattress to raise the bed clothing so that no material touched his raw skin. As he turned the sheet the doctor made a sucking sound through his teeth. The nurse leaned forward to look and the doctor pointed out something. Craning over the narrow expanse of his bed, they looked at his leg as if it were something of deep and sympathetic interest. Max wondered if there was any mutilation that frightened them, any agony they could not meet with their soft, dark eyes. How might they have responded if one of their own children had been lying in his place? Would they have turned away then?

His leg had been severed a few inches above the knee and was wrapped in white bandages, already soiled with blood and yellow fluid. There was a slightly sweet, sulphurous smell that reminded him of mussels slowly turning bad on hot rocks at low tide. The skin on his thigh had been shaved and felt flat and cool to touch, not like skin at all, more like cold, white paper. Below the knee, the missing part of his leg itched; even though it had been cut from him, it still itched and burned.

The nurse gently pulled the sheet back across the bridge. She smoothed down the white folds across his chest, but did not touch him. He looked at her. She had one of those kind African faces that glow with a sort of protected goodness. She must have been only twenty or so, but her features were those of someone much older and more experienced in the world. He swallowed. The nurse asked if he wanted water. He shook his head; his throat was filled with tears and he did not want to give way in front of her because he felt that if he allowed himself to break he would never be able to gather himself up in one piece again. He shifted away from her. She remained by the bed for a few moments and then walked away down the ward where some men called out to her in her own language. By the time she had reached the double doors of the ward his pillow was soaked.

He wondered what they had done with the rest of his leg. It seemed odd to him that such a large part of his own body was now somewhere he didn't know about. He would like to have had the missing limb next to him, in a box by his bed, so that he could lean over every now and then and check it. For some reason he thought of it as a child, a newborn with its umbilical cord still attached, skin puckered and bruised. The thought of it made him yearn in a way he might have yearned for any sick creature to survive.

After the shooting his leg had suffocated. Dry gangrene had developed, killing tissue, destroying muscles, tendons, ligaments, bone; all the internal engineering before turning his skin black as charred meat. The crepitation was not painful, it rendered his leg drily unconscious, sloughing the skin from his toes, turning them grey and silky. All his nails came off and sometimes he would catch his thigh on a sharp piece of himself snagged inside the folds of the sheets. He felt the decaying leg as a heavy presence; the more diseased it became the heavier it got until it seemed to be the whole weight of him. It was his entire body. It governed all his thoughts and moods, and infected his memories and dreams. It had become everything he had amounted to, and he fully expected it to kill him.

Joshua had looked after him at Marsden's old bush house where Max had dragged himself like an animal. The elderly cook, who had looked after Wing Commander Marsden in his last days when the malaria fever had pinned him to his bed, was used to sickness. He brought Max tea made from bush herbs and roots and tried to coax him to eat from the bowl of *nshima* he brought every morning. Max could only manage a few spoonfuls of the sticky yellow maize porridge before he felt full. He drank the bush tea gratefully. Even though he expected to die, he didn't want to dishonour the cook by refusing his offering.

Max waited for death, stoically bearing his injury, expecting the gangrene to travel up through the rest of his body, devouring him with its toothless jaws. He had turned into a kind of food for the disease, a hump of flesh that was being sucked dry piece by piece. He knew the state of his leg worried Joshua because when he came to clean it with a freshly boiled cloth he sometimes closed his eyes as if in denial of what he saw.

One bright afternoon the door burst open, disturbing the mosquito nets across the bed and Joshua announced that the security guard wanted to see Max. Geoff Seven was dressed in uniform. He was much thinner than when Max has last seen him and ignored questions about what had happened to him. With a tight look on his face he lifted Max from his bed and carried him out to a waiting jeep.

The guard had driven fast across the bush, jolting in and out of the holes that pocked the road like the marks of small dark explosions. Max had shuddered in the back, cold sweating inside the blanket Geoff had placed over him, the trees passing overhead in a nauseous spin. At a crossroads they stopped and the guard twisted round to check on him. When he saw the spewed mess on the blanket he got out and with a deliberate motion went over to the side of the road where he picked a handful of dry grass. He returned to the jeep, puffing slightly, and then gently used the grass to mop up the vomit from the blanket. Then, in an extraordinary gesture, he took off his uniform shirt and wiped the sourness from Max's face.

They set off again, Geoff driving more slowly this time, his eyes flickering to the back, his body tense inside an immaculate white vest, the soiled green shirt smirched into a ball on the passenger seat beside him.

It was dark by the time they reached the hospital. Max had woken to the feel of gentle hands lifting him from the jeep and on to a trolley. Geoff had stood apart, drinking a Pepsi, his eyes streaked with red. Max had put his hand out to him as he was wheeled inside and the guard had nodded. Max knew he would get back into the jeep and drive the eight hours back across the bush just as soon as he had finished his drink.

The guard would still have been driving as they removed his leg. The operation took less time than the journey, and he would not have reached the plantation by the time Max was awake. He imagined the guard would make the journey again just as soon as he had been to the police. Or perhaps not. Perhaps he would not come again. He would get to hear about it, though – how the police had come and placed Max under hospital arrest.

But by the end of the first week no one had come. A month passed and then another and gradually Max stopped waiting, although there was still a part of him that remained alert, like a dog sleeping with one ear cocked for danger. He asked to be moved closer to a window because of not being able to breathe at night, and the orderly pushed his bed across the ward. He left the window open with the fly screen pulled across.

It was a little easier near the window although he could still hear the sounds in the surgical ward, the mutterings and occasional screams of the other patients that filtered through the faded green curtains around his bed. The hospital was owned by a mine company and trucks arrived daily with new casualties, mostly young men with broken, crushed or missing limbs from mining accidents. They were pushed on to the ward on trolleys, silent after their amputations, stumps bound in clean, new bandages.

The trucks provided a rhythm for his days. From his bed he could hear them coming and going, wheels scratching across the dirt, sending up plumes of white dust that billowed into the sky like smoke. His world became a patch of sky covered by fly mesh through which he would watch clouds moving with agonizing slowness. There were never two moments when the sky was the same. It endlessly shifted, the clouds forming new lakes and valleys every hour. He saw jets and small planes and once a dark powerful mass of eagle, feathered wing tips like ragged black gloves streaming against the blue bowl of sky. Sometimes when he woke there would be such a strange pure light around the rim of the clouds that he almost could not bear to look.

As he lay inert, his mind turned over his time of flight. He recalled the journeys he'd taken to Landless Corner, following the line of the Great North Road, which wound like a dry red river through the flat open country, then over to the Lukanga Swamp before turning back across the plantation fields where his coffee pickers worked, bent in the middle, like people broken in half. He remembered ground lessons with the wing commander, the flying manual he read nightly when the old man was dying, the effects of rudder, airspeed, gliding approaches, sideslipping across wind, climbing, gliding and stalling. His first solo. Lying in his hospital bed, he relived every lesson in detail, recounting entire pages of the manual by heart, its homely phrases ringing clear in his mind as if someone were speaking them aloud to him. Sometimes he felt that the flying manual was the only thing holding him together. It stopped him from falling.

The wound around his stump became infected and Max saw more of the doctor who spoke quietly around him as if he were a sick horse. The doctor's fingers were cool as he searched his arm for veins, his forehead smooth, untroubled by the process of dealing with disease that seemed to Max to be the worst kind of attack on humanity, so muted were the patients, so profoundly bound up in themselves. The infection made his blood race, his body swim with sweat. At night he woke trapped in a sticky lake of his own making, a great pounding in his ears that sounded like drums, but was actually his own heartbeat. The nurse bathed his forehead with cloths soaked in iced water. The pouch of blood was exchanged for a clear bag of saline solution and clean white sheets were pulled on to his bed. He was watched at night. At some point he became delirious and begged the nurse to cut the saline bag down because he believed it to be poisoned by soul thieves. The nurse sat solemnly by his bed, a bag of knitting in her lap, eyes the colour of infinity. She lifted his hands and put them on his chest whenever he tried to snatch the IV line.

He spent days drifting in and out of consciousness, the limb aflame under the sheet, tormenting him with its absence. He could feel the impact of the bullet, the actual moment when his hamstrings tightened, his ligaments popped, his bone ruptured.

His missing knee ached and when he moved it pieces of grit grated together under his skin. He was so convinced that his leg was still attached that many times during the night he would drag down the sheet to look, thinking perhaps that there had been a mistake, that they had taken someone else's leg instead. The bandages and oozing stump seemed incomprehensible, a trick of some kind. He did not understand how he could feel pain in something that no longer existed. How could he flex toes that were no longer there, or turn his ankle, or bend his knee? Maybe he was suffering from some kind of mental disorder that made him see things as missing when they were present. Or maybe he was under some kind of black magic curse. He didn't want to believe this, but he could not rule it out. The doctor said his experience was normal. He explained that the limb was a kind of phantom, which in time would disappear.

Gradually the infection subsided and he was able to look at the sky again. He felt weak and not quite inside himself and he had lost a great deal of weight. His arm felt hollow as if his muscles and tendons had melted, leaving only the remains of dry bone. Further down, his hip bones protruded into sharp points that snagged against his exploring hand. He didn't dare go any lower. The nurse fed him *nshima*, but he was unable to keep anything down for long and regurgitated a thin yellow stream from the side of his mouth. She wiped his chin and persisted.

One morning he woke to a full white sky. Standing by his bed was a woman in a pale apricot dress and he was momentarily confused, thinking that he had somehow summoned her from his memory, creating her phantom presence. He sat up and the woman moved a few paces closer. She had drawn her hair back and was carefully made up as if for a dinner party with two pearl drops swinging lightly from her ears. She looked for somewhere to sit down, but there was no chair near his bed and so she stood awkwardly, her eyes staring at the tented expanse of sheet drawn over his body.

It was a moment before either could speak.

'Max,' she said carefully and lowered her eyes. She brought her thumbnail up to her mouth and twisted it against her teeth. Her hands were rough and seemed older than her face. He had forgotten how young she was. She was really no more than a girl. She let out a long breath and pulled at her lower lip and then in a sudden impatient movement pulled her hands down and clenched them in front of her.

'What are you doing here, Elise?' The words came out harsher than he intended.

She flinched. 'I needed to see if you were . . .' She pulled her eyes down, unable to complete what she meant to say.

He looked at her and then turned away. Through the window the sky rolled and tumbled heavily, the white clouds seeming to strain against a powerful force that was trying to break them open.

She took a step closer, but stopped just short of the bed. 'I'm so sorry, Max,' she said gently, her eyes aghast. 'I came before, a few weeks ago, but they wouldn't let me see you.'

He closed his eyes. He felt tired and he did not know how to talk to her.

'I won't stay long,' she said. 'They told me not to tire you.' He could hear her breathing, the slight wheeze he remembered. 'I just wanted you to know that we've made all the arrangements.'

He thought she meant prison, but she continued: 'The police have dropped the charges.'

'It was my gun.'

'Look at me, Max.'

He kept his eyes closed, his head turned. He knew it would be far worse if he faced her. 'I know what happened.'

'But you mustn't speak about it.' Her voice wavered. 'Tambo admitted shooting a white man; there's nothing for you to worry about. You are free.'

He continued to stare at the sky. He understood that she needed some version of events that she could believe in, some story that she could live with.

'Look at me,' she said again. 'Why won't you look at me?'

He summoned his strength. 'You must tell them the truth.'

He heard her gasp. 'I can't. Max, they nearly killed you. They could come back, even here.'

'It doesn't matter,' he said. 'It makes no difference what happens to me now.'

She moved closer and reached out and touched his shoulder. He flinched. 'I'm sorry,' she said and pulled her hand away. He remained where he was, facing her with his back, the touch of her skin burning into his mind.

'I also came to tell you that the little girl is with me. I went looking for her after . . .' She swallowed and he listened to her breathing snag. 'Her name is Memory. She's been living with me in the house, and it's helping . . . we're helping each other really. My father has come over. He's made the arrangements. We want to take her home with us; we're waiting for the rec-ommendation from the welfare officer. It will be a new start for all of us, Max.'

He heard wrenching hope in her words. She continued, her voice barely faltering even though she had now begun to cry. 'You'll recover. I *know* you will. You're a survivor. Nothing can beat you, Max, I've always felt that. You're indestructible. The strongest person I know.'

He thought she would leave then, but she stood quietly by the bed, no longer crying. 'I love you,' she said and he heard defiance in her voice. He envied her courage. She was the one who would survive. She was young enough to forget. He heard her inhale sharply. 'I'm so sorry this has happened to you,' she said in a whisper. He knew she would leave soon. He hadn't told her. He would never tell her. He couldn't express how much he felt for her because now it was impossible. She was the horizon of his life, the point he would always look towards. He waited for the longest possible moment before turning to look at her.

Her hair had loosened in the humidity and the make-up around her eyes had smudged, but the impression he had was that

9

she was now freshened. She wiped her nose with a tissue and swept back a few strands of hair that had fallen forward on to her cheeks. She looked at him with shining eyes. Max felt his throat constrict. He tried to speak but all the words he considered in his mind sounded inadequate for an experience he held infinitely in his soul. He reached for her hand.

She cried again. He felt her hot tears on his wrist. 'It wasn't wrong,' she said, looking at their hands held together on the white sheet. 'It can't ever be wrong to love another person. That wasn't why it happened.'

He let his eyes rest in hers for the last time.

After she'd gone he lay without moving in the bed. The hospital was silent around him, most of the patients sleeping through the hot afternoon. The air felt thick and humid, its flat heat rebuking the emotions that had been stirred. Max closed his eyes and saw an image of Paul Cougan's open face, swivelling round on a barber's red chair, laughing.

The doctor and then the nurse appeared and both found chores to do around the wounded limb. It seemed as if a long time had passed before they pulled the green curtains around his bed and left him alone with his thoughts. The delay between Elise leaving and him lying with the lights lowered, the sounds subdued, the pain pinned with a new dose of morphine, had fooled Max into thinking he would not react. The first splutterings were reflexive and closer to the sensation of vomiting than sobbing. But then it came, an outpouring of rain, a buckling grief that flung him to depths of pain he did not know existed. It was as if all the departures of his life, all the losses, frustrations and disappointments had happened to him all at once. These two people he had loved. These two people had given themselves to him, both of them had handed themselves over, and he would have to live with the knowledge that he had let them down. He had not been careful enough. He had ignored what he knew, and now the shame he felt, the deep flooding of humiliation caused him to cry out, and he bit on the pillow to muffle the sound.

The next day they taught him how to walk. As the nurse lifted him from the bed, her arms warm across his back, he realized that he was being shown how it would be from now on. He was entering the second half of his life whether he wanted to or not: the transition from air to being on the ground.

He was wheeled in a chair to a small and dirty hot room with a bundle of sticks in the corner all leaning against one another. He wasn't asked to choose. The nurse made the decision for him: a pair of crutches with the arm rests padded with a worn strip of red towel. The nurse got him to stand. He felt eerie, suddenly giant. A floaty sensation bloomed in his head as the nurse helped him on to the crutches. 'Try, just try,' she said, even though he made no attempt to resist. He swung between the crutches and tried to adjust to his new lopsided weight. He did not know how to orient himself. What had been joined up and obvious before was now broken. The nurse put her hand on his shoulder and urged him forward. He took a halting, limping lurch on the crutches and tottered, feeling the rough pads dig under his armpits. 'Good,' the nurse said.

After his first lesson, he practised alone. Swinging on his crutches, he realized how delicate a two-legged skeleton was. To lose a limb was to lose a way of seeing. He had no idea of how he walked because he had never had to think about it until now. He had simply relied on his body to remember what to do and he had to learn to ignore what was stored there because it was useless to him. Pushing forward, leading with his chest like a butterfly swimmer, he thrashed his way through his first strokes, measuring his progress by the squares on the tiled floor. It took him ten days to reach the end of the corridor.

When he grew stronger he explored the hospital, lurching by the kitchens where staff in blue hairnets stood over huge aluminium basins. They did not look up as he went past. Now he was moving he was invisible, no longer a patient to be watched over as a matter of life or death, but someone on the fringes, in limbo. The doctor who had treated him so kindly even failed to recognize him one morning. Max understood that he was no longer part of the place, but it was unclear whether he was free to go. There seemed to be no one who made such decisions.

The skies continued monotonously white and heavy and he knew the rains would begin soon. His early morning excursions around the hospital took on a new urgency. He didn't want to be stuck on the ward during the rains. He wanted to be back on the farm, smelling the rain and dirt and feeling part of the outside again. His foreman had been to visit once and told him that the coffee was the healthiest it had ever been. With good rains this season Max would be harvesting his best crop yet. Grimly he swung his body on the rickety crutches and tried to harden his mind to thoughts of profit.

The rains broke through one morning as he lurched down the corridor. When he returned to his bed there was Geoff Seven dressed in a fawn suit, trousers hemmed with a band of red mud, his waxed shoes splattered at the sides. The guard sat quietly, hands held gently in prayer. He looked up as Max approached and bowed his head. In one hand he held a slightly crumpled caramel-coloured hat. Propped up against the bed was a pair of dark wooden crutches.

A little while later the nurse brought his things and the security guard helped him dress. The familiar clothes were bigger than Max remembered; the shorts waistband slipped down past his navel and his shirt billowed across the shoulders. Even his boot seemed to have increased in size. It slopped against his white ankle as he stood one-legged, leaning against the guard who tusked as he laced him up, as if he were telling off a child.

When Max had finished dressing, the guard took a step back and nodded his head firmly. His eyes were gently lit. He thrust out a large dark grey hand, enfolded Max's hand in his and drew it up to his chest in a warm capacious grip, more of cradle than a shake.

Max met his eyes. Immediately the guard dropped his hand and lowered his own gaze. His arms hung straight by his sides, his pose resembling that of a mournful grey heron. The expression signalled deep courtesy towards the other person. Nothing spoken could have said as much and Max knew he had been forgiven, even though he did not understand why.

The guard helped him on to the new crutches, turning away as Max made his first movements. Then he collected his hat from the bedside and placed it on his head, pinching the top to ensure it sat at the right angle. He let Max lead, walking slowly alongside him down the ward and out to the front of the hospital building where new trucks were coming in, churning up the ground which smelled of rain.

2

FORWARD FLIGHT

In their forward flight the wings attack the air at an angle (angle of incidence). The wings therefore resist forward flight; this is known as DRAG.

London, 1996

Memory makes her last call of the day to a photographer caught in traffic at Victoria. 'Can you take the photocall at Christie's tomorrow at ten?'

'So long as it's not rock star stuff.' The photographer's voice splinters. 'Hang on, let me pull over.'

Holding the phone away from her ear, she waits, glancing up at the wall-mounted television where the early evening news begins with the sound turned down low.

'Memory, I can't fucking hang about . . .'

'Sorry.' She pulls the receiver closer, still watching the TV screen where the Princess of Wales leaves the London Lighthouse. The photographer sighs. 'Forget it,' she says. 'I'll book someone else. You still OK with the premiere tonight?'

'I'm on my way to put the ladders up now.' The photographer's voice fades into the surrounding violence of traffic and then comes back like an echo. 'If I ever get out of here.'

She laughs. 'Maybe see you later?'

'I'll try.' His voice is spiky with tension.

She disconnects and draws a line through the photocall. She won't send anyone to Christie's. The Japanese magazines will have to fill their pages with something else. The press agency she works for as diary editor feeds the world with photo features. From Norway to New Zealand, Britain is misrepresented as a land of green hills and large breasts; a milky village offering silver spoons, sporting heroics, slinky girl groups, kitten rescue homes and vintage motorcycle clubs in the form of a curdling culture. She wonders sometimes what the readers of these foreign magazines must think when they visit London and find not the promised land of Burberry rain bonnets, but a dark, spewing, hot-headed place.

The red light on her desk phone flashes. 'Memory, call on line two, your mother.'

She hesitates then buzzes the operator. 'Tell her I'm on another call.'

Putting the phone down, she goes through the jobs for the next day: Planet Hollywood, Tower Bridge, Prince Edward's Theatre, all covered. That just leaves the job in Brighton: the Holiday from Humanity Club featuring Bob and Sarah who intend to gallop across the beach wearing nothing but zebra body paint. Memory reads the accompanying press release. 'We find freedom in expressing ourselves as animals.'

'Bunch of freaks,' Adam, one of the staff photographers, snorts behind her. He starts to massage her shoulders. 'Relax, you're so scrunched and tense.' His fingers find dull sore patches and prod them into points of pain.

'You're making it worse.' She squirms away from him.

He makes a face at her and drifts off to the knot of people gathered under the TV. She knows he enjoys this time of day, the half-hour wind-down when people leave their light boxes and talk to one another as human beings. At this time of day her colleagues are fresh and enthusiastic, confiding and joky as they never are during the grim hours of the morning or long headachy afternoons. She watches Adam talk to a thin young man dressed in clothes so outsized he appears to be emerging from a collapsed army tent. Most of the staff dress this way – drab, utilitarian, surprisingly fussy – but just occasionally one of the girls will come in wearing a flirty vintage coat or pair of pastel leather boots and everyone will talk about it all day.

Adam touches the tall young man on the shoulder, using his fingertips to move him slightly so that he can see the TV better. For some reason this tiny gesture enrages her. Then Adam turns and looks at her. He mouths something; she doesn't know what he's saying because she's still feeling hot with outrage. He looks over at the group under the TV and then back to her. This time the mouthed words are deafening, as if he'd shouted them across the office. 'Love yoo.' His mouth stays in the shape of the 'yoo' for a moment, a cartoon blown kiss. One or two people have picked up the semaphore, including Aidan from the library who sends Adam an affectionately mirrored 'fuck yoo' before sliding his eyes back to the TV screen. But Adam can't turn back immediately; he needs a response from her, some kind of confirming gesture. It's there: a minute, hard panic in his eyes, which won't go away until she does something. Without thinking she lifts her hand with her palm facing towards him and sees him actually flinch, as if the air had slapped him.

She thinks of last night's dinner with Adam and her mother. They'd gone to one of those incredibly expensive, highly uncomfortable places in Hampstead with metal seats that dig into the soft part of the back. Elise, who had a top job in medical research, had paid; she always did, and she'd sat next to Adam, quite close so that their elbows touched on the table. Every time she turned towards Adam she seemed deliberately to slow down her body and make her blonde hair fall slightly across her face. Memory sat opposite watching. It was routine, this play intimacy; this little excluding joke. It had started when Adam first met Elise and had discovered to his delight and fascination that she was just fifteen years older than Memory. 'Great, I get two for the price of one.' But last night the joke had fallen a little bit flat.

'You two could be sisters,' Adam had said, looking at Elise, immaculate in heavy dark trousers which swung when she walked, white linen shirt, the sleeves pushed back to show a cuff of solid silver at her wrist, linguine-thin leather sandals. Adam was also carefully dressed in white jeans with a beige smooth T-shirt and buckskin jacket. The two of them shared a passion, or, more accurately, an obsession, for grooming.

'Isn't there something you've failed to notice?' Memory had said, glancing at her bare arms. She hadn't had time to wash and still smelled of the office.

'Oh, darling.' Elise had glanced down at her menu card, the smile fading on her lips. 'Red or white?'

'White please,' from Adam.

'Memory?'

'I don't want any.'

'Oh, come on, we're celebrating. You can't not drink.' Adam had looked at her, hurt, surprised, dumping in her lap a whole bag of emotions that shaken up would mix into a sort of perplexed disappointment.

'I can.'

'How about some champagne. My treat?' from Elise.

'I really don't feel like drinking. Why is it such a big deal?'

She should have dropped it then, should have accepted the champagne, got a little drunk, pretended to laugh and enjoy herself, but something needled her on, some urge to bite through what felt like a paper mask stretched tightly over her face.

'As I said.' She'd leaned forward towards them and they both stiffened, perhaps anticipating what was coming. 'There's something Adam always forgets, some tiny little thing about me that he prefers to overlook.'

'Memory.' It was a warning in a low voice from Elise.

Adam was watching her now, a frown creasing his blue-black Irish looks, his mouth tightening.

Memory put her elbows on the table and turned her palms over so that they were looking at the back of her hands.

'Don't be childish, darling,' Elise said quickly and glanced towards the waiter. 'Could we have some service over here, please?'

The waiter came trotting over obediently. Memory covered her black face with her black hands and sighed. For a moment, she enjoyed the sensation of being truly invisible. Then she put her hands back down on the table. Adam had given her a look of real disgust then, as if she had taken off her clothes or something instead of merely showing her hands. But it was true, he didn't think of her as being black. Rarely mentioned it. It was supposed to show her how cool he was about her colour. Oh, you're *black*, I hadn't noticed; it's because I'm interested in you as a person. I love the inner you, the real you, your spirit and soul. *Love yoo!*

Adam wants them to get married. He's already asked for Elise's permission and between them they're planning it. They are 'in it' together. Memory is their pet project, their ultimate make-over; their blank canvas. They've spent hours designing her dress, making sketches on tablecloths in restaurants and wine bars all over north London. Their current favourite is coffee-coloured lace. White being too, well, obvious.

She's going along with it because she doesn't know how to stop it and also because if she does say, 'No more,' or 'I can't do this,' then she needs something to replace it with, and that's scary; that's the big one, bigger, in a strange sort of way, than getting married. Even stranger is the fact that she loves Adam. She loves him for all the things he does that annoy because it gives her something to pit herself against, something to measure herself by. Without Adam, without the tension, she feels she might dissolve into nothing. Being with him is easy as long as she doesn't resist. As long as she lets him take care of the details. He needs to do things in a certain way and she finds comfort in that. For instance when she goes to his flat she knows exactly what he will want to cook that night and how he will want things chopped, that is, extremely finely: he does these micro-surgery meals, Vietnamese and Thai. He reads the cooking columns in the Sunday newspapers and has a shelf of hardback cook books which he periodically wipes with a clean cloth. Sometimes, Memory thinks, she could *be* Adam, she knows him so well.

Quite often on her way to work on the rare mornings they don't sleep together either in his flat or hers, usually when he's out of town on a photography assignment, she slips into being him, paying for her bus ticket in the way *he* would, thinking about the passengers with *his* mind, holding on to the rail with his hand. It's something she does with other people too, although not as much as with Adam, and somehow it makes her feel *definite*. Or what she imagines it must feel like to be definite. To have a defined and clear-cut way of doing things, being *obvious* about who you are, must be a luxury, she thinks. It's not that she lacks tastes, habits or opinions of her own. She has her likes and dislikes, but she doesn't *live* by them. She would never put them on display. She couldn't say: I'm a white wine person, or I need order. Most of the time she feels provisional, as if she has taken on her current self just for a while. This is difficult to articulate, but she's always had this sense that there is somehow *more* to her than she knows.

Over at the TV the boys are bored and talk through the news, pausing only when the newsreader turns to sport. 'Mem,' Adam calls, trying to attract her attention. Adam can't bring himself to call her by her full name. He's always shortening it. She pretends not to hear him and he turns his attention back to the TV. If she marries him, she'll lose her name. She hasn't thought of this before. Of course, she could always keep the Cougan. Splice it to his Collins. Memory Cougan-Collins. It sounds wrong; that double-barrelled C is too much. She knows Adam would insist on one C, if only for the sake of aesthetics.

But she's being unfair. It's not his fault. She's twisting things. He would say that she's finding reasons to resist. It's a habit of hers apparently. He might even remind her that there had been a time when she had been embarrassed by her name, particularly during her teens when she always seemed to be adopted by slightly cruel girls called Melissa or Francesca. In the region of Africa where she was born it was not unusual to name children Gift or Precious or Happy. But her young friends were suspicious.

They didn't believe those kinds of names were real. One girl said Memory had made her name up simply to appear different. 'You think you're *so* special.'

It made her defensive and protective. One of her earliest memories is of writing her name over and over in different handwriting styles, covering exercise books, inside the desk, on the wooden frame around her bed: inside her wrist. *Memory Cougan.* However, the more she wrote her name, the less familiar it seemed. She would look at her page covered with globby fountain pen script, the big, angular M, the smudged C and wonder how she could make her name belong to her.

Later she started sketching characters: first she drew her mother and then herself, holding her mother's hand. There were not enough characters for a family and so she added a dad, whose name was Paul because that was the name of the man her mother had met at university, married, then travelled with to Africa to build a school. Memory had never met him. He died in Africa during a plane crash. She made his expression sad. She added other Cougans, imaginary brothers, sisters, aunts; a clutch of cousins around her own age. They had a tree house, she decided. And horses. There was always a dog poking between the legs of someone. In these sketches Memory made everyone white, even herself, although she used a darker pen for her hair.

The girls at school were interested to know about her black parents, or 'real' mother and father. They had died from malaria when Memory was still a baby and she'd been looked after by another family. 'What was it like in Africa?' the girls would ask, but she didn't want to speak to them about her early life. She told them Africa had been wiped almost clean from her memory.

Gathering up all the loose papers on her desk, she finds the remote control hidden under a press pack from a cosmetics company. She turns off the news and then bins the press pack in the recycle box.

'Got anything planned for tonight?' Emily sidles over and picks out a free sample of city block from the recycle box. She breaks the seal, sniffs, and lets the sample drop back into the box. A powerful soap-charged scent fills the room.

'Adam's invited a few people to the Jet Bar later. You're welcome to join us.'

Emily smiles, showing a set of pretty white teeth. This is her first job in the media and she is permanently broke. Every week she shows off something cheap from the market she is unable to resist: a velvet top embroidered with little mirrors, a cuff of trinket bracelets, ponyskin shoes. She cadges cigarettes all day from the boys downstairs in the darkroom.

'Thanks, I'd love to.'

Memory watches Emily drift over to the group and ask sweetly if someone could lend her twenty quid. The boys pat pockets and tell her to try someone who isn't skint. Eventually Aidan obliges, telling Emily she can pay him back on pay day.

Adam comes over to her desk and offers to drive her home. She tells him she wants to walk and his face falls. He watches her pull on her coat and then waits for her on the stairs.

'The car's at the back.'

'I need the exercise.'

'You don't, you're getting too thin if anything.'

'It must be the diet.'

'It makes you look ill.'

'Thanks,' she says savagely.

Adam sighs. 'You don't need to diet any more.'

'I know, I don't *need* to do anything.'

He looks at her puzzled and then suddenly kisses her hard on the mouth. People file past and wish them goodnight.

Her hands rise behind him and she finds herself gently patting him on the back.

'Don't be late,' he says, his voice thick, almost slurred.

Something within her aches as she watches his familiar form shrug down into his padded jacket and step out into the sodium-lit street.

She waits for a few moments then flags down a black cab.

'Newington Green.'

Someone has left a bunch of flame-coloured tulips wrapped in brown paper on the seat. On impulse she claims them and puts them across her lap. She watches her own reflection as the cab rolls through the clogged streets at the speed of a stately procession. The driver flashes her a weary smile in the rear-view mirror. 'How you doin'?'

'Great.' She leans her head back against the seat and closes her eyes. The tulips feel cool on her lap and give off a soft grassy smell.

Guilt grips her as she pays the twenty-pound fare. The driver looks her in the eye. She shifts her bag on her shoulder. 'Sorry, no tip.' She feels annoyed that she has to apologize. The driver rests his fingers on the outside of his liquid black door for a moment and she notices that his skin is close in colour with hers, a kind of dark violet brown. The cab inches forward and a panicky feeling blooms inside her as she lets herself into her flat.

The bedroom smells extinguished. Spooning warm cereal into her mouth, Memory stands for a while looking at the bunched hangers in her wardrobe. Most women she knows have a co-ordinated style, a way of inhabiting whatever they wear, but her clothes represent different moods and attitudes. And there is not one outfit that seems right tonight. Wrapping up in a dressing gown, she is suddenly in hot tears.

She continues to cry as she arranges the taxi tulips in a heavy square glass, one of many presents that Adam had bought for the flat, and carries them with sopping hands to the windowsill where the traffic hurls past, rattling the panes. Going into the bathroom, she washes her face in cold water and stands for a while inhaling the comfort of her towel. There's a sharp pain around her breastbone and she senses the first glimmer of a migraine.

She returns to the kitchen and gripped by a stab of hunger nibbles on a piece of bread. Feeling guilty for breaking her diet she eats only the doughy white inside and chucks the rest in the bin. The telephone begins to ring in the bedroom. Ignoring it, she pads back to the bathroom where she turns on the hot tap, sprinkles in oil from a dark bottle, and begins to fill the bath.

'I love your colour,' a snapper from a rival agency breathes in her ear. 'You could be a model.' He looks her up and down. She's in black. It was easy in the end. She just put on the same black top and skirt she wore for work, which felt kind of extravagantly careless after she'd soaked for such a long time in the bath. Different shoes, though, high-heeled mules with beads. Normally she wears flats; being nearly six feet tall she doesn't feel comfortable towering over everyone. But tonight she needs all her height.

'Put your tongue away, Fisher,' Adam says, working his way through the crush of perfumed party people to claim her. 'What the hell have you been doing? You're two hours late.'

'Getting ready.'

Adam looks her up and down, his brow furrowed. He has dressed entirely in shades of ironic vanilla. Great. She meets his eyes and he looks away for a moment. Then he steers her over to the bar. The place is supposed to suggest a private cocktail lounge onboard an exclusive jet, but there are too many loud people and mirrors for it to succeed.

'What will you have?'

'Coke.'

His jaw stiffens. '*Coke?*'

'Yes, Coke.' She wants to explain that she has a hovering migraine and wine would not be a good idea, but somehow she can't. It might begin to open something up.

'Coke,' Adam tells the barman in a flat voice.

'Ice and lemon?' the barman trots out, looking at her.

'No, thanks.'

He puts the drink down on the bar and she sips it through a straw, enjoying its childhood smell and sugar fizz on her tongue. The steel bar feels icy under her elbows and the blue, slightly strobing light freezes everyone for a moment: the girls with their jeans rolled up, tight tops and twisted hair, clipped with tiny butterflies, laughing towards the boys, who are in the same kind of clothes they wear for work only cleaner. The sound system is playing Tricky.

She sips her drink and then through the haze of light and smoke sees the bar manager coming towards them carrying a silver bucket, white napkin draped over one arm, smiling that smile that means something is about to happen.

She looks at the crowd. Everyone is talking louder than usual and loosely putting arms around one another, rubbing faces wet with shine. Fisher pops a champagne cork, and like a rally driver aims the spurting bottle towards the girls who shriek and hold up glasses to catch the foam. Fisher licks his bare arm and then starts to form everyone into a semicircle. Adam takes her hand.

'Haf conflession,' he says, leaning towards her and nuzzling her neck. He always speaks with a fake Chinese accent when he's nervous. It used to make her hysterical. Now it makes her flinch. 'I couldn't wait. I've told everyone that I asked you to marry me and you said yes.'

She stiffens into a cold shock. Adam smiles at her and then nods to the manager who steps forward from the smoke, bearing his cold silver tray. A weightless glass is pushed between her fingers and filled with champagne. Feeling its brittle rim against her lips, she has to restrain an urge to bite down. The crowd pushes in and she is smothered by congratulations.

The next morning she wakes with a sore face. She realizes she has been lying with her cheek against the digging claws of a zip fastener from a rumpled dress she chose not to wear.

She had left the bar soon after the champagne; she didn't intend to, but after slipping outside to drink in some cold air, she somehow couldn't go back in again. She decided to walk home, but she hadn't got far when Fisher pulled up and offered her a lift; he was on his way to another party, he said. Near Archway she had to ask him to stop because she was going to be sick. She got out; there was traffic all around and she was sick as she had never been sick. Some people rolled down their windows and shouted. Fisher stood at a distance asking in a low voice if there was anything he could do. When she climbed back into his car he had put a box of tissues in her lap. She told him she'd just puked her heart out and then she began to cry. He drove her home very slowly, the window wound down, music turned off, the petrochemical smell of night-time fried food prickling the air.

She sits up. There's a dull hard pain in her head as if a band has been tied around it too tight and an empty feeling in her stomach. Needing water, she leaves the bed and goes out to the kitchen. The light hurts her eyes and she pulls down the blind. There's a poster on the wall, a Klimt print Adam had given her for her birthday showing a man kissing a woman, and she's never noticed this before, but the man's hands seem to be throttling the woman.

The phone rings and she picks it up. It's Adam. 'What have I done?' he says.

A long pause. She cannot think. She toys with the cord on the blind and lets it snap up a little way so that she can see what kind of day it is outside. The sky is white and swollen as if it could soon burst.

'Why did you leave?'

She hears him catch his breath and almost blurts out that she's sorry.

'Mem . . . Memory,' he says. 'Don't do this.'

She chews at the skin inside her mouth. Her jaw feels stiff as if she has spent the night gnawing at a tough piece of meat.

'I'm coming round,' he says.

'I don't want you to.' She hears him breathe once sharply and then he breaks the connection.

She goes immediately to the front room expecting absurdly to see him there already. A bus looms past and she shrinks from the faces on the upper deck. One thing she hates about her flat is how it exposes her to the world. Her living room is on the Angel bus route and she sometimes feels as if her whole life were being offered in tiny pieces to a passing audience.

Unable to settle, she flits from room to room, opens drawers and cupboards and sniffs them. In the bottom of her wardrobe there is a square tin with dented corners. It rattles when she shakes it and smells of wood smoke and earth and rain and dried leaves. She opens it now and pulls out a tiny photo of a girl with rough hair and dark hopeful eyes. The photo is cut into the shape of a heart. Memory had worn it around her neck, sealed inside a gold locket given to her by Elise soon after they arrived from Africa. Memory had carried on wearing the locket up until last year when she had woken one morning in Adam's flat and found it detached in the bed, its fine chain twisted into knots.

She closes the tin, sealing its memories, which are to her like faint shapes that slip through clouds, sometimes picture-clear, more often blurred and out of focus, and goes back into the kitchen. She stares out of the tiny window and a thrush with speckled camouflage comes to pick at some unseen scrap on the window ledge. She watches it dipping its head; the peculiar fixed expression in its eye unnerves her slightly and she moves into the other room where she perches on the tip of the sofa facing the blank TV screen. Flicking the remote, she hears a burst of derisive laughter from a morning chat show which seeps slowly into the screen in a glare of colour. Across the bottom of the screen a caption reads: *She is angry with him for giving her presents he likes.*

The male presenter says, 'So tell us what he bought you for your anniversary.' The audience bursts into anticipatory laughter as a blonde woman, immaculately made up and dressed for a nightclub, reaches into a large carrier bag and lifts out a shimmering motorcycle helmet, holding it aloft with both hands, twisting it with a triumphant smile. The audience jeers as the camera seeks out the husband who stares at the lurid helmet as if it is his own severed head.

Adam lets himself in with her spare key. She had it cut for him early on because she was always losing hers.

'Hi,' he says tenderly. His long pale face is pinched and wary as if he has already received bad news.

She kisses him on the blade of his cheek. His hair gives off the sweetish odour of polluted streets and his fingers, momentarily brushing her neck, feel cold.

'I'm about to make some coffee,' she says, needing to lead him away from the open front room with its window of curious eyes. He looks round once as if expecting someone else to be there and then follows her to the kitchen where he leans awkwardly against the sink, allowing her room to move about. She finds a packet of real beans in the fridge. Normally they drink instant, but she needs to take her time over this because she is not sure how things are going to come out.

'Did you sleep with Fisher?' he asks as she sniffs the beans.

She pulses the grinder and screws up her face at the ugly jagged sound.

'No.' She unscrews the cap of the grinder and pours the fresh coffee granules into a glass cafetiere. She fills the kettle with filtered water and turns to reach for a saucepan to warm up milk. The look of relief on his face makes her bite her lip.

'I'm sorry,' he says. 'I should have waited for you. I just felt . . .' He lifts his hands and opens them as if offering an invisible gift. 'You were so late and I don't know, I felt it wasn't fair to keep everyone waiting. I thought that as soon as everyone knew we could start the party.'

The kettle rumbles to boiling point and clicks off. The water makes two dents in the layer of coffee, which she notices she has ground too fine.

She understands how the situation appears to him as a breach of promise. She agreed to marry him back in the summer one long weekend in Cornwall. They spent the day on an Atlantic beach with sand the texture of hard sugar, lying side by side, all the sharp points of their bodies lightly touching. She remembers that he didn't really ask her. He announced in a drowsy, easy voice that he was thinking they should tie the knot. There was a liquid quality to the day and the sea and sky seemed to shift all at once. She watched a wave rise and fall on to itself before she answered. But afterwards when the gulls burst out screeching above them she had felt afraid as if something small and flinty within her had flown and was receiving greeting in that sound.

She pushes the plunger down and it catches on the side of the cafetiere, spurting a glob of scalding coffee up through the lip and on to her hand.

'Careful,' Adam says. 'You should let me do that.'

'It's all right,' she says and watches him shrink back against the sink.

He looks down at his hands. 'You need more time, or something?'

'I suppose so,' she says. Again she has to push down the urge to apologize. He is wearing his favourite buckskin jacket, and she notices it is wet around the sleeves. His hair is damp. He must have rinsed his face in water before he came. It's a nervous habit of his.

'That's fine,' he says, his face tight. 'There's no pressure.'

She pours coffee into large white mugs, another present from him, adds steaming milk and a sprinkle of chocolate powder. They sip their drinks and look away from each other.

The timer on the cooker suddenly bursts the silence by springing into a fit of nervous ringing. Awkwardly they both move to turn it off, scrabbling fingers against small switches tacky with burned-on grease. The ringing stops but the subsequent silence is charged. Nervous hysterical laughter swells inside her.

Adam puts his coffee mug down sharply. 'You don't mean this,' he says, his eyes accusing.

She feels a prickling at the back of her eyes and at the same time a stab of anger. 'I'm not sure I can explain how I feel, but you shouldn't take it personally.'

'I don't see how else I can take it. You're giving me the push.' His face has a stubborn closed look.

Hearing him voice it sends a bolt through her. If she is breaking things off with him, she needs him on her side. She needs him to see that she is doing this because she has no choice. She's not being deliberately hurtful. She's not withholding herself, something he's always accused her of; she's actually taking a step in the direction towards herself. Absurdly she wants to get close to him now. 'Adam, there's something I need to do, but I don't know what it is yet.'

He looks at her bleakly. 'Why now? I thought we were . . .' Again he opens his hands. 'I just don't know what to say, Memory.'

'I know. I'm sorry.'

'Why haven't you brought this up before? We've been together for five years and nothing like this has happened. I don't understand, why now?'

She shakes her head. She could be honest. She could tell him that he has been directing the flow of her life for too long and now she feels that she wants to try it for herself. She could tell him that she feels on the cusp of something extraordinary, something life-changing, but she can't because at the moment there is nothing to grasp hold of, nothing she can point to. It's just a feeling.

'I just don't understand how you can throw us away,' Adam says.

'I'm not throwing *us* away. I don't expect you to get this, but I need to go back.'

'*Go back?*' He frowns. 'What are you talking about?'

'I need to go back to the beginning. I need to work it all out. I've got to have the whole story.' She feels trembly and leans back against the cooker for support.

Adam looks at her in silence for a long moment. 'You know what I think? I think you're being very selfish. You're just looking for excuses, that's all; why don't you just come out with it and admit you're shit scared?'

His words slap her. She feels on the edge of something huge, the tip of a wave. She looks at him. 'Adam, I *am* scared. I'm terribly scared.'

He turns his head and brushes his eyes with the back of his hand. 'Mem, please . . .'

'No, listen, you have to listen. It's not you. I'm not rejecting you. It's just that I haven't yet reached who I'm supposed to be.'

'That's obvious,' he says. 'You're floundering. You haven't got a clue, that's always been your trouble. You have no idea how to do things properly. You just go from one thing to another, nothing structured or thought out. You have no loyalty to anything and that's why you always mess things up.'

'That's not fair.' She feels her anger rise.

'Two hours I waited for you last night. *Two hours!* Is that *fair*?' he shouts, setting glasses on the drainer ringing. 'Have you any idea how ridiculous I felt, thinking you weren't going to turn up? Thinking you were just going to leave it like that? After I'd told everyone!'

'It wasn't deliberate.'

'Oh, please!' He is up close to her now, looking into her face. She thinks he may be about to hit her. 'Have you told Elise about this?' he asks, his face tight and white.

'This has nothing to do with her.' She can't help it, she's sobbing now. She hadn't expected such bitterness.

'She knows what you're like,' Adam almost spits at her. 'She warned me that you'd be hard work.'

'Just go.' Her face feels hot and heavy with tears.

'All right, if that's what you want.' Adam gives a sound halfway between a gasp and a sob and then slams the mug into the sink, breaking off the thick handle. He turns on her with glittering eyes.

She holds her breath, wondering what is coming next. The situation seems to be spinning out of control and she can't shake off the feeling that she is breaking some kind of taboo.

'I hope you find whatever it is you're looking for,' he says. He picks the mug out of the sink and carefully wraps it in kitchen roll. 'What a waste.' At the door he pauses and gives her a long searching look, and then, realizing that he still holds the bandaged mug, efficiently drops it into the steel waste bin.

London people come from everywhere. The man in the newsagent's is from Zanzibar. He keeps Dime Bars in the freezer for her, asks what her special drink is, whether there is anything he might order for her. Special cigarettes or snacks? Anything you want, you tell me. Memory knows he talks to her because he thinks she has time on her hands. One of her habits is to spend ages looking at the magazines, which sometimes she consumes during guilty evenings, lured by promises of a fresh start, a new way of life. Healthier, happier, in harmony. Today the magazines disgust her and she leaves without buying anything. The man behind the counter glances up from his newspaper spread open on a double page of classified soulmates. 'Nothing for you?'

The street outside smells old and sour. She jumps back from a bus, startled by its warning horn, like a ship lost in fog. She passes fruit and vegetable stores offering trays of oranges wrapped in silvery tissue paper and boxes of yams cut open to reveal the white heart like freshly sawn timber. She walks in the direction of Highbury. Here, the houses have a cloistered look, the entrances guarded by clipped bushes and trees in tubs. She imagines lives of quiet order, drawing rooms and thick oriental rugs. Couples speaking quietly to one another. She remembers a house she used to visit as a child where there was a painting in the hall showing four people standing around a table: two women in plain white dresses with ribbons under their bosom, hair curled into stiff ringlets, and two rotund men in dark tailcoats. Each of the characters had been given an unnatural pink flush, which made them appear as if they had been painted not from life but from a collection of china figurines. But the most striking aspect of the painting was a three-legged table, which provided a focal point for the group. It had been painted with care and its wood glowed like a live thing. More remarkable was that the very same table stood delicately under the painting. It could be touched. It could even be picked up and moved, although she never dared to put a finger on it. She spent a long time looking back and forth at the table and the painting and it seemed to her like some kind of optical illusion. An intriguing little situation so delightful it was like a burst of music each time she visited the house.

When she told Adam about the painting he immediately said that it was like hanging a photograph of a table over an actual table, but she didn't think it was the same at all. At the time she kept quiet, but later, she remembers, they argued.

In trashy magazines love doesn't end, it *withers*, suggesting that love naturally decays or fades slowly away. But what of love that grows stronger with resistance? Adam's love had been indestructible, like ivy, needing only the slightest nourishment to grow wild. She'd had to hack it from her, but now it's gone she feels a space like a hunger, a craving for something she cannot name.

A bus comes towards her and seeing that it's heading towards Victoria she steps aboard. She sits upstairs on a seat sticky with drink and watches the grey-fronted houses with clouded windows fold in on themselves. The sky is the colour of milk.

At the office Memory receives a nod from a receptionist who wears a dark blue uniform. The receptionist tells her to wait. Mrs Cougan will be down soon. She settles on a cream leather sofa piled with cushions made from African cloth. A small gallery of photographs features dusty villages and half-naked African children with a grey pallor as if they had been rolling in cement dust. The photographs are uplit by needles of white light. A low wooden table displays literature about disease control in the Third World. She's about to pick up a magazine when she hears the lift skim down and come to a whispering halt.

Elise steps out into the foyer, her heels ringing across the floor intimate as a heartbeat. At the sound Memory stands up. 'I was in your area.' She feels suddenly exposed, like a child refusing to go into school.

Elise inclines her head. 'You *have* lost a lot of weight.'

Memory can't tell whether this is admiration or criticism. 'Have I?'

'Yes, I've never seen you so skinny. Come on, let's go across the road and pick up a couple of sandwiches.'

After the intensely lit foyer, the street outside appears dull. They cut across the pent-up traffic, each looking out for the other, lifting their arms, but not touching, just guiding the air.

'Now!' Elise says as a gap appears.

Memory's stomach dips as they reach the glistening sandwich bar. The racks of chilled rolls, cabinet of candy-coloured drinks and wire baskets piled with polished fruit for some reason fill her with dread.

Elise chooses swiftly: smoked salmon on brown bread, no cream cheese, a plastic cup of freshly squeezed orange juice, a small bottle of mineral water. Memory stands before a rack of tortilla wraps aware that Elise is waiting at the till, a ten-pound note held in mid-air, her expression simultaneously apologetic and urgent. Memory feels a swell of people behind her and at the same time hears Elise make a joke about her daughter suffering from option paralysis. Memory imagines the young man's inward response. Your *daughter*, but she's black . . .

She selects a bacon and avocado wrap with pesto, a combination that sounds curdling, and carries the little frozen bag to the till, releasing with relief the suspended ten-pound note.

'You don't have to pay.'

Elise gives a small, exasperated sigh. 'My treat, we rarely meet for lunch.'

'This is hardly meeting for lunch.' Memory is surprised at the edge in her own voice.

'I know, sorry. We'll make proper time. Towards the end of next week?'

They both know it won't happen. People break engagements all the time. In Memory's office it's called *blowing people out*. In Elise's they probably still speak of *crying off*. It's not because people don't want to meet. Often it's simply too complicated to arrange, and so people stay at their desks or go straight home. If they do go out, it's usually to one familiar place. It's *less hassle* that way. Everyone understands, but sometimes it seems to Memory as if there is an unspoken war going on that imposes a curfew.

Carrying their lunch in two separate brown carrier bags, they cross the street. The traffic fumes make Memory's eyes stream. Back inside the foyer Elise tries to ignore the receptionist who has put her feet up on a swivel chair to eat her lunch from an identical brown paper bag. They ride up to the fourteenth floor in silence, the heat in the lift drawing a smell of cold eggs from their lunch bags.

Stepping into Elise's office, Memory decides to make an excuse to leave as quickly as possible.

Their lunch bags face each other across the desk. Elise dips into hers with a sigh and takes out the orange juice. She pours some into a water glass on the desk.

'I'm sorry, you don't have a drink.'

'It's all right. I'm fine.'

'Here, have some of mine.' Elise pushes the orange juice glass towards her.

'I don't want it, really.' Memory pushes the glass back towards her mother.

Elise drinks from the water bottle and avoids her eyes. The glass of orange juice sits on the desk between them. Neither touches it. Elise sighs and stretches her feet under the desk and loosens her shoes, releasing a slightly sour butter smell. 'It *is* good to see you,' she says.

Memory unsheathes the wrap. The bread has sweated to room temperature and its lumpen weight makes her think unaccountably of Adam's penis. She puts it down on a paper napkin on the desk.

'Wrong choice?' Elise's eyebrows draw together enquiringly.

Memory puts the wrap back in the bag. 'I'll eat it later.' She half rises from her seat. 'Actually, I've got to get back. I really only popped in for a second.'

Elise's grey eyes become still for a moment. 'You seem a little strained. Is everything all right between you and Adam?'

Memory stalls, wondering what she should say, *whether* she should say. She notices Elise's hands: French-polished nails, the thin gold wedding ring. She wonders why she still wears it.

'Fine, we're really . . . great.'

Elise bites serenely into her second sandwich. 'Adam is such a considerate young man and he so admires you.'

If you could have seen him a couple of days ago you wouldn't have thought so.

'I'm very lucky,' Memory says automatically.

Elise finishes her sandwich and dabs at her mouth with a paper napkin. 'I know you've had your ups and downs,' she says, glancing at a lipstick stain smudged on the greasy tissue. 'But I feel he's a good choice for you. You need someone stable and dependable.'

Memory sits up abruptly. Through the window a cloud in the shape of a ripped star drifts across the sky.

Ups and downs, that's a bit of an understatement. If only you knew. One day I'd really like to tell you the truth about Adam and me.

'Meaning that I'm a mess, I suppose?'

Why do I always have to snap at her?

'Oh, darling, why do you have to take everything the wrong way? I just think he's a smart bet, that's all.' Suddenly she reaches towards the orange juice glass and takes a sip. 'I also want you to know that I'll help you in any way I can. I know it will be difficult for you both to raise the deposit for a house in London. Consider it a wedding present.'

Oh, my God, what now?

'Thank you.'

Elise gathers their lunch wrappers and presses them into one of the brown bags, cracking the plastic inside.

'You know, it's been really good to talk with you. I feel we don't and it's mostly my fault. I'm sorry.' Elise wipes her hands on a napkin and briefly smooths her gleaming hair.

I need to tell you something.

They both stand up at the same time.

'Do you mind seeing yourself down?' Elise says, wrinkling her forehead, eyes roaming her desk where a report awaits her attention.

Memory picks up her black shoulder bag and shrugs out of the office. At the door she glances back, expecting to see Elise already at work, but she is standing up with her back turned, staring out of the window.

Say something to me now. I haven't left. I'm waiting. I want to tell you something.

At Victoria Station Memory pushes through the crowds. The need to find somewhere to dispose of her lunch bag has taken hold, and she feels the beginnings of a throbbing rage at the lack of bins. She pushes against the flow and people knock into her, muttering curses. Eventually she drops the bag on the floor and watches it become carried downstream by the human tide.

She wanders over to a coffee shop and sits for a moment on a stainless-steel chair. She feels light and empty partly because she hasn't eaten properly for days, but there's something else, a sense that something vital is missing, and then she realizes what it is. Her shoulder bag has been taken.

Keeping her eyes down, she walks all round the edges of the station hall, hoping that she might find the bag washed up in some dirty corner. A young man sitting with a brown dog on a paper sack lifts pleading eyes to her.

'I've just lost everything,' she tells him.

A pair of police officers, a head taller than everyone else, cut across the station. The crowd gives way to them, and they pass through chatting easily, their soft faces animated but wary, like a pair of teenage brothers on their first weekend away from home.

When Memory tells the officers about the bag they glance at each other, an expression of minute sympathy passing across their faces, as if she were a child holding up a thumb pricked by a pin.

'Did you see who took it?' the first officer asks, naturally taking on the incident while his colleague stands a little apart, raking the crowd with his eyes, a tiny pulse twitching in his jaw.

'No.' She feels as if she has failed some small test.

'What did it look like?'

'It's black, about this size.' She shows them with her hands, sensing already the futility of the situation. The officers shrug. A lost black bag is ridiculous.

'What was inside?'

'Purse, travelcard, cash card, address book, house keys, driving licence. Everything.'

The second officer winces slightly.

'Much cash?'

'No, about ten pounds.'

'We'll have a look around. You'd better get to the bank and cancel everything. We'll let you know if it turns up. Sometimes miracles happen.'

He takes from his pocket a small black notebook with an elastic band across the cover.

'I need your name and address.'

For some reason she feels scared.

'My first name is Memory.' She pauses, expecting some comment, but the officer merely writes it down.

'Surname?'

'Cougan, that's C-O,' but the officer doesn't need her help.

She gives him her address and telephone number and he says that she will need to go to a police station near her home and fill out an incident report form. He writes down a number on a piece of paper and gives it to her.

'This is your crime reference number. Can you read it to me?'

'3762 PTY?'

'Don't lose it.'

She folds it up and puts it in her pocket.

After cancelling her cards at the bank she walks towards Holborn in the rain. The network of streets in this part of London lies just beneath her skin. She would know these streets if she were blindfold; the rhythms and smells, the sounds bouncing off buildings. A burst of freshness and Jockey's Fields opens up to her left. She pushes opens the cold iron gate and sits for a while on a bench under a great splashing plane tree, twisting the paper with her crime reference number between her wet fingers.

She walks home, wishing she'd had the courage to tell Elise the truth. Why couldn't she have told her quietly and simply that she and Adam had split up? It would have been a completely sane and normal thing to do, but it now felt revolutionary, especially after her offer. She wonders why Elise had said Adam *admired* her. She hadn't really done anything to be admired for. She shouldn't have left the office so abruptly – if she'd stayed her bag might not have been taken – and she might have been able to see a little more clearly why it is that every time she visits Elise she comes away feeling subdued and ungrateful.

On her last birthday, her twenty-ninth, Elise sent money on her behalf to Médecins Sans Frontières. Adam gave her a pair of tiny diamond earrings and took her out to the Jet Bar. The staff at work clubbed together to buy her a set of Companion Saucepans, which was Adam's idea. Emily manned the phones while they went to Al's for lunch, and as they came back late, a little bit pissed, someone said, 'Whose turn is it next?' Memory had laughed, of course, but the comment had stayed with her. She'd had a sudden glimpse of the future: an airless round of birthdays, parties, engagements and marriages – a sort of exhausted festivity – and it had made her feel guilty to want more, or maybe she wanted less than other people. Perhaps that was why Adam had been so disappointed in her.

Some nights alone in her flat, a certain mood would come over her and she would find herself going to the memory box.

Sometimes it would be enough just to see the tin and she would shove it back under the tangled shoes and belts and not think about it for weeks. Other times she would tip out all the contents on her bed and look at the documents. Along with her passports, British and African, the box contained her adoption papers and her first school exercise book with her African name, Memory Edna Yamba, pencilled inside the red cover. There was another name inside the book, written in a thin, sloping hand. Whenever she saw this name it would in a strange way make her feel better. There was also an airline ticket in the box, unused and now expired. She'd bought it on her credit card in those first heady weeks of meeting Adam during which she felt her world expand. In a burst of courage she had booked a return flight to Lusaka. But when she told Adam she was going to Africa, just for two weeks, his face had hardened. She'd felt her courage deflate, her plans stall.

She reaches her flat and asks her neighbour for the spare key. Once inside she goes straight to the memory box. Her British passport feels warm inside her coat pocket as she holds on to it all the way back on the bus to Holborn.

At the bank the young male assistant recognizes her. 'Did you find your bag?'

'No.'

'Bad luck.'

'I want to take out all the money in my current account. My salary has been paid in today, and I would like it in twenties and fifties please.'

The assistant swivels to the screen. 'You don't know your account number, right?'

'Right, the only number I have is a crime reference number and that got shredded in the rain.'

The assistant laughs. 'You *are* having a bad day. OK then, give me some other ID.'

She slides her passport under the glass.

'Memory,' he says. 'That's cool.'

He taps in her details. She leans her stomach against the bank's brass rail. Why, she wonders, does brass smell so sour? A man behind her coughs and she hears the clatter of wings from pigeons outside and the gentle backfiring of taxis. She feels suddenly tired. She could fall asleep with her arms on this old brass rail. She could stay here in the warmth of the bank with its quiet screens and tall windows and not decide. The assistant says her name again softly and then it is done and she is back out on the damp street with her pouch of money and her passport and her intentions and her fear that if she doesn't take this chance soon, she never will.

3

MARINER OF THE SKY

The more work you do on the ground, the easier it will be in the
air. Unless you are an experienced pilot, you must not contemplate
going up through the cloud, even if you do fancy yourself at blind
flying.

Zambia, 1996

Max cuts across a field of stubbled maize. He swings urgently,
propelling his body with his bunched shoulders. There's
something about the way he's ploughing forward taking deep
lungfuls of breath that suggests a rower nearing the end of a race.
The points of his crutches keep slipping and skidding on clods of
dry earth, spraying dust behind him in a fine pink wake.

He reaches the middle of the field where a movement from the
opposite side makes him start and lose momentum for a second.
Then a woman bearing a child in a sling of red cloth with a yellow
butterfly design comes swaying across the field. She veers off
course when she notices him and quickens her stride to reach the
perimeter where she leaps a ditch with a light, dazzling movement. Her child's hands reach out automatically and cling to her
neck, dark bobbled head swivelling round to stare at the white
man. Max watches them go, resting on his crutches, underarms
dark with sweat, hands loose by his sides. When they have
disappeared he continues on his way, less violently now, as if
he'd just spent some kind of passion or talked himself out of
an instinct.

He has dressed differently this morning. Clean khaki shorts and a pale blue cotton shirt, the sleeves rolled up, showing skin burned all over in big camouflage patches. In its natural state the skin would be white with a layer of ginger freckles, but years of sun-blasting have altered its texture so that it now appears tender and raw. On his face, especially around the jaw line, there are white patches where the pigment has faded giving him a slightly ill and exhausted look. Burned coral lips. Small nose, a fine curve around the eyes which are habitually narrowed against the sun, sometimes revealing tiny chips of the most startling blue, like a thin slice of Atlantic Ocean glimpsed on a bright winter morning.

Viewed from the waist up he appears strong, a man who has spent years outdoors and has forgotten all ways of living except the physical. His chest is deeply muscled and matted with thick grey hair, which moves in shadow inside his shirt, rising and falling in time to his breathing.

By contrast his lower body is cruel. Impoverished hips taper into one thin womanish leg ending in a slight foot currently clad in a dusty desert boot. There is no foot on the left side merely a gap between ground and knee. The stump, round as a thumb, has the soft scaly texture of rose quartz.

From a distance his asymmetry is arresting; a work of sculpture interrupted by war, or disease. But up close his expression is intensely human, his emotions unsettlingly present. Flies skim his arms, briefly suckling the moisture from his skin, and buzz his eyelids. Flicking his head, he looks across the field at the horizon shimmering with oncoming heat and tries to calm a growing sense of apprehension.

In an hour or two a Boeing jet will be landing at Lusaka and what started a few weeks ago with a letter and then a short phone call to London will properly begin. Max cannot see beyond arrival. To go further, even to try to imagine what might happen, seems outrageous. At least, he thinks, the conditions are good for flying: the sky clear, not too hot. *Memory*. He's glad that she's kept her African name. She didn't sound African, though, during the phone call. Completely English, and it threw him. He hadn't expected her to sound so *familiar*. Memory. The last time he saw her was more than twenty years ago. A tall girl with defiant eyes. She'd be nearly thirty now. Pushing down hard on his crutches, Max heaves himself forward again. In the distance across a red gritty area a tattered landing sock lifts and fills with air.

Reaching the airstrip, he goes slowly down its length, checking the surface for any obvious obstacles, branches or rubble, new ruts or potholes. The runway is no more than a wide red patch of earth scraped from the bush. Flying is difficult without knowing the terrain. From the air the waves of bush are black-green, the vegetation tightly packed, layer upon layer of it, like seaweed laid down on rock. A plane could easily drown in these trees. Not that many aircraft pass over. Out here if a plane goes over, most people know who's up in the cockpit. The community of farmers, crop-sprayers, school teachers, flying doctors and missionaries is spread across a large area, neighbours living a half-hour's drive from each other, but no one comes in or out unnoticed.

Max reaches the end of the strip. From a tangle of acacia trees a pair of pink and grey doves takes off, snapping muscular wings. The sky still holds the pale softness of dawn, the top branches of the trees misted with peach-coloured light. Leaning on his crutches, Max heads towards a concrete stand where a small blue and white aeroplane rests lightly on her wheels.

A group of African women, who have come to the strip to take advantage of the free water supply, glance up as he makes his way towards them, wet ropes of coloured cloth held still for a moment, eyes meeting eyes as an amused murmur passes among them. One of the older women points to his stump and laughs. The others mimic her, raucously, patting their own brittle black pegs. Max briefly nods his head. He is used to the mockery and even welcomes it. The Africans consider him more of an equal now that he is so obviously disadvantaged. The women watch him pass and then spread their cloths out to dry in the sun, dipping their broad backs as they slip into a dawdling song. Mist fizzes from the sky.

43

Mazungu, he hears in their music. *White Man.* The word used to follow him around when he first came and he hated it. He remembers being chased one morning by a horde of children as he made his way through a market. *Mazungu! Mazungu!* As if he were the answer to a question. *Mazungu!* Now the word, which also means stranger or friend or tell me who you are, is no more bother than the wind.

Max reaches the plane and runs his hands over her flank. Her blue and white fuselage has a faded deckchair glamour, dusty and blistered in places, although the letters of her name still stand out in strident white across one side of her belly. 9J-RHJ. *Nine Juliet Romeo Hotel Juliet.* She'd had a lively history, flying through a number of ownerships, including a Polish priest, a farmer or two and an emerald mine syndicate. Each pilot had left something of themselves behind, a certain kind of attitude or presence that had been absorbed into her fabric. When Max first started to fly solo, the knowledge that others more experienced than he had inhabited the tiny cockpit space and had navigated the plane through storms and bush fire was reassuring to him. Especially during those times when he had become lost and not known which way to turn, usually during one of the solitary night flights to Broken Hill he took back then. He would let the plane drift and find her own way through the mass of cloud, guiding her by instinct rather than instrument and was always amazed when he came through safely.

Juliet was not built for distance. She was really only a pleasure craft, intended for weekend circuiting. Her features included chrome ashtrays and a neat walnut fold-away drinks table. At one time she would have been quite smart, but all her trimmings were faded now, bleached by sun; her seat covers torn, her instruments sticky. When she took off with a heavy load it was like a Christmas goose attempting lift-off. She should have been grounded years ago and would have failed any safety test but her engine was sweet and sound and she still had class. 'That plane has spirit. Whatever happens, she won't let you down,'

Max remembers Marsden saying one night towards the end, when the old boy's own spirit was preparing for final departure. 'Keep her going for me. I'd like to think of *Juliet* still flying when I'm gone.' Max wishes Marsden were still here. He would be able to advise him on how to handle Memory. He would know what to do.

Max checks the wings and flaps and gives the black propeller a twist. He stands back, one hand shading his eyes against the sun. He has always loved the early mornings in Africa. The sense of a clean start. Some days standing on his veranda with his first cup of coffee, watching the morning star, he feels close to understanding what it means to be given another chance.

The plane feels warm under his hands, almost like skin. He moves round to check the tail and a memory slews into his mind. A dirt runway at night with a Land-Rover parked at one end, lights on full beam. Coming in low, clipping the acacia, a *chandelle* for the sheer hell of it, then another reckless circuit, freed for one delirious moment from all that had shaped him and held him in place up until then, all caution and quietness dissolved, the sense that he was breaking through his own membrane, almost as if he were being pulled out of himself, or what he thought of himself and into someone new. Someone more real. Someone more himself. It lasted seconds and then he was pulling back, steadying, coming down, drifting soft as a cinder into the yellow home-coming light, and breathing as if it were his last breath the warm scent from the co-pilot's seat beside him. Then landing. Then sitting quietly for a while listening to the jewellery chink of the plane cooling down. Then hearing her catch her breath, and say, 'Well, that's it . . .' Unclenching his fists, swallowing what felt like his choking heart. Then climbing out of the cockpit and into the sudden shivering brilliance of the stars. Letting go of her hand at the very last possible moment. Stepping on to solid ground with both feet, feeling the grit scrape his soles. Then Paul Cougan coming across, his eyes steady in torchlight, taking *Juliet* from him easy as unfurling a rope. Sliding her into the galvanized metal hangar with a backward glance at his wife standing on the runway, her arms folded against the cold.

'Hey!' The shout breaks into his thoughts. Max turns and looks down the runway where a figure is running towards him waving both arms over his head.

'You're late,' Max says as the pilot, a young man called Kennedy Kaluwana, comes to a skidding halt and swings his arm into a stiff salute.

'Sorry, boss.' The young man breaks into a cracking laugh. 'I was sleeping.'

Frowning, Max reaches into the pocket of his shorts and pulls out a thick wad of brown kwacha notes. He feels uncomfortable counting the money out. *Kwacha* means freedom but the currency has become so devalued as to be virtually worthless and bundles of the filthy stuff are required for a trip into town. Max was never rich in his own country; here he is a millionaire several times over. He gives up counting and pushes the entire wad at Kennedy.

'Don't forget cigarettes, six hundred if you can get them.'

'You want a couple of bottles of Johnnie Walker and a case of Mosi?' the pilot asks.

'Three.'

The pilot's eyes widen. 'You shouldn't drink so much.'

'You shouldn't sleep so long. You're late. I told you it was important to be here on time.'

'I'm here, now.'

'OK, whatever you do, don't overload. Throw out the whisky if you have to. I want the passenger here in one piece.'

'She's from London, you said?'

'That's right.'

'I'm going to ask her to marry me!'

Max shakes his head. 'Are you going to make the pre-flight checks or just stand around here talking bullshit?'

Laughing, Kennedy climbs up into the cockpit and fetches down a small cloth bag containing a plastic syringe. He inserts the syringe into the fuel tanks in each wing, nods when the aviation gas comes up clear then wipes his hands down his red and black tie-dye baggy trousers which he wears with a formal white shirt. Max had bought the shirt on a trip to Harare a long time ago when he was able to walk without crutches. The old man and the young man look at each other critically for a moment.

'What are you wearing?'

'Good clothes, boss.' Kennedy pinches the sides of his trousers. 'Do you think I look beautiful?'

'I think you look like you forgot to get one half dressed. You're still in your pyjamas. Where are the flying trousers I got you?'

'Too big to wear, boss.'

Max's face falls. 'You're not sick, I hope,' he mutters and then glances at the horizon where the sun slides up fast and clean. 'You'd better get going.'

'You ever think about getting one of those artificial legs?' Kennedy enquires, putting his head to one side. 'I seen them in Lusaka and they look same as real. You could fly again with one of those legs.' He takes a pair of mirrored aviator glasses from his shirt pocket and puts them on. 'Permission to take off, sir?'

Max leans hard on his crutches. He can see his own reflection in the glasses: a tiny half-man with retreating features. 'You crash her, and I'll kill you.'

Kennedy snaps his heels together, pats the pocket of money and grins. 'Yes, sir.' He takes a step towards the plane. 'I mean, no, sir!'

Max shakes his head again. 'Don't try any fancy stuff on the way back, keep her nice and steady. No aerobatics. No showing off.'

'No, sir.' The pilot puts his foot on the rung leading up to the wing. Max sees that he is not wearing shoes. His toes are long and bony, the ankle slim and taut.

'Kennedy?'

'Sir?' He has his hand on the cockpit door ready to swing inside.

'Refuel at Lusaka. Use my account.'

47

'Yes, *sir.*' He hovers for a moment, the ribs across his long dark body suddenly visible under the near transparent shirt. The rainbow pants billow with air and he pats them flat before ducking into the cockpit. Max watches him settle inside before giving him the thumbs up.

Juliet quivers like a racehorse and darts forward on her wheels. Max steps back from the propeller as the plane turns in a tight circle, jittering and jumping on the rough ground. Kennedy brings her round so that her muzzle points down towards the end of the runway and holds her for a moment. Her propeller spins invisibly fast, a ripple in the light morning air. Through a side window Kennedy waves and Max feels his throat constrict as the plane moves off down the grit, spitting red dust, yawing slightly to the left before lifting into the air over a bank of dark feathery trees. Watching her climb, he feels an old ache. Some days the urge to break free from the ground pulls at him like gravity.

Max came to flying in a roundabout way. All his early life was spent on water, and it was the sea that defined him, was an elemental part of him. Brought up in Cornwall, he worked on a fishing trawler from the age of fourteen. His father had fished and going to sea was the one certainty in young Max's life. There was continuity in the ocean, the endless swell and rhythm of water.

During the stormy season salt waves licked at the fishermen's cottages that lined the harbour where he lived. Some wives lit candles for their husbands at sea. But there was no candle in his cottage. His mother wasn't superstitious. She didn't believe in all the nonsense that went on around boats, the forbidden words, sayings and taboos. One cold morning she told him that his father had drowned. She had the breakfast things in her hand at the time, a teapot with a rough wool cover, a small chipped plate and a tarnished silver knife. Something about his expression must have made her put the tea things down. He felt her hand on his shoulder. She kneaded his bones with her thumb, just once and quite roughly. Then she took her hand away, picked up the tea things and carried them out to the kitchen, leaving him to explore his shoulder with tentative fingers, as if looking for something she had left there for him.

He left her a note in the teapot and went to sea. It seemed the right thing to do; he knew she would not miss him. He went at night, carrying his things in a green fishing bag that had belonged to his father. It was easy to find a boat. The men laughed when they saw him and asked how old he was. 'Sixteen,' he lied.

No one came looking for him, not the school, which was no surprise to Max, nor the police. He was free to find his own way and the men on board the boat soon tired of asking questions and accepted him once he made himself useful. Night after night he braced himself on deck, feet splayed, face set against the flitch of salt water, steering across the dark swell. His oilskins became fouled with fish blood and diesel oil; his hands red-itchy with dermatitis; his mind stained with the stunned brightness of fish eye. The older fishermen slept below in gassy warmth, stirring only when they needed to piss over the side of the boat. He dreaded it when they came stumbling up, cursed out of sleep, wondering what the fuck he was doing sitting up on the prow with his legs clinging to the damp skin of the boat, the spray sluicing over, sometimes completely drenching him. When he brushed his face, the stars would momentarily swing and smart, blurring with the lights from the distant harbour.

Once he saw a castle strewn with festive lights appear like a dream ocean liner on the blank horizon. The light on the water was a rippling freeway of silver, tempting as a mermaid. He had placed his hands on the slippery rail then and hoisted himself up ready to leap when he was hauled back to reality, the smell of fish and guts and pain, by a great gob of ocean pelting his face.

Not long after he gave up his fishing job and travelled across the Channel to Brittany where he worked on a seaweed harvester, a curious craft that was partly boat and partly dinosaur with a long plunging neck that dipped in and out of the water. He spent his evenings in the bars among men with great brawling chests and arms who sang ballads and roared poetry. One of the bar girls had waist-length hair in rust-coloured coils. He watched her over his drink. Sometimes she glanced in his direction and when that happened he mostly looked away. Once or twice he'd had enough to drink to let his eyes stay with her and the physical shock when she returned his glance left him paralysed. He was sixteen by then and no one had ever touched him or looked at him with desire or even fondness. No one had ever cupped his face or held his hand or spoken softly to him before he went to sleep. He imagined these feelings, longed for them to happen to him. He had heard the saying that you couldn't miss what you'd never had. But Max knew that wasn't true. He missed love. It was simple. He missed it as if it had always been his. It was like the feeling he got when he looked into the stars, huge and aching and yet small and piercing at the same time. He wanted to love the girl, but she left the bar. Someone said she'd fallen pregnant by some other seaman.

He left Brittany and went to work on an oil rig tethered in the North Sea. The smell of men in the sleeping quarters was like that of a rank dog fox. Most of the men on the rig were married and carried photographs of their wives in their wallets. They pinned up pictures of blond children near their bunks and spoke to him of riches to be had elsewhere.

One of the men on board the rig had lived in Africa. The man, whose name was Andy, became a sort of friend and played cards with Max, coaching him through tricks he instantly forgot, all the time talking in a low, nasal, nagging voice of how Max had to 'get out' and see the world which was for Andy a great casino, a place of rolling chance, glittering dice and lady luck. According to Andy, the first thing Max needed to do in the game of life was to recognize his chances. Then he had to ignore small temptations and focus on potential big wins. Only once in a blue moon could he gamble everything. Andy had spent eleven years farming in a remote part of Zambia, the Copperbelt region, which he said was like the Wild West, a frontier place where normal rules did not apply. 'You could do anything there, pal, be whatever you wanted.' There was tenderness in his voice as he spoke.

When Max arrived in the Copperbelt with his belongings stuffed into his father's fishing bag he was twenty-three and had spent all his life in work. On a piece of paper tucked inside his passport was the name and address of a coffee farmer who was looking for a field supervisor. Max didn't have the slightest clue about farming, but his reputation as a hard worker accompanied him in the form of handwritten letter from Andy. It was composed like a school report. 'This boy spares himself no effort. He works to the best of his ability at all times. He is reliable and sensible.' Reading the letter made Max feel strange. It was the first time he had discovered what someone really thought of him. His early school reports he 'lost' on the way home to the cottage or dropped them over the grey harbour wall. He couldn't write; it made him panic because he got the letters mixed up and back to front. Whenever the teacher gave his work back it was covered in a scowl of red.

The plantation was owned by a white Zimbabwean called Joe Baxter, a solid blond bull of a man with tiny chubby hands. He read the letter from Andy greedily and carefully folded it before putting it into the pocket of his shorts. 'Shame,' he said and looked at his new arrival with obvious disappointment. Max didn't know what to say in return because his head still felt light from travel. It seemed impossible, almost a miracle that he had woken up in Aberdeen and was now in Africa. After a monosyllabic meal of oxtail and beer, served so cold the froth stuck out of the neck in a slender iceberg, Max was shown to his quarters by a watchman who gave him a candle, a rough towel and a mosquito coil. That night when the generators shut down it seemed as if the engine of the world had been unplugged.

The work in the coffee fields was long and hard and Max found it difficult to motivate the pickers who were often ill. During the afternoons they lounged about the fields, a milky, listless look in their eyes. When he tried to urge them to action they turned their faces and ignored him. They complained of hunger and headaches and constantly asked him for medicine, which he did not have. Every day a line of workers would come to ask his permission to attend a funeral. They spoke English only when they wanted something, and then, he felt, grudgingly. He felt cut off from them, lost in a sea of accusations he could not answer. Baxter told Max the pickers needed to hate him in order to respect him. 'What every African needs is a good leader. If they're led well, they're all right, but blacks cannot rule blacks. They tear each other to pieces.'

Gradually Max adjusted his expectations. He grew used to the rhythms and routines of the pickers, and after a while their eyes lost some of their wariness and became almost friendly. There were some, though, he knew he could never trust. They sat under the trees in groups of three and watched him with supreme contempt, turning back to each other as they mimicked his looks and gestures.

Every month after pay day the pickers got drunk at the drinking dens in the bush where *shaky shaky*, a maize brew the colour of chocolate milk, was sold. At night the drinkers spilled out along the network of dust roads between the coffee fields. Max had to watch his driving. The pickers appeared without warning from the darkness, lurching into the path of his Land-Rover, eyes wild and rearing in the headlights. Others moved like waterless swimmers, arms embracing the dark. One night he saw his chief picker slumped over a bicycle like a dead cowboy pitched over his horse. Baxter said *shaky shaky* was the devil's brew and tried to make Max ban his workers from drinking it. 'Tell them I'll dock their wages if they miss a day through drink.' Max told them, but it made no difference.

On Sundays no one drank. The Africans went to church at the small chapels dotted about the bush like mushrooms. Max generally slept through Sundays. It disoriented him not having to work and it was easier to sleep than sit in his cramped quarters with the generator rattling away for nothing. One Sunday Max woke up with an image of his father clear in his mind. He was sitting in the dark kitchen at the cottage in Cornwall, his face slack with tears, the collar of his shirt soaked. Max had woken in what he thought was the middle of the night and some instinct had taken him downstairs. Seeing him in the open doorway, his father lifted his fist to his mouth and rocked his head slowly from side to side. They had looked at each other for a moment, both shocked, and then Max had turned and gone back upstairs, understanding that his father needed to be left alone. Climbing back into his still warm bed he had felt vaguely comforted because he now understood that it wasn't just he who suffered at night. There was perhaps a source for what he felt, if his father felt it too. Moments later he had heard his father leave the cottage for the last time.

Max dressed and walked out into the wind. It was the dry season and the sound of the trees curiously echoed the sea; seed pods and branches hissing in a wash of reaching surf. Still thinking of his father, he began to walk across the bush.

The chapel was tiny and reminded Max of the seamen's mission where the service had been held; men in rubber boots at the back, no coffin because the body had never been found. No fishermen in his village had learned to swim because it was better to drown quickly than die slowly of cold.

This chapel was full and everyone turned to look as Max went in, disturbing a reading from Isaiah. '*The wilderness and the solitary place shall be glad for them.*' Taking a seat at the back, he looked down at his knees until the gathering turned round again to face the preacher, an elderly white man dressed like a sea captain in full uniform with braid. The elders among the coffee pickers wore brown suits with wide trousers, buttoned waistcoats and held soft-brimmed hats. They sat straight-backed and listened to the high, refined voice of the captain who urged them to be strong and trust in the Lord. '*With my soul have I desired thee in the night; yea, with my spirit within me will I seek thee early: for when thy judgements are in the earth, the inhabitants of the world will learn righteousness.'* The congregation muttered approval and one of the elders shouted, 'Hallelujah!' Max kept his head down and prayed not to catch anybody's eye.

After the service the preacher stood at the chapel door shaking the hand of everyone who left. Unsure of what to say to the preacher, Max decided to let everyone else go first. The preacher clasped the hands of a thin young man who was struggling to walk on wasted legs and asked him how he was feeling, listening with his head held to one side as the young man explained something in a low, halting voice. Behind the young man a clutch of children looked up at the preacher with wide dark eyes. The girls had their black hair twisted into braids and wore white socks and tiny black shoes. Their mother, wrapped in a blue and orange *chitenge*, stood quietly behind them, her expression heavy with exhaustion. The family left, the girls skittering in their unfamiliar shoes like show ponies, and other people took their turn. Max was impressed that the preacher seemed to find just the right thing to say to each person and so when they left they walked a little lighter. His turn came and he shuffled forward, aware of his own meaty smell. In his hurry to be up he had forgotten to wash. Close up the preacher looked smaller, almost shrunken in his uniform. The four rings on the sleeve were not navy but air force, Max saw, as the preacher took his hand and introduced himself as Dr Peter Marsden.

'I'm Max.'

'Why haven't I seen you before?'

'I don't go to church.'

'You did this morning.'

Feeling caught out, Max looked at his boots.

The preacher closed the chapel door and stepped out into light. 'I recognize you now. You're Baxter's supervisor, aren't you?' He peered at Max through foggy grey eyes, jabbing his head forward to see him better. His hair was white with patches of pink skin showing on his scalp.

Max nodded. 'I've been here a year.'

'Like it, so far?'

Max shrugged.

The preacher laughed and scratched at a bite on his mottled hand. 'It's hell at first. Came out after I retired from the air force. Thought I'd come to the end of the world. And I was used to watching people die. But I stuck it out; the place gets under your skin after a while.'

Max remembered his friend Andy's comments on getting Africa in his blood. Every white man he talked to had said something similar. The preacher adjusted his cuffs, which seemed too weighty for his frail wrists.

'Can you fly?' the preacher suddenly asked.

'*Aeroplanes?*'

'Yes, of course aeroplanes, what else?'

'No. I don't fly.'

'Well, I don't either, too ancient, but I'd like a pupil. Could I teach you?'

'To fly?' Max felt his hands go clammy.

'Come over to the house and we'll see if you're up to it,' Marsden said. 'You'll need a medical first.'

'A medical?' Max repeated.

'Yes, yes, won't take long. Come over soon, ask one of the natives to show you the white house.' Then with quick, light steps he strode off through the trees, the sun glinting off his braid.

The medical consisted of the doctor punching Max between the shoulder blades and asking him to cough. Afterwards Max was given his first ground lesson. In Marsden's opinion there was only one book that matched the importance of the Bible and that was *The Complete Flying Course* first published in 1939 and based on the Gosport system of training evolved during the First World War. Max was told to learn passages from the manual by heart, and this he did diligently, for the doctor was adamant that the principles of flight began with the feet planted firmly on the ground.

Lessons were held in the small white house which nestled in the bush like an egg and attracted people from all over the region, some walking through dense woodland for miles to reach it. When they arrived they were always given tea and something to eat. Most often they sat for an hour or two, straight-backed with legs outstretched, in the shade thrown by the bushes around the house, resting before they made the journey back across country.

Ill health had forced Marsden to retire from his post as a medical missionary. He'd suffered malaria several times which had affected his eyesight and forced him to ground his Piper Cherokee single-engine *Hotel Juliet*. It marked the end of a second career spent flying around the Copperbelt, swooping down from the skies like a blue and white angel, being greeted by communities whose only experience of medical treatment had been at the hands of the local herbalists and witch doctors. Mostly it was hopeless, Marsden told Max: all he could do was dispense advice on hygiene and nutrition, not having the drugs needed to contain diseases that swept across the bush communities like fires, wiping out entire families, creating odd untouched groups of pot-bellied children who spent their days throwing stones at birds.

Missionaries were known locally as Devil Dodgers and Marsden had adopted the name as his radio call sign. It amused him greatly to see the look on the faces of Church visitors from England as he requested permission to land at Lusaka. 'This is Devil Dodger in *Hotel Juliet*, do I have clearance? Over. I repeat, this is Devil Dodger in *Juliet*. When are you boys going to wake up and let me sodding land? Over.' Max learned that the Duke of Edinburgh had once flown with Devil Dodger and had been at the controls when the plane strayed illegally over the border into Angola.

When Marsden gave up missionary work his houseboy Joshua was given the duty of looking after the plane, making sure she was kept up to scratch. Every Sunday after church the cook went to the airstrip with a bucket and brush and scrubbed the dust off the fuselage and cleaned the windows. Some days Marsden came by and watched, squinting; his eyesight by then cloudier than the Windolene Joshua loved to smear across the glass.

The doctor had never married. Hurt or rejected early on – Max never learned the details – he resolved to live life on his own terms. Educated, experimental and endlessly energetic, he was one of those breeds of Englishmen who obeyed an inner moral code kept stoked up inside him like a furnace. He had many other dependants and correspondents. He treated Joshua's children like grandchildren and had promised to send the latest, a son called Kennedy, away to school when the time came. He had ambitions for him to become a flight engineer. There were a clutch of other Africans at boarding schools who wrote him cards and diaries, one or two university students in the United States studying medicine, another reading law, someone else studying to be an opera singer in Paris. Marsden kept up with them all, typing letters on his old Olivetti portable, the carriage ringing into the night.

He was unexpected in other ways. Once Max arrived early to find the doctor stretched out on the floor in a dark green ball-gown with eyes closed as he listened to Beethoven's Ninth Symphony. Seeing Max, he roused himself from his supine splendour and with great dignity announced that he adored the feel of silk against naked skin.

Marsden loved God but was highly critical of the Church. 'Same as a ship if you ask me. There's bound to be trouble when a lot of men spend time close together. It's about power, being in charge. All men dream about killing each other, especially when they feel unmanned. Men are tribal; they need to compete to feel alive. Stay out here long enough and you'll understand.'

He drained his glass of champagne and sat back in his cane chair. Max thought of his workers, the way violence would erupt over the smallest of things during the *shaky shaky* time. But he guessed that Marsden was talking about another kind of violence.

The old doctor grew frail and began to walk with a cane. He had several but his favourite was one made from African satinwood.

It had a varnished walnut embedded in its top that had been carved by a witch doctor as a gift to Marsden for curing him of headaches. Scores of tiny faces, some sleeping, others laughing or crying or shouting like a crowd of squashed souls, had been worked inside the grain of the nut. Marsden claimed it brought him luck. Along with many white people who worked among the bush people of remote Africa he acknowledged the power of witchcraft without believing in it himself. 'I've seen too many men die from fear of it,' he told Max.

Their talks still continued on the veranda, but Marsden often fell asleep before he finished what he wanted to say, white head lolling on his chest, claw fingers gripping the chair. Sometimes he would startle Max by waking suddenly and uttering a few words he seemed to have gone looking for and then nod back to sleep again. Their ground lessons continued slowly and took the form of Max reading from the flying manual while Marsden dozed. Max suspected that the old doctor only wanted company, but he didn't mind. He was content to sit under the flickering candlelight reading at his own pace. He found that for the first time he could enjoy words without fear of being judged for using his finger to guide his eyes and mind. One of his favourite passages was the introduction to the lesson on Air Navigation.

'The navigator on a long-distance flight at night or over the sea might well be called a mariner of the sky, for like his nautical brother, he, too, has to make stellar observations.

'For comparatively short distances over well-mapped country, matters are much simpler, and largely resolve themselves into the ability to read a map quickly and accurately and to hold a good compass course.'

A few fine days they flew in *Hotel Juliet*. Marsden believed that learning to fly was principally a mental skill. Any hint of impulsiveness or frustration prompted instructor to order pupil out of the cockpit and take a moment or two to study the way the wind stirred the branches of the torchwood tree that grew near the runway. Sometimes pupil was told to count to one hundred, slowly. Those seconds seemed to last for ever. Max recalled a lesson in forced landings during which he had to practise recognizing various types of field. Grass, stubble and sand near the water's edge made for the safest landing. From the air grass looked a dull or brownish green and stubble buff. Root crops were dark green, ploughed land brown or red. Cereal crops were lighter and brighter and rippled in the wind. The manual advised avoiding those. In the event of engine failure the pilot had to select a suitable field and glide to its downward side. In a large field the undercarriage could be lowered, but if the field was small or had a bad surface, the wheels were to be kept retracted.

Then after a couple of months of lessons the doctor went down with malaria, collapsing in his garden where a small group of patients waited under the trees to see him. The doctor had been carried to his bed by the time Max arrived. Walking into the quiet, dim room swathed in ghostly nets, Max imagined he was already too late. But Marsden was sitting up drinking Earl Grey tea from a tiny Japanese cup. He had a stack of books by his bedside, a pen and some writing paper, a Bible and, of course, the flying manual on top of the pile.

'Come on, don't look like that. Come and read.' The doctor swivelled his head and indicated with filmy eyes a chair pulled up by his bed. Max took a few steps forward. The doctor's head on the white pillow was a skull covered with old glazed paper, and the eyes in comparison seemed shockingly alive. 'Come on, what's the matter with you?'

'It must be the heat,' Max said as he picked up the flying manual. 'Where would you like me to start?'

The old man's eyes were half closed. 'At the beginning, boy. Start at the beginning.'

Max turned to the introduction and began to read. '*Perhaps of greatest importance is the necessity of winning the absolute confidence of your pupil. This depends largely on your personality and manner. From this follows a natural and effortless authority which is not undermined but improved by a friendly disposition to your pupil.'* Max glanced up and saw that Marsden had a faint smile playing on his lips. He continued: *'No pupil ever forgets his first instructor, and all the world over this is the hour of birth of the very powerful camaraderie which exists between all flying men. The authority of "I have wings on my chest" or "More rings on my sleeve" is the wrong attitude. The pupil may be frightened of you and possibly dislike you, in which case he will be slow to learn, and you will think that he is a dunderhead, etc., etc., when really the fault lies at your own door.'*

The doctor opened his eyes and pulled himself upright to give Max his full attention. His eye sockets were rings of bone and his breathing quick and shallow. His slick yellow appearance gave the impression of a creature that had just laboriously shed a skin. 'I need to ask you something.' He struggled to get comfortable, waving away Max's attempts to assist. 'How much money do you make from coffee?'

Max wondered at the question. Recently he had moved away from Baxter and set up his own small plantation.

'I don't know exactly, but a profit at least. Should do better this year, depending on the rains.'

'Got enough spare to set up a school for the children?'

Max looked at the doctor. 'What are you saying?'

'You know I don't believe in giving something for nothing. You can have *Hotel Juliet*. Haven't got long left, want to leave her in good hands, but in return I'm asking you to do something for me and build a school in the bush.'

'I could afford to do that, if it's what you want, you don't need to give me anything,' Max said slowly.

'Are you turning down my offer?' the doctor asked sharply.

'No, I suppose I don't feel ready.'

'Ready, you're more than ready. What are you waiting for?' He reached over to his stack of books and took a sheet of paper and wrote a few lines. He glanced over at Max. 'You're stalling, why?'

'I can't take the plane. I haven't flown solo.'

'Not to worry. Go up in the morning, take her for a good spin and think about what I've said. You'll need a strong building team, get Baxter to help you. This school is important. It was always my dream to set one up here, but now I've run out of time. You'll do it for me, won't you? There isn't anyone else I trust.'

'You've still got time,' Max said. 'A few weeks, you'll be well again. You could do it.'

'Listen, old boy, we both know that's not true. Here.' He handed Max the sheet of paper.

Max looked at it, hands trembling. In an attempt at formality the doctor had scripted the change of ownership in fine copperplate writing, but the flourishes had skittered out of control in places, smattering the document with ink. Max blew on the paper and carefully placed it between the pages of the manual. Then, excusing himself from the doctor who was already nodding asleep, he carried it out with him into the garden. He turned the page to Air Lesson No. 11.

THE FIRST SOLO

I am getting out of the aeroplane now, because for the last few hours you have been the pilot entirely, and I the passenger.

Now you are going to fly without a passenger, and that's all there is to it.

Without my weight you will find the aeroplane lighter, so that the tail will come up quicker when taking off; she will climb faster, and when landing will float longer before sitting down.

Otherwise there is no difference from what you have been doing.

Make a circuit and land. If there's anything in your way, on with the engine and round again.

If your approach does not plan out as it should or your landing is doubtful, don't bother, just open your throttle straight away and go round again.

I don't care how many times you do this if you make one of your 'daisy-cutting' landings.

Taxi in, and if you see me struggling over the aerodrome with my parachute, stop and give me a lift.

Well. Cheerio! Off you go!

Max climbed until he reached the point where all he could see were waves of white rolling endlessly before him like a rough, brightly lit sea. All traces of the earth had vanished, suspended somewhere under this magical carpet of white, so tantalizing and fresh it could have been an undiscovered island. He wanted to leap out and bury himself in it, grab handfuls of cloud and stuff it into his mouth. The cloudscape made ground life seem small and forlorn, almost secondary. *Juliet* hummed and creaked against the wind, her dials flickering gently back and forth. The hot metal smell of aviation fuel caught at the back of his throat. Protected only by a thin metal fuselage, he was flying alone. He'd made it. He wanted to cry and shout all at once. He was flying! Look, he was flying. For the first time in his life he felt something close to love.

Dropping altitude, he cut down into the blue. Fields with their puny sprinklers came into view. He could see tiny cubed buildings and huts, a few smoking fires, the Great North Road carved into the red earth, but no cars or people. He was looking down on a world that had just been freshly created. Clearing a telegraph wire, he held the plane steady for a moment, checked the nose and wings, and then lightly came down. Then he taxied round and sat in the cockpit for a while, his heart thudding, hands still gripping the elevator column as if frozen on to it.

When he reached the white house, Dr Marsden was sitting up in bed, a tray with tea things across his lap, a half-smile on his mouse-coloured lips. The tea in the pot had gone cold, Max noticed as he took the tray away and carefully laid the dead man to rest on his back.

The sound of a plane passing over the house makes Max look up from the veranda where he has been dozing in an old wicker chair, crutches propped beside him. He goes inside and drinks a glass of water and finds that his hand is shaking. The kitchen is cool, the fridge sighing in one corner. The cook has already been and prepared five different types of vegetables for that evening's supper. Covered aluminium saucepans sit on top of the gas stove; the beef will go in later when Joshua comes back on duty, wearing white gloves to serve, not that Max asks him to make any special kind of effort, but because he understands from the way the boss has been acting these past few days that the visitor from London is significant. The plane drones over the house again. Max imagines Kennedy pointing down at the white shape sprouting from the trees, perhaps indicating the flamboyant trees around the garden, or the Rhodesian boiler smoking away with hardwood logs ready for the visitor's bath. Max will be staying at his farm while she is here. A green fishing bag packed with spare clothes, towel and razor sits by the kitchen door. Crutches clicking, he takes one last look around the bedroom, which smells unfamiliar, the curtains and mosquito nets washed and hanging in pale folds, the blankets aired, the pillows changed for fresh ones. Then he goes out into the bright light where the jeep, which also has been hosed down for the occasion, is waiting, droplets on the windscreen sparkling like diamonds in the sun.

4

READING THE COMPASS

Imagine yourself sitting in the middle of the compass, then your direction of flight is always straight out from this centre position to the lubber line.

Africa, 1996

Memory lifts the aircraft window shield. The lights of Johannesburg fill the space and she finds herself looking down on a city of diamonds. The noise inside the Boeing shifts, and for a moment the plane hovers in silence. The lights glitter below. She buckles her seat belt and quickly finishes writing the postcard she bought at Heathrow which has a picture of a red London bus on the front. '. . . *about splitting with Adam. It happened so fast. Coming to Africa (finally!) just seems the right thing to do. I'm sorry I didn't call before I left . . .*' She wonders how to explain; a postcard seems inadequate, almost an afterthought. She shoves it in her bag. An uneasy urgency ripples down the aisle. A slim young man with liquid black eyes pulls down a jump seat opposite her.

'Don't worry, miss,' the crewman says. 'The aircraft is very safe.'

'I'm not a particularly good flier. Hate landings.'

'Here.' He offers her a boiled sweet.

She doesn't want the sweet, but his eyes refuse to leave her. She puts it in her mouth. It tastes of pepper.

The jet engines begin to scream. The crewman draws his fingers together and points them in an attitude of prayer. His hands are beautiful, the fingers straight and slim, like new pencils.

The Boeing drops suddenly and she grips the armrest tightly. She can feel her tail bone trapped like a small hard bead in the crease of her seat. A low bell tone sounds.

A sound whooshes down the plane like the sea sucking in its tide. She feels caught inside a membrane of very thin rubber that is being pounded from the outside. The plane plummets and she braces herself for a jolt, but the wheels hit the ground smoothly. An airy feeling blooms in the pit of her stomach, making her feel suddenly alone. People are smiling and there are a few desultory hand claps. Memory stays in her seat, picking at her fingers, looking out at the halogen brightness that is her first sight of Africa.

Johannesburg Airport is an unattended shop. She drifts between the display cases where there are tiny specks of diamond sealed in clear plastic pouches. She looks at the prices written in pencil on the white tags, and thinks how nice it would be to send Elise a diamond for her forty-fifth birthday. But the smallest glittering fleck costs a thousand dollars. A wave of tiredness sweeps over her and she sits down for a while on a rank of yellow plastic chairs. The flight information board is blank with all shutters drawn. She has three hours to wait.

A message board on the wall near the gift shop suddenly spools into green neon life. ERIC DE SPOT PLEASE CONTACT ME. Memory watches the message feed through and then start again. In the row of seats next to her a fat man is sprawled asleep, his feet dangling over the edge of the seats, the soles of his shoes glittering as if he has just waded through diamond dust. His arms are folded across his chest and rise and fall in time to his pinched breathing. Is he perhaps the mysterious Eric De Spot?

The message spools on. It could be a code, she thinks, some kind of secret airport language that alerts the staff to a crisis. Perhaps something is happening right now. That would explain why the airport seems so deserted of staff. Perhaps a plane has come down. Perhaps a terrorist has taken over air traffic control, and all the workers are being held in a back room, their arms bound to chairs, mouths sealed with tape. There will be searches, questions. Did you pack your own bag? She won't be able to catch her connecting flight. They'll send everyone home. Back to where they came from. Perhaps it's a sign. It means her journey is doomed. It confirms her fears. She shouldn't have come without letting anyone know. She thought it was being courageous, adventurous even; but it was just stupid. The giddy feeling of doing something purely by herself and for herself has finally worn off and a thousand accusing voices are now waging war in her head. *You shouldn't have . . .* but she needs to stop this right now and go and find coffee.

By the time Memory returns to her seat the sleeping man has moved on. She sits with a styrofoam cup of scalding coffee in her lap and watches the message continue its circuit. Sipping her coffee, she decides that it's too personal for an emergency, besides which if there were a crisis there would be alarms, surely, and instructions to evacuate. Anyway Eric De Spot is such an unlikely name it has to be genuine.

That *me* is intriguing. Somehow it manages to be anonymous *and* personal, so confident of its own identity. The messenger is calling the shots here because the messenger assumes that when Eric receives the message he will know *exactly* who to get in touch with – *me, me, me.* She watches it go round and wishes she had someone to share it with. Elise would have appreciated the scenario. She might have come up with something better for De Spot. She had a good instinct for games. Or used to.

Suddenly tired, she finishes her coffee and tries not to look at the message board. Her mind always gets a little wired when she's exhausted and she hasn't slept properly in days. Reaching into her bag for her book she finds the postcard, adds another 'sorry' and a solitary kiss after her name, writes in the address, and then realizes there's nowhere to buy local stamps. She turns over the card, decides not to send it, to phone instead, but as she opens her wallet for her credit card to make the call – *what is the time in London, now, anyway?* – she finds a book of English stamps, and decides to risk it. Posting the card, Memory thinks that this is the second time in the past few weeks she has sent a message not knowing if it will reach the intended recipient. After buying her ticket to Lusaka, she had written to the bush school in Chingola, asking if anyone there had known anything about Paul Cougan.

She heard nothing. Time was running out. Looking up Chingola in her *Times World Atlas*, she saw that there was only one main road that went through Zambia, and Chingola was on it. Surely it wouldn't be difficult to find? She could go there and find a place to stay and make further enquiries when she arrived. It would be an adventure. Maybe she could do some travelling on her own around the yellow torn piece of country that, she had to admit, appeared like nothing much in the great shape of Africa. With Angola on one side and Tanzania on the other, Zambia was landlocked. There was a lake, Lake Kariba, but no dramatic mountain ranges or great rivers. The main distinguishing feature was the crossroads: a V-shaped junction that spread a sprawling length of road right across the left-hand side of the country up through Lubumbashi (Elisabethville) to Likasi, Kananga, past the Kasai Occidental and on through Kikwit, finally coming to rest on the shores of the Congo at Kinshasa (Leopoldville). To the right the road wound its way across the Muchinga Mountains and came to rest at Dar es Salaam on the Indian Ocean just below Zanzibar. Closing the atlas, Memory had been struck by a feeling that all her life until now had been played out in small rooms filled with nervous smoke.

Then one night she was woken by a telephone call. Thinking it was Adam, she ignored the ringing for a while. Buses and taxis boomed in the street, signalling the start of the dawn traffic chorus. She pulled her blanket around her head, but she could still hear the phone.

'Memory Cougan?' The voice was deep and slightly accented, although she couldn't say where it was from. It was a bit shocking to hear someone she didn't know say her name so confidently and she wondered for a moment if she were not speaking to the police. The thought occurred that someone may have found her bag, and she was at once relieved that she had taken the last piece of advice Adam gave her, and changed the locks.

'Yeah, that's me.'

'I'm calling from Chingola. I knew Paul Cougan.'

Then the line broke into fragments. When the caller came through again she heard his name: Max Searle. Somehow she managed to get her flight details across the static. In return the man told her that he would send a driver to Lusaka to collect her. She put the telephone down and sat for a while, her mind turning over with the realization that something essential had started.

At Lusaka Airport Memory pushes through the crowds, dragging her suitcase, which has lost a wheel. There's a prickly sensation at her throat and her legs feel heavy from flight. She glances at the people, mostly men, pressed against the barrier, eyes eagerly searching the passengers filing through slowly. The soft blackness of the people oddly shocks her. There's a rawness and vulnerability about the crowd, as if everyone has been turned inside out. At the end of the barrier a tall young man with prominent clavicle bones jutting from the neck of a near transparent white shirt stands with a yellow paper banner bearing her name written in bold red letters. Its cheerful audacity makes her swallow.

The man, whose name is Kennedy, looks at her suitcase critically.

'Is that heavy?'

'Very. I can barely lift it.'

His eyes sweep down her body coming to rest at her toes, which are varnished *rouge noir*. He bends down and picks up a couple of shopping bags and asks her to wait for a moment. She watches him cross the airport in long loping strides. He doesn't hurry. He reaches a check-in desk where he leans over the counter and talks to the attendant there, resting one bare foot, exposing the creamy arch crinkled with tiny brown tributaries. After a while he reaches down and lifts the plastic bags on to the counter. The attendant rises from his seat, looks inside and breaks into a broad smile.

'I had to give my friend the frozen chickens,' Kennedy explains on his return. He picks up her suitcase and she follows him out of the door and into a soft white heat. She thought they would be driving, but he's taking her to another part of the runway where there are small planes all lined up with their pert tail fins sparkling as if ready for a parade.

'I've never flown in a small plane before,' she says.

'It's easy,' he says, heaving her suitcase up to the cockpit.

'Where do I sit?' she asks when he comes down.

'In the co-pilot's seat at the front.' He stands back to let her climb up.

'I'm not sure . . . I don't know if I can, I . . .' She falters, one hand on the side of the plane which feels warm under the sun. 'I've flown in two planes already. I thought we would be travelling by road.'

Kennedy looks at her with his head held to one side. 'I thought you would be white.'

'What?' The sun feels warm around her legs. 'Why did you think that? Didn't Max tell you who I was? I mean you had my name written on the paper.'

'He said you were from London.'

'Well, there are blacks in London, you know.' She doesn't like the sharpness in her voice, the slightly patronizing tone. The way she said *blacks*.

He looks away for a moment. 'I'm sorry. I have offended you.'

'No!' She tries smiling at him. 'You haven't. An easy mistake, I'm often taken for a white person. My mother is white, you see.'

His eyes lighten. 'Can you manage to climb up?'

'Of course.' Ignoring his steadying hand she steps up into the cockpit and slides into the seat. The plane has a worn, slightly musty smell. Her suitcase sits in the back under a raft of more shopping bags and a case of beer. There's a boxed bottle of whisky at her feet. Kennedy climbs up beside her and reaches over to help fasten her seat belt, his fingers cool against her stomach. 'Ready?' he says.

'Can you try not to go too fast? I'm really not used to this.'

He laughs as he opens the throttle. 'She has one speed.'

'Really, I mean it, I might be sick.'

'*Really*,' he repeats, mocking her English accent. He glances over and smiles at her as they roll down the runway and lift into the sky.

The tiny plane drones. Memory keeps drifting into sleep and then nodding awake. In the background she can hear Kennedy talking on the radio. He says something about Romeo and Juliet. She wishes she could open her eyes, but the warmth in the cockpit is like being wrapped in a blanket in a room filled with light and it's delicious, not frightening at all, but then she hasn't looked down, won't until they're back on the ground.

They land on a red dirt track in a clearing. A white jeep waits for them, a bulky, dark, tanned man at the wheel, greasy canvas hat shading his eyes. He shakes her hand firmly. 'I'm Max Searle.' He looks away. She gets the impression that he would like to say more but has forgotten the words. She is offered the front seat, but says she will travel in the back. Kennedy climbs into the front. The wheels of the jeep kick up dust as they drive, it seems, straight into the sky, thick and blue and heavy. Light flickers through trees as they swing on to a wide dirt track, swerving around potholes, slowing to let an occasional figure walk past. People wave and salute at the jeep as if they are arriving dignitaries.

They turn into a farm marked by white gates and a lawn where a man tends a hose, spraying it in a high loop over a border of bushy plants with small pink and white flowers. Against the parched brown land, the greenness of the lawn seems unnatural, almost forced.

Max asks them to wait for a moment and climbs out of the jeep. Part of his left leg is missing. He uses a crutch to balance on, leaning against it lightly as he limps across the lawn, says something to the man with the hose and then goes into the house. Kennedy puts his feet up on the dashboard as if expecting a long wait.

'What's he doing?' she asks.

'This is his house,' Kennedy says.

'I gathered that.' Again, the sharpness. She must try to tone it down. 'Where do you live?'

'Next village.' Kennedy waves an arm out of the window. She looks down the red dirt track where the dust of their arrival still hovers. Beyond that there are fields with a dark green bushy crop, sprinklers rotating one way and then another with a high ticking sound.

'How did he lose his leg?'

Kennedy pulls his feet down off the dashboard. 'He was shot.'

She considers this for a moment. 'How?'

But Kennedy doesn't answer. A moment later Max comes across the lawn, followed by a servant carrying a pile of cushions, a small reading lamp balanced on top, the frayed cord dangling down. Max opens the back door of the jeep and the servant slides the cushions in next to her. She can see they have been made from old velvet tablecloths or curtains faded by the sun. Her hand sinks into their feather softness.

They drive down a narrow red track and reach a clearing where there is a wooden building with a thatched roof. 'This is the school,' Max says from the front. 'Would you like to take a look?'

He holds open the jeep door as she climbs out. His hat shades his expression. Kennedy walks on ahead and glances back at her.

'Is this the school Paul Cougan built?' she asks Max. She feels a little breathless, her limbs cramped from hours of travel.

'The first school burned down. We rebuilt.' He stands aside to let her enter. Inside the school is cool and dim and smells of earth. Rows of wooden benches face a huge blackboard chalked with the names of animals and their young: Cow – Calves. Sheep – Lambs. Cat – Kittens. There are pages of sums pinned to the walls and a map of the world with Africa outlined in green.

'Where are the children?'

'It's Sunday,' Max says.

'Of course.' She had forgotten.

Kennedy lifts the lid of a desk. There's a name written on paper taped inside. JUBILEE M. She walks over to him.

'Could I look?' He shrugs. She peers into the desk. It's empty. She moves over to the next desk and lifts the lid. It belongs to someone called SPLENDID S and is also empty. The next one, GIVEN P, contains a pencil and rubber.

'Thank you,' she says to Max as they return to the jeep. 'But could we come back on a school day?'

He nods and starts the engine. After a short drive down another red track they come to a small white house, thick with overgrown honeysuckle and bougainvillea. A gardener sweeps the lawn of fallen leaves. All the windows and doors are open.

Max stays in the jeep, leaving Kennedy to carry her suitcase inside. The gardener is told to fetch the cushions and the reading lamp. Memory follows. Paint peels from the white windows and the fly screen across the door is rusted, but inside the rooms are immaculately clean. Kennedy carries her suitcase in both arms, holding it against his chest.

'I'm sorry it's so heavy,' she says, following him into a room containing a small table and a bed made up with white sheets and a yellow cotton cover. A mosquito net has been carefully folded back around the head of the bed. 'Oh, just put it anywhere.' She wishes the wheel hadn't broken.

Kennedy puts the case down near the table. 'Did you bring a lot of books?' he asks.

'No, it's mostly clothes, I'm afraid. And shoes.'

'Shoes,' he says doubtfully.

She notices his feet; the long, dusty toes. As she turns to unzip her case, she feels him watching her.

'What's it like in London?' he asks.

Oddly she cannot think of anything to say. The city she'd left just twelve hours ago is suddenly unintelligible. 'Big, noisy, fast, oh, I don't know, I can't really describe it. Have you never been?'

'No.'

'You should one day.'

'Why?'

'Because it's an experience. Everyone should visit London for the experience.'

'What could I do there?' His eyes meet hers, so dark they seem to be composed solely of pupil matter, missing out the stuff of irises.

'Anything you liked, there's so much, galleries, theatre, museums. It's actually really wonderful when you get used to it, the pace, I mean.'

'When I finish my studies maybe I will.' Kennedy smiles.

'What are you studying?'

'Engineering. I am on leave from my university course. I have one more year to do.'

'What will you do when you finish?'

'Fly. I would love to train to be a commercial pilot'.

She looks at him as he lifts his arms into imaginary wings.

'It's my dream to fly everywhere in the world.' He laughs. 'It's a crazy dream.'

'Have you always flown?'

'I learned when I was fourteen. Max taught me the instruments and ground techniques and then I went up with a crop sprayer.'

She hesitates. 'Did Max ever talk to you about Paul Cougan?'

Kennedy looks directly at her. 'My father worked for him.'

'Your father worked for Paul Cougan?' She feels a rush of something, not quite excitement, more of a glimmer, a tiny flash.

Kennedy nods casually.

'You knew him? You *met* Paul Cougan?'

'I was a boy. I don't really remember him.'

'What do you remember?'

'I remember my father crying when he died.' His eyes slide from her face.

'After the crash?'

Kennedy frowns.

'The plane crash?' she says.

He looks at her, again the same direct clear gaze. 'The witch doctor killed him,' Kennedy says. 'Everyone here says this is what happened.'

'He was killed by a witch doctor?' She almost wants to laugh, the idea seems so preposterous. But something about Kennedy's glance makes her falter. A shudder passes through her, a rippling chill, unbalancing her for a moment. 'What?' she says, but then she pauses because there standing at the doorway is Max leaning on his crutch, his arms dark with sweat, his hair the colour of a storm cloud. Max, who now regards her with steady blue eyes.

'Everything all right?'

'Fine, thank you, it seems very comfortable.' For some reason her heart is racing.

Both men leave. She walks around the room, cooling her feet. Near the bed the stone is worn so smooth it feels oily. She wonders who lived here. It has the feel of a quiet person's room, there's something simple about it, something deeply private. She glances at a pile of books on a desk near the window. There's a medical dictionary, an old leather-bound Bible, a volume of *Diseases of Africa* and a hardback flying manual. She touches the cracked spines gently. She feels herself start to wind down. She can't believe she's come this far. So soon. She lifts the curtain and looks into the early night. No stars yet. The blackness has a soft look to it, almost like animal fur. She imagines it warm and velvety against her cheek.

Calmer now, she walks back to the bed, unlaces the mosquito net and climbs under the sheets still in her London clothes. Outside the wind pours through the trees and birds call low hooting songs. She hugs her arms against her body and rolls around trying to find a soft place. The bed sighs a deep note. She closes her eyes. She mustn't sleep. She needs to get ready for supper, but the sweet comfort of the bed acts on her like a sleeping drug. When she wakes again she finds a delicate cup of steaming bergamot-scented tea on the little wicker table next to her.

5

SUNDRY AEROBATICS

An inverted spin is recognizable by the feeling of being thrown on to the shoulder straps and being on the outside of the spin.

London, 1996

From her office window Elise looks out on a grey sky where a tiny plane no bigger than a silver ball bearing begins an almost vertical descent. She watches the ribbon of vapour stain the sky and wonders whether anyone has ever worked out just how much aviation fuel gets dumped over London every day. Sometimes, working here, in the heart of the city, surrounded by the crazy spew of waste, excess and poverty that seems to sum it up these days, she feels a twinge. She doesn't know what it is exactly, but her guts recoil at everything. *Everything*, including her own decisions.

Tonight she's stayed on after work and every few seconds or so she leaves the window and goes over to her desk and takes a sip of water. Then she carefully retouches her lipstick in a little compact mirror. Each time she catches sight of her face she notices some tiny flaw in her skin, a burst capillary, a patch of dryness, a shadow under her eye. Moving to the window to catch the last of the evening light, she bares her teeth in the mirror, and there caught between her two front molars is a tiny transparent fleck like a fish scale. She removes it with a shudder.

He chose the meeting place, a club, and said that he would leave her name at the door, so that *if she got there early*, she could settle inside and not feel uncomfortable. He spoke carefully over the phone, his voice cultured, but with a trace of arrogance or impatience. She has to confess that she doesn't remember much of what he said because she was thinking about how it might feel to have sex with him. It's difficult to admit, but it's sex, not love, or long walks or twenty-four-carat conversation, or opera or any of the other lures advertised by sophisticated soulmates she craves: sticky, shouty sex.

How wonderful it would be to forget her tiny fish scale worries. It has been a while since she last felt sexually exuberant. The last time she'd bedded someone had been embarrassing, one of those Foreign Office cocktail parties when she flirted heavily in a lift with some sort of cultural adviser who told her she had elegant calves. The sex had been elegantly restrained, middle-aged, middle class, middle of the road. Afterwards she had walked home to Highgate in high heels, feet burning, furious with herself. She used to be able to have dinner with men and not expect or want it to lead anywhere, but recently impulses or instincts Elise thought she had under control were beginning to stir again. It was unsettling, almost as if she were going through a second adolescence with all the blushes, rushes of emotion and awkwardness associated with that time. But she should be grateful, she supposed. She had few real troubles. The exterior of her life was, to some, quite perfect. Her flat in Highgate had a wonderful light carpet and cream sofas; high ceilings, fresh flowers. Elise had created the ideal white space for herself: a retreat from the ugly business of life. Even her involvement in disease was detached. She handled no blood, saw no wounds, was devoted to relieving suffering on clean white paper or glistening computer screen. She travelled first class to conferences and enjoyed the attention from waiters, managers, assistants who took her bags, held open doors, left chocolate on her pillow, treated her like a mature princess.

Over the years, however, a certain ugly perfectionism had begun to creep in. She had always been one for detail, tying up loose ends, checking the fine print. It was part of the reason she'd risen so quickly at the British Medical Research Foundation where she worked as project director for malaria research. But lately she'd found it harder to begin assignments and end them because the details would overwhelm her often to the point of exhaustion. She knew the answer was to delegate, to hand over some of the more intractable research assignments to her team of colleagues and advisers, but somehow she couldn't let go. A part of her had always felt that leaving work to others was a sign of failure, an inability to cope, and that was the last thing she wanted people to think. Elise prided herself on being a manager who got things done.

She needed a diversion, something to take her mind off the details, the ripple of figures, negotiation and argument that swirled through her sleep at night. She had thought about further study, perhaps working towards a PhD, but realistically she did not have the time and any extended period of academic research would involve getting buried in documents and that was exactly what she needed a break from.

And so she has come to this . . . experience, date, event, she doesn't even know what to call it. She looks at the fish scale poised on the tip of her little finger, a small meniscus, a foetal moon, and realizes with relief that she isn't going to be early after all.

'Elise? How delightful,' he says. She has an impression of tallness, money and a slightly strained confidence poured into a tight skin. The club staff stand back a little as he guides her towards a small bar furnished with tables made from wicker and glass. The place is so clean and primrose-lit it puts Elise in mind of a nursery.

They settle down in their seats, pulling cushions out from behind them and wondering where to put them.

'What will you have?' Richard rests his hand on the glass tabletop, and she is surprised at the little rim of dirt under the nails.

'A gin and tonic, please.' Better to stick with what she knows. Not try anything out of character.

Instead of waiting for someone to take their drinks orders, Richard gets up and goes to the bar, talking quietly with the bartender, as if he knows him, which he doesn't. It's a feature of male behaviour, Elise observes, to bond immediately with any strange male, however unlikely, rather than talk closely to an unaccustomed woman. She watches his back: the dark blue suit hangs well, cut loose across the shoulders. Something about him suggests order and precision, but there's also a hint of performance. It's there in the slightly too-chummy way he's chatting with the bartender, an older man in his late sixties, who looks like a former jazz musician, and the way he's looking at her now with a faint glimmer of apology, as if to say: 'I'm really sorry I'm doing this.'

He carries their gin and tonics over to the table, glancing around the club, walking a little too carefully, as if expecting some scenery to be suddenly unrolled in front of him or an alarm to go off. She tries not to look at him.

'Elise,' he says, sitting down and crossing his legs, revealing a line of pale blue sock.

'Richard.' She sips her drink and looks at him. They don't speak for a while. It's as if they need to confirm that they are who they say they are.

'You haven't been here before?' he asks.

She shakes her head, lifts the lemon-scented glass to her mouth and looks around. A few couples talk quietly around other glass tables, and one man, dressed in a business suit, takes a woman's hand and squeezes it. The woman looks close to tears.

'Tell me about your work, it sounds fascinating,' he says.

She leans forward. 'At the moment I'm putting together a document of the latest research on malaria. It's a huge project. We work with universities and institutions all over the world. My job is to try to classify the research, and pull together what we know about the disease so far. There's a lot of rubbish written about malaria and I spend most of my time weeding out some of the more unscrupulous claims by drug companies. I'm setting up a database of new developments. I often work with doctors.'

79

She sits back and inwardly flinches at what she's just said. Too cold, as if she were at a job interview.

Richard leans towards her. 'You said you lived in Africa?'

'A long time ago.'

Richard clears his throat. 'I worked in Delhi. Extraordinary place, India. Fucking awful, really. You know, seeing people lying half dead in the streets next to some opulent hotel.'

The expletive makes him appear friendlier.

'How long were you in India?'

'Two years. Working in any London hospital is paradise in comparison.'

'Which hospital is it again, I'm afraid I've forgotten?' She feels herself flush. She should have remembered this piece of essential information.

'The Royal Free.'

'Of course.'

He leans back in his seat and smiles. She can see his knees under the glass table. What do doctors think about when they make love? she wonders.

'The menu here is very good,' Richard offers. 'Shall we order something?'

A waiter arrives with a list of Italian-inspired dishes printed on plain white card. No prices.

'I'll have the white truffle risotto,' Richard says without glancing at the card.

'The same,' she says, feeling the minutest pressure. She really wanted the crab.

'I thought we might look at a play afterwards if that's all right with you,' he says as the risotto arrives on huge white plates. The thought occurs to Elise that the ultimate sign of wealth must be massive tableware with small amounts of prosaic food.

'Fine,' she says through a mouthful of hot rice. 'What's the play?'

'*Who's Afraid of Virginia Woolf?* My daughter's playing in it.'

'Wonderful,' she says and Richard looks shy, but delighted.

'I didn't know whether it would be a good idea, or not, but thought . . .' He trails off, unable to put the thought into words. A pool of sweat has collected in the deep groove of his upper lip. Steady hands, though, which is a relief.

She covers her mouth with her napkin. 'No, really, it sounds perfect.'

Excusing herself after they have eaten, she goes to the Ladies where she looks at her reflection in the moonbright mirror and waits for the redness in her face to die down. Coming out, she is startled to see Richard standing right outside, folding a credit card slip into his wallet.

'We'll take a cab, if that's all right with you.'

A young waiter with a white cloth tucked into his jeans dances out into the traffic, hailing them a cab. Richard watches him, his eyes still, mouth slightly set.

Inside the taxi they sit with thighs touching in the slippery seat.

'How long were you married?' Richard asks. 'I can't remember anything of what you said. I was a little nervous when you phoned to tell you the truth.'

Nervous. So, he is new to this.

'My husband died in Africa.'

'You didn't tell me that?'

'No!' Laughing. 'It's not the sort of thing you launch into on a first phone call.'

'Of course not. Was it malaria?' he asks, face composed. But she notices a tiny light has lit up his eyes.

'He . . . died in a plane crash.'

'How dreadful . . .'

The cab passes over the Strand where the Thames, trapped between grey concrete ramparts, appears exhausted of life. Lost for words, they each look out of the window on their side of the cab.

'Such a waste,' says the cab driver to no one in particular. A moment later he eases the cab to a halt, as if reining a slightly unruly horse. 'Woah, there you go!'

Richard leans towards her and confides in a stage whisper, 'I don't know whether it's a sign that I'm becoming a pedant, but I can't help noticing this tendency among cab drivers to speak like Australian stockmen.' The attempt at wit is awkward, but she smiles anyway.

Elise's stomach rumbles and burps all the way through the performance and she tries to quieten it by covering it with her programme, which has a luminous photograph of Richard's daughter on the cover. She has long red hair trailing down her back and cream skin. A little too slender for the part of Martha, though, Elise thinks. Richard watches his daughter intently, his face cupped in his palm. She delivers her lines with a savage yet squeaky accent. She is so good it is strangely appalling, and Elise feels uncomfortable, as if they had somehow stumbled on Richard's daughter having sex in a public place.

After the performance they walk through Soho in silence. All the young couples on the streets appear locked in combat and there's a screechy tension in the air. Richard suggests a last drink somewhere.

They settle into a pair of deep blue curved armchairs in a quiet corner of a cocktail bar. Swirling her drink she says flirtatiously, 'Urbane heart surgeon WLTM seriously good-looking older woman with a passion for theatre, art and *mashed potato*.'

'I was trying to be amusing. Actually, I never eat it.'

'I thought a heart surgeon would be quite terrifying, intellectually.'

'Well, thanks.'

'I didn't mean . . . I'm sorry.'

'The play wasn't a good idea, I know,' he says quietly.

'Your daughter is an excellent actress.'

'She has fire in her soul. She gets it from her mother.'

'Really?' Elise looks down at her drink and wonders whether she should ask.

Richard plays with a book of matches on the table. 'My marriage broke up because I worked too hard,' he says flatly. He twists the little book of matches which has the name Jet Bar written in silver. 'What about you, has there been anyone else since your husband died?'

She hesitates. 'Nothing serious. I've also been working too hard.'

A companionable laugh. How might it be, she thinks, to wake up on a Sunday morning and argue about whose turn it is to fetch the newspapers?

'You know,' she says, still laughing. 'For ages I thought *WLTM* meant would like to marry!'

'Your place in Highgate, is it a flat or a house?' he asks mildly.

'Flat. Perhaps you'd like to come over for lunch one weekend. I find those are usually the worst times. Don't you?' She flushes, wondering whether she's revealed too much.

'I nearly always work at weekends,' he says, suddenly putting the matches down on the table.

'Well, so do I, I don't mean immediately, of course.'

Richard looks at her wearily and suddenly the table in the window has become a cold place to sit.

'I'm getting rather tired,' he says apologetically. 'Would you mind awfully if we left? I have an early start tomorrow.'

'Of course.'

She feels a familiar mixture of anger and guilt. She doesn't understand why it is that whenever she relaxes enough to start really talking with a man, especially an older attractive man, he immediately loses interest.

As they leave Richard tries to help her with her coat, but she politely shrugs him off. They stand in the road for a moment looking for a space to cross. She's grateful for the roaring traffic, the snarling scooters and hard-edged shiny cars, the hot smell of rubbish and strong tobacco. The young gobbling up London. It suddenly seems to her more honest than the encounter that has just taken place. A young man wearing a leather jacket with the collar turned up gives her an appreciative glance. The *once-over*, or *checking her out*, as Memory would say. Maybe she could go to Memory's flat now, just turn up for another nightcap, but she dismisses the thought. She would probably be out somewhere anyway. It is after all Friday night.

Now Elise turns to Richard and smiles at him, graciously. Frowning at the noise around them, his hand already raised to halt a cab, he kisses her fleetingly on the cheek.

'I had a wonderful time,' he says. 'Thank you.' Then he slides into the cab and does not look round.

At home Elise takes a long bath scented with Sanctuary oil, a present from Memory given last Christmas Eve in the street outside Selfridges where they had met for coffee. What had they talked about? Elise has forgotten. Sometimes it seems as if they have stopped talking altogether. When did that happen? Again she doesn't remember, things just drifted and when they did meet it was awkward, as if they were both suppressing something. Maybe she should arrange to meet Memory properly, have supper somewhere. She had seemed strained the last time she came to the office, as though she had something on her mind. Perhaps it was work. Memory was probably getting bored. The job at the photo agency had never really been right for her. Memory was too restless to be pinned down by a desk job; she needed something more stimulating.

Sliding deeper into her bath, Elise looks at her stomach, the skin stretched pale and smooth; her stomach is the only part of her that seems ageless, still ripe. She wonders whether she could still conceive and the thought makes her breasts ache. She puts her hands under them and feels their weight: they have become smaller and more insular over the years, shrunk in on themselves, quiet inside her expensive bras. She runs her hand down her thighs and checks her skin for flaws, raised moles, secret lumps; she has a fear of developing a malignancy; collapsing from the inside. The skin on her shins is thin and dry and bluish; her thighs are ruddier and flare red when she steps from the bath.

Wrapped in a deep white bathrobe Elise checks her complexion. She rubs moisturizer into her skin with the upward sweeping movements she learned during a facial. The mirror is an unremitting oval, alluring as mercury. She'd caught sight of herself in its magnifying face one stale afternoon in Boots, and had not recognized what she saw. A wild impulse to sweep up all the mirrors had come over her, but she had taken just the one, this steely one, over to the till. As she searched in her purse, the assistant had asked, 'Anything to redeem?'

She flosses her teeth and then brushes them with the tap turned off, a habit from Africa. She watches the water swirl down the sink, carrying away the bloodied thread, like a tiny umbilical cord, and then as she turns to reach for a towel to dab her mouth she remembers what it was Memory had asked in Selfridges. How could she have forgotten? It was a question about Paul. Unexpected, out of the blue. Utterly devastating.

'Who taught Paul Cougan to fly?'

She'd stalled and said she couldn't remember, but Memory had pressed her, and so she had told her his name. It was the first time she'd spoken the name in years and it had tasted strange in her mouth.

'Max Searle his name was. I don't remember much about that time. It's all so long ago.' Elise had looked at the backs of people bent over scrambled eggs and smoked salmon. Here, surrounded by murals in pink, blue and gold, everyone talked in muted tones as if in deference to the tinkling of fine china and cutlery, delicate as wind-chimes.

'Max Searle,' Memory repeated, causing Elise to grip her chair hard. 'Was he a friend of yours?'

She stirred her coffee slowly, lifted the spoon, looked briefly at her reflection, then quickly put the spoon down on her plate where it skidded and clattered. 'Not really. He was a farmer. He showed us around when we arrived.'

'Is he still alive?' Memory was leaning forward, her own coffee untouched.

'I don't know.' Her bag was at her feet. She dropped her head and fished around, feeling for her purse. Opposite her Memory waited, twisting a bit of skin on her lip. Elise lifted her purse and put it on the table between them. 'Listen, why don't you go and pay? My treat.'

'They'll bring the bill.'

'Of course.'

'What's wrong, you seem upset?'

'It's nothing.'

She had placed her fingers on the table ready to rise for the bathroom when Memory said, 'Why have you never spoken about him?'

'Who?'

'*Max Searle*. He must have known Paul pretty well, I mean if he taught him to fly. I imagine that would create a bond?'

'I suppose so.'

'You never heard anything from Max after you left?'

'No, he wasn't a writer.'

'What was he like?'

'Look, why all these questions, Memory? We're supposed to be enjoying ourselves. Come on, let's go.'

Memory looked down into her coffee. 'It puzzles me, that's all. There's so much I don't know. You've never really told me the details.'

'I suppose I've blanked most of it from my mind. It's not something I want to dwell on. It was an awful time.'

Memory had winced and then smiled. Her face had a wonderful purity when she smiled. 'I'm sorry, it's Christmas Eve and I can't believe I'm being so insensitive. I'm really sorry.'

They had got up from their chairs and gone to the bathroom together. Facing each other in the mirror over the sink as they washed their hands Elise had felt a beat of panic at the bright look in Memory's eyes.

The message on the postcard also says 'sorry'. Elise turns it over in her hands, wondering when it came. She hasn't checked her post in days. The handwriting is so familiar, so heart-stopping.

'Sorry, I just didn't know how to tell you . . .' She reads it several times, but is unable to take in the message. She walks around her flat turning the card over in her hands, her mind ringing. Eventually she sinks into the sofa. She feels suddenly chilly. But when she tries get up to turn on the central heating, she finds that she cannot move. She twists the card over. The red London bus on the front leers. A telephone begins to ring in the flat upstairs. She listens to its sharp tone. She has the beginnings of a headache. Unfolding her legs carefully, she manages to get up from the sofa and walk over to the window. The sky is a familiar pale orange, brightened by the lights of passing aircraft. She presses her cheek against the cool glass. Memories she's worked so carefully to conceal start to play through her mind in cinematic detail. She begins to shudder. Clutching her robe, she looks up at the London sky. There are no stars. She misses the stars. Every night in Africa she used to look at the stars. She can see her reflection in the cold glass. It looks young and far away.

6

AIR EXPERIENCE

It should be remembered that a point visible to the instructor is
not necessarily visible to the pupil.

Scotland, NewYear's Eve, 1971

Paul Cougan took the hill roads to the party at the Torphins
Hotel. The dress suit he wore still breathed his father's smell,
a blend of hair oil and scorched starch. It was the suit his father
had worn for his wedding. Cut less generously than the baggy
jackets Paul was used to wearing around college, it pinched him
under the arms and gripped his neck so viciously that he was
beginning to regret his decision to wear it.

Frost beamed in his headlights. Up here in the swarming hills
it was difficult to keep track of distance. The hills seemed closer
than they actually were. But one thing was certain, it was getting
colder by the hour and soon all the roads would be iced. Paul
didn't know if he was ready for a party. He was going because he
didn't know what else to do. It would be a kind of test: his first
social event since his mother and father had died.

He turned the heater dial up a notch and the suit smell spread
until it filled the car, so pungently close his father might have
been sitting in the passenger seat next to him. But driving out
anywhere with his father for a drink or a meal had been inconceivable, and not simply because his father had suffered from
heart trouble even though he was no drinker (he went down
among the trees when his heart burst) but because it was

somehow shaming. On the few, odd occasions they had gone out, once for his mother's birthday to a local bar where it was so silent you could hear the ticking of the clock and the sighing of the barman, Daniel Cougan had sat stiffly as if waiting for someone to give him permission to speak. He preferred to live outside and his job as a woodcutter meant that the sky and trees were part of his inner landscape; his language was the movement of the clouds, the voice of the wind. A deep, slow intelligence showed in his face, but he had never in his life said a word about his thoughts. So seldom did he speak that words when they came were an embarrassment, something to be swept away quickly, like tears.

Paul shoved one sleeve of the scratchy suit across his face and drove fast across the top of the hill. He had started out a little later than he intended and he needed to make up time. He followed two tracks of grey mashed snow, keeping to the centre of the road because if he went into a skid it would have been quite easy to plunge into the valley. He couldn't see the valley in the darkness, but at the bottom of it there was a deep black loch where his father had gone swimming the day before he married his mother. It was the only intimate piece of family history Paul knew. His mother had told him about it one day when they were out driving. The image had stayed in Paul's mind for years: the silent man stripped naked on the eve of his wedding, bare feet planted on the black shore of the deepest loch in the Highlands, clothes in a quiet bundle behind him, all his future ahead of him.

He kept to the right side of the road where the snow had banked and, in some places, drifted into frozen islands. A chemistry student's family who owned the hotel were paying for the party, and although he barely knew the student, she had insisted he came because, and she said this with her head tilted towards her shoulder, *she had heard,* and what she had heard was that Paul's father had died on the morning of his birthday followed, two days later, by his mother. The news had rippled around the campus, and Paul had achieved a certain glamour because of it. People slowed in the corridors when he went past and asked him to join their table in the dining hall. But they also left space around him as if expecting him to fall over. Girls he wanted to sleep with smiled at him. Lecturers stopped and spoke with him. He was asked if he wanted to defer on his examinations. It was easy. It was appalling. It wasn't what he expected. He felt as if all his thoughts and feelings had become a slow frozen river and that made responding to the attention awkward. Whatever he said sounded inappropriate, too brightly grateful or too subdued and humble. Sometimes in the middle of a group of friends he would catch himself laughing just a little too loudly.

There were other bizarre symptoms of grief: he couldn't eat fleshy food; just putting meat or fish near his mouth made him gag; and he was constantly cold. At night he slept in his narrow student bed with his clothes on, feet bound in a sweater. It seemed to him that he was suffering the first vague twinges of an illness that would take months to brew up into proper symptoms. Sometimes, as he fitfully slept, there would be a soft knock on the door. But he ignored all temptations.

Taking a corner, he felt the wheels crackle over ice and the car momentarily slip from his grasp. He needed to take things a bit steadier, not drive so fast; the party wasn't going to go away, as his mother would have said. She was always on at him to slow down: 'Why the rush? You go on as if you're going to run out of life.' But she would have been pleased that he wasn't going to sit around moping in his room, especially on New Year's Eve. His mother had approved of celebration, anything that shook a person out of himself was a good thing, not that she had gone to many parties herself. New Year had always been a quiet time at home because of his father. She usually made a cake, though, filling the croft with warm scents of almond and orange. Near midnight his mother would drink a tiny glass of whisky and eat a slice of cake as she toasted the future.

His father slept through these small ceremonies, flat on his back upstairs. Much of ordinary life was simply incomprehensible to his father, who was so inhibited it made him utterly incorruptible. Paul used to think that even if someone had offered his father a million pounds he would have merely nodded and continued working. He was so rooted to his way in the world that he didn't even know it limited him. He acted as if he were the freest man alive and Paul envied him. It was his father's certainty, he supposed, his absolute attachment to his circumstances and refusal to yearn for something better that made him so admirable.

At home, there had been a kind of simple comfort in living alongside his father's routine, his *way*, his lukewarm bath every night, his simple meals and Sunday sleep; his solitary work in the wood. Sometimes Paul, looking up from his homework and seeing his father silently absorbed in his thoughts, had the sense that he was obeying orders from an invisible source.

Snow streamed towards him in straight lines and he flicked his windscreen wipers to clear his vision. Every snowflake was different, a unique pattern. The thought made him swallow. He remembered his mother standing at the sink the day after his father died, her face red and swollen, looking up at the heavy white sky. 'There's snow coming later,' she said. He thought he heard a note of regret. Maybe he wanted to hear it because the next day she was gone. He had stood in the garden staring at his own solitary track of footprints as he waited for the doctor.

Having them both go together was stupefying, but also oddly coherent. Even though they had not been obviously close, they were a pair, like swans who stay with partners for life. He'd always felt excluded from them, not quite of their world; not humble enough to be so content with so little. The sympathy gifts that seemed to be coming his way as a result of their deaths made him feel like a fraud.

Needing to breathe, he wound down the window to let in some cold night air. A cracked blue moon hung over the hills, a mournful grin across its face. Sometimes Paul imagined the face of the moon reflected his own mood, which was romantic for someone supposed to be studying environmental science. He wished he had chosen philosophy instead because all the philosophy students he met seemed to be in love with the subject. He had tried to switch, but was advised by his tutor to stay in science. He would not find employment within philosophy, and that was what it was all about, wasn't it? Paul didn't argue. He needed money. He needed a job. Several science students had already been approached by drug companies or laboratories with job offers. But Paul had been waiting. He told himself he didn't want to take the first opportunity that came up. He would wait.

He saw the eyes shining in his headlights just as he realized they belonged to a young deer. For a split second they stared at each other. The deer stood on an island of snow, its four slender legs streaked with dark melting water. Paul could see its breath and all its young muscles quivering; the veins standing out on its neck. It dipped its head and then leaped under his wheels.

There was a hollow bang, a sound like stones being tipped from a bag, a scuffle under the belly of the car. Some instinct made Paul speed up, and the sound carried on in belting shudders, which leaped through the car, jarring every bone in his body. Stiff with tension, craning forward, his eyes sweeping the road for signs of blood, he pressed on and after a short while the terrible sound died. He stopped the car and stepped out on to the road.

Inexplicably the air felt warm around him. He undid the pins holding his shirt and loosened the collar to let in some air. The black bow tie he scrunched up in his pocket. The road was shining with new ice, the air cold and clear. All around him the hills lay in solemn silence, summits drenched in snow. He guessed the deer had escaped, but he decided to walk up the road just in case.

The road bent around slightly to the right and he came across a small stone bridge where there was a stream. He could hear the water gulping. Just beyond the bridge a dark shape like a full sack lay in the centre of the road.

The deer's head was turned to one side, eyes open and glassy, the expression in them one of surprise. She – somehow Paul knew that she was female – appeared gently beautiful with a soft russet coat dappled with cream markings in smudged half-moons. He knelt down by her side and put his hand under her muzzle. It was beaded with fine droplets of water. Looking down over the body he saw that her belly had been split open. Her guts protruded in a mass of corded red, as if she were giving birth. He touched her neck. The red needles of fur lay stiff and cold. He picked up the slim head and cradled it in his lap.

The road felt gritty beneath him. He looked at the hills. He felt he couldn't breathe properly. He let go of the head and pulled at the deer's front leg. The tiny hoof in his hand felt warm, but the leg was sickeningly loose as if broken or dislocated. He took hold of both her front legs and pulled. As she shifted he could feel the small bones move under her skin. She weighed more than he did and he had to work hard to drag her clear. He pulled her to the edge of the snow-covered verge and then, sweating inside his suit, pushed her further with his feet. He had to sit on the cold road to do this. The deer rolled inch by inch, her spine curved towards him; she looked perfect, undamaged. 'Sorry,' he kept saying as he pushed her. 'I'm just so sorry.'

He stood up and caught his breath, wiping his face which was warm with tears. Then he crouched down, scooped up a handful of snow and scattered it across the dark body. He walked back to the car. Unable to drive immediately he sat for a moment with the heater turned on high, the small hot stink of death all around him.

'Go on, blow your mind.' The barman slammed a shot glass with alternate layers of clear and murky liquid down on the bar.

'What the hell is it?'

'B52. What you want is three of these.'

What you want. Paul looked into the drink and then took a cautious sip.

'No, you've got to down it, so the layers mix. Imagine you're a human cocktail shaker.'

Paul did as he was told and downed.

'Same again?' The barman turned towards the optics and Paul tried not to look at his reflection in the mirror behind the bottles. He put his hand in his pocket and his fingers broke through the thin satin lining. Strange there hadn't been any blood. He thought his hands and shoes would be covered with it, but there were no obvious signs of the killing at all, just that hot, musty smell which was beginning to fade now.

Turning around on his bar stool he looked across the ballroom. Crystal chandeliers illuminated small islands of girls in ball-gowns of evergreen colours with red tartan sashes and bows. The young men, who wore dinner suits or kilts, were smoking and talking to one another, occasionally glancing up to the stage where a piper played a ballad. Down one wall a trestle table covered with a white cloth was being attended to by a group of elderly women bearing plates of sandwiches, small rolls, pastries and cakes. The kitchen led off from the ballroom through a swing door with a round porthole behind which heads wearing scarves could be seen moving up and down. Every time the door opened a slice of acid light spilled across the dance floor.

On every table there was a raffia wine bottle with a red candle stuck into it. Wreaths of holly and evergreen were strung on the walls. The dance floor had been smoothed with chalk. Familiar faces appeared fleetingly in candlelight, glossed and urgently talking. Paul couldn't follow any of the conversations because there was too much movement, too many hands up to mouths, too many obscuring wine glasses and cigarettes. There was a ringing in his ears. He looked down at the bar where another B52 waited serenely.

A red-faced caller urged dancers to take their places. Paul watched. A space cleared and a line of women stood talking to each other, stroking creases from dresses. The row of men stood silently looking at the women. The caller stamped his foot, swinging the red chequered sack of his kilt, and the women stopped talking and linked hands. They looked up at the caller expectantly while the men bunched ever so slightly closer together.

It was a walking kind of dance that started off with partners strolling diagonally across the floor, turning, delivering a few sharp steps, then moving on and repeating the process with a new partner. Almost imperceptibly the dance got faster. Paul watched the women move around. He was interested to see how they greeted each new male partner and although nearly all the women smiled at nearly all their partners he could still tell whether the woman really liked the man she had been paired with. Her shoulders might soften or her head might move just that tiny little bit closer to his than it had with a previous partner. There was a woman he could not take his eyes from. She stood out because of her dress, simple, black, sleeveless, showing off pale slender arms. Her hair flowed a dark honey colour and she had clasped it at the back of her neck with a pink flower clip, like an orchid or hibiscus.

Paul watched her move smoothly from partner to partner. There was something a little detached about her, Paul thought, as if she were holding herself in check. He was struck by the thought that she was the only woman among all those dancing who did not appear to be attracted to any of the men. It made him want her. Not really knowing what he was going to do, he slid from his stool.

The dance ended and Paul was caught for a moment in a brilliant white spotlight. He put his hand up to his face to shield his eyes. People bumped past him as they made their way back to tables. The girl with the flower stepped off the polished floor and gave him a backward glance before being absorbed into the soft fug of smoke and candlelight.

'You all right?' It was Thomas, his friend, in unfamiliar white tails, blond hair stiffly corrugated with spray. 'I didn't think you'd made it. I heard the roads were bad across the top.' He gestured to Paul to sit down at his table where two girls in identical magenta gowns chattered to each other in French.

'I got held up. I hit a deer on the hill.'

The girls stopped talking and looked at him.

'Bad luck,' said Thomas. 'I hit a dog once, not very pleasant. It shakes you up a bit.' He looked at Paul sympathetically. 'Much damage?'

'It had a hole in its stomach.'

Thomas laughed. 'I mean damage to the car, idiot!'

'I don't know, I didn't look.'

'Did you have to kill it yourself?' one of the girls asked brightly.

'With your bare hands?' her friend added. 'I've heard it's almost impossible to break a deer's neck.'

'No, I killed it outright.'

The girls looked down at their laps.

'It wasn't your fault, these things happen,' Thomas said quickly. 'Join us, have a drink.'

The girls looked at him expectantly. Paul brushed his hands down his suit. 'No, thanks all the same. I've had enough.'

He retreated to the bar where he grimly lit a cigarette. Refusing another B52, he settled for a pint, drinking it slowly in the hope that it might sober him. He caught a glimpse of the girl again, laughing at a tall man who escorted her off the dance floor with his hand around her waist. At the trestle tables a row of elderly women, wearing white aprons and lipstick, stood at intervals, nervously looking down at the food.

One of the magenta girls wandered over to the bar with a plate of sandwiches and offered Paul one. When he refused her face hardened a little and she leaned up against the bar and turned away from him. She toyed with the cheese cubes and tiny silver onions speared on cocktail sticks, deliberately pricking her finger until she had squeezed out a little pearl of blood. 'I've been thinking about what happened to you,' she said.

Half listening, he sipped at his pint. The girl was watching herself in the mirror and seemed drunk.

'My friend over there' – she waved her arm vaguely – 'is a vegetarian and a Christian.' She swung her eyes round to rest on his. Her breath had a smell that was like soiled hay. He sipped his pint, and prepared to endure some kind of lecture. 'She says that when a man kills an animal, *any animal*' – and here she looked at him intently – 'he kills God. What do you think of that?'

He drained the rest of his pint and walked away, feeling her eyes on his back. At the door there was a queue for the cloakroom. Paul pushed his way through and walked around the outside of the hotel, his feet crunching on the sandy gravel. The sky was soft and black with a sprinkling of stars. He lit another cigarette and smoked it in quick bursts. The smoke felt warm around his face. He could hear faint music; a wave of talking, rising and falling. He dropped the cigarette and ground it into the gravel with his shoe. The black narrow lace-ups he wore had also belonged to his father. A sprinkling of powder had fallen out when he first tried them on, the buttery leather offering no resistance as if the shoes had been hand-made especially for him. Now here he was, cold and alone, literally standing in his father's footsteps. On the eve of the New Year.

He left the wall and came to the back of the hotel where a long rolling frosted lawn opened out on to a hollow space holding a swimming pool. Drained for winter, its sides glittering with ice, it had attracted a group of young men in tuxedos and their silken women, one wearing a tiara. The men tossed gravel into the pool and the women laughed, their voices like crystal. A noise from the hotel made everyone look up. Then the men and women divided into pairs and began to kiss and hug each other. Paul watched a man pick up a woman and swing her across the pool, laughing as her shrieks cut open the air.

Overwhelmed by a sense of heaviness, Paul walked over to the car park. New snow dusted the roofs and he had to search a bit to find his car, an old yellow Triumph Herald, which had been his mother's car and treated by her like a dear friend. He used a cigarette packet to scrape away the skin of snow from the windscreen. He had forgotten gloves and blew on his stinging hands to warm them. From the hotel he could hear people singing 'Auld Lang Syne' and letting off party crackers. His breath flared in front of him, thick with the smell of alcohol. He climbed inside the car and sat for a few moments looking out at the spooling darkness. There was a small hole at the base of the windscreen with a fracture across the glass in the shape of a half-moon. When he collided with the deer a stone must have come flying up like a bullet.

When a man kills an animal, he kills God. When a man kills . . . Why hadn't he braked at the first sight of the eyes in his lights? The icy roads were a familiar hazard. He should have stopped. He had killed an animal. It had to mean something. Perhaps it was an omen of some kind. He remembered the feeling he'd had after he pulled her clear, the strange glimmering thought that somehow he'd been given an additional *soul*. There was something he needed to take care of, although he wasn't quite sure how.

Blackness spread in front of him. It was an ordinary night, quiet, still and cold. He felt a sudden lull in his thoughts. Perhaps it was just the alcohol thinking; the strange elation he felt was probably only tiredness. He'd run over a deer. So what? Thousands of animals were killed every day on the roads. His accident was nothing special. A road kill. He only wanted it to mean something because he felt guilty that he hadn't been able to stop. He took a deep breath and turned the key in the ignition.

The bullet hole in the windscreen was a glittering frozen eye. Turning the wipers on to brush away the last smears of ice, he felt a breeze around the back of his neck, a cool presence, as if someone were breathing behind him. Instinctively he jerked his head round. Curled up on the back seat, wrapped in his mother's old plaid blanket, was the girl asleep, her long hank of hair hanging over the seat, the flower clip fallen to the floor. He turned back and put both hands on the steering wheel and clenched it hard. The girl was breathing brokenly through her mouth, wheezing a little as if her airway were slightly blocked. Her feet were drawn up on the seat under the blanket. The top of her shoulder was uncovered like a smooth white stone. He leaned over and then withdrew his hand quickly. Perhaps if he just sat still he would be able to work out what to do.

Leaning his head on the steering wheel, the engine thrumming warmly, he closed his eyes. He was so deeply tired he could sleep for days. Why had she climbed into his car, of all places, and why her? Maybe someone was looking for her, the big man in the kilt she'd been dancing with. He could see a few people standing around at the front of the hotel looking down towards the car park.

The heater churned out its musty warmth and he wound down the window a little to breathe in some fresh air. At the dry sound of the window lever the stowaway stirred and clicked her mouth a little before nuzzling deeper into the blanket.

'I'm sorry, but you're going to have to leave now,' Paul announced, trying to calm the nervous tremor in his voice. The girl gave a little snore. He wondered whether to return to the party. In his rear-view mirror the hotel seemed smaller, a condensed castle looped in white light. The people he'd seen outside had gone.

Reaching over to the back seat, he gently jogged the blanket, feeling the girl's warmth. She stirred crossly. Maybe if he drove very slowly around the car park she might wake up.

At the hotel gates, he paused with his foot hovering over the brake. The gravel crackled under his tyres as he pulled out on to the road and headed for the hill roads. At first he drove slowly with the window wound down thinking the night air would wake her. She slept on soundly. He picked up speed. It wasn't his intention to do anything: he would make sure she got home safely. Eventually. For now he wanted to enjoy this sense of adventure, of taking flight with a girl he did not know to a place he hadn't yet been. He pushed the car on, wheels bumping against solid lumps of snow.

She woke as he drove across the small stone bridge sitting suddenly upright, her hair falling all over her shoulders. 'Where are we going?'

Paul slammed on the brakes and skidded on a patch of ice.

'Shit,' the girl said levelly. 'A kidnapper who can't drive.'

'I'm sorry. I'll take you back now, wherever you want to go. You say.'

The girl rubbed her face and flicked back her hair. 'You're Paul Cougan.'

He kept his eyes on the road and looked at the snowy verge. They were nearing the place where the deer had leaped.

'How do you know that?'

'I just know.'

The hills were deep white canyons with sparkling slopes. He felt clear-headed. He liked the way she had said his name, as if she'd somehow chosen him.

'What's your name?'

'Elise. At college I'm known as Ellie, but I really prefer Elise.'

'Elise,' he repeated.

'I like your car,' she said. 'It has a comfortable smell. I found it open, you know.'

'I never lock it.'

'You should, someone might steal it.'

Or steal into it, he thought. He wondered where he could take her. It would have to be somewhere extraordinary. A café or garage would be too, well, rough and ugly. What he needed was an old place that would be open for breakfast at six in the morning, somewhere with a fire and a telephone. He knew of a place maybe twenty miles on. Taking a corner a little too fast, he skidded again on ice.

'What's the rush?' said the girl from the back.

'Sorry.' He slowed right down. He would take his time over this and do everything properly. He glanced in the rear-view mirror. The girl was now leaning back against the seat with her eyes closed, breathing through her mouth. The car smelled of her. He took a long breath and drove on, this time taking the corners smoothly across the spreading hills.

The castle was further away than he thought and it was dawn by the time they arrived. The grey granite building was surrounded by pine trees, middle boughs weighed down with great platters of snow. Around half a dozen cars were parked in front on a semicircular drive, some with canvas covers over bonnets and windscreens. He looked round at the girl before he got out. She was sleeping, her head tucked into her neck, the blanket drawn up over her shoulders. He called her name. 'Elise?' He loved the sound of it, the feel of the name on his lips. But she stayed asleep, snuffling gently, completely unaware that they had stopped. He opened the car door and a blast of cold air hit his chest, making him cough.

The castle was closed. He tried peering through the keyhole in a black iron lock mounted on a heavy wooden door, but there was no sign of light or life. He rattled the door handle once, hearing the sound echo down what he presumed was a long corridor. Wind whisked snow from the trees. It was getting light, the sun slowly making its appearance as a faint pink glow behind pearl-coloured clouds. He turned back towards the car.

Not knowing what else to do, he took the road that led eventually to the croft. At least, he thought, it might be still warm. He'd lit the wood-burner when he'd been back only a couple of days before, sorting through his parents' clothes which he'd bundled into garden sacks, except for one or two pieces he couldn't bear to give away, the dress suit and shoes belonging to his father, which he now wore, and a pair of garnet earrings belonging to his mother. Everything else he'd decided to keep: dishes in the kitchen and bed linen and towels stored behind a curtain near the bathroom. He didn't know what he was going to do with the property; it was too soon to make decisions, but for now he found it consoling just knowing that it was still there and he could visit any time he wanted.

The girl yawned from the back and Paul looked round at her. She smiled at him through watery eyes and lifted her hair from her neck, rubbing a space under her ear and grimacing. 'I think I slept awkwardly,' she said, yawning again, showing milky, slightly pointed white teeth. There was something feline about her mouth, and her dark gold colouring. 'Where are we going now?'

'To my parents' place.' He kept his eyes on the road, his voice steady.

'Oh.' He could tell that she was surprised. 'Will they mind us arriving so early in the morning?' Then with a sharp intake of breath she clapped her hand over her mouth and rolled her eyes. 'Oh, my God, I'm so sorry.'

'That's all right,' he said. For some reason he felt strangely comforted by her blunder. 'I've been half living there since they . . .' He hesitated. It was still difficult saying the word *died*. And 'gone' sounded as if they'd left the country, or got lost. '. . . left. I've just needed to sort out a few things.'

'It must be so hard for you,' she said, leaning forward, propping both arms over the front seats. 'I think I'd fall apart if I lost my mum and dad, especially my dad.'

She was so close he could smell the stale cigarette smoke in her hair. He wondered what her parents were like, probably posh and intelligent. There was something about her that made him feel old and set in his ways, just like his parents. Maybe that's what happens when you meet someone new, he thought. You offer them a mirror of your origins almost without knowing it.

'What does your dad do?' It sounded childish, a primary school question, but he had to know.

'He's a professor of anthropology and a writer.'

'Is he well known, I mean would I have heard of him?'

'I doubt it.' She sighed as if there were more she wanted to say. 'But I don't want to talk about *me*, we should be talking about *you*. Tell me about what happened to your mother and father, that's if you feel all right talking about it.'

He drew breath sharply. She leaned her head on her curled palm just near his shoulder and he could feel her lazy interest. He began to tell her about getting the call while he was eating breakfast in halls on the morning of his birthday on 2 December. He remembered the shout, the brief knock on the door. 'Paul Cougan, call for you,' and finding the phone dangling on its cord as he went up to take it. 'I thought it would be my mother ringing to wish me a happy birthday, but . . .'

'Go on,' Elise said.

'She said Father had been found in the wood. He'd had a heart attack and could I drive round, but only if it wasn't too much for me. She knew that I probably had plans, and she wasn't even going to phone, but she didn't want me to think she'd forgotten my birthday.' He paused and swallowed. 'She said she was sorry. I couldn't believe it.'

'Wow,' Elise breathed. 'What a terrible moment that must have been for you.'

He turned his head slightly and saw that there were tears in her eyes. He felt awkward then, but she urged him to continue, pressing him for details when he faltered and he managed to tell her the rest as he drove, finishing his account of the funeral and the first odd days back at college just as they pulled into the turning that led up a rough track. 'This is it.'

When he opened the door the first thing he saw were the two forgotten sacks of clothes side by side in the middle of the sitting-room floor. With a surge in his chest he heaved them up in both arms and carried them to the bedroom and put them on top of the bed. His mother's old travel alarm clock showed the time was 8 a.m., too early or late for sleep. He went back into the sitting room and found Elise crouching by the wood-burner screwing up pieces of newspaper and pushing them under charred pieces of log. 'Here, let me.' He knelt down beside her and felt her hand touch his shoulder. Embarrassed, he kept his head down as he busied himself in arranging small pieces of kindling. When the fire was roaring they both sat in silence, watching the flames flicker up the sides of the blackened walls.

7

TAKING OFF (INTO WIND)

Visualise yourself coming out of the big end of the windsock: you
will then be head to wind.

Scotland, 1972

Paul changed into work clothes and washed, feeling slightly
uncomfortable for being able to go about his usual routine
while Elise slept on the sofa, still in her party dress, dirty bare feet
dangling. As he shaved he thought about the way she had climbed
into his car and let him drive her away without a care for what
might happen later. She'd said that she was drunk and had got the
wrong car by mistake; the big man in the kilt was supposed to be
taking her home, but she couldn't find his car and it had got too
cold to carry on looking and so she had tried a few car doors until
she found the Triumph open. The sequence of events had seemed
to Paul like a small miracle, but now he felt worried about how
things were going to turn out. At some point, he supposed, he
would have to drive her back to the big man's house because that
was where she was staying for the rest of the holiday.

He rinsed his razor and began to clean his teeth, his eyes straying to his father's bristle shaving brush squatting on the side of
the sink, and the two worn, stained toothbrushes standing up in
a mug. He dried his mouth on a towel and went back into the
sitting room.

Elise had not stirred. He hovered over her for a moment. Her
ability to sleep so soundly in a strange room made him feel

uneasy as if he had to keep watch for both of them, although he was not quite sure what it was he was looking out for. He just felt as if someone might burst in on them at any moment and ask what they were doing. He pulled the blanket over her naked foot and went over to check on the fire. Bending down, he noticed that the log basket was empty.

The woodshed smelled of the dark. His father's overalls hung on a nail, stiff with grease, the wide legs bowed through daily use. When Paul touched the hems of the trousers they felt cold. His father's hammers, saws and chisels were arranged in order of size, each tool occupying its own careful space on the wall. A wooden work shelf ran around three sides of the shed and this held boxes containing screwdrivers and small clear trays for screws, nails, hooks and tiny hexagonal nuts. He bent down and groped under the bench for a rope, his fingers ripping cobwebs apart with the prickling sound a sweater gives when it's pulled over the head.

The rope felt greasy and heavy and made him sweat when he dragged it out of the shed. He needed it to tie around a severed branch of an old Douglas fir that had come down in a storm a few months ago. His father had promised his mother he would cut it up for wood, but the limb had lain in a deep trough of snow, untouched for weeks. Paul knew it would have embarrassed his father to see the fir lying there every morning as he went to work. Maybe he had tried to move it and got stuck. The tree was a giant, almost 200 years old with a thick scaly bark. Beached in the snow its whorls appeared like dark eyes. Approaching it with a chain-saw and rope, Paul felt he needed to go carefully.

The saw gave three beats and ran out. Down the valley a flock of rooks took off from the trees with a black cry. Paul watched them go. His mother had disliked the rooks; their constant blatant hawking. She'd wanted his father to shoot them, or cut down the trees. She'd come to Scotland for peace; the egotistical rooks ruined it. His father said there were too many rooks to shoot. Instead he put a scarecrow in the garden. It wore a blue apron and a painted toothless grin.

Paul pulled the cord again. This time the chainsaw surged into life. The blade sliced into the old fir with a thin sound and the resin smelled sweet and heady. He piled the logs into a wheelbarrow and pushed it back towards the shed where he intended to chop it up into smaller pieces for kindling.

The exertion hurt his arms and chest and he rested for a while in the shed, rubbing his knuckles to stop them seizing up from the cold. He was built like his father, low-slung with short springy limbs and small hands and feet. But unlike his father he had no stamina. Student life had softened him and he felt out of touch with his body, his attitude towards it remote, as if it were a younger brother he used to enjoy play-fighting with, and had now grown tired of. Grimly he picked up an axe and weighed it in his hands. He remembered how his father had the knack of being able to place the point of the axe at precisely the right position to cleave the wood cleanly. Paul had watched so many times he imagined that the technique would come naturally, but when he swung the axe it bit into the wood and stayed embedded, tight as a cork in a wine bottle.

A movement by the door made him glance up and there was Elise, wearing a baggy sweater he had left behind one weekend. 'I'm going to cycle into the nearest town,' she announced calmly.

He stared at her. She had put on some orange lipstick and seemed to have got ready for something.

'Wait a minute,' he said. 'I'll take us in the car. You won't be able to find the town.'

She stepped back a pace. 'I've got a good sense of direction.' She flung back a few strands of hair. She had put on his mother's green wellingtons and rolled up her dress or belted it somehow so that it no longer hung down to her ankles. There was something about such practical presence of mind that both impressed him and made him feel uncomfortable, as if he had already failed her in some small way.

He looked down at his boots covered with sawdust and then back to her. 'Down the track and turn right, follow the road round and go straight on through the crossroads. There's a small town about a mile from there.'

'I remember it from last night.'

He looked away from her.

'There's nothing in the house,' she said. Her eyes wandered around the shed, rested on his father's overalls and came back again. 'We need some supplies.'

'Good idea.' He hauled the axe out of the wood for something to do.

'Pancakes,' she said. 'When I woke up I thought of pancakes, isn't that odd?' She laughed at herself and he felt something lurch in his stomach. His mother had made pancakes, thick with syrup and butter on slow Saturday mornings. 'I looked at the flour, but it seems too damp. Now I've thought about pancakes, I just have to make them.'

'Sounds good,' he said. The axe dragged at his arms and he yearned to put it down, but felt he couldn't. He was caught in a conflicting desire to make his physical presence as large as possible and also as small.

'See you in a little while.'

He nodded and bent over his pile of wood. A moment later he heard the crunch of bicycle tyres as she wheeled his mother's old sit-up-and-beg bicycle up through the garden. He watched as she mounted and pedalled effortlessly away down through the line of birch trees, her river of hair bouncing down her back.

The pancakes were doughy on the inside and black on the outside. A smell of burned butter hung about the croft. They drank their tea in silence, each looking a different way. Icy rain melted down the windows. Elise got up and went to the back kitchen. He heard the tense scraping of plates. He wanted to clutch at the air she'd left behind. Every time she moved he felt a vibration just under his skin. The soles of his feet felt tender, his tongue tingled and he seemed to be sweating all the time. He was restless, his reactions on the tip of ignition. He had no idea that one person could generate such fragile electricity. By just moving the air she made him feel stingingly alive.

'Well,' she said as she came back and looked at the table with its plate piled with inedible pancakes. 'What now?'

They drove up to the hills. He wanted to show her the places he'd explored as a boy, all his secret dens and hide-outs, but after a few miles of climbing he was lost.

He stopped the Triumph.

'I'm sorry, this isn't it.' He knocked his fist on the steering wheel. His knuckles were tender from cutting the fir. Water blisters welled on the soft parts of his hands. The hills spread before them in brown and white folds, the highest peaks submerged in snow. The icy rain had cleared, but the sky was still swollen in patches with the promise of more snow. A few sheep with matted tails grazed savagely by the side of the road, skittering together as Paul and Elise got out of the car. He scanned the landscape and a despairing feeling came over him. He felt her beside him, breathing.

'It doesn't matter,' she said, her hand dangling close to his. 'If it's not the right place, it's all wonderful.' She spread her arms out wide, embracing the sky, her eyes clear. He watched her. There was a certainty about her that he lacked. She wasn't afraid to face life head-on. He thought back to their conversation by the fire. He had talked to her about his parents, the small things he remembered, their routines, their way of doing things. It seemed impossible that he would never again watch his mother stand at the window as she washed up, or listen to his father suck his tea. They were still so close he could almost hear them breathing. Elise hadn't said much in return. She had simply held his hand and stroked it. And it had made him cry later, in the cold bathroom with his face deep in the towel so she wouldn't hear.

They walked down a black peated path. The sheep had carved out thousands of little trails, no wider than a human foot, right across the hills. He let her take the lead and watched her from behind as she strode off, her legs carrying her firmly. She was taller than he was, although not particularly graceful; what she had was a muscular directness that was powerfully feminine.

They continued walking until they came across an old barn where they stopped. It had a rusted tin roof, the colour of a blood orange, and looked as though it had been cut out and stuck against the cold blue of the sky. Light green paint flaked along the sides and around the door. Every one of its eight paned windows had been smashed. Further down the path they discovered a decomposed carcass of a sheep lying in a flattened hollow of heather, and after pausing for a moment to stare at its grim yellow jaw with the teeth all exposed like a skull in a museum, they changed direction and took another track.

Paul saw that they were heading towards the loch. There was a car parked beside the beach and an old couple sat on fold-up chairs, a tartan blanket stretched across their knees. They waved as Paul and Elise stepped out of the Triumph.

'You young ones brave enough to take a dip?' the old man called out.

'Don't be foolish, they'll catch their death,' the old woman said.

'Come on,' Elise said. 'Let's just jump in and out.'

'I don't think it's a good idea.' Something about her impulsiveness made him feel shyer than he actually was.

Elise moved behind a bush and quickly stepped out of her clothes. Her hands moved to the back of her bra, but to Paul's relief, she changed her mind about removing it completely. Her stomach was naked and white, her belly button girlish. Around the seam of her pants a few curls of gold hair flowered. He averted his eyes and stripped off his own clothes down to a pair of grey shorts. He felt her watching him.

They walked to the cold gritty beach. The old couple waved again from their chairs where they sat drinking steaming cups of thermos coffee.

'We'll save some for you for when you get out,' the old man called.

'Shush,' the woman said and pulled his arm. 'Let them be.'

Paul entered the water. It felt like cold oil lapping around his knees. He walked a little way out, stiffly holding his arms up to keep his balance. Elise had plunged on ahead and he could see her drawing across the glassy surface of the loch, giving little shivering gasps, her hair streaming out over her back.

'Go on, laddie!' the old man cawed from the shore as if cheering a horse from the grandstand. 'Catch her!'

Stuttering at the cold, Paul slipped forward and let the water close over his shoulders. His feet touched cold, soft silt.

Elise breast-stroked up to him. Her hair was slicked down over her shoulders in thin strands and her eyes were reddened. She laughed, her mouth wet and clean, and showered him with a splash.

'Look, there's a hawk,' he said.

'Where?'

'It's circling us, maybe it thinks we're huge salmon.'

She flipped over, spreading her arms and swimming fingers. Her thighs were white and long under the water and gently knocked together. 'It's fantastic the way it keeps so still,' she said, watching the hawk.

They lay on their backs, fingers drifting in the water, sometimes touching. The hawk screamed once and then swooped off over the trees. After a while it began to snow in soft spirals ruffling the waters of the loch. The couple at the beach packed up their chairs and left.

Paul turned towards Elise. There was a rising sensation in his chest. 'We're swimming in the snow!'

'I know,' she said.

He wanted to kiss her, but his nerve failed. He held his nose and put his head under the water. Green-grey clouds swirled around him. He couldn't see the bottom. When he pulled his head up it was snowing hard.

A few days later Elise went to see her father in Durham. She didn't tell him she was coming. She wanted to surprise him with her news. All the way down on the train she perched on the edge of her seat, looking out of the window, her thoughts snagging together as her mind leaped from one possibility to another. She knew she had started something with Paul, but she had to be careful not to let her enthusiasm show too much because it might scare him off. She could be intimidating to men; she always wanted to go so much faster and further than they did. What she needed to do was take things slowly. But it was difficult to hold back when she was bursting with energy. It always happened when she was about to become ill; a sort of rush of activity that was a precursor to the chest infections that hit her every January. The previous winter she had decorated the big man's flat in a frenzy because she wanted him to be amazed when he came back from a weekend trip to London. Illness always made her feel a little wild, as if some protective bubble around her had been pricked, deflating her inhibitions, making her want to live more brightly.

Hovering outside her father's office, she heard him talking on the telephone and decided to wait. There was a notice on his door written in large red letters: STUDENTS BY APPOINTMENT ONLY! A wire post basket marked 'Essays and Submissions' was empty. She looked at the noticeboard, which advertised a conference on hominid research and a seminar on hunters and gatherers past and present, both events several months out of date. There were notices about grant submissions, scholarships to the United States and a letter from a mission in Africa requesting student volunteers for the summer to help set up a bush community school. Bored, she walked up and down the corridor for a while smelling its familiar worn old carpet smell. Without students the place seemed shabbier than usual. She heard the phone bang down and her father shout, 'Come!'

He was sitting as usual behind his desk with his back to the window. She stepped into the room, her chest tightening as it always did at the sight of him barricaded behind his tottering books and papers. A rhino horn sprouting from the thicket on the desk was a familiar navigational landmark as was the motorbike helmet perched on a stool. The rugs were covered with brown box files and enlarged photocopies of what appeared to be a skull. As she picked her way through, her father stood up behind his desk and took off his glasses, an expression of utter astonishment passing across his face. 'Good God, I thought you were Anne for a moment. You *have* got to look like her.'

Elise didn't know whether to be pleased or not. Her mother Anne and her father Robert were divorced, had been since Elise was twelve, and each parent now lived defiantly independent lives: Anne in Highgate within reach of wine bars, boutiques and the all-night supermarket; Robert in a spindly Durham house with his four red setters, his old motorbike, his papers and his unravelling manic depressive artist housekeeper who never wore any colour except black. Her parents still telephoned each other for an hour or so each week, usually late at night when one or the other had drunk a bottle of wine.

'Sit down,' he said, coming round to her side of the desk and sweeping off a stack of essays from a chair. 'I must say you look awfully well. Have you got a lover?'

'You don't waste time in getting to the point, do you, Dad?' She laughed. 'It's good to see you.'

Robert ran his hands through the wings of long grey hair that fell down into his eyes and smiled wearily. Outside a student without an appointment tentatively knocked on the door.

'Bugger off, I'm busy!' he roared. From the corridor outside came the sound of giggles and shuffles. 'It's supposed to be a bloody holiday! Can't get anything done.'

'You shouldn't be so popular, Dad.'

He snorted, but she could tell he was pleased. It was well known that Robert found people irresistible. Despite the written warnings he would spend hours with tearful students, anxiously mopping up their problems, sending them away cheerful. Her father was one of life's defenders; no matter how hopeless the cause he would have to give up his time. What he got from it, Elise knew, was an endless source of diversion. Without it, he would have shrivelled and died from lack of nourishment.

'What are you working on at the moment?' she asked.

'Broken Hill Man, one of the earliest humans to be discovered in Africa. Here, take a look.' He raked through some papers on his desk and passed over a photograph of a huge skull labelled *homo sapiens rhodesiensis*. 'Handsome, isn't he?'

The eye sockets were deep caves and the material of the skull looked more like polished wood than bone. In the margin of the photograph her father had written: *Man at the Crossroads?*

'Not my idea of a pin-up.' She laughed and handed the photograph back.

'Let me show you something fascinating,' her father said, taking a nub of adhesive and sticking the photograph against the window so that they both could see it clearly.

He pointed to the crumbled jaw. 'Look how the teeth have rotted away, all those gaps, see?'

She nodded. 'I suppose they weren't too hot on dental hygiene in those days?'

'Absolutely,' her father said. 'Ten of the sixteen upper teeth have cavities, and we can see that abscesses have formed in the jaw. But look at the left ear, just below it, see?' He pointed at a small hole. 'Truly extraordinary.'

She peered at the skull. It was grotesque, how she imagined bone would look if it could melt and solidify again, but even so there was something compelling about it.

Her father pointed to the hole under the ear again. 'Can you see it?' She nodded. 'It's a wound mark, possibly caused by a stone tool, or maybe a carnivore tooth.'

'How did it happen?'

'We don't know. Maybe someone bashed him. Maybe he was bitten by a wild dog.'

'Maybe he ran into a tree?' she said.

'Unlikely. The wound is too precise.'

'So?' He seemed to be leading to something.

Her father pointed to the hole under the ear again. 'The wound was serious enough to cause our friend to lose a lot of blood.'

'Yes.' She peered beyond the photograph and looked through the window where the light was watery bright.

'He could have bled to death from such an injury?'

'I suppose so. Dad, when are we talking about, how long ago did old skullbones live?'

'We're not really sure, but he could be as old as 250,000 years.'

'Wow. A quarter of a million years. Are we sort of talking Neanderthal?'

'I'll come to that in a minute. If you look closely at the wound you'll see that it's partially healed which means there's a possibility that he was patched up. He wasn't left. He was *helped*, given some form of nursing or treatment.'

'You mean he didn't die from the wound?'

'No. And that's the exciting part.'

'I don't get it. Why?'

'Because what we're looking at is the first evidence of altruism in our early ancestors.'

Elise stared at the image pinned in the window. There was something strange about it, almost poignant in the way that pumpkin ghouls sometimes are with their intolerably lonely expressions. Now she remembered that her father had visited Broken Hill as an anthropology student. She had a faint memory of him telling her a story a long time ago about a bone cave filled with layer upon layer of animal remains: elephant, rhino, antelope, birds, bats and other kinds of small mammals, like a fossilized Noah's Ark. Her father was saying something about the skull belonging to a sub-species of early mankind, but she had stopped listening and was looking instead beyond the window and out to the sky filled with clouds like racing yachts. Her chest felt tight and there was a swimming sensation behind her eyes. In one corner of the office a calor gas heater fumed and then began to putter out.

'I see him as being at the crossroads of two lines of human ancestors,' her father said, 'more primitive than the Neanderthal,

perhaps the key to the missing link between humans and apes—'
He stopped abruptly. 'You've come to tell me something?'

In the weak light his facial marks were clearly outlined; the mauve thread veins on his cheeks, the feathery lines around his lips from when he used to smoke and the V-shaped scar under his lower lip where his teeth had bitten through after a motorbike accident.

'Oh, Dad.' She watched him remove the photograph gently from the window and place it in a plastic folder.

He flapped around his papers for a while as if looking for the exact place to put the folder, his face reddening slightly as he became aware of her scrutiny. Finally he put the folder down on top of the nearest pile on the desk. He looked directly at her.

'You're not pregnant, are you?'

'Dad!' She sat up straight.

'You look pale, that's all, and a bit . . .' He paused and looked carefully at her. 'Nervy. Has something happened?'

'I think I've fallen in love.'

'*Again?*' Her father swung back on his chair and put his hands behind his head. 'Now what's happened to Angus?'

'He's too old. We were never more than friends really.'

'That's not what you said when you first met. I distinctly remember you saying something like – I think this may finally be *it*!'

'Dad, I did not!'

Robert gave a tiny frown. Elise looked down at her lap for a moment and then swung up her eyes defiantly. 'This really is different. He's in a bit of a state. It's big, Dad. Both his parents died, close together. Things haven't been great for him.'

Her father shook his head slowly.

'Stop that. I didn't come here to ask for your approval.'

'Yes, you did. You always do.'

'All right, but don't try to talk me out of it.'

Robert gave a snort. 'Not much chance of that, but I have to ask: weren't you engaged to Angus?'

'Not really, he gave me a ring, but it wasn't a real one. Anyway, I don't wear it now.'

Her father sighed.

'Dad, aren't you just the slightest bit pleased that I'm happy?'

'You'll go your own way, whatever I say.'

'I know, but you *were* twenty when you met Mum, and don't say that's different.'

'I wouldn't dream of it,' Robert said. 'But I suspect your friend probably has many young ladies all desperate to take care of him. Think about it. Have some adventures of your own first. Live a little.' He paused and opened his desk drawer. 'Can't bloody find it, but there's a mission in Zambia looking for a young thing to help out, build a school or something. Give you something useful to do for the summer.' He pushed the drawer shut. 'You could travel a bit afterwards, go up to Victoria Falls. You always said it was your dream to go to Africa. I could come out and have another look at the mine. Useful research.' He chuckled. 'It would be good to see the old place again.'

Her father always pushed what he hoped would be life-enhancing experiences on her: kibbutzim in Israel, orphanages in India, the Red Cross anywhere and now Africa. It was quite sweet and old-fashioned really, the idea of seeing the world before settling down. It was what he had done. He'd spent months at a time living in remote areas, relying on the generosity of locals for food and lifts. In Africa, he'd been looked after by a retired wing commander who had become a flying missionary. He had taken him everywhere in his old aeroplane and nearly got them killed once or twice when they ran out of fuel. Her father was by nature adventurous, but she wasn't so sure about the benefits of travel. It was different now. Her generation travelled because they couldn't think of anything else to do. The idea of community service bothered her, the grubby worthiness of it; she'd seen people at college return from summers working in Nepal with their sun-bleached hair and tatty string bracelets, and loathed the way they flaunted their thin experiences and the deliberate way they made everyone else feel inferior. Most of them came back dumber than before they left, but of course it was impossible to criticize without being accused of envy. Real travel, she felt, would be different, and she would do that on her own terms. 'I'll think about it, OK?'

Her father glanced at her across the desk. 'Hungry?' he asked. She nodded. Actually she felt queasy, but around this time in the afternoon her father usually succumbed to a craving for sweet iced cake and strong tea.

Over a pot of tea served by grim waitresses in a near silent tea shop, her father told her he was thinking about turning the story of Broken Hill Man into a book. An academic publisher had expressed an interest after seeing a proposal and some notes, but the trouble was finding the time to discipline it all into something more substantial. 'I just can't seem to find enough quiet time, except when I'm asleep!'

She poured him more tea, thick and orange and strong, just how he liked it. 'Write it in your head, Dad, while you're out on the motorbike.'

He looked at her, his eyes widening slightly. 'You're really serious about this young man?'

She sipped her tea. She was too churned up. She shouldn't have come. Her father knew her better than she thought. 'I think I am. I mean can you ever be sure?'

Robert glanced away then, eyes brimming for a moment, which shocked her. She wondered whether he was thinking of her mother. No matter how close she felt to him, there were still places she couldn't stray into. The love affair between her parents had always baffled her. When she was younger she had asked them both why they couldn't all live together. Her mother had said that it was too complicated to explain, while her father had looked pale and serious, as if the blood had drained from him. She had never known exactly what it was that had driven them apart.

'Fancy a walk with the dogs?' her father asked, his fingers straying towards the sugar bowl ready to snatch up a few lumps.

Since he had given up smoking he had not been able to resist the bowls with their glistening cubes. He liked the rough brown crunchy stuff with a texture like rock salt.

'Dad, that's terribly bad for you,' she said as he popped a lump into his mouth. 'You'll end up with teeth like the Neanderthal.'

He crunched down on his sugar and looked about the tea shop guiltily. 'You're right, it's an awful habit,' he said and pushed the bowl out of reach across the table, a woeful smile crossing his face as if he were remembering something that happened a long time ago.

'So, Dad, how are things with you and Isobel?'

'Fine,' he took a slurp of tea and looked at her over his cup. 'Nothing much to report. She's busy with her art. You should try talking to her some time. She has interesting views.'

'She's too dark for me.'

Her father looked startled. 'She's not, really she's not. If you got to know her you wouldn't think that.'

Elise looked away. She didn't want to talk about Isobel and wished she hadn't mentioned her. One of the waitresses caught her eye and scowled. 'Perhaps we should go.'

She reached down under the table for her bag and when she came up again caught her father with his fingers in the sugar bowl, which made her laugh so much her chest hurt. Reaching across the table she took her father's hand and squeezed it.

'I love you, Dad, I really do.'

Her father smiled. 'That's what you say to all the boys.' He patted her hand. 'Come on, let's go home and fetch the dogs. They'll be delighted to see you.'

8

LOW FLYING

Low flying is often necessitated by conditions of poor visibility or low cloud. Be very careful of your airspeed near the ground and always open the throttle on turns.

Scotland, 1972

The events leading up to the wedding had an unreal quality. Paul wondered what he had set in motion or rather what Elise had. It was she who had asked him to marry her one evening when they were walking away from the library, muffled in coats, hands in pockets, their breath forming funnels through the freezing fog.

Her offer was irresistible. It seemed to come direct from the cold night, and it pierced his heart. The simple fact of having been chosen filled him with an overwhelming sense of relief. There was a reason for how things were turning out. The way that his greatest happiness seemed to be contained inside his greatest loss made him feel that Elise was almost a reward for the suffering he had endured. She had singled *him* out, after all; he had not gone in pursuit of her.

He dressed for dinner in his best clothes. He wanted to make an impression on Elise's father, who had booked rooms for them in an unfamiliar hotel where they would all spend the night before the wedding.

Paul brushed his hair and looked at himself in the mirror. He seemed older than twenty. The death of his parents had robbed him of his boyishness and he was pleased. He felt ready now to take his next step in the world without them. He still missed them, but their deaths did not haunt him, mainly because he forced himself to stop thinking of them whenever an image appeared in his mind. He walked down the red-carpeted stairs and into a dark wood-panelled hall. There, standing staring up at a great stag with antlers like gnarled oak branches, was the anthropologist. His eyes crinkled when he saw Paul. 'Nice to have a little live company. Come, what will you drink? We've got at least ten minutes to get to know each other before my daughter comes down.' He held out a long arm and guided Paul towards the bar.

They settled down with pints of heavy before a log fire. Robert slipped his shoes off and toasted his feet in their socks, one of which had a hole. His trousers seemed too short for his legs and he kept hitching them down over his knees. He asked Paul about his course and then his parents, keeping his eyes on him as he replied. Then Elise joined them, wearing the sleeveless dress he'd first seen her in. Paul felt his stomach jolt as a memory of his drive across the hills swirled into his mind.

She groaned when she saw her father in his socks. 'Dad, what will people think?'

Robert gave her a fond look in reply and put his shoes back on, his grey hair flopping over his face. When they went into a back room for dinner, Robert made a point of sitting between them so that neither felt excluded.

They sat in deep cracked red leather chairs with wings that so blinkered movement from the sides Paul would jump whenever a waiter appeared with dishes.

'How's the book going, Dad?' Elise asked as soon as they were settled.

'Well, I've made it beyond the note stage and on to the type-writer so it feels like proper work at last.' Robert took another forkful of food. He ate rapidly without much chewing, looking round in the soft almost guilty way a dog does when it is eating.

'Dad's writing a book about one of the oldest human beings ever. Even older than him!'

'Cheek.' Paul watched him wave his fork at his daughter. 'Actually, I need to thank you. It was good advice you gave about writing it on the bike. It's helped me to imagine it. I'm ending with a scene in the cave with Broken Hill Man and his helper.'

'You've written the ending first, Dad?'

'Yes, why not? Sorry, Paul, this is probably terribly dull for you.'

'No, it's not at all. Are you writing the book as part of your work at the university?' Paul felt his palms go clammy. He wanted to ask the professor a question that sounded intelligent.

'I pretend to be doing academic research, but mostly I make wild guesses about things that no one can possibly know. For example, we know that early humans formed relationships, but just what kind of relationships these were, we can only imagine. Was there tenderness or compassion or empathy, or are these modern feelings? Was there rivalry? I've been wondering whether love is not something very primitive indeed. Something much older than we think. Maybe, and this is just a theory, love is what makes us human.'

'Oh, Dad, you're such a romantic,' Elise said, throwing her napkin at him.

Paul sat on the edge of his chair, waiting for more. But Robert simply smiled and returned to his food.

The room simmered with rich smells and Paul felt a sumptuousness wash over him. Everything he could ever desire was here and it was incredible, but also inevitable, as if he had always known he would end up sitting in this particular chair looking across the table at the woman he was going to marry because that was the way things had to be. Now she was leaning forward and reaching for her water glass, her eyes darting with mock disapproval at her father, her hair shimmering in the firelight in streaks of red and dark gold. She reached her hand across the table and touched his wrist, shocking him with her heat. Between them Robert laid down his knife and fork.

'Dad's always the first to finish,' Elise said rolling a fragment of roast potato around in the bloody juices left on her plate. 'He says it's instinct, I call it greed.'

Robert made a 'woof' sound. 'Nonsense, I just don't like my food getting cold.'

'There's no chance of that,' Elise said through a mouthful of potato. 'I'm surprised you could even taste it.'

'It was delicious. Very tender for venison.'

They both laughed. Leaving the rest of his meat untouched in a small mound in the middle of his plate, Paul quietly put down his knife and fork. A waiter appeared and whisked his plate away.

Afterwards they sat by the fire with large tumblers of whisky and the professor spoke about his travels in the Middle East and Africa and his fascination for rituals and sacrifice. He also spoke further about his Broken Hill Man project. Ever since Robert had visited Zambia as a student he had wanted to return to the lead and zinc mine where the skull had been found by a miner, who after unearthing it jammed it on a pole where it sat for three days until it was rescued by a doctor who recognized its importance. Robert chuckled at the thought. Paul let his head loll in the deep recess of the chair, his mind drifting to his father, another working man, but one who had made no significant discoveries in his life, none that were obvious anyway. Across the hearth Elise and her father began to engage in an exuberant debate about evolution. Paul half listened; they were talking too quickly for him to follow the thread of their arguments. During a pause, Elise asked her father how long it had taken for humans to evolve from apes and Robert replied, 'About five million years.' Robert's face in profile was pale and amused, clearly delighted. He looked across at Paul and winked.

Elise apologized. 'I'm sorry, we're getting carried away. We always do this.'

Paul drank the rest of his whisky feeling it bite and then warm his stomach. He wanted to tell them not to stop on his account, but somehow he had lost the power of speech. They continued sparring anyway, gesticulating at each other with slightly clenched hands, unconsciously mirroring each other's gestures. Whenever her father made a point Elise particularly disagreed with she would admonish him by leaning forward and slapping him on both knees. Paul watched them through a mist of whisky warmth, his senses filled to the brim. When they had finished, Robert hauled Paul out of his seat and after patting him gently on the back steered him up the stairs and pointed him towards the room where he was going to sleep alone.

The next morning Paul stumbled into the hotel bathroom, head buzzing and found his father there, work overalls undone, doggedly carrying the breakfast teapot to be emptied down the toilet bowl. Gripping the edge of the white bath, he wondered whether he had seen a ghost. His father's eyes had been blank, his movements curiously lifeless and empty. Perhaps he had been given a glimpse of another realm, a parallel world where the dead enacted all the habits and routines of life in endless ritual. The encounter shook him. Going down for breakfast he found Elise and her father deep in newspapers and bacon and eggs and found that he could not say anything.

They married later that afternoon at a register office in Aberdeen. A handful of university friends came, wearing their usual jeans, holding plastic bags over their heads to protect them from the rain. Paul wore his father's suit, chemically cleaned since New Year's Eve, and a pair of new black shoes. Elise wore a smart cream wool suit bought by her mother Anne, who flew up from London for the day and sat between Robert and the housekeeper who wore a black feathered hat. The dogs waited in Robert's old Volvo outside, leaping up as the wedding party left the register office in a celebration of barks, smearing the steamed-up windows with saliva.

After tea and sandwiches in the same back room of the Aberdeen hotel where they had dined the night before, Paul and Elise got into the Volvo and Robert drove them up to the forest where they let the dogs go. Isobel had stayed behind for an afternoon nap and so Robert and Anne walked together. Paul heard them laughing. Every now and again one or the other would knock gently against a shoulder or hip. They still looked married, he thought, unused to being apart, almost as if they had been one body at one time and then separated. Elise strode on ahead. She had changed from her wedding suit into jeans and sweater and seemed energized. Next to her the dogs streaked russet through the trees. It had stopped raining and the air felt thin and clean. Elise stopped and waited for him to catch up.

'What are you thinking about?' She linked her arm through his and hugged it to her.

'Oh, I don't know, what it means to be married, I suppose.' He felt oddly embarrassed by her question.

'It means whatever we make it mean. We can do anything we like with our marriage, isn't that an amazing thought?' She pulled a branch with her fingers, showering droplets down on to them.

'I suppose so.' He felt a prickle of unease.

'Don't look so worried. I only mean that we're free to decide what to do with our lives.'

'Your father has other ideas.'

'I know, we have to humour him.' She looked over her shoulder at Robert whose laughter was reverberating around the forest. 'You still want to go?'

'Of course.' Ever since they'd talked about it with her father he'd felt a leaping sensation as if a tiny rodent were running around inside his chest. 'I still can't quite believe it.'

She took his hand. 'Oh, Paul, you're so wonderful. You remind me so much of him.'

He was taken aback. Just occasionally he felt as if they were talking at cross purposes. Her hand felt warm against his and he walked for a while in silence, wondering how to respond.

She put her mouth against his ear so that he could feel her hot breath. 'Anyone awake in there?' A pulse of desire for her stirred inside his jeans, and he reached for her, wanting for a moment to hold her, but she pulled away, leaving a cold space between them. 'Come on,' she said. 'Let's run and catch them up.'

Under a large beech tree Robert and Anne waited for them, heads close to each other as they inspected a mound of dark earth. 'We've lost one of the dogs down a badger hole,' Robert said as they caught up, breathing fast after their run.

'Typical,' Anne said, but she smiled. She wore new clothes, a stiff wax green coat and high black leather boots, now speckled with mud and stuck with wet pine needles.

Robert gave a high-pitched whistle and the other dogs came, holding ragged tails high. They looked at the badger hole with wet eyes. One dog whined.

'Johnson, come out of there,' Robert said, exasperated. All the dogs were named after big game hunters, but did not live up to their names because they rarely caught anything. Robert said it was the housekeeper's fault. She fed them too much.

Theodore whined again and pawed at the earth. Baker (after Sir Samuel Baker, one of the first governors of Sudan) gave a bark, and then they caught sight of a streak of red hair, then a length of bony tail, and finally the hindquarters of Johnson wormed out of the hole, his eyes glowing with adventure. 'Look at him,' Robert cried and slapped the dog affectionately on the shoulder.

The party continued through the forest and Elise broke away from Paul to walk with her mother. He watched them from behind. Elise had lost weight for the wedding and her young tallness emphasized Anne's petite rounded figure, which seemed too soft for the unaccustomed country coat. As he observed them Robert came up and casually slipped an arm around Paul's shoulder. 'All right?'

For some reason tears welled up in Paul's eyes. He swallowed.

'Lot to take in?' Robert asked as he squeezed his shoulder. Paul drew in breath sharply. 'All happened a bit fast?'

Paul nodded and kept his eyes down on the ground which was still winter black.

Robert fell in step beside him and after a comfortable pause announced, 'You're mad about her.' It wasn't a question.

'I can't imagine loving anyone or anything more in my life.'

Robert chuckled. 'I believe you are going to be good for her. She doesn't quite know herself yet, but I feel that you do. You've got a sense of where you're going and I admire that in a person.' He picked up a stick and threw it for Theodore. 'She needs to slow down a bit and learn to grow up naturally. A lot of the others . . .' He tailed off, perhaps realizing the inappropriateness of his comment, and busied himself with one of the dogs which had a burr caught in the silky tendrils of his ear. 'Sorry.' Robert straightened up, the blood bright in his face. 'None of that matters now, of course.'

'How many?' Paul heard himself ask. Robert glanced at him with surprise and Paul's heart began to pound. He felt as if he had crossed an invisible line.

Robert picked up a stick and watched the dog dance around, anticipating the throw. He hurled it down the track, but his aim was slightly off and the stick caught in the branch of a fir tree where it dangled to the frustration of the dog who braced himself in front of it and tried to bark it down. 'A few,' Robert said carefully. 'I suppose she's told you about Angus?'

'Yes, oh, yes, the Big Man we called him.' Paul heard his own breathless laugh.

Robert smiled thinly. The dog continued to bark at the trapped stick, the noise echoing down the forest sending birds into a panic. Anne's face twisted round and looked pointedly at Robert who strode up to the tree and lifted the stick free. With a matter-of-fact grace the dog jumped at it and took off with it between his jaws, tail working in a delirious circle of delight. Robert turned to Paul. 'You may have to get tough with her every now and again, but don't worry about that. She'll respect you for it.'

Paul nodded. He understood what Robert was saying. Elise could be quite daunting at times and he instinctively knew that being with her would require strength on his part. Getting to know her properly would necessarily involve getting to know himself and the prospect filled him with a kind of exhilarated anticipation for the adventure they were about to begin.

Africa was Robert's idea, given in the form of a wedding present of two airline tickets to Zambia, an act of generosity that had stunned Paul. His gasp on opening the envelope at breakfast had been drowned out by the sound of Elise laughing in a you-can't-be-serious way. And then a lot of things had happened very quickly: the waiter had come to take their order for coffee and Elise's mother had arrived, which meant another chair had to be brought up to the table and more coffee ordered, and then a round of greetings and introductions – strange to be meeting these people for the first time on his wedding day – and the tickets, half out of their envelopes, had been shoved under the newspapers and general fuss not to be retrieved until Elise had gone upstairs with her mother to dress. Paul had sat at the table alone staring at the tickets in his hand, feeling as if he had just been granted a trip to the moon.

'I didn't thank you properly this morning,' Paul said. 'It's difficult to know what to say because I've never been anywhere, and it just seems too good to be true, but really it is a most amazing gift. Thank you.'

'Well,' said Robert, bending down to retrieve the stick Theodore had dropped neatly at his feet. 'If you insist on marrying then I insist on adventure.'

One of the conditions of Robert's acceptance of the marriage was that they travel. Every year he would pay for them to visit a country of his choosing. He didn't want grandchildren. He wanted them to explore the world fully. It was unusual. Paul didn't know how to behave in the face of such extraordinary generosity and openness. He thought of his father's deep pride; his insistence on struggle and denial. He would have been ashamed of his son right now for taking what seemed to be an easy route. His mother would have been kinder, but afraid. Travel for her meant leaving security, opening up to forces outside your control, dicing with the unknown, which could only lead to harm. In going to Africa he was betraying them in a way.

Sensing his discomfort, Robert looked at him. 'You don't owe me anything.' He hurled the stick for his dog, and this time it landed straight. 'Except honesty – to yourself that is. Best piece of advice I've ever been given is don't ignore what you know.'

Unable to reply, Paul looked up at the sky where a line of cloud hung in a dense mauve curtain.

'Looks like there's going to be more rain,' Robert said.

'What I know is that your gift means the world to me.'

Robert clapped him on the shoulder. 'Come on, that's enough about it. Let's go and find the girls and think about getting back for some strong tea and cake.'

They returned to college life and the unfamiliarity of a married room overlooking a row of roofs. Most days Elise cycled to the library while Paul stood at the window and thought about Africa, wondering how he should prepare for the trip, what he should do to mark the transition from college student to adventurer. He understood that he was looking for some kind of defining moment, a sign that he was beginning a new phase, but things stayed pretty much the same. Elise slipped back into college life easily, spending her time researching the pulmonary system in the library – she was thinking about converting her biology degree to medicine – or shopping with friends. She told Paul she never imagined it would be so easy, being married. When he asked her what she was doing about Africa, she said she would think about it nearer the time. Maybe they wouldn't go.

He was surprised. Shocked even. She didn't seem to be taking her father's condition seriously. When he asked why she wasn't committed to the idea of adventure she mocked his anxiety, his willingness to honour the gift. 'You know, it's just his way of getting back at me,' she said one night as they both lay awake after an attempt at sex that had somehow dwindled into nothing, all promise and possibility, but no real passion. 'He's furious really. He didn't want me to get married at twenty and the trip is his way of showing it. It's a form of control.'

Paul felt a wave of heat wash over his body. He rolled his head and looked at her. 'I don't think so.'

She widened her eyes. 'He's having a joke at our expense.' She shifted on her pillow to free a tangle of hair that had got caught up during their earlier struggle. 'I wish you'd stop thinking about it.'

'I can't.'

She turned away from him, wrenching the covers from his side of the bed. Paul lay in the dark, watching the headlights from the passing cars slide across the ceiling. A new worry wormed its way into his mind. What if Elise refused to go? What if she decided to hand the gift back unused? He wanted to tell her how important it was, but he kept quiet. It was too enormous.

The term dragged on and Paul neglected his land economy assignment because he found he couldn't write. Each time he shaped a phrase it would escape him before he had a chance to write it down. Looking at the words he'd compiled already, the notes he'd taken, he felt no recognition. It was as if his own writing were a code that was being kept secret from him. He felt walled in on himself, tired of breathing the same stale air in the same small room. To try to motivate himself he walked into college most days, taking a grim pleasure in the bus fumes, the exhausted feel of the streets, the drawn faces. He looked around for Elise and not finding her in the science rooms or library he walked back.

Gradually he pulled the assignment together, working late at night while Elise slept. Sometimes he would leave writing to go and look at her. She slept with her face turned to the doorway, slightly hunched into her neck so that he could see the long curve of her jaw, the slight swell of her cheek, her hair pulled to one side revealing the soft patch of golden down at the base of her neck. He would stand and listen to her breathe in and out with the tiny sucking and snuffling sounds she made due to blocked sinuses, and a fearful tenderness would come over him. The life they were leading was small and secure, but perhaps it was enough. It had been enough for his parents and generations before. What was it in him that needed a new frontier? Why wasn't he content with what he had? It was already more than either of his parents had.

When he handed in the assignment two weeks late the girl at the office said it probably wouldn't be marked. Didn't he know about deadlines? He did. He told her he was going to Africa to build a school.

'How do you know you're not coming back?' the girl asked, leaning her arms on the counter to peer at him. She looked vaguely familiar and then he recognized her from the New Year party. She had spoken French and she'd told him about her vegetarian friend.

'I didn't say that. We're just going for the summer break.'

She sighed as she took his assignment. 'As I said, it probably won't be marked. Deadlines are very strict. If you were having problems, you should have let us know.'

'I wasn't having problems,' he said.

The girl looked at him levelly. 'You're married now, aren't you?'

'Why do you ask?'

'Just curious.' She peered at him again then sharply pulled down a metal grille, closing off the submissions office for another year. 'Have a good time in Africa,' she said through the bars of the grille.

Coming into Lusaka Elise fastened her seat belt and began to prepare for descent. During the night flight she had read *The Voyage of the Beagle*, which her father had stuffed into her bag at the send-off. Robert had also supplied them with anti-malarials, torches and notebooks along with instructions to fly out to Broken Hill if they got the chance. Glancing back at him after they had put their hand luggage through passport control, she saw him flick his hand across his eyes before he turned and walked away with the long bouncing stride he used when he needed to work something out. She had wanted to call out to him; she had a sudden need to see his face, but Paul had already gone through and was waiting for her on the other side.

She slept through most of the flight, a heavy exhausted sleep that left her feeling groggy when she woke to Paul jogging her arm. His eyes were bright with another kind of exhaustion. As they prepared to land at Lusaka, she tried to quell a feeling of apprehension. For some reason she wished they could remain airborne for a few hours longer so that she could get used to the idea of coming down, she supposed. Paul was up on his feet, pulling down their bags from the overhead locker, talking with a few of the other passengers, occasionally glancing over at her. She looked out of the window at a landscape that seemed composed entirely of flat brown dust fields.

The airport was hot and quiet. A group of Africans waiting near a glass door flickered eyes towards her, faces the colour of dark ripe plums. She could not stop herself from staring. The heat was so thick she could feel it resting on her face like an open palm. There was no console or row of trolleys, simply an empty area where, looking oddly abandoned, their luggage waited for them. Carrying a suitcase each, they headed towards a wooden booth marked passports. A sprawling immigration official gave their documents a cursory glance and waved them through.

Behind a rope, standing back from the line of greeters, a tall, athletic man with a burned complexion waited for them. His khaki shorts were frayed above his dark brown legs and his pale blue shirt was damp with sweat. 'I'm Max Searle,' he said and marched off with their cases without so much as shaking hands. Momentarily stunned, she watched the crowd part for him. Beside her Paul let out a caught breath but did not say anything.

Outside the building a white glare pulled tears from her eyes. She wanted to look for her sunglasses, but Max had already slung their cases into the back of a pick-up truck. He glanced at her feet as they walked up and then jerked a piece of canvas over the cases, securing them with a piece of baling cord. Tied up to one of the safety bars around the edge of the pick-up was a small, shivering brown dog. Elise put out her hand encouragingly towards the creature.

'Don't touch him,' Max barked. 'I just picked him up on the road, he could be rabid.' He wiped his hands down his shorts. His legs were thick with hair, the colour of copper wire.

'What are you going to do with him?'

Max gave her a swift look. 'Shoot him, probably.'

He opened the driver's door and got in, leaving them to make their way to the other side and slide across the red cracked front seat. She got in first. The pick-up had a dry, warm smell. The seat was hot and pricked the back of her thighs. Her arm brushed against Max and he jumped away from her. She noticed then a shotgun lying in the footwell, the dark muzzle pointing straight at them. Max saw her look. 'Don't worry, it's not loaded,' and although she didn't need proof, he took from his shorts pocket a handful of cartridges to show her. He started up the engine, his eyes fixed on the road. She could feel the stickiness of Paul's body beside her and on the other side a close, dense warmth.

Max drove fast and relaxed, one arm propped along the open window. Elise tied her hair off her face to stop it from being blown. Small tornadoes of red dust rolled from their wheels, forming a great billowing cloud, through which ghostly African figures, one carrying a basket of white chickens on her head, could be seen, moving thickly and slowly along the roadside as if wading through deep water. The sound of the tyres smacking against dirt made talk impossible and she felt herself drawn towards the shifting horizon, a liquid band of two colours which slipped into one another as they rode on. Even when she closed her eyes she could still see the red of the road dipping beneath the white of the sky, and feel the dust shaking and shivering beside them.

It was dark by the time they arrived at a white house set in a bowl of trees which formed a dense canopy over the grounds. A tall servant carrying a torch came forward. He shook their hands, keeping the light low so as not to shine it in their faces, and gave a glimmer of a smile. It was difficult to get a whole sense of a person in the darkness that seemed thick enough to grab in handfuls. Behind the servant, a boy of around five years old glanced up at them with fascinated eyes, but when Elise went to take his hand the boy shrank behind the servant.

'Kennedy,' the servant said. 'Show the people where to go inside.' His voice had a low, musical quality.

They found themselves in a large white room lit by an open grate on which burned a huge branch of red wood. A branch of hibiscus had been cut and stuck into a jam jar. In one corner there was a desk with a stethoscope and blood pressure sleeve hanging from the back of a chair. The room smelled as if it had been recently swept with a smoky brush. The boy poked at the fire and watched them wander around.

Instinctively they went to the bookshelf, the rest of the room being too strange and personal to navigate, and found stiff copies of paperbacks by Somerset Maugham and E. M. Forster, pages caramel yellow, and a few old Bibles bound in crumbling leather. Paul pulled out a flying manual and read aloud the introduction:

'*One of the objects of this book is to reduce the talk in the air to the minimum, yet giving it in full, and keeping it colloquial, so that the pupil is free to concentrate on cause and effect.*' He grinned at her in the firelight. '*The shortness of the air talk simplifies the synchronisation of words with demonstration . . .*' He paused and she became aware that someone had come into the room behind them. The boy ran over to him and she glanced round to see Max pat the child on the shoulder. He saw her looking and averted his gaze, muted now in the firelight. Into her mind came the thought that she wanted to see his eyes in full. Unsteadily, she moved closer to Paul.

'Oh, Max, we were just having a good nose around,' Paul said.

Max nodded. 'I hope it's all right.' He swallowed. Elise felt he wanted to say something more but was unable to locate the words.

'Thanks for coming to meet us,' Paul said. 'Will you join us for a drink? We brought some malt whisky with us, a present from Elise's father. Apparently he came out to Broken Hill and met the wing commander many years ago.'

Max's eyes leaped. She saw him hesitate. He seemed torn. 'I need to get back. I want to see to the dog.'

'You're not going to shoot him, are you?' she asked in a quiet voice.

Max glanced at her and then looked away. 'I'll see how he is in the morning.' He took a step backward. His face was in shadow. She could see the outline of his body, the bulk of his shoulders filling the dark space of the doorway. 'The cook will stay.' His voice was gruff. 'He'll get you anything you need. I'll be over tomorrow to take you out to the school site.'

After he had gone, they opened the bottle of malt and sat drinking it by the fire, the light reflecting off their glasses.

'He seems pretty uneasy,' Paul said. 'Probably not used to visitors.'

'I don't suppose many people pass through.' She shivered despite the warmth of the fire. 'My father was right. It is so remote, it's practically *nowhere*. I hope we don't get stuck here.'

Paul shifted closer to her and rested his hand on her shoulder. 'Listen.'

She took a sip of her drink and listened expecting to hear the pick-up leaving, but all she could hear was a singing in her ears. 'I hear ringing.'

'So do I, isn't it amazing?'

She was not sure. All her senses felt jolted out of place and her head seemed to be floating some distance away from her body.

'I'm so glad we're here.' Paul stroked her arm. 'Are you?'

'Of course I am.'

'We're so lucky,' he said.

'Yes.'

'Elise, we have to make the most of this for your father.'

She remembered his look as he crossed the airport, as if he'd forgotten to tell her something important.

Paul continued to stroke her arm. 'Let me hold you.'

She moved into his arms and felt his face against hers, his skin smooth and cool. Her hand brushed his hair which was soft and vaguely damp. When they made love it was as easy as swimming, skins slipping together without tension or friction. Afterwards they always slept soundly, a secure distance apart from each other.

'Come here.' He pulled her head up and kissed her with his eyes closed. His breath was whisky sweet, his eyebrows soft in the firelight. She held on to his young body, with its boyish ribs, flat hips and winged shoulders, breathing slowly as she took in the dim room. Beyond the solid wooden furniture and coloured woven mats was a darkness of a kind she had never experienced, a night so deeply black it was as if the moon and stars had momentarily ceased to exist. In a sudden panic she pulled her head from Paul's shoulder and took a gulp of air, afraid that she would forget how to breathe.

They made love afterwards in a sagging bed draped with white folds of mosquito net, fine as a bridal veil, Paul smoothing her hair and calling her name as he slid into her. She kept her eyes fixed on the tiny blade of yellow moon hanging in the slice of darkness between the curtains while he arced over her, pleasing her, holding himself back. At some point she slept and then woke again to a granular chill on the sheet beneath her. Her legs were sticky as she pushed them through the netting and went naked out to the hallway which separated their room from the main room and the kitchen. The stone felt cool under her feet and she went cautiously, feeling her way around the unfamiliar contours.

At the entrance to the kitchen she paused at a slight snuffling sound, the hairs rising on her arms as she imagined an intruder, or worse, some kind of African animal she had not heard about. She made out the shape of something resting on the centre of the kitchen table and moving closer saw a cardboard box with one side ripped out to make a kind of bed and there inside was the sick dog, breathing shallowly, his pale tongue lolling from the side of his mouth. On the other side of the box, head down on his arms, hair in dusty red tangles, was the sleeping bulk of Max Searle. She stood frozen for a moment, her arms pressing backward. She heard him breathe deeply and then he slowly moved his head. His eyelids fluttered and she thought she saw his lips move. His skin was pock-marked on the hollows of cheeks and there were white creases around his eyes, and deep lines running from his nose to his mouth. As he shifted his head she noticed tiny bristles of gold light on the cleft of his chin. Keeping her eyes on his face, she moved away.

At the doorway she heard him swallow thickly. Her back was turned to him now and she felt a flutter, as if someone had brushed a finger down the length of her spine. She paused, heart leaping in her ribcage. Behind her the dog whined slightly and stirred in his box. She crossed the hallway and returned to bed where she lay for a long while, her mind wide open.

9

STEEP TURNS

The steeper the bank the higher must be the airspeed to provide the extra wing lift necessary to keep the vertically upward force equal to the pull of gravity. Otherwise the aeroplane stalls.

London, 1996

Malaria is ancient. It was known by Socrates and described in writings by Homer and Aristotle. The Chinese canon of medicine, the Nei Ching from 2700 BC, also discusses malaria, a disease that has, perhaps like no other, become part of mankind, riding on his back, refusing to die, merely changing and adapting to drugs and all other attempts to eradicate it. The Italians coined the name mal'aria for the disease in the sixteenth century, believing it came from bad air. In Africa it is still thought by some that malaria comes from the sun, an idea that is perhaps not so surprising considering a parasite invisible to the human eye can in a few hours suck as much as a quarter-pound of haemoglobin out of the blood . . .

Elise stops writing and her page of work dissolves into the screen saver. Swinging her chair away from the computer's demanding hum, she considers her notes. It was optimistic of her to agree to speak at the World Health Conference at such short notice, but the organizer had been very persuasive. She'd been out to dinner with him a few times. A well-exercised Californian with a breezy manner, Jonathan Pool had told her: 'I'd like a kind of aerial view of the disease and what's been done to prevent it. You're the only one I know with the right intellectual credentials; we need someone high profile.' Flattered and excited, she'd agreed after a third glass of wine. Jonathan's second invitation she had somehow managed to resist.

Now she is not so sure whether she can pull the speech together. Malaria is such an elusive disease; it has no defining shape or pattern, no obvious target point on which it might be attacked, nothing tangible. It's as if it really does come from the air, borne on malignant, invisible wings.

She has twenty minutes to speak. Twenty minutes in which to deliver a message that will be heard by doctors, scientists, fellow researchers, drug company representatives, diplomats and the press. In Paris – in two weeks. Her palms sweat thinking about it. Malaria is more like a war than a disease, a battle for blood, and the parasites are winning, killing millions each year, twice as many as Aids, according to one estimate, and leaching the will to live from many more, sucking the health from the veins of communities in Africa, Asia, America, Europe; there wasn't a continent that didn't suffer malaria, and she had somehow to convey all this, inform people that there was a war going on, a silent, deadly plague.

She rubs the space between her eyes and decides to call Jonathan to cancel, but the thought of his hopeful voice puts her off. He wouldn't let her wriggle out of it that easily. He'd come up with a plan, a scheme, perhaps suggest another dinner, and she doesn't want that. She doesn't want to explain why she can't do it, and that, perversely, makes her decide that she will. She will finish the speech and mail it to him by the end of the day.

Turning back to the screen, she reads over what she's written and adds a few more details from her research files. Now that she's decided to do it, her speech seems better constructed than she first thought, as if she had only to acknowledge it to realize its worth. Scrolling through, she wonders whether she ought to say more about attempts to destroy the disease. During the

1930s the Americans succeeded in obliterating malaria with an eradication programme in the South during which the army literally went to war on the swamps, dropping insecticide bombs across millions of acres of mosquito breeding ground, carpet-bombing the area until there was not a single pair of the insects left. The attack worked for a few years and malaria was kept at bay, but gradually the mosquitoes returned, not just to America, but other places where similar tactics had been tried. Insecticide poisoning was eventually abandoned in favour of drug treatment, but the malaria protozoan learned to evade the new attempts to wipe it out. Sometimes, Elise had thought, it was as if the mosquitoes and protozoan were somehow working together to destroy the world, which was ridiculous of course. It was only a disease.

She sits back and her lurid screen saver of an engorged mosquito suckling a human arm blossoms into view. A young assistant had customized it as a joke one weekend. He had since offered to remove the image, but Elise had let it remain. It reminded her that her enemy was real.

The mosquito was in fact quite innocent: on its own it created no harm, destroyed no life, but in combination with its deadly partner, the protozoan *Plasmodium falciparam* carried by female mosquitoes in their saliva, it was a serial killer. It could infect birds, snakes, lizards, mice, rats, as well as monkeys and humans. The mosquito itself was simply the syringe that delivered the deadly dose; the hand that delivered the fatal blow; the gun that delivered the final bullet.

A sudden fume-filled gust from the open window flicks her papers and she turns away from the screen. She goes to the window and stands looking down on the street, working her shoulders back and forth, releasing the knots in her muscles. The pain between her eyes pulses. She wonders whether she should book a Thai massage after work. It would help to release the tension that has been building since she arrived at the office, earlier than usual because she hadn't slept well, to the sound of a car alarm bleating down the street. It has continued its wail all morning, like a sick child.

She presses her forehead against the cold glass. From this height the traffic looks like one long jointed machine made from shiny pale metal. A masked young cyclist breaks away from the chain and speeds down the middle of the road, neon back taut as a bow. Cycling is now an extreme sport, she thinks, as dangerous as abseiling or ice hockey. People need protective gear: helmets, gloves, visors, masks. She used to adore cycling, the raw feeling of wind in her face, hair flying. Her old bicycle had a basket on the front, which she filled with biology books, pedalling around madly like some romantic undergraduate from a film. How absurd! Or, as her colleagues would say: how retro! What cute times you lived through.

But now, thinking about it, the seventies seem loose, woolly and unravelled in comparison to the tightly wrapped, shiny-packaged, go-getting nineties – a hand-knitted, bobbly rainbow scarf against something sleek and black nylon. The nineties were a different continent, a new frontier, of gloss and glass. And she has somehow crossed from one place to another, one decade to another without really noticing. She never imagined the future would be like this, but then nobody of her generation did. It's as if the new modern way of being had hatched outside the old comfortable world and then pushed its way in. Move aside! We're the nineties! We're cool and hard and swift and unbreakable. We'll overtake you in a flash! She steps back from the window. It isn't that she's worried about getting old; it's more that she's just realized that her time of being young has actually gone. And some part of her, she's always supposed, would one day have that time back.

It wasn't something she thought about consciously, but it was there, an imperceptible force that had over the years somehow impeded her. It was as if she were waiting for something, some sort of signal. She didn't really do anything, she thought, except go to work.

What else was there? What lay beyond the orbit of work were other people with their hurts and needs, their urge to share and sometimes probe. 'Have you ever been loved?' she remembers one of her weekend companions asking her one cold night in the Cotswolds. 'Really truly loved by someone who cared for you more than themselves?' A log fire had been burning and she had looked into the flames before she answered.

'Yes, I have.'

How much she had weighted the 'yes' became apparent later when after leaving the bar and finding a double room they had not been able to think of anything more to say to each other.

Now she wonders whether it is inevitable that the past decides the future. Would she always be in some way the girl she was at twenty-one with her great grief and hope for the future? Would she never be able to leave Africa behind?

'Yes.' Her weekend companion had resembled him in some way. A certain bulkiness across the shoulders, but without the grace. He had been more educated but less refined.

The window grows warm under her cheek. Down in the street below the line of cars, most carrying a single person, remains frozen. She can see a man jerking his head to some tune. Another driver is slumped forward, arms cradling the steering wheel. A red bus is caught in the middle of the traffic, the faces onboard pale oval cut-outs like those odd little people chains children create from newspaper. She remembers making them at school, endlessly cutting them out, rows and rows of people, working very carefully with the scissors so that they would all be identical. Why? What were they for? What was any of it for?

She lifts her palms and places them against the window. The glass feels hard and unyielding, probably toughened in some way. Most of the buildings in this part of Westminster were reinforced against terrorist attacks. She feels tired. She always feels tired. She's been tired for years. Everyone she works with is tired, but no one says anything, too exhausted even to protest. She looks down at the people in their cars and sees that everyone there is tired, too. Most of the faces have the resigned, closed-in pallor of city workers who survive by shutting their senses down. She recognizes every one of them.

Rattled by her thoughts, she tries to pull away from the window, but finds she can't. It's as if the sheet of plate glass is somehow the limit of where she can go. She could hurl herself out of it, but drama is not her style; there's a certain part of her that has always been committed to cold survival: a bleak, stubborn force that grits its teeth and holds up its hands in the face of oblivion. But the biologist in her doesn't believe in wilful forces, doesn't believe in fate or destiny. Maybe all that stands between her throwing herself from the window and survival is a single selfish strand of DNA, a tiny mortal coil that cannot *not* live. Perhaps that's all there is.

She turns back towards her office and looks across its space. Every day for the past twenty-three years she has sat at her desk and worked almost unconsciously, writing reports, compiling data, tracking drug developments, and passing up opportunities to study in the field because of her responsibilities to her daughter. It was comfortable in the early days, almost homely. Things had been a little more chaotic and accepting back then. The carpets had been shabbier, the desks messier, the office doors always open and occupied by adventuring Oxbridge types who kept wine in their filing cabinets and hung about reading Henry James while they waited for funding and made plans for trips to Cambodia or Swaziland, or just anywhere they liked the sound of. They didn't feel as if they had to save the world, they simply wanted to see something of it.

Elise had risen quietly, some would say stealthily, to the top, or almost the top. She was the most senior officer below the chief executive who was due to retire in a year. There was a part of her that desperately wanted the job, not because of the status, someone in her position was used to that, but for the opportunity to make the foundation truly her own. For many years she'd worked almost invisibly, consulting only a few trusted colleagues about her ideas, building her research meticulously layer by layer into an impressive body of work. Now she wanted to do something with it. She wanted to make sure that her efforts amounted to something before it was too late.

The foundation had changed since she first joined, but it was difficult to define what the change was exactly. There were still plenty of bright young researchers only too keen to fly to Thailand or Bangladesh, where multi-drug-resistant malaria was spreading, but their attitude was less diffident, less ironic. Around the office the atmosphere had become tighter, almost severe. The new researchers believed in hard work and stayed after hours staring dry-eyed at their computer screens as they compiled anxious reports. They all looked hurt in some indefinable way and their problems both touched and appalled her: the secret abortions, addictions and debts. Some were victims of intense emotional blackmail or bullying. The stories were vivid and complicated. She didn't know why they came to her, she wasn't known for her compassion, but something drew them into her office at the end of the day, something she recognized, but could not put into words.

The flow of trouble made her aware of a kind of sickness that lurked under the impeccably groomed surface of the young. A sort of panic that made them seek solace in drink, or drugs, or each other. Some mornings on her walk to work what she saw was a stream of mournful young eyes, people who should have been in their prime, hobbling under duress, the same clenched look in every face, as though they were being forced to undertake a journey without any sort of reward. On those mornings she would pick up the phone to speak to Memory as soon as she arrived at the office. And the response would be short.

'What? What are you ringing me for now?'

To hear your voice, to know that you are alive and still part of me even though we never see each other.

'Oh, I don't know. I just thought about you on the way to work. Doesn't matter, I can tell you're busy.'

'Look, if we arrange to meet, you'll only cancel.'

'I know, it's been hellish here, too. I just wanted to know if you were all right, that's all.'

A long sigh from Memory. 'How about coming over after work?'

You want to see me, you're not just pretending?

'To your flat? Well, it's a little bit out of the way.'

Why can't she say more? Ask how I am?

'Out of the way? It would take you half an hour in a cab.'

'Don't pressure me, darling.'

Don't punish me for wanting to see you. Don't push me away.

'*Pressure you?*' A sharp laugh. 'You phoned *me*, remember, to see how I was. If you didn't want to see me, why bother?'

'Oh, darling, don't . . .'

Don't, let's . . .

'I've got to go, another call . . .'

. . . start again . . .

They never completed, never resolved anything. There were simply pauses and gaps in the same conversation. A few days or weeks would go by with no contact at all and then it would start again, the tentative crabbiness, the frustration over the complicated arrangements. Impossible to believe how difficult it was for two people in the same city just a mile or so apart to meet. When they did manage to settle on a mutual arrangement, they celebrated it. 'We've done it! Now are you sure? *Are you sure?*' They both knew that if either cancelled there would be no more attempts for weeks. It was too exhausting.

Elise goes over to the small refrigerator filled with bottles of mineral water and pours herself a cooling glass. She stands for a while looking across her desk and wonders how it would feel to walk away from it all. She would take no notes or files, just her bag with keys and purse. That's what Memory had done. She hadn't even called. Just sent her devastating postcard. It was almost an immaculate disappearance. Of course, Elise had gone to the flat – Memory had given her a key in case of emergency – and looked around. The place had smelled abandoned, but looked oddly occupied. A bowl of tulips Memory had forgotten to throw out were gently rotting on the windowsill. Cushions still held her shape, clothes her scent. Going into the bathroom, Elise had found cosmetics dropped in the sink, as if the morning of departure had been hurried, nervous, a scramble to get things to stay in their correct place. Long black hairs corkscrewed against the sides of the bath, a book lay face down on the bed, a dressing gown was scrunched on the floor, its thick folds unbelievably still damp. And it was this Elise had picked up, cradling it in her arms, its weight oddly consoling as she walked around looking for other clues.

The telephone rings on her desk, jolting her back into the present. 'Mrs Cougan,' a flat young voice announces. 'Adam is here to see you. Shall I send him up?'

She closes her computer file. 'Give me a minute.' Then she checks her make-up and hair in a compact mirror. The lines around the corners of her mouth are deeper than usual. She looks old and creased as if she has been sitting in one position for too long. At the knock on the door she snaps the mirror shut.

Adam brings with him the smell of damp city and sits down heavily, refusing her offer of coffee. He seems to have lost weight. Seeing him sitting on the edge of his chair, his face so pale and hopeless, causes some primitive impulse to fire up inside her. She pulls her eyes away from him.

Adam swallows through dry lips. 'It's quite some office you have here. I didn't realize it would be so—'

'Difficult to find? Most people walk straight past. We're not obvious, as a building I mean.'

Adam gives her a weak smile. 'I was going to say impressive.' He lifts his head and looks across her desk and out towards the window. From his position he would be able to see the sky. He swallows again. 'I need to know if you've heard anything from Memory.'

'I had a card,' Elise says gently. 'She's in Zambia.'

He looks at her bleakly, his full blue eyes appearing in the afternoon light like soft bruised berries. 'Did she say . . . did she tell you what happened with us?'

'Only that you had split up . . .' Elise pauses. 'I'm so sorry, Adam.'

He looks down at his knees and then jerks his head up quickly. 'She didn't talk to you before she left?'

'No.' She lets her reply hang in the air.

Adam shifts in his seat. He places his hand on the edge of the desk. 'Did you have any idea she was planning this?'

'I don't think it was planned. I think she just decided to go.'

His eyes darken for a moment. The office is quiet except for the persistent hum of the computer.

'Excuse me.' She shuts down the computer. Adam waits patiently. But when she faces him again his eyes have taken on a glittery edge.

'You lost your husband suddenly, didn't you? Tell me, how did you cope?'

Panic sluices through her. 'I don't know that I did.'

He looks away from her. She sips water and offers to pour him some, but he flicks his head in refusal. 'It's the suddenness I find so difficult to accept,' he says. 'I didn't even know anything was wrong. We were getting married for God's sake.'

'I know,' Elise murmurs. She realizes he hasn't come to be consoled. He's come to be heard.

'She *agreed* we would do this. I just can't accept that she would throw it all away so . . . *casually*.' He kneads the desk as if trying to make an impression.

'I don't understand it either,' Elise says.

He glances at her. 'There is something you should know, something she perhaps didn't tell you. I was, well . . . a bit presumptuous the night of the party. She was late, very late, you know how she is, and I thought, well . . . I thought I needed to get on with it; you see the bar people had it all timed and kept asking me when I wanted the champagne and the flowers and the cake, we had a special cake with fireworks that she never even got to see . . .'

'You had put a lot of effort into organizing it, I know.'

'I kept telling them to hang on and I could see they were getting twitchy . . .' He pauses and wipes his nose with the back of his hand. 'I *told* everyone. I made the announcement without her. I know I shouldn't have, but I just couldn't wait any longer.'

'And then she arrived.'

'That was the crazy thing, I'd only just told everyone a few seconds earlier and then she walked in, looking amazing of course. I couldn't believe it. What timing.' He looks up hopelessly.

'You couldn't have known, Adam.'

'I messed it up. I really wanted to surprise her and I blew it.'

'And now she's surprised you. Surprised us both.'

'I can't deal with it.'

'You can.' Elise gets up from her desk and Adam looks startled as if she is about to dismiss him. Slowly she walks away from him and goes to the window where she looks down on the traffic which has now broken up and moved on slightly. 'You will learn to live with it.'

'You sound as if you know something. Are you sure she didn't say anything?'

'I know her quite well, remember.'

Adam exhales and she continues. 'What I know is that it will hurt for a long time. Every morning you'll wake up and there'll be a short time, a blissful moment, when you won't be aware of anything, but as soon as you get up, it will be with you and you'll think about it until you fall asleep at night. Then gradually you'll go through a day or two when you feel that something's missing and you don't know what it is. You'll become absorbed in a job, maybe find someone else . . .' Adam shuffles in his chair, but she goes on. 'Slowly your memory will fade. It will seem as if it never happened. It will seem like a story. When people ask you about it, you will search your mind for the details and find they have gone. You'll make something up. You won't mean to lie, but you'll find something to say that's less painful, something that doesn't make other people uncomfortable. Something easy so that people don't ask any more questions. You'll realize that you can cope.' She turns from the window.

There's a silence as Adam absorbs what she has said. He runs his hands through his damp hair. The sleeves of his jacket are wet. 'You're telling me what happened to you?'

'I understand how it is to lose someone close.'

'You make it sound as if she's not coming back.'

'Adam, the best thing you can do is to let her go. Move on with your life.'

'She was my life.' He looks down and rubs his damp sleeve across his face.

Elise looks away. His passion unnerves her.

'She's got to do it properly,' Adam continues. 'It's all right you saying, move on, but I can't until she's said something definite, made it clear what she wants.'

'Hasn't she made it clear?' Her voice trembles slightly.

Adam stares at her. She sees that he wants to protest, but something holds him back. His fingers are white against the desk, his lips ghastly pale as he slowly realizes what she is trying to say.

'Memory can look after herself. She's pretty tough. She's gone to a remote area, but she'll be all right. There are people there who will look out for her . . .' She pauses. 'She's not in any danger.'

Adam glances at her hollow-eyed. She wants to sink down on to the floor. What a relief it would be to tell him now, spill the truth on to the carpet, like blood.

He nods and stands up. 'Could I come back again?'

'Of course. Any time.'

He goes. She sits down, her chest tightening, throat closing, and grips the edge of her desk, thinking she is about to have an asthma attack. Breathing deeply and slowly, she closes her eyes. Voices drift from the corridor outside.

After a moment she turns the computer on and pulls her speech back on screen, scrolling through it, deleting awkward and unnecessary words, trimming it to its bare essentials. She works solidly for an hour. After rewriting her conclusion she sits back. How would it be, she thinks, if she could do this with her life: reorder passages, delete the ugly parts? She hadn't handled things right with Memory. She had always meant to go back and set some things straight. She'd been waiting for the right time, a significant moment. But something had always come along to stop her telling the truth. She'd never intended to obscure what happened in Africa, if anything it was the opposite: she'd always *wanted* to tell the truth, but she had avoided it because it was too important to reveal casually. Her explanation had come out unthinkingly a long time ago when Memory had come home from school wanting to know some details so that she could satisfy the curiosity of her friends.

'Mum, people keep asking if I have a dad at home and I don't know what to say.'

'You can tell them that he was killed in a plane crash.'

And Memory had seemed satisfied with that, pleased that she had something impressive to report to her friends. The explanation was temporary, a way to hold things together for a while. Elise had not meant for it to go on so long.

But it had. And she'd been aware of it constantly. Like the bronchial infections that laid her low each winter, it made it hard for her to breathe freely. Even when she felt healthy it was always there: a clotted darkness close to her heart.

It took a long time for Memory to settle. At first all her English words were spoken in lists, and it took nearly a whole year before she would engage in a conversation. The child psychologist said it was trauma. Post-traumatic stress disorder. The little girl had been through some terrifying events. With time she would recover. But there were so many fears to be overcome. Getting Memory on to the aircraft to leave Africa had been the worst and Elise could still feel the pain of being pummelled in the stomach by the girl's feet as she kicked in protest, screaming like a wild thing. Her father had taken over, carrying Memory in his arms up the steps to the plane. Elise remembers the sight of the girl's dark head buried tight into his shoulder, her tiny black palm resting on his back.

When they got her home she had been frightened of the big white bath and had to be scrubbed clean with a flannel. She wouldn't sleep in a bed, preferring to curl up on the floor under the open window. Buses, tubes and taxis made her tremble, and for the first couple of months they walked everywhere. Working then had been impossible for Elise who had relied on her father for financial support. He had stayed with them, sleeping in the spare room which he had set up as a study to continue his research in between writing countless letters and telephoning people he knew in various government offices to help secure the adoption.

Her father had taught Memory to smile again. He encouraged her to draw, supplying her with soft coloured pencils and endless sheets of watercolour paper. While he was making his telephone calls, he would sit her down on the rug and let her draw whatever came into her imagination. At first she drew almost exclusively flames in fierce abstract scribblings, sometimes ripping through the paper in her attempts to express what she saw. Other times she drew children with their hands over their ears, or lying on the ground in rows, their eyes absent from their faces. Some of the drawings made the hairs rise on Elise's arms, and a strange prickling feeling come over her. One November night she had found Memory standing by the ashes of a bonfire muttering words in a dialect her father identified as Bemba. Memory also had nightmares. Elise's father would go to her. He would sit with her in the soft night-light, sometimes reading to her passages from *The Hobbit*. The child psychologist said she would forget her memories in time. Her father said Memory needed nurturing.

The word haunted Elise. Each time Memory was sick she wondered whether it was because of a lack of nurture. She had no nature to give the child, no part of her own biochemisty would ever bond them; she couldn't look at Memory and say, as other parents did, 'Oh, you're just like your father.' She could only watch her grow up.

At first, all treats and outings were experimental. The zoo overwhelmed her, the parks were too windy, but ice-skating at Alexandra Palace was a success. Elise remembers Memory's dark face lit with joy as she wobbled to the safety bar, her stubby little hands awkward inside her woollen mitts. Once she got her confidence, she would kick off, skates spraying chips of ice, and turn perfect circles. Memory went alone when she was old enough, coming home flushed and smelling sometimes of drink. But Elise never questioned her. It had taken the child so long to find any sort of freedom that she didn't want anything to break the spell. She wanted Memory to grow up without fear.

Skating was eventually replaced by trips to Brighton and then long weekends away with friends when Memory sometimes neglected to tell Elise where she was going. 'Don't fuss, Mum. I know what I'm doing, you just have to trust me.' And Elise had learned to let go.

Sometimes the temptation to reclaim her was just too strong. She thinks back to the birthday tea she arranged in Claridge's that year. The Foreign Office friends who came had congratulated Elise on Memory, who looked dazzling in a red silk dress with diamanté in her professionally straightened hair. As she blew out the twenty-one candles on a white iced cake, someone had said: 'Amazing, just amazing – you must be so proud. You've done such a good job.' Elise had looked at Memory. There had been something in her smooth, young face, a sort of flickering darkness that had made her wonder.

In the crowded years of Memory growing up, Elise had forgotten to tell her daughter the truth. The story she'd told was provisional: a reassurance until she felt that Memory was ready.

All children believe that there is some kind of secret being kept from them. All children go looking for clues when they think there is a mystery to be solved. Elise had been careful.

After her return she had made sure that there were no traces of Africa for a curious child to find: she threw away photos, clothes, even books she had read because of the scent in their pages. The only thing she kept was a flower, a once headily scented frangipani bloom she had picked after leaving the hospital, which had dried to paper thinness. Sometimes she looked at it sitting in the jewellery box along with a pair of pearl earrings she no longer wore, but mostly she forgot about it. She had been planning to give the earrings to Memory to wear on her wedding day.

Maybe it was impossible for parents to bring up children without lying to them. How many other lies had she told? *I'll only be half an hour. I'll come as soon as I can. I would love to have been there. Do you mind, darling? We'll go another day. You wait and see.* How many promises had she broken? How many gifts had she bought to compensate?

It was strange how easily the lie had become the truth even though she did believe in her heart that it was an *honest lie*. Elise had repeated the story of the plane crash so many times, she almost believed in it herself. In a way it seemed more *real* than the truth, singularly convincing in its simplicity.

Over the years the story had become a reference point for colleagues, new friends, lovers – she hasn't realized this before, just how embedded one single piece of false information can become – and every new encounter added to an ever widening and deepening net. The story made sense. It was rational and immediate; it was the ultimate explanation after which no further enquiry was necessary. It was final. People tended to react in the same way. A gasp and then: 'I'm so sorry,' before changing the subject. She had been lucky, that way.

But luck didn't have anything to do with it.

She stares at her computer screen. She has lived a narrow, covered-up existence, almost like a spy who has seen things he can never make part of his ordinary life, and thereby closes in on himself, making his existence as small and innocuous as possible in order to protect what he must not talk about. The thought frightens her, but she also feels an odd sense of relief, almost a glimmer of hope.

The sky fills the window, glowing blood-red in between shredded purple clouds. She watches the mosquito fade from her shutdown screen. How simple the truth is, she thinks. She gathers her keys and security pass. We always think we have to dig for the truth, scrabble for it in dark buried places, but in reality we don't need to struggle because the truth never hides. It's us who hide. We elude the truth. We step into the shadows. Truth merely bides its time and waits for us to find it. No wonder it takes us by surprise.

10

SIDESLIPPING (BASIC)

You should always be able to approach an aerodrome, glide in, and land without the necessity for sideslipping: it is a good practice and a sign of polished flying. Nevertheless, there are times when you overestimate your height, and it is then that the ability to slip off excess height is useful, even although an admission of misjudgement.

Zambia, 1996

Memory looks down at an undulating shape imprinted across the red dirt road. 'Kennedy, I think I've found a snake track.' At the sound of her voice he turns and walks lightly down the road, his long naked feet seeming to float across the ground.

He kneels and traces the wave-like imprint with one long brown finger. 'Mmm, she's pretty big.' Hugging his knees, he peers into the matted bush grass sprouting at the side of the track. 'She's hiding in there somewhere.'

'How do you know it's a she?'

He shrugs and then gets up and brushes off the dirt from his yellow trousers. He stands for a while looking down the road, his brow furrowed almost as if he is expecting someone.

'If we wait, do you think we might see her?' She feels excited at the thought. At a street party once in London she had spotted a man wearing a python draped around his neck and had wanted to go over and touch it, but Adam had pulled her away, his arm encircling her protectively.

'She won't come out while we're here. Snakes are shy.'

'But they attack humans?'

'Only in stories.'

'Oh.'

They walk side by side. The sun has not yet risen to its full height and a rosy glow spreads behind the trees, which are still dark at their bases. The air is filled with the sounds of doves and wood pigeons and a bird she has never seen which makes a noise like an old Morris Traveller winding its way slowly down a steep hill. Every now and then huge white butterflies fly up from the grass, sometimes landing on her arm. One lands and lightly suckles her skin. 'She – it – thinks you taste sweet,' Kennedy says.

She throws him a look, expecting a grin, but he appears impassive, almost withdrawn. He walks ahead of her slightly and she can see the small rickety bones down his spine showing up like an X-ray. A butterfly the size of her palm with wings made out of ripped white paper buzzes his shoulder. She wants to point it out to him, but for some reason stays silent. More butterflies slip in and out of the light and she wonders whether it is true that they live for only a single day. They are an appropriate metaphor for a place that seems permanently temporary.

She couldn't imagine anyone she knew wanting to stay any longer than a day or two and she had been here nearly three weeks already. The country was so utterly remote it seemed inconceivable, almost as if it did not exist outside her imagination. Being here felt like entering a dream state, and just as some dreams gave her the unsettling feeling of knowing somewhere, yet at the same time doubting it, this place seemed constantly to shift perspective. Like countries in dreams, it was made up from various bits and pieces that did not fit into one coherent whole. It had no real contours of its own, only borrowed frontiers from other places, no real centre, beginning or end. It was somewhere that invented itself from day to day.

It was most disorienting at night. Then the bush became swamped with such terrible blackness it seemed to have substance.

More than once she had woken and put out her hands into the choking softness, wanting literally to rip away the folds of darkness.

One night as she woke she heard drums. The sound caused her heart to race and she had sat up, her chest heaving, a smell of wood smoke in the room, and a darker, riper odour. She thought she'd been having a nightmare from her childhood in which an old man grabbed her and squeezed her until she could hardly breathe. He always took her to the same place, a flat, dry area where there were stones and people dressed in white. The drums beat louder and she had reached under the bed for her torch. She had kept it next to her until the batteries ran out.

At a fork in the path Kennedy stops and waits for her to catch up, one hand resting on his hip. He lowers his eyes as she slips into step next to him. They are going to the plantation to pick up the jeep for a trip into town for supplies: the usual beer, spirits and cigarettes needed by Max to numb the pain from his leg. A few nights ago while they were out drinking at the club bar Kennedy had confided that Max slept with a shotgun under his mattress. She had wanted to ask more, but someone had joined them, one of the farmers, a florid man called Joe Baxter who was angry at losing his fence wire. The conversation had been rapidly cut and not returned to later. She remembers how Baxter had complained to *her*, as if she were personally responsible for the teenagers who snipped his fences and stole lengths of wire to make toys. She had seen roadside displays of these silver toys, intricate helicopters with hinged parts and motorcycles with moving wheels and tiny wire riders, and had been impressed at the industry. The toys stretched as far as the eye could see, as if they were lining up to take part in a race. She had even thought she might buy one to take home. But they hadn't gone back to the place where they were for sale.

Now she wonders why Kennedy had mentioned the gun. Perhaps he was trying to impress her, but he hadn't talked about it in a boasting kind of way. He'd dropped it into the conversation quite deliberately, almost as if he were trying to include her in something, or maybe even trying to warn her.

It was frustrating, but there was an aura around Max that prevented direct questioning. She had the sense that Max was profoundly injured at his core. Somehow his entire being had been deeply wounded.

A few days ago he had come to the house and joined her in the garden for morning tea. He'd sat with her for a while looking up at the trees. The light seemed particularly radiant, and rippled in the spaces between the trees like golden saris that had blown on the wind and become snagged in the branches. Max drank his tea with delicate sips but did not look at her. His fingers picked at the raffia on the garden chair. His bulk and brooding presence emanated a shuttered sadness made all the more poignant by the light that seemed almost to be laughing around him.

Placing her cup under her chair, she had turned to him and felt him stiffen as if anticipating a blow. His eyes swung around the garden, desperate for something to settle on. Eventually his gaze alighted on the Rhodesian boiler squatting like a displaced chimney some distance from the house. Logs jutted from the boiler door, limbs of hardwood burning for her morning bath. She turned her gaze away guiltily. 'I need to know the truth about what happened to Paul Cougan,' she blurted out suddenly.

Max looked at her then in a fierce blaze of blue. She thought he was going to say something, but he tore his eyes away and glanced up at the trees as if they might save him from scrutiny. His single foot nervously rasped the dry grass. She looked at his boot covered in red soil. With both legs intact he would have towered over her, physically intimidated her. He remained seated, his head turned slightly away from her. She looked at his sunburned neck and the golden hairs on his stubbled cheek. He hadn't shaved that morning and she wondered why. She softened her tone: 'What I mean is, I would like to see the spot where the plane went down. I think I need to do that.'

Max's jaw twitched and his shoulders slumped forward. His brow was contorted, and she noticed a vein pulsing like a tiny heart on his temple. He slowly cleared his throat. She thought he was about to speak, but he just looked at her with a single, piercing glance.

'Well, maybe not now, whenever you're ready. It's not as if I'm going anywhere, is it?' She attempted a laugh, but Max sat simply in his chair looking somehow smaller and younger.

After a few moments he grunted and lifted himself up. She watched him hobble across the garden on his crutches, his shirt drenched in perspiration. A feeling of shame came over her as she shaded her eyes against the sun. There was something about Max that was utterly overwhelming. She did not know why, but he made her feel wrong about everything. He was like the country itself, completely unanswerable.

For days after, Max avoided her. Kennedy came to check how she was and when she asked him about Max the reply was always: 'He's working, it's the planting season.' Memory wondered if she had lost her opportunity. Maybe Max would never be able to talk to her about what had really happened. She had been wrong to come looking for answers just to fill in some gaps in her own history. There was something deep and unsettling going on. The really fine choice, the right choice, would be to give up on what now seemed a monstrously self-indulgent quest and return home. At the same time Memory knew that having come this far, *this close*, it was the last thing she was going to do.

'Hey, dreamer!' Kennedy calls out to her from some distance along the path. 'Do you London girls know how to run?'

She looks at him standing with his hands on his hips, a challenging look on his dark face and she breaks into a sprint. 'Watch me!'

When she catches him up, laughing and bending over to recover her breath, she has to resist an impulse to link her arm through his. Nudging shoulders, they walk down a short dusty track that leads to Max's plantation. They go first to the farm office, a low white building made from concrete blocks, but there's no sign of Max or the jeep. She watches two kittens box each other with tiny paws from behind a plastic carton sprouting a dried-up plant. At one point she reaches down and then jerks back, remembering warnings of rabies.

Kennedy tells her to wait inside the office while he goes to look for Max. She watches him stride off towards the coffee fields, which seem artificially green against the flat brown land, his long legs making scissor shadows across the ground.

The office is dark, and it takes a while before her eyes adjust. Every surface is coated with a floury dust, as if a sandstorm had once whipped through the office and nobody had bothered to clean it. A tiny bell sound rings from one corner and she registers the presence of a petite African woman sitting at a desk with her back to the window, working at an old Imperial typewriter.

The woman stops typing and investigates her visitor coolly. 'The boss is not here,' she says and resumes her work.

'My friend has gone to look for him,' Memory says. 'We've come for the jeep. Is it all right if I wait?'

The woman shrugs and continues typing at a faster speed, cropped head bent, her brown cleft chin jutting from a slender neck.

One wall of the office is covered with yellowed notices. She wonders whether it was Max or perhaps someone else who had written down the list of names for the Kapenta Cofee Footbal Teem. Pictures of old planes torn from magazines, curling stiffly at the edges, are also pinned on the wall along with a faded birthday card, showing a pink thatched cottage. In a childish hand someone has written: *When I begin a new project, I like to forget past problems and approach it as if it is my first. Lionel Ritchie.*

The woman at the desk continues to type monotonously, occasionally flicking her eyes towards Memory's bare legs and painted toes. The kittens roll under the door space and quiver on the floor, a pile of snagged cobwebs with four bright eyes.

Memory shifts her feet away from them. On the floor she finds an old copy of the *Zambia Times* and flicks through it, her eye drawn towards a story about the deaths of three-year-old twins called Emmanuel and Saviour in a farm hut that caught fire while they were sleeping.

The kittens squeal and roll around her ankles. The typist picks up a piece of blue carbon paper and carefully places it between two pages of typing paper which she winds into her machine. Memory reads through the rest of the newspaper which is dominated by stories involving documents and bureaucratic slip-ups. There are many curious advertisements, one of which invites Copperbelt farmers to a Poultry Chat.

Sliding the newspaper back under her chair, Memory wonders what the woman sitting typing so solemnly would make of her city office with its water cooler and coffee machine, its screened windows and wall of chrome clocks showing the time in Los Angeles, Rome and Sydney; its pristine white computers with curved keyboards and silent mousepads, its muted telephones and self-watering plants. Even to Memory it seems like a fabrication. And yet, Africa is no more real. It hasn't revealed anything so far. She came expecting answers, but all she has is more questions. Why, for example, hasn't Max kept his promise to talk to her? The woman stops typing and looks directly at her.

'The boss is coming now.'

The jeep scrunches to a halt outside and a few moments later Max lurches into the office. In one hand he carries a piece of torn plastic with something dark and pungent oozing inside, the other grips a crutch. Putting the plastic down on the desk, he wipes his hands down his shorts before looking at her. 'Sorry . . . I had to go and rescue one of my workers from some bees.'

'Bees?'

'He climbed a tree after honey and the bees swarmed.'

Something in the room gives off a smoky liquorice smell. She imagines a furious cloud of bees, all pointing in the same direction. 'Is he all right?' Her mouth feels dry.

'He's in shock.' Max leans against the desk, his face shiny with sweat. All the hairs on his arms are raised and one hand trembles slightly as he pushes a grey strand from his eyes. 'Kennedy's bringing him in now.'

She tenses at a sound from outside. The woman at the typewriter suddenly stands up, an alert look on her face. Kennedy pushes the door open with his back and comes in carrying the shoulders of a slender young African. Another man holds the boy's feet. Walking with careful, tiny steps the men bring him into the space between the two desks and look for somewhere to lay him down. The young man's body is rigid, his fingers and toes stiff and dusty pale. His eyes are partly open, showing rolling whites shot with flecks of blood. His pale lips move as he murmurs something: the word *mass*, or maybe it is *grass*. The men gently lower the young man down and put his head on the newspaper where it rolls from side to side. He is wearing a pair of football shorts and a grey vest which rises up and down as he breathes rapidly like a dog that has been tied up for too long in the heat. He has been stung in all the tender parts of his body: in the creases of his arms, on his ears, around his mouth and eyes, the stings swollen into lumps the size of small pebbles. There are more swellings down his thighs and on the pale undersides of his feet. He stirs and moans a different word this time: *Mulenga*.

'He's saying his name,' the woman at the typewriter says, her eyes dark. 'I know the boy. His name is Victor Mulenga.'

Max orders Kennedy to fetch water. When he returns with a bowl filled from the tap outside, Max gestures for the boy to be given a drink. Kennedy offers the bowl of water up to the boy's swollen lips. His eyelids flutter up and down like tiny shutters and he clenches his fist as if trying to signal that the effort of drinking will be too painful for him. But Kennedy persists with the bowl, pushing its lip against the boy's mouth, which is darkly engorged, the colour of meat that has been left to dry out. After a few minutes the boy begins to lap with his tongue and Kennedy tips the bowl to make it easier for him to drink. The boy's taut features soften slightly and he even lifts his head to take the last drops of water. When he puts his head back down he sighs. Kennedy lifts the boy's thin wrist in one hand and takes his pulse, looking up at the wall of notices as he counts. For a brief moment he meets Memory's eyes, and nods, as if affirming something, and then looks away. The boy visibly relaxes, his legs slacken and his feet fall on to their sides. The woman at the typewriter sits back down.

'Shouldn't we take him to hospital?' Memory asks. 'We could take him with us.'

'He needs to be quiet,' Max says. 'It's better for him to stay here.' He glances at Kennedy. 'You should get going before it's too late.'

Memory wonders whether she should insist on taking the boy to hospital. The prospect of leaving him behind and driving into town for food seems absurd. 'Look, we're going anyway,' she blurts out to Max as he prepares to leave. 'We ought to take him, he might die.'

He turns and studies her for a moment with what appears to be incomprehension. His glance switches to the boy on the floor and he says flatly, 'He's too sick. The drive would kill him.' Then he lurches out of the door.

Kennedy sighs and throws her a look almost of apology before following Max outside. The woman at the typewriter makes a clicking sound in the back of her throat and then resumes her work. Momentarily disoriented, Memory peers through the window screen and sees that the front wheel of the jeep has gone down with a puncture. Deflated and frustrated at having to wait again, she sits down heavily. The woman at the typewriter glances up, a minute beat of irritation flickering across her face. 'All right,' Memory wants to say. 'I'll be out of your hair soon.' The boy lies on the floor, muttering his name: *Mulenga, Mulenga, Mulenga*; his face swollen as a melon, eyes rolling with pain.

The window has a dirty wire mesh across it composed of tiny hexagrams immaculately interlocked as in a honeycomb. She can see the outline of the men as they change the wheel, but they seem remote and indistinct, their voices muffled. Behind her the boy on the floor continues to moan, his voice rising and falling. Maybe he will die. There is nothing she can do to prevent it. She turns away from the window, and catches the woman at the type-writer staring at her. Their eyes meet for a moment and then slide away. We are the same age, Memory thinks. If things had turned out differently, I might have had her life. She smiles at the woman who glances at her suspiciously and narrows her eyes. Then, perhaps sensing something genuine in Memory, points to the desk with its curious, pungent plastic packet.

Prompted by the woman, Memory goes over to investigate. Prising the packet apart she finds a comb of dark almost black honey with bees stuck inside, still twitching, and pieces of twig and tree bark massed together like some dense sticky living organism. She looks over at the woman who nods vigorously and then, slowly understanding, dips the tip of her finger into the mess and brings it up to her mouth. The woman smiles and nods again. The honey is the most incredible thing Memory has ever tasted: a woody, syrupy, mushroomy concoction, dark and intense. She dips her finger in again. The boy on the floor groans and rolls his head across the newspaper. She goes over to him, bends down and offers him some honey to eat from her fingers. His eyes flicker. He feels hot and his breath smells sour. Gently she picks up the bowl and lets the boy lap some more water, cradling the back of his head with her hand. Across the bare office she is aware of the woman watching her.

When eventually the jeep is ready, she is startled at how still and white the sky has become as if the season has changed. They drive off, wheels crackling, spraying dirt. Max stands watching them, his body like a hurricane-damaged tree. Memory tracks him in the wing mirror, watching him grow smaller and smaller until he becomes just a dark blue blur on the dusty red road.

They park in the marketplace near a statue of a young African hurling a stone. The heat from the parked cars burns her legs as she walks through them. A woman carrying a huge iron pot on her head sidles up and tries to show her some hand-painted cards, but Kennedy shoos her away.

'Wait a minute, that's a beautiful pot. I wonder how much she wants for it?'

'Don't talk to her.'

'I'm interested in what she has to sell.'

Kennedy rolls his eyes and walks on a few paces before he stops and turns round. Emboldened by a sudden feeling of space around her, Memory steps up to the woman and touches her shoulder and then the pot. She smiles as the woman lifts it from her head and holds it in front of her. The metal is warm from the sun. The woman stands patiently, her eyes clouded, fixed not on Memory but at some point further down the road.

'Don't give her money,' Kennedy calls out.

'I want to buy the pot,' Memory persists. She addresses the woman: 'How much do you want to sell it for?'

The woman says something in a thin, high voice.

'What's she saying?' she asks Kennedy who leans against a wall under a green shop awning, one leg drawn up showing a dull, lean length of thigh.

'She doesn't understand you,' he says. 'She says if you want the pot you must give her what you think it's worth.'

'It's so beautiful.' Memory touches the pot with her palm and the woman makes a sucking sound. 'Maybe I should go away and think about it.' The woman, perhaps reading some subtle signal, adds something in a low voice.

'If you want it, get it now,' Kennedy calls out and puts on his mirrored sunglasses, his mouth moody under the shaded awning.

Memory reaches for her purse and pulls out a wad of notes. The woman stands very still. Memory takes the pot from her and turns it, tracing its leaf patterns with her fingers. The metal is the colour of dirty copper pennies, and she sees that its neck is exactly the same width as the woman's arm.

'Don't give her too much,' Kennedy warns.

Memory presses the wad of money into the woman's hand. The woman rapidly thumbs through it, gives an almost inaudible gasp and then quickly tucks it out of sight into a roll of material at her waist. She bobs before Memory in a movement that is partly a curtsy and partly a genuflection. Tears pour down her cheeks.

'How much did you give her?' Kennedy asks as Memory joins him under the awning, leaving the woman to make her way across the marketplace.

'I don't know. Not much, probably about ten pounds in English money.'

'You shouldn't have done it here where everyone can see. Come on.' He leaves the shade and pushes through the crowd around the supermarket entrance. Inside he selects a trolley and grimly starts filling it with tins and packets he barely looks at. They have brought an ice box for the meat and he goes over to the counter and asks the man there to fill it with packets of steak and half a dozen chickens.

'Slow down,' Memory says. 'I want to look at everything. It's all new and interesting for me.'

But Kennedy pushes the trolley on until he reaches the last counter, a metal padlocked cage containing spirits and cigarettes. He places an order, glancing up and down the shop as he counts out thousands of notes. Memory hovers behind, sensing her presence to be an embarrassment.

When they are in the jeep again she asks, 'Kennedy, what happened to Max? How did he get shot?'

'I told you before, an accident.' Kennedy swerves to avoid a pothole, setting the drink bottles clanking in the back.

'But *how*?'

'You ask too many questions,' he says and drives on, his face suddenly closed. She looks down at the big warm pot in her lap. The metal is the colour of a river in flood, strangely comforting.

'That woman was blind, you know,' she says to change the subject.

But Kennedy turns on her, his eyes white and clear. 'You think I don't notice anything? You think I'm some stupid African who drives you around?'

'I don't think that at all.' She's shocked at the vehemence in his voice, the tension in his body as if all his supporting lines and guy ropes are about to snap 'What's wrong?'

Ignoring her, he turns the jeep down a dusty street lined with industrial sheds, covered with rusting metal signs advertising seeds and farm machinery. He drives slowly as if looking for a certain place. Then abruptly he pulls the jeep to a stop and gets out without looking at her. She watches him stride towards a long shed, his yellow shirt clinging to the small of his back, his thighs loose under his trousers. He walks as if his feet have natural springs. She releases a long-held breath. Then silence folds around her, inscrutable and oppressive, suddenly making her want to weep with frustration.

Africa is getting to her. She hadn't expected it to be so vague, so diffident and difficult to get hold of. She'd had a clear picture of it in her mind, somewhere more brightly coloured and sure of itself, like the Afro-Caribbean parts of London with their healthy polish and arrogant swagger. But *this* Africa could not have been more opposite with its forlorn sheds and dusty streets, its wide-eyed pot-bellied children; its sullen stare. It was a place with all the luck drained out of it, a dried-up rag of a country and that was difficult to accept because it was *her* country and now it seemed like a con. Her own country had nothing at all to offer her. Her own country did not want her, was not the slightest bit interested in her. Her own country, she was beginning to realize, did not give a damn. It was like arriving at an elderly relative's house after years of imagining a tender reunion only to find an exhausted old woman asleep in a chair.

She puts her face in her hands and listens to the jeep engine ticking as it cools. She could go home; she could tiptoe away without making ripples or stirring memories. Or, and this thought makes her lift her head, she could shake the old girl awake.

She climbs out of the jeep and walks over to the shed. From inside comes the nasal sound of electric saws. She walks round to a side entrance and there her eyes take in a large area filled with zinc sinks and baths. Inside the baths are grey blocks of what appears to be stone, but turn out to be blocks of solidly frozen fish. Men, wearing cut-away vests, are bending over the baths and hauling up the blocks on to a long table where a gang of workers cut the ice with chainsaws, carving the solid slabs of mummified fish into new geometric shapes, odd triangles and squares that are then packed into plastic bags. The shed floor is inches deep in grey crystal sawdust flecked with blood and the smell is a potent mix of oil and fish and human sweat.

Eyes swivel towards her as she stands uncertainly at the mouth of the unlit shed, taking in the scene. A dark energy emanates from the bodies of the men as they lift faces hostile with curiosity and open-mouthed greed. She folds her arms across her chest. At the far end she can see Kennedy talking to a man with a vivid face, who is using a small hand saw to cut off the head of a long fish. She can see the eye glittering inside the ice, flattened as if pressed against a window. The man wraps the fish head in a plastic bag and Kennedy hands over a few notes. A young boy standing near the blocks with a duster of soft feathers to brush away flies gives her an alert look as Kennedy begins to weave his way through the workers who turn their shoulders against him almost sullenly. Reaching the entrance, he shoves the bag of fish at her playfully, and she shudders at the cold sharpness against her skin. 'For my father. He makes a special stew with fish heads.'

'Sounds disgusting.' She receives another slap from the freezing bag. Clambering back into the jeep, he briefly takes her hand.

They drive down a wide street lined with shops, awnings spilling long tobacco-coloured shadows. Baskets placed on the ground offer plastic shoes and cheap coloured towels. They pass a shop with bolts of material hanging from a pole and she asks if they can stop. She wants to buy some African cloth because she doesn't like wearing shorts. He glances at her legs but doesn't say anything.

Inside the shop is muffled and dark, all sound and light blocked by the vivid bolts of material arranged in ranks from floor to ceiling. It is like standing under a great coloured tent and for a moment she is stunned. The chemical smell of new cloth prickles her nostrils making her sneeze. A grey African, wearing a waistcoat and braces, slowly looks up from a counter, which has a brass tape measure running down its length. 'Welcome, you are most welcome.'

Kennedy drifts about the shop, occasionally plucking out colours for her to try. He comes up to the counter with a fine green cloth embroidered with gold. He unwraps it, holding it tucked under his chin and gestures to her. She realizes that he wants to try it against her and she stands very still as he pulls it around her waist, and then softly winds her into it. His breathing is slow and concentrated as he pulls the material taut. She lifts her arms slightly as he tucks in the folds just under her ribcage. He keeps his eyes on his fingers the whole time and when he has finished steers her over to an angled mirror in one corner of the shop. 'I think this one is the best,' he says and rests his hand on her shoulder. She meets his eyes in the mirror.

Then before she has time to say anything he goes over to the counter and pays the old man. She stands looking at her unfamiliar self in the mirror. I appear African, she thinks, but it's obvious I'm not. I don't walk in the same way as African women, or carry my head from my spine. I'm too thin, too waxed and polished, and my hair is too light. She smooths her new *chitenge* and catches Kennedy looking at her.

'Thank you, you didn't need to do that,' she says when they are back on the street.

'I wanted to.' Kennedy holds out his hand as they cross the road and she takes it. His grip is warm and dry.

'It's a gorgeous present.'

'*Gorgeous*,' he says, mocking her British accent.

'You're awful,' she says, dropping his hand and standing to face him in the road. 'Why don't you take me seriously? Why am I so amusing to you?' She keeps her face straight and at that moment sees that he doesn't understand her. He is flinching at the sudden loss of contact and standing in the road, looking embarrassed and uncomfortable. A battered silver Toyota, filled with faces, arms, legs, children with wide, gleeful smiles, comes towards them at speed, horn blaring and they step out of the way. The windows are wound down and she can hear the children laughing. A hollow feeling comes over her. She remembers the natural warmth of his hand, and the way he had gently folded her into the cloth. She tries to catch his eye, but he turns from her and begins to walk down the road.

They look for somewhere to eat, but everywhere is closed except a tiny shop selling scalding chicken pies, which they eat under a torn umbrella on a forecourt bristling with feral cats. She throws scraps of pastry on the ground expecting the cats to pounce but they stay crouching in the shade, eyes hungrily fixed on the food. Kennedy rubs his hands together to clean them of grease and takes a long swig on his bottle of frozen cola. She does the same. The cats hang in the shade, waiting. A breeze flicks a yellowed umbrella, joggling it on its pole. The metal table has been eaten by rust around the rim and one of its legs has lost its foot so that it tilts at an angle too steep to hold anything still. Their Coke bottles wink light as they drink, spreading diamond patterns across their faces and arms. Kennedy glances at her, takes a drink and then looks away. He seems tired. She remembers the bee-stung boy lying on the floor of the plantation office and wonders whether he has survived the afternoon.

'Where shall we go now?' Kennedy asks suddenly.

His question takes her aback. 'Nowhere. We shouldn't be back late, Max will worry, and anyway aren't you tired?'

A squiggle of a frown appears between his eyes. 'Let's go.' He pushes his chair back and ducks out under the umbrella. The cats arch their backs as they cross the forecourt and dive on to the pastry scraps. Kennedy drives out of town and at a dusty round-about he slows and asks, 'Do you want to see Max's house?'

'What? Max has a *town* house?' For some reason she feels a beat of fear.

'You must not say we went there.' Kennedy's face is impassive.

'Of course not.' Fear turns to excitement as he pushes the jeep down a wide avenue lined with jacaranda trees. Their luxuriant mauve perfume drifts in through the open window and makes her head swim.

The house, a squarish villa painted a pale green, is set back off the road and fronted by a garden tumbling with wild roses, frangipani and tall grass. There are burglar bars across the windows. Sweat trickles down Memory's back as she waits for Kennedy to open the solid oak door. It requires two keys, which sit on a ring attached to the bunch belonging to the jeep.

They enter a dark hall. The place smells hot and stale. Leading off from the hall is a large sitting room where a pair of leather sofas sit angled near a fireplace filled with ash. The curtains are drawn and the air is so dense it feels recently occupied as if a crowd of people had just left.

'What does he do here?' Memory asks.

'He never comes here. He asks me to clean the place sometimes.'

They move through the other rooms, a large kitchen with empty cupboards, a small utility room, a bathroom with a few dried leaves nestling in the bath. The feeling of occupation persists. Sweating, she follows Kennedy up a flight of stairs, which seem heavy with something, some kind of thickness she cannot define.

They come out on to a large wood-panelled mezzanine. A sweet muffled smell lingers here and she realizes why the place seems occupied. Almost every wooden panel exhibits the head of an animal: a wildebeest looking down its nose with glassy eyes, a fine muzzled zebra with thick velvety ears, a luminous-eyed leopard, an antelope with long curving horns, a rhino, an exquisite gazelle. Each animal has been mounted with extreme care, where the skin has been torn it has been finely stitched. It's awesomely terrible, but also somehow touching and beautiful. Even though the eyes have been replaced by glass, the animals still have expressions; there's fear and defiance, betrayal, love, hope and, most movingly, forgiveness and acceptance. Kennedy points at the final trophy, a great matted head of a lion. 'This one always reminds me of Max.'

'I see what you mean.' She looks over the grim parade. 'Did Max shoot them?'

'He shot some, mostly the old or injured ones. He used to take parties to private game reserves.'

'It's a dead safari park.' Shuddering, she turns away from the animals and looks down into the well of the house. From this angle she can see two chairs in the front room. They are heavy leather chairs with solid winged arms, the kind you see in old Scottish hotels, and they look as if they have been pulled as close to each other as they can get.

'I think I've had enough now. Can we go?' she says.

Kennedy puts his hand on her arm and she realizes that there is something else he wants to show her. 'Over here.'

She follows him into a bedroom furnished simply with a single bed covered with a rough brown blanket. On the bedside table is a book showing various types of aircraft in construction.

'I feel like a spy,' she says, looking round.

'One moment,' he says, pulling open a drawer filled with papers. 'I thought you might want to look at this.'

It is a photograph of a young man standing near a small aeroplane.

'Wait a minute, this is your plane. *Hotel Juliet*?'

'Max owns the plane. He just lets me fly it.'

She frowns and then looks more closely at the photograph. She had assumed she was looking at a photograph of a younger Max, but now she sees that the man is slighter in build with finer features and a curve of neck and upturned mouth that seems curiously familiar. She sits down on the bed, almost knocked off her feet by a wave of dizziness.

Driving back, Memory wishes she had taken the photograph, but she had been unbalanced by the sudden intimacy, the way

Kennedy had sat with her while she cried, stopping her tears with his thumb. He'd put his arm around her afterwards and rocked her like a child until she'd recovered. Now he is silent, his face soft in the dark, his eyes flickering over the road, hands loose on the wheel. There is a deep concentrated strength in the way he sits. She leans her head against the jeep window and looks up at the night flooded with rivers and waterfalls of stars. They seem close enough to grab in handfuls. The only constellation she knows is the Plough, the neat way it points to the north star. She thinks back to the animals in the mezzanine and the way that they had almost pointed her to the image of Paul Cougan, her first sight of him. Of course, Kennedy had known about the photo all along; he'd recognized how important it would be to her. But there was something about finding it in the presence of so many dead that was unbearable. Maybe that was why she hadn't taken it; it would have felt like desecrating some sort of shrine. The house seemed filled with memories someone was trying to forget.

11

NIGHT FLYING

Take everything quietly and use all controls smoothly. Remember that red signals of any kind are negative, and if a red signal follows a green one, it cancels the green signal.

Zambia, 1972

A week after arriving, Paul started work on the school. Early every morning Max collected him in the jeep and drove them to a deep part of the bush dominated by a circle of mupundu trees that had been growing it seemed since the beginning of time. Paul moved around them in awe. It was not just their size – the Caledonians and Douglas firs of Scotland were familiar giants – or the curious bark that bled a golden red sap which gradually crystallized so that each tree wore an amber necklace, or even the powerful scent that impressed him; it was the sheer force of the trees, their massive indifferent aliveness. He felt that he had arrived at a place that belonged to an older time, a more spacious and unhurried place. The bush was perfect, he thought, it needed nothing or no one, nothing could be added to it, and yet it didn't seem quite complete; there was a great sense of expectancy about it as if the bush existed somehow on hold in one single, beautiful, extended pause.

It made him think of the times he spent walking in the hills in Scotland. He remembered climbing to the top of Bennachie behind his parents' croft and looking out across the land. No village or house could be seen. The sky dominated, seeming somehow fresher and more optimistic. He had lain down, the bracken closing around him, tickling his face, its brown bread smell comforting and vaguely exotic, the fronds curled tightly like baby seahorses. He learned to become watchful in order to receive what he felt the world was trying to tell him. Ever since he'd been born he'd had the strangest sensation that something was trying to get through to him. It wasn't a voice or a person; it was more diffuse, unspecific, the kind of understanding that made him aware of what he didn't know.

The intensity of it diminished as he grew older. He became more closed and cautious. He doubted what he felt. Sometimes, though, flashes of the old feeling would come back, jolting him like a reminder, or a pointer to the future. In Africa the feeling had almost leaped at him, coming over in strong waves. It was especially potent deep inside the bush. He felt as if he had reached the centre of everything. It made him realize that the world was all made up of the same substance; that the same essence permeated everything.

The mupundu formed a natural boundary around the area they were going to clear for the school. All smaller bushes and trees inside the boundary had to come down, and the first to go were the mupane trees with their rotten hearts and turpentine smell. In one day they felled five. Paul watched them topple and crash, their falling branches sending the bush into a twitching panic, stirring up leaves, seeds and forest dust, which rose in a great head of steam. When the last tree fell it emitted a deep groaning sound and the silence afterwards was dense as if the bush had been momentarily knocked unconscious.

They used machetes on the smaller trees and bushes, hacking at the acacia, hook thorn and umbrella thorn. Paul asked Max the names of the trees before he felled them. It seemed important that he should know some small thing about them before he cut them down. He remembered his father saying that each tree had a nature, and it was the woodsman's job to respect it by *going in clean*. According to his father, badly butchered trees were the same as badly butchered meat: unfit for the table. Paul remembered how his father had smiled into his shirt collar after he'd told him this, almost as if he'd given away some small secret about himself. Paul had laughed and his father had smiled again, but then caught himself quickly, and looked down at the table where the three of them sat, each with their coats on because the woodburner had gone out. His mother had cleared away the breakfast things carefully, her eyes moist, as if some small sadness had occurred. Paul remembered going out later and gathering up fists of snow and stuffing them into his mouth so as not to scream, and then sitting down under an immaculate sky with his frozen hands in his lap, looking up at the rooks ripping through the blue.

Chopping thorn bushes was tough, especially the umbrella thorn which were the most stubborn of all and reputed to have been the source of wood for Noah's Ark. Max, once in a rhythm, seemed as if he could go on for ever, cutting through the scrub with powerful strokes, piling bush upon bush, creating a pyre as he went. Occasionally he would stop and stand bow-legged, wiping the sweat from the back of his neck, all the time looking hard at the area he'd just cleared as if he expected new trees to begin sprouting while he was off guard. Sometimes his gaze settled on Paul, and for some reason Paul felt he had to look away.

There was a physical wholeheartedness about Max that Paul envied. The bush absorbed him so utterly that anyone wanting to break his concentration would have had to put a gun to his back. As he chopped and pulled at the undergrowth the awkwardness he showed around people melted away and he became lighter and more definite in his movements, wielding his axe with nonchalant grace, his back muscles moving in synchronicity. Max rarely needed to stop and rest or even drink water. Paul, on the other hand, took frequent breaks mostly because the drenching heat sapped his energy and left him feeling faint. Seeking cover in the shade, swigging from his water bottle, he would watch Max moving about like an animal foraging intently. It was the deliberateness about Max that most impressed Paul. He was absolutely unwavering; everything he did he carried through right up to its hilt.

A day's work left Paul incoherent with exhaustion and he was unable to do much when he arrived back at the house except wash and sleep. Elise was usually in bed reading. At night the house became quite cold, but she didn't like to light the fire, preferring to climb into bed with all her clothes on, her books piled beside her in two unsteady towers. She'd brought along some biology books, which amazed him because he did not know how she could concentrate on reading when there was so much around them to think about. She would usually be awake when he got back and he'd try to talk to her while he showered, but her responses would be flat, her attention fixed on an article about the eye or diagram of the circulatory system. When he came into the bedroom naked she would sometimes look up and stare at him with a puzzled expression as if she were observing his muscles or bone.

During the day she spent most of her time reading in the garden. He had asked her to come out to the bush to see what they were doing and every morning she said she'd come along later, but she never showed up. Her lack of enthusiasm disappointed him and made him feel as if he were failing her in some way. But when they were alone he felt unable to talk about it. Her books seemed to prevent him getting through to her. Climbing into bed, he would sit up for a while, pillows supporting his shoulders, and listen to her breathing. She was able to fall asleep almost the second he turned off the light and he envied this ability while at the same time not quite trusting it. He would remain awake and leaning his head against the cool wall with her near scorching heat a few inches away from him he would imagine how the bed might appear to someone else. Wrapped in its cocoon of mosquito net it seemed secure and deeply private, even romantic. It suggested a wartime field hospital, or perhaps a Bedouin tent, a place of mystery, sickness and hospitality. The net hung from a wooden crown that swung slightly, twisting on its axis. In the thick folds at the top of the tent clusters of insects were trapped, desiccated bodies of flies, wasps, beetles and the paler husks of moths and dragonflies. The netting material felt surprisingly heavy when he pushed it aside on the nights he found the bed too hot and cloying.

In the mornings, though, Elise wanted him and would pin him greedily to the bed, flicking her hair across his chest as she kissed him, her tongue restless in his mouth. He would go to work unwashed, the heat and smell of her still potent on his skin. Climbing into the jeep he would catch a waft of her strong scent coming at him like a wave, secret, briny and powerful, knocking him sideways. Glancing over, he would wonder whether Max could smell her too.

Every other day they burned great bonfires, sending funnels of smoke across the bush, sometimes blotting out the sun. While the burning was going on the dog crept closer to Max, his fur stiff along his back. Since Max had rescued him from the road he had not left his side and most days lay in a shady patch watching them work, his blunt yellow head resting on outstretched paws, nose quivering, eyes following his master back and forth. When Max finished clearing one area, the dog got up, scratched himself with a hind leg, and took up a new position. No one except Max could get close to him. If anyone tried he would lay his ears back and sink down into himself, drawing his buff-coloured fur protectively in a stiff ruff around his neck like porcupine quills. He never barked. The only sound he made was when Max had finished work for the day. Then he would open his mouth and yawn a high-pitched whine of pleasure. Max had christened him Lucky.

Now Max stood by the fire scanning the tops of the trees for changes in the direction of wind. Sensing Paul's stare, he drew his hand across his face and wiped his palms down his shorts. Little droplets of soil clung to the wool fibres in his socks which he wore rolled down in a thick wad around his ankles. Gold hairs, all curling in different directions like seedlings, sprouted from the top of the socks, continuing in patches up his sunburned legs. His whole physique carried a curving strength, an athletic fitness and rightness. Looking at him, Paul thought that this was the shape that every man wanted to be.

He remembered one of the last visits he'd made to the croft when he'd found his father uncharacteristically slumped in his chair, his tea on the arm in a wide cup jiggering slightly on a wooden coaster with a rucked image of a Scottish castle. Seeing him, his father had struggled to his feet, knees cracking, a tightness in his blue eyes, puffing as a slow red flush rose in his face. Paul had suppressed an urge to apologize and had followed his father out to the hallway, standing back slightly among the sour-smelling coats, watching his father pull on his work boots, his breathing sharp and almost indignant.

Later, standing next to his father in the garden, smelling his familiar smell, the slightly oily sawdust scent so similar to his own, Paul had fought two conflicting impulses. One was to put his arm around his father; the other was to turn and walk away from the garden and never return. He did neither. He simply stood and watched his father work, just as he had always done. Walking back to the croft with an armful of muddied leeks, he noticed that he was a good head and shoulders taller than his father, which added to his shame and confusion. It was as if he'd overtaken the old man by stealth.

Max spoke, breaking into his thoughts. 'You tired?'

'Not really.' Paul stepped out of the shade. He felt guilty for stopping, but the tightness across his shoulders had become so unbearable it was almost as if his bones were trying to break out through his skin. 'I was just hot.'

Max looked at the sky, humming with rich blue colour. His eyes carried a narrow amusement. The dog stretched a hind leg around to his ear and scratched. A clatter of sparks took off from the fire, spiralling up against the darkening sky. 'Forget it, let's call it a day.' Max flung his axe into a fallen tree trunk. Lucky, sensing a shift in time, gave a yawn and then uncharacteristically went over to Paul and pushed his hot, dry nose into his palm.

'He's telling us it's time to go for a beer,' Max said, glancing affectionately at the dog.

Paul rubbed the bony yellow head and the dog returned to his master where he waited, eyes bright with anticipation. Paul wiped his hands down his T-shirt and then sank his own axe into a softened stump of wood. Smoke was clearing from the sky as they left the forest and headed towards the bush club.

There was a barbecue going on and the little clearing with its lean-to thatched bar area was unusually full. African farm workers stood at the bar drinking beer while their wives and children remained outside, sprawled on white plastic chairs, occasionally sending young messengers in with requests for more Sprite. There was a settled atmosphere with a streak of festivity, heightened by the squeals of delight from the children diving into a tiny green pool filled with water lilies. Under the trees African wives, wrapped in vivid cloth and gold jewellery, chuckled quietly as they relaxed in wicker chairs below which plates of char-grilled meat had been discreetly left.

'What will you have?' Max asked at the bar, kwacha note already down on the counter.

'Just a cold beer.'

While Max paid, Paul glanced around. A couple of the white farmers looked at him with curiosity as they continued conversations filled with complaint. Theft and the unreliability of the African worker, not the middle classes drinking shoulder to shoulder with the whites but the invisible underclass who were paid less than a dollar a day, shaped most of the conversations Paul had heard so far. Each white person he'd been introduced to had offered him some version of the complaint, often in a wounded tone, as if appealing to him for justice. He found it discomforting and confusing. From what he had gathered so far the farmers were not ungenerous towards their workers. He had listened to enough worried talk about servants falling sick with malaria to know that they cared for them and were prepared to make a two-hour drive across the bush to the nearest clinic to have them treated. He also knew from Max that the same farmers who complained so bitterly about 'the blacks' were also helping a number of Africans by paying for their education or medical treatment. But their philanthropy did not extend to friendship, or what Paul regarded as friendship. These farmers would never have sat with the Africans or addressed them on equal terms. In turn, the Africans maintained a polite reserve around the whites, revealing nothing of their attitude or real feelings. The Africans Paul had met so far kept their distance from him. He remembered one night catching the eye of an old grizzled servant who was wearing white gloves to serve beer to a farmer and seeing a look in the man's droll, sad-clown's face that seemed heavy with irony, but he may have been mistaken.

Paul reached for his drink. The first sip caught him between the eyes with its sweet stale coldness and feeling slightly out of breath he put his bottle back down on the bar. Max drank beer as if it were lemonade, taking long, delicate draughts, cradling the bottle against his chest. He was talking to one of the other farmers about coffee prices. Sometimes when Paul was included in farm talk he found it difficult to concentrate. The farmers seemed to assume that because he came from Scotland he would know about the awkwardness of land and the frustrations of climate. He didn't like to admit that he actually understood very little despite a year at college on a land management course. Against these emphatic farmers, his own knowledge seemed artificial and unrelated to anything he could discuss with authority or even interest. Listening to them talk, Paul would feel a sense of excruciating dullness, which sometimes threatened to overwhelm him. He would look at Max leaning on his elbow, deep in conversation about a mechanical problem and feel a strange mixture of shame and envy. Paul knew he had nothing to offer these men. He was simply a visitor, someone they tolerated, and would not think about or remember once he'd left. He shifted his position slightly and the white farmer who was talking to Max cocked his head towards him. 'So, what d'yuh reckon?'

Paul gave what he hoped was an it's-great-to-be-here grin. The farmer, a tall, well-muscled man with a thick head of white-blond hair, waved his bottle. 'At least the beer's good, eh?'

'Sure is.' Paul narrowed his eyes and tried drinking with a swagger, but ended up clinking the bottle against his teeth.

The farmer looked him up and down and chewed a little. Max pulled another kwacha note from a wad in his pocket. The farmer waved him down. 'Let me buy our young English visitor here a beer. He looks like he needs one.'

Paul understood what the farmer meant by this. His slight build made older men protective towards him, but in a way that always made them seem bigger and stronger. Without really trying, he seemed to bring out an impulse in other men to boast and preen. The farmer dug him in the ribs slightly as he shoved his way up to the bar. His smell was full, like a sack of something warm and bloody such as a brace of freshly killed pheasants. He didn't look at Paul while he ordered; he simply spread his smell and his whistly breath across the bar and waited to be served.

The African barman danced over and took his order. The farmer pushed the bottle of beer, which seemed colder than usual, across the bar with his fingertips ever so casually as if buying a stranger a drink were the lightest gesture imaginable. Paul felt that to say 'thank you' would almost be an insult to the man. He kept his eyes down as the farmer paid, leaving the change on the bar top where it sat in a stubby little column. The farmer drank confidently, holding his bottle high and swallowing smoothly. When he eventually put the bottle down Paul saw that there was only an inch of beer left.

Propping an elbow on the bar, the farmer belched softly and then cupped his fingers against his chin. 'How's that young wife of yours?' His thumb rasped across coarse blond bristles.

Paul waved his bottle. 'She's fine, thanks.'

'I bet she is.' The farmer leaned into his fingers so that his thumb was now tickling his own throat. 'How does a little boy like you keep up with her?'

Paul felt his elbow jerk as Max made an abrupt movement beside him. 'Watch it, Karl.'

The farmer opened his fingers in front of his eyes and stared at them as if he had just performed a magic trick. He looked as if he were about to say something else, but a sharp glance from Max made him reconsider.

Paul finished his beer. He felt a mixture of gratitude and humiliation at the speed with which Max had reacted, almost as if he himself had been insulted. The farmer edged away and went to talk to a group of men at the other end of the bar. Paul wished now he'd said something to the farmer. He would have enjoyed telling him to mind his own business, showing him he wasn't just a puny visitor from Scotland (he'd put him right on the England thing too). He just hadn't been quick enough on the draw. He'd reacted too slowly, and that had left a gap for Max to step into.

Feeling a sudden stab of misery, Paul glanced outside. In the shade of a red and gold flamboyant tree a tall good-looking young African in an immaculate pale blue shirt and white chinos was holding court among a group of men seated on chairs. All the men were leaning forward with arms resting on knees, laughing uproariously, their intense animation exerting a pull. Paul slipped off his stool and wandered outside to take a look.

The good-looking man had a pistol in a shiny brown holster which he was showing off to the group who passed it around, each man taking a turn to weigh the weapon in his hands. Paul watched them stroke the oiled black metal and touch the sharp muzzle and neat trigger. The gun looked like the kind of weapon the dying man in films always pulls out at the end. Its owner smiled fondly, his eyes following it as it went round the circle. When it was returned to him he replaced it in its toffee-brown holster and patted it. Someone called from the group, 'Tell them about the first night you used it.' The good-looking young man gave a snort and rolled his eyes.

'Go on,' a round man in a fawn safari suit called out, slapping his fat knees and jiggling up and down in his seat. The good-looking man stroked his holster, precipitating a sputtering of suppressed laughter from the audience who were watching him closely, eyes occasionally flickering to one another. The good-looking man cleared his throat. His vivid face suggested a natural performer, someone who was used to being in the centre of things. He radiated ease and polish, just like his gun.

Speaking in an accent that sounded to Paul like a mixture of American and African, he began his story. He'd bought the gun because he was fed up with being burgled. Robbers had come to his house regularly even though, he said, there was nothing much to take. Anything of value was kept in a locked safe or at his father's house where there was better security. One night he left the window open and went to bed as usual, putting the gun under his pillow.

'They always came at the same time, so I knew I'd wake up,' he said, rolling his eyes, miming someone springing awake, hands clutching at invisible bedclothes. The group laughed and leaned forward, all eyes trained on him.

'Anyway this night there was only one robber and he couldn't believe his luck when he saw the window open. I waited for him to climb right in and then I sat up with the gun in both my hands, like this.' He demonstrated, fixing his teeth in a cartoon grin as he pointed his gun at the audience who laughed in one loud, hard round, one or two men patting their knees with their fists, thumping quite hard, and then wiping away tears.

'Well, he started to shake and beg me not to shoot him, going wild, like this . . .' And the young man acted out the part of the robber, trembling and champing his teeth with fear. The audience gave a collective moan of pleasure and leaned further forward, necks all held at the same angle, like hunting dogs.

The speaker paused and looked around at the eager faces, his eyes glowing with pleasure. 'So, I told him to come over to the light. Then I ordered him to take off his clothes.' He mimed with his feet the actions of someone reluctantly stepping out of a pair of trousers then awkwardly pulling a shirt over his head. 'When he'd got undressed I tied his shirt around his eyes, nice and tight so he wouldn't be able to see where he was going.' The group was silent. Paul kept his gaze on the young man. There was a reck-lessness in the way he sat, legs wide apart, chinos hitched above a pair of glossy leather loafers.

'I led him out through the house, telling him to turn left and right and he kept getting confused because he didn't know which was which.' The group tittered at this. 'We were nearly out of the house, but then the children woke up and came out of their room to ask, "Daddy, what is going on?" So what do I do? I take off my pyjamas and tell the man to put them on because I don't want the little ones to see the robber's privates.' The group collapsed into loud giggles.

'Well, I'm pretty wound up by this time, I'm yelling and yelling and telling them kids to go back to bed, but they say they're scared and I have to go back with them and tell them a story. All the time I'm doing that this bastard has taken off the blindfold and is running through the house, ripping me off, taking cash and spoons and food and anything he can grab from the kitchen and stuffing it down the pockets of my own pyjamas.'

The group folded up with laughter and the young man waited for his audience to recover before continuing, using his arms to make wide sweeping movements.

'When I'm done with the children, I run after him and catch up with him in the garden. I grab him and I make him kneel down in the dirt and swear on the Bible that he will never come near my place again because if he does he will get a bullet in his neck. Then to make my point I shoot at a tree, but the bullet bounces back and hits a stone which flies up and shatters the goddam kitchen window. My wife is up out of bed this time, screaming and crying and threatening to call the police. She comes out and finds me standing in my underpants in the garden pointing a gun at a man wearing *my* pyjamas, and then starts screaming at me telling me *I'm* crazy!' The group exploded. One man even left his seat and did a little dance, acting out the parts of the captor and captive.

A hush fell over the group as the man went on. 'Well, I manage to calm my wife down and she goes back inside the house. I am mad by this time, Jesus, I am really going crazy, and I'm waving the gun and the robber is saying his prayers and begging for mercy. I'm really close to shooting him, but seeing him down on his knees like that I can't do it. I say to him he's free, and he gets up. He stands in front of me with his head down looking at the ground. I tell him to go before I finish him off with a bullet, but he still stands there not moving. He just looks like he's got nothing in the world to run to and then I ask him what he wants and he says he needs a job and could he come and be my gardener?' The group sat back tutting and shaking their heads with disapproval.

'I tell him to go home, but in the morning I hear him outside and he's sweeping leaves, still wearing my pyjamas . . .' The young man paused, but no one laughed.

This is like a parable, Paul thought, looking at the now thoughtful group.

The young man continued: 'The first day he worked until night in the garden and I thought that would be it, his repayment for trying to rob me, but the next day he came back and, you know what, he'd washed the pyjamas and left them on the kitchen table. Not only that, he'd also left the money he stole on top and a bag of groundnuts for the children.' The group murmured and one or two whispered comments which Paul could not hear.

Sitting straighter in his seat, the good-looking man went on with his story. 'And now he comes every day and tidies up the garden and he's even planted melon and sunflowers. He's the best worker I've ever had and I haven't paid him a penny yet. I just want to see how long he lasts and he knows it. He keeps coming and doing the work. He knows I'm not going to turn him away.'

The man looked round at the sober audience. 'The thing is, if I'd shot him, I'd never have known what he was. I'd never have known how honest he really was. You know, I'm even thinking of sending him to college soon because he's so smart. In trying to rob me, he won himself the best chance he could ever have. What do you think of that?' The group looked rueful and one or two men smiled and shook their heads. A few necks craned towards the bar.

Sensing that things were about to break up, Paul edged away and returned to Max.

He jerked his neck up when he saw Paul, his eyes darting, hand trembling slightly as he brought his beer bottle up to his mouth and drained it.

'I just heard a great story,' Paul said. He pointed out the man in the blue shirt and briefly told Max the tale of the robber, hurrying over the details because he could sense Max was not paying full attention. As he spoke he could see the man laughing with two women sitting under some trees, one leg propped behind him.

Max scooped up the loose change from the bar top and put it in his shorts pocket, his manner thoughtful. He looked down and tapped some soil from his boot. 'We haven't seen him in a while.'

'He sounds American. Who is he?'

Max grunted and picked up his keys. 'He's the President's son.'

Paul gaped. 'What's he doing out here?'

'He owns one of the big farms. He likes to come up from Lusaka and work on the land; he has a small place up country where he goes fishing.' They were walking towards the jeep now and Max was having to talk louder than usual to be heard above the shrill insect chorus. A slim moon had slipped into the sky, and the first stars were lighting up.

Paul leaned his head back against the seat and watched the sky slide past the window. He let his mind drift over the events at the bar, remembering the moment Max had leaped to his defence. But

187

it didn't seem to matter so much now. It was as if they had gone to the bar several days ago instead of an hour or so ago. Time was somehow more expansive in Africa: an hour encompassed a day, a morning, a week; an evening could contain an entire lifetime.

Men behaved differently out here, Paul thought. It was the opposite of everything he had ever known. In his life it was the women who had fought the battles, the women who had called the shots. The women who had spoken. He thought of his mute father and his quiet friends, the remote bars where the men sat with their pints and listened to each other breathe. The men in the bush bar had not stopped talking all evening; everything had been open to vibrant discussion. The farmers didn't hide behind themselves, they spoke out proudly, confident in what they were saying even when they were wrong. He couldn't dislike them, which was confusing because he found their comments, especially about their workers, offensive. But behind their words there was a rough warmth, a rugged interest in the people they were abusing. Joe Baxter had kept glancing at him as he talked about his cook, a man who had been with Baxter's family for fifteen years and still couldn't make toast without burning it. 'Every morning I have to come down and open the flaming kitchen window because the bastard's forgotten how to do it again. I've bought three different toasters for him to try, but he still gets it wrong. I can't believe I'm employing a cook who can't make toast.' Everyone had laughed and Paul had joined in. Looking round at the tough, red faces at the bar, he had felt something stir in his guts. It was disconcerting; it was intoxicating. It was like diving naked straight into the wild heart of the world.

Gradually the school got built. Beam by beam out of the good clean hardwood they had cut down. Paul threw himself into the work. As the weeks went by his confidence grew as his muscles hardened and his body changed shape. He sawed until his arms ached, sawdust spitting in small storms around him. In physical labour, he felt fully present and the relief it gave was luxurious and almost sexual. Every day he felt as if he had passed some small test, whether it was fitting a window frame or door, or digging a trench outside. He discovered a stubborn resilience in himself, a refusal to give up until he had completed whatever he was working on to precise standards of his own.

As the time for completion drew nearer Max drafted African workers in to help finish the roof. The men perched on the rafters and called across to each other as they worked. The women stayed at ground level, clearing away smaller branches and stones, sweeping the dirt so that it lay flat and smooth like a beach at morning tide. Their babies clung to their backs. Whenever Paul stopped to draw breath he would catch one of the brown babies staring at him levelly. He had tried talking to them, but they shrank from his touch and burrowed against their mothers. The women were friendlier and clucked at Paul, beaming at him as he watched them. He decided that he would try to learn a local language as soon as he could. He longed to be able to speak to the people as freely as Max.

A gang of children came to watch the building take shape. One boy of around fourteen with narrow eyes twirled a piece of knitting between his fingers, regarding the proceedings with a bemused expression, as if he had never seen anything more preposterous in his life. The younger children threw stones at each other or tried to tempt Max's dog with sticks. When it was hot they lay in a heap under the trees, like a farrow of brown piglets, dusty bodies pressed together, sides heaving as they breathed. Sometimes a girl came. She was around five years old and seemed different from the rest. Her manner was more inquisitive and she liked to be alone. The first time she came she walked right up to the school and strutted around under the open roof with her hands on her hips while the other children giggled from the sidelines. Afterwards she sat under the shade of a tree, bony knees drawn up, picking at a hole in her long green shorts, impatiently flicking flies from her tiny heart-shaped face.

One afternoon Paul looked up and saw to his amazement that the framework was complete. Standing airily in its clearing, the structure made from twelve triangular A beams looked like a medieval barn that had been uncovered rather than built from scratch. Immediately the children claimed ownership, the younger ones slapping and shoving each other under the open beams, dappled light flickering across their faces. Alert to something new, Lucky watched them, his tail minutely stirring the leaves. The girl, however, walked about quite solemnly and proudly as if getting the measure of the place. 'It's not ready,' Paul tried to tell her. 'You need desks, books, pens.' He mimed writing, but she looked at him blankly. He tried to smile at her, but she gave him a haughty look and then left. At the edge of the clearing she glanced back over her shoulder and he saw that she was smiling, a sweet, hopeful smile that made him feel somehow validated.

Paul drove over to Joe Baxter's to collect the galvanized metal they were going to use to clad the roof. Baxter greeted him in his farm kitchen where three pale blond children were curled up on a sagging sofa in front of a TV. The youngest child sucked his thumb while the other two stared at the screen, their eyes unwavering. All three were wearing yellow flannel pyjamas with reindeer pictures on them.

Baxter offered Paul a drink and they sat down at the kitchen table. Baxter seemed agitated as he swigged his beer. His eyes were pink-rimmed and the fist curved around the bottle was nicked with lots of tiny cuts. 'All of it went last night,' Baxter said, his eyes irresistibly drawn to the television, which showed a star soccer match. The sofa was in front of them and Paul could just see the softly messy crowns of the three children fixed on the screen.

Paul put his beer down on the table. '*All of it?*' The metal sheets had been stored in Baxter's barn for safe-keeping. There must have been over a hundred sheets of the stuff.

'The whole lot,' Baxter took a savage swig of his drink. 'Every single sheet.'

'Have you any idea who took it?'

'Yeah, I've got a good idea and when I catch them I'm going to give them one hell of a blast. You have to nail everything down in this place.' Baxter slammed his bottle on the table, making the three blond heads jump. 'They help themselves to everything. *Everything*. There's no respect for property, no respect at all. I'd like to shoot the lot of them, they are such liars and thieves.' His eyes blazed. On the sofa the children squirmed and kicked each other, bored because the match had stopped for half-time.

Paul wondered how he might escape. Baxter's anger was so fierce it made Paul feel almost as if he had been responsible for taking the roofing. From the sofa a small voice said: 'Shut up, get off.'

Baxter roared. 'No, *you* shut up. Any more noise from you and it's straight back to bed.'

Paul watched a tiny pair of shoulders slump down further into the sofa.

Baxter got up to get another beer from a small fridge crammed with bottles. 'You children want Cokes?' His voice was ragged.

Three heads twisted round and then three necks rose slowly over the back of the sofa and bobbed like three meerkats rising from the grass. 'Yes, please,' they all said together.

Baxter served his three children with a Coke, spiking each bottle with a coloured straw. 'I want a red one,' one of the children said. Baxter went back to the fridge where there was a glass filled with straws and dutifully swapped the green straw for a red one. He sat back down opposite Paul and shoved a beer across the table towards him. It had already been opened.

'What would they use the metal for?' Paul asked after a moment.

'I don't know. Building stuff in their villages. But it's useless, they don't do anything properly. They don't take care of their own places. They just let everything fall to pieces and rot. When it's all gone they start sneaking round to see what's on offer at the farms. Useless,' he said again, shaking his head, his red fist clamped around his beer. 'Bloody useless.'

On the TV the players were jogging on to a field so sickly green it made Paul's teeth hurt.

'Now we're on,' Baxter said, suddenly cheering up. 'Stay and have another drink?'

But Paul's head was already swimming. He said he needed to get back. Baxter shrugged and turned his attention to the soccer. One of the children saw Paul out, standing on one leg with a blonde head hunched on a shoulder, a girl he thought, although he wasn't sure. Her reindeer pyjamas were too short for her legs, ending just below her knees. She had a silver ring on one of her toes and it glinted in the sun. 'Bye!' She waved at him as if she knew him and then turned and ran back into the house. Climbing into the jeep, he noticed a row of barns some distance away from the house. An electric fence around the barns had been cut, the gap almost invisible in the shimmering daylight.

When he delivered the news at the school Max flinched slightly and put down the screwdriver he was using to fix a window frame. Taking a step back, he glanced up towards the roof and cast a critical eye over the structure. 'There's a space there, see where the beam is not quite flush?'

Paul followed his gaze up through the exposed timbers to the sky where a few pale clouds drifted. 'Looks all right to me.'

'No, there's a small gap. I need to go up and fix it.'

'What about the metal for the roof?'

'We'll put something else up,' Max said.

More workers were drafted in to help, arriving in trucks, faces grey after a day's work in the coffee fields, muttering to each other as they climbed up to the roof with sheaves of straw tied to their backs. Max had promised each of his workers two kilos of mixed beef cuts if they completed the job in three days. Despite their obvious resentment they worked quickly, slotting straw into place, expertly laying the thatch in a thick crust of pale yellow quills all facing the same direction. On the last day they stayed later and hung candle lanterns in the trees, which cast a swinging gold light over the school, transforming it into the listing bridge of an old ship, vibrating with African murmur and the occasional outbreak of song. At two in the morning the oldest worker, a skinny man with grey knees poking from green football shorts, slid down the roof and announced it was finished and where was the meat?

Max had come prepared and sent Paul to unload the four scuffed cold-boxes from the back of the jeep. Then under the sloping eaves of the new thatch that gleamed silver in the moon-light there was a solemn handing round of packets of mixed cuts bulging with blood under cellophane. Each worker genuflected before each white packet as if it were a holy gift. When all had received payment the old man in the football shorts said they wanted to throw a party to celebrate finishing the school. They would invite the chief and send the word out. It would be a great party with food and dancing. Clutching their meat, the workers exchanged broad smiles. It was one of those rare moments when everyone involved in a project comes away with the feeling that he has gained something. Still, Paul couldn't help secretly won-dering whether the Africans smiled so heartily partly because of the new galvanized roofs he had seen adorning all the huts in their villages.

The next few days were spent painting the school from buckets of fuming orange paint, donated by a supermarket, and arranging the benches and desks that had come in a crate from a church in Pennsylvania. Paul would sometimes sit on one of the benches and close his eyes and think about how much his life seemed to be changing. It felt as if his old life was gradually being covered up, rolled over smoothly and slowly like a great thick bed of turf being put down on dry ground.

One morning he arrived to find the young African girl sitting with her elbows at a bench in the front row looking up at the empty blackboard. She glanced at him expectantly.

'Good morning,' Paul said. The girl locked her eyes on to his. 'Good morning,' he repeated deliberately.

He watched her slowly push her tongue around the unfamiliar words. 'Gud normin.' She frowned.

'Good. My name is Paul.' He pointed to himself.

The girl nodded vigorously and pointed to her chest. 'Memory,' she said.

'Memory?' He looked at her, surprised, and she nodded and smiled the same sweet, shy smile he remembered from before. Turning round, he found a used stub of chalk in the groove under the blackboard and wrote out the letters of her name across the board. M-E-M-O-R-Y. 'That's really unusual.'

The girl smiled at the letters on the board. He wondered if she had ever seen her name written before. 'These letters spell your name,' he told her. She looked at him blankly, a bubble of snot blooming at her nostril. Her eyes had the familiar bloodshot look of all the African children. He wondered whether she was dying.

On impulse he wrote the letters of his name across the board under hers. P-A-U-L C-O-U-G-A-N. The girl stared, her brown eyes fixed with concentration as if she were trying to remember something.

'OK, Memory, I'm going to teach you how to count. Are you ready?'

The girl stiffened and seemed to pay attention. He realized that she was probably reading his body language. He held up one finger. 'One,' he said clearly and crooked his finger back down. The girl stared at him and giggled. 'One,' he repeated, straightening the finger. The girl chewed on the inside of her mouth. Her eyes blinked a few times and he could tell that she was thinking about what he was trying to do. 'One,' he said, looking at her with all the encouragement he could muster.

'Wan!' she suddenly shouted out, holding her finger towards him in a show of proof.

'Great, now try this. Two.' He held up two fingers in the peace sign. 'You try. Two.'

The girl responded immediately. 'Too!'

'Three.' He held up three fingers.

'Free!'

'Four.'

'Faw!'

When they reached ten they went back to the beginning and started again. After a couple of rounds the girl was picking up the numbers and throwing them back at him, her face bright with achievement. He wondered if she had ever had any schooling. Maybe this was her first lesson.

The girl looked at him with her chin cupped in her hand. Her eyes were curious and strangely sympathetic, as if she knew what he had been thinking. He began to take her through the alphabet and then became aware of someone behind him. The girl stopped at E and then he heard a light voice say: 'I didn't think we were open yet.'

Elise came up to the blackboard and kissed his cheek. 'Hello,' she said to the girl who dropped her eyes and began to pick at a scab on her elbow.

Paul stared at his wife. She wore a long blue skirt with buttons up the centre and a loose blouse tied at her midriff. Her hair was damp at the ends, newly washed, and he felt his throat constrict with a mixture of pride and embarrassment. 'Memory,' he said, smiling at the little girl. 'Meet Elise.'

The girl gave a shy glance and continued to pick at her arm. A drop of bright orange-red blood oozed from the scab and she dabbed it with her fingers. She licked them clean and then folded her hands in her lap.

'Hello, Memory,' Elise said. 'What a pretty name.'

The girl ran a delicate tongue over the gap between her two front teeth and appraised Elise who continued to smile at her, leaning slightly forward so that her hair swung between her breasts. The girl sucked on her finger and looked at the blackboard. Elise followed her gaze and when she saw the two names chalked up there she smiled. She straightened up, her eyes skimming the classroom with its new beams and old wooden benches glowing in the sunlight.

'It looks like a school.'

'You sound surprised.' Paul wondered why he felt defensive when she seemed so impressed.

She glanced at the girl and then looked away. 'I haven't given a thought to what I might teach.'

'You've got a bit of time yet,' he said. 'We need to wait for books.'

She nodded and looked around again. 'I'm not sure about this orange colour.'

He shrugged. 'It's all we could get. Beggars can't be choosers.' She glanced at him and flicked her hair over her shoulder. The girl at the front shifted in her seat. 'Sorry, Memory,' he said. The girl flashed him a smile so melting and tender it made his heart lurch.

'I'll leave you to it,' Elise said. 'I only came to say hello. By the way, where's Max?'

'I don't know, probably something happening at the farm.'

'Oh.' She paused. 'Is he coming here later?'

'I think so.' He wondered why she seemed nervous. 'But you never know with Max. Some days he doesn't come until the late afternoon. He flies into town in the mornings.'

'What does he do in town?' She lifted the lid of a desk and peered inside.

'I don't know.'

She put the lid down, her cheeks slightly flushed. 'Haven't you ever asked him?'

For some reason he felt annoyed. 'It's up to him what he does. I don't like to ask too much, you know how he is.'

'Aren't you even the slightest bit curious about him?' She stood facing him now with her arms folded.

He felt taken aback by her challenge. 'We've just been working, that's all. We haven't had much time to talk.' But even as he said it, he felt uncomfortable. He was intensely curious about Max but he did not want her to know that. He didn't know why; there was just something about being with Max that he wanted to keep for himself, a kind of pure and whole feeling.

Elise rolled her eyes. 'Oh, you men are so useless.'

Paul stiffened. 'If there's something he wants to talk about, he will in his own time. One thing I have learned is that you can't hurry him.'

Elise pouted. 'I reckon he's hiding something. I mean why would he choose to cut himself off from everything for so long?'

'He's a solitary person, he doesn't need a lot of people. He's not like us. Max is here because this is where he belongs. You know, I envy that.'

'I can tell,' Elise said quietly.

Sensing a change in mood, the little girl slid off her seat and came up to him. She offered him her hand.

'Memory,' Paul said. He had almost forgotten she was there. She looked at him with hungry, dark eyes. He noticed that her belly was slightly distended, her hair rough and dry. From the top of her head came the smell of pee and musty smoke. Outside a jeep pulled up and the girl dropped his hand, her eyes shifting towards the door where Elise was now standing, her arms casually folded. Paul looked at her eyes, half closed against the sun. The girl looked, too, and Paul felt a moment of understanding pass between them, a recognition, which held them suspended for a moment. Then it was broken. He watched the girl rush out of the school and into the hard slicing light. She reached the bush and carried on running, zigzagging between the trees. She was swift, almost weightless, like the dry brown twigs on which she made no impression at all.

Max lifted the wooden crate from the back of the jeep, arms buckling under the strain. He saw her watching him, her face cool in the shade. She called out a greeting and he replied to her. The words felt warm in his throat.

Paul came out and together they wrestled the crate across the ground, rocking it with their shoulders, grunting when it shifted. They dragged it over the threshold and into the school where they stood for a moment, wiping their hands over their faces. Max used his pocket knife to cut the plastic tapes which gave a noise like a small explosion when released from the crate.

She wanted to look inside the box. Her face was excited when she dipped her arms into the yellow straw and felt the packages there. It was mostly books, old school books from Britain and

197

America. There were also exercise books, maths books with damp red covers, a black dotted line for the pupil's name. Inside the pages were yellow and perforated with tiny holes like blight on fruit. Max went outside to fetch another smaller crate while they arranged the books and talked about them.

When the crates were empty, the books stacked in columns against the back wall, Paul asked Max whether he would drive them into town while it was still light. Was there a place where they could get a haircut? The party to celebrate finishing the school was the next evening and they needed to get cleaned up. Elise watched him while he thought. He knew a place in town, but it was not for women.

They drove to Ibenga. At the Fabs Barber Shop, Elise asked him to stop. It was not the place he wanted to show them; there was somewhere further along that was more enclosed, but she insisted on getting out. A young man wearing a black and white knitted ski hat sat chatting with a couple of other traders. He stood up when he saw her and waved exuberantly. His friends watched her, too, smiling and bending their bodies around as if they were all listening to the same beat of music. She came over to the jeep, her face flushed. 'He says he'll do us all. Isn't this great, Paul?'

'Fab.'

Laughing, they linked arms and Max followed behind them through a woven grass screen where, improbably, a pair of fat red leather chairs waited and a set of disembodied pink electric hairdryers, domed plastic hoods nodding above the rustic fence like rather surprised aliens who had landed in the wrong place.

Paul and Elise looked at each other gleefully before they climbed up into the red chairs and swivelled around. Max settled on a wooden stool and looked at the jars where combs and brushes were submerged in a deep blue liquid. The barber worked his foot on the pneumatic pump and grinned as they rose to greet their reflections in a fly-blown mirror hitched to a dried-out tree. When the barber lifted her hair from her neck and placed a white towel across her shoulders, Max had to look away.

'How much do I take?' the young man asked her.

Afterwards they walked about the township, the heat fierce on their freshly shorn necks, hands loose by their sides. It was by now the hottest time of the afternoon and the place seemed dry and exhausted. Few people were about. The traders they passed were pleased to see them and called out excitable greetings from shops constructed entirely from salvaged rubbish; bits of twine held doors together, roofs were patched with yellow plastic bags and plants sprouted from blue and white milk cartons. The painted cardboard signs appeared childishly optimistic: *Lovily Tailor, Fun Dress, Sweet Drink.*

'So many tailors,' Elise remarked as they passed a Singer sewing machine moored in dust on a trestle table. The machines with their gold leaf etchings had always appeared to Max strangely beautiful and he stopped and looked. She stood just in front of him. The barber had taken off an inch of her hair, which was the colour of pale coffee beans, and now bounced lightly on her shoulders. He imagined taking the weight of it in his hands and the thought made him catch his breath. The tailor in residence, a young man wearing a grey suit jacket and red jeans despite the deadening heat, looked up and smiled. Over his stall a wedding gown decorated with silver crystal beading swung in a slow spiral, its glitter startling amid the dried-up surroundings. It reminded Max of a photograph he'd seen once of a chandelier left intact in the rubble of a bombed-out ballroom. The last shop in the row was a crumbling hut that sold odd bits of machinery. The outside was painted with flowers and someone had daubed on the wall: *True love never dies.*

Walking had made them all thirsty and so Max took them to the Welcome Again Bar. In the flat, cool darkness, a few Africans slouched at a chipped red counter drinking beer. They slowly lifted their heads as the whites approached. Max ordered a Castle beer for them all and they leaned up against the counter and drank without talking. A cartoon on the back wall showed a man in exaggerated patched clothes looking up at a well-dressed woman. The message in Bemba read: 'I may look poor, but I can afford to buy beer.' There were other notices which made Max feel strangely embarrassed. 'Mr Credit is on Holiday, but Mr Cash is here.' 'My Beer is My Life.'

Rectangles of light filtered on to the dusty floor. Elise wore brown leather sandals and he could see crosses of skin on the brow of her foot that were still white. Paul glanced up as a swing door slammed open and two young African men came up to the bar. One wore flared faded jeans, a Coca-Cola T-shirt, beads and a silver pendant with the letter T around his neck; the other a blue pinstriped suit with wide trousers, pink shirt and dark glasses. The man in jeans asked for two beers, but the barman ignored him and went out to the back where Max saw him settle down into an old armchair. The man in jeans rapped the bar, his face taut. 'Two beers,' he called out. He leaned his chest right over the bar and scowled at the barman who sat in his chair and turned his face away.

'Here,' Max said and pushed over a few kwacha, which the man at the bar snatched up.

'Hey,' he called towards the man at the back, holding up the limp, dirty money. 'I asked for two beers.'

The man got up slowly, putting his hand against the small of his back as he stretched and yawned and then ambled his way to the bar. He took a cloth from a hook under the counter and slowly polished a couple of glasses, holding them up in the gloomy light to check for smears. Then pointedly he served Max with two beers. Max pushed them towards the men and ordered two more.

'To my friends,' said the man in jeans, holding on to his beer bottle tightly, his eyes warily flickering towards the barman who stood in shadow watching them. He chinked the flat end of his bottle against theirs, and drank his beer in gassy gulps, giving a sharp gasp as he finished as if he had just swum a length underwater.

His companion drank more slowly. 'Thank you, friends,' he said, his gentle face brimming.

Max asked the men what they were doing in the township.

'We work here,' said the man in jeans. 'I'm Christian Tambo and I have a clinic in the bush. This here' – he indicated the man in the suit – 'is my disciple, Sylvester.'

'What sort of clinic?' Elise asked.

'I'm a famous witch doctor,' said the man in jeans. 'But I don't have any money.'

'I can see that,' said Max.

'You could help me,' said the witch doctor. 'I need to buy equipment for my clinic.' He looked over his shoulder and then turned back to them, his expression vivid and urgent. 'I need your help, my friends.' He lowered his voice. 'I am in a desperate situation.'

Elise and Paul exchanged glances. Max took a long pull on his beer. There was something unsettling about the witch doctor's manner, the agitated way he kept looking over his shoulder as if he were expecting someone. It affected the other customers who kept shifting in their seats and looking towards the door.

The witch doctor tried to smile at them through the slits of his bloodshot eyes. 'I will show you my clinic. No white man has ever been before.'

Paul's face leaped 'How far is it?' He looked to Elise who gave a brief nod, but did not meet his eyes.

'Eight kilometres. We will walk.' The witch doctor gave a sullen laugh. His teeth at the back had decayed into brown stumps.

'OK, we'll go,' Max told him. 'But we won't walk, we'll drive. Are the tracks up to it?'

'Yes, yes,' said the witch doctor, a pleased look on his face. 'One more beer and then we go. He gave a sickly smile and grabbed Max's arm. Max slipped off his stool and the witch doctor lost his grip.

'No funny business,' Max said. 'If you try to rob us, I'll smash that little head of yours to pieces.'

'Hey.' The witch doctor raised his hands. 'Mister, you just bought me a beer. I wouldn't rob you.' He glanced at the others for support. Paul made a thin line with his lips while Elise seemed bemused as they left the bar.

They drove into the bush. The witch doctor and his disciple sat in the back, leaning forward giving directions when the track ran out. The smell of beer and sweat was strong and Max kept the windows open as they went deeper in, engine revving, bucking over red gullies and climbing banks of dirt as hard as concrete.

They passed through villages where emaciated dogs ran at their wheels and children with big brown balloon bellies wobbled at the sides of gullies, faces blank, mechanically knitting with little sticks and long ragged scraps of wool. Termite mounds loomed among the trees, curiously beautiful like crumbling rose-coloured temples. After another mile or so during which Max felt the top of his scalp grow tender from being knocked so many times on the inside of the jeep, the witch doctor leaned forward excitedly and told him to stop.

They got out at a clearing surrounded by a few capsized huts. The witch doctor and his disciple led the way towards a grass corral. Various attendants came forward and arranged seating of tree stumps covered with pieces of cloth. They were all told to sit down. They waited. Outside, little fingers poked through the grass, parting it, making spaces for small brown eyes. There was rustling and giggling.

The witch doctor left the corral and the attendants continued with their preparations, placing a grass mat on top of a piece of old velvet curtain laid on the ground. A white cloth was laid on a small table and a chair arranged. A battered sports bag was placed on the mat. The attendants took up crouching positions at the sides of the corral, their expressions serious and intense.

The witch doctor returned. He had changed into white overalls, which he wore with a beaded fur hat and dark glasses. He said he had brought them here to tell them something. His life was in danger and he needed their help.

'There are people out there who want to kill me.'

'Who are these people?' Max asked.

'They are jealous of me because I cured their chief. He brought me here from my homeland and built this clinic because he was suffering from fits. He stayed here for a month and I looked after him. I cured him and now his people want to kill me.'

'But surely they would be glad you helped their chief?' Paul said.

'No, they want my life. They think the chief gives me money.'

'Does he?' Max asked.

'He has nothing left. His family is very large.'

'Why don't you go back to your homeland?' Elise asked. She was leaning forward from her tree stump, her hands clasped in her lap. A few tendrils of hair had curled into spirals across the top of her forehead.

'My work is here. You must help me.'

'Why should we?' At this she received a warning glance from Paul who sat with his legs crossed, a slight frown on his face.

The witch doctor grew agitated. Every now and again he looked over his shoulder as if he expected someone to be spying on him outside the corral. He lowered his voice. 'I'm telling you these people are very dangerous. They are soul thieves.'

'What do you mean?' Paul asked, his eyes bright.

'They steal children in the middle of the night and take them to the graveyard to sacrifice their souls.'

'Why do they do that?'

'Because they believe the young souls will bring them luck in business and protect their money from becoming bewitched. Most of my patients are children whose souls have been stolen. I keep them here and give them herbs and make them well again. There is a girl . . .' He paused and again looked over his shoulder, then he said quietly, 'Sylvester will get her.'

The young man in pinstripes stood up and walked quickly out of the corral. The witch doctor nodded at him and blew through his nose and clenched his hands from tension. A nervous glance rippled across the faces of the men. Max felt his back stiffen. He stared at the ground. The earth here was thick and red like powdered blood.

Sylvester came back into the corral holding the hand of a small girl in a torn red dress. She kept her head bowed as he led her up

203

to the witch doctor who ordered her to kneel on a mat. 'Di!' the witch doctor called. 'Di!' She lifted her chin and he drank from a plastic cup, which he then handed to her. She received it in both hands, but did not drink. The witch doctor laid his hand on her dark head and closed his eyes and looked away from her. Then he turned back to her and helped her to drink from the cup, his expression gentle, almost like a priest at communion. When she had finished, the witch doctor gestured at her to sit on a mat at one side of the corral and she went, stiffly obedient on her thin, scuffed legs.

The witch doctor looked at them. 'She is thirteen years old.' Max was surprised. The girl was so small he thought she must be around six or seven. 'She was bewitched by an old man from the Catholic Mission. He wanted to open a shop and he needed a human soul to bring him wealth. So he took her spirit. She stopped growing and then she started having fits. Her grandmother brought her to me.'

'How long has she been here?' Max asked.

'Two and a half weeks. She will stay here for a month.'

'Is she cured?' Elise asked.

'We found the old man who bewitched her and brought him here. We ordered him to cure the kid, but all he can do is destroy. He has no powers to make someone better. So we ordered him to surrender all the witchcraft he has. I am trying to cure her now, but it is taking a long time. I need money. I need your help.'

There was a silence. Elise looked at Paul, but it was impossible to tell what she was thinking. Eventually Elise said, 'Why don't you let the little girl go back to the hut? She looks tired.'

'Di!' the witch doctor called in a rough voice and the girl jerked her head towards him. Her eyes were filmy, Max saw. She got up and followed Sylvester out of the corral.

'What did the old man do to her?' Paul asked after the girl had gone.

'He took her to the graveyard at night and he used voodoo on her so that her spirit would join with the spirit of the dead.

Sometimes children are found there unconscious. I'm telling you, mister, this problem is very real. I am the only person in the region who knows the cures. You must help me.'

Sylvester came back into the corral carrying a green and white sports bag.

'Let me show you something,' the witch doctor said.

At a sign, the disciple dipped into the sports bag and lifted out several small objects which he arranged carefully on a white cloth.

'What's he doing?' Paul asked.

'I'm asking him to show you the voodoo I confiscated from the old man. Sylvester is the only one besides me who can touch it because I have given him medicine to protect him.'

They all leaned forward. 'You can look, but you must not touch anything,' the witch doctor said.

'What would happen to me if I did?' Paul asked.

'You would go into a fit as your soul left your body, and then you would die,' the witch doctor said.

Sylvester stepped back and wiped his hands down the trousers of his business suit. Max stared at the objects spread on the mat. The smell coming off them was foul and made his head swim. He heard Elise ask the witch doctor what they were.

One dark object had been shaped into a crude representation of a bird, another made from the decomposing flesh of an electric fish had been moulded into a thumb-sized piece and wound with ribbons of black cloth. The other piece of voodoo was part of an elephant tusk bound with a bracelet of tiny red seeds.

'I have confiscated many others, but I don't have the right medicines to protect me from them, so I can't show you,' the witch doctor told her.

Max felt dazed. The grass clinic was peaceful and yet he had the sense that things had happened there that superstition prevented anyone talking about. A chicken squawked behind the screen and he almost jumped out of his skin.

'Now do you understand?' the witch doctor said. 'These people are fighting for my life.' He explained that wizards were trailing him constantly. These wizards could take any form: dogs, snakes, cats, rival witch doctors or ghosts.

'I can look at a wizard approaching in the form of a dog and know this is very dangerous. I can look at someone and know this is not a man, this is someone I need to fight. These people will not stop until they kill me. You must help me.'

A deal was struck over a pack of cigarettes. Max agreed to give the witch doctor a weekly allowance to continue his clinic and sell his herbal medicines. In return, Max wanted information: times, names, sightings of the so-called soul thieves. 'I will send my man from the farm every week and you will tell him everything you know. *Everything*. Do you understand?'

'It will be very dangerous, but for you I will do this,' the witch doctor said, puffing and nodding over his cigarette as if he were enjoying a particularly fine cigar. The disciple grinned and shook their hands. Everyone seemed in good humour now that some transaction was taking place. Max handed over all the money he had in his pockets and said he would return the following week to see how things were coming along. The witch doctor stuffed the wad of money into the top pocket of his overall and asked Max for the rest of the packet of cigarettes. As they left he suddenly burst into song: 'Do you believe in Jesus Christ? Jesus Christ, do you believe in Jesus?' he sang as the disciples watched, their faces rapt. His voice was surprisingly light and sweet. Holding the packet of cigarettes in his open palm, he grinned and waved as they climbed into the jeep.

Rattling their way back across the bush, Paul asked Max, 'Do you really believe in all that witchcraft stuff?'

'No, but you have to take it seriously. People die. I've heard about the kids being taken before.'

'So, do you think that little girl was bewitched, instead of just being terrified out of her mind?' Elise said from the back seat. Her arms were so close Max could smell the saltiness of her skin.

'I don't know.' He felt the air move as she leaned back.

'But why give him money?' Paul said. 'He'll only spend it on beer.'

'I need him to keep an eye on things. He knows what's going on and the main thing is that these gangs need to be stopped. I'll ask my guard to check on him. He knows about these people.'

Paul turned and looked out of the window and the jeep fell silent as they rolled on through the night. Max felt more comfortable driving in silence. He was able to concentrate on avoiding the potholes that, if he were not careful, could cost them a wheel and a delay to change it. His eyes swept the track, watching out for the strange pennant-winged nightjars that would sometimes fall across the headlights and lie paralysed, snub bodies twitching. The eyes of the nightjar had always reminded him of a frightened child.

Max knew that Paul was right. The witch doctor would take as much as he could and possibly give little in return. Max would have to watch him carefully. He would ask around, find out where the soul thieves operated, which villages they targeted and put some of his men on watch. His security guard Geoff Seven was reliable and he knew the bush better than anyone. Max would ask him to help. He drove on into the night, feeling a sense of relief now that he had decided what he was going to do. Both his passengers were asleep. Paul's chin had dropped to his shoulder and his neck showed white in the darkness. He looked like a child himself curled up there and Max felt a surge of something, a clear instinct to protect. He must not let harm come to these people. He must keep them safe. He also knew that as long as he kept this in mind, he too would be safe.

It was pitch black by the time they arrived at the house. Max stayed in the driver's seat as they let themselves out, rubbing faces crumpled with exhaustion. He watched them walk across the lawn. They both carried torches, beams criss-crossing over each other. At the door Paul turned and waved his torch light indicating that Max could go. But Max remained behind the wheel for a moment, craning his neck slightly forward, thinking she would turn around, but she slipped past Paul, her head suddenly dark above his, and went inside. When the kitchen light flared yellow, Max jerked the wheel and scraped out of the drive, pushing the jeep fast towards his farm.

12

GLIDING

When an aeroplane is gliding, it is losing height, but not falling in the ordinary sense of the word. It is still flying and is airborne.

Zambia, 1972

Paul stood on the runway. He felt a little dreamy and unfocused, still surprised at being pulled from his bed at dawn by the sound of the jeep and the sudden appearance of Max framed in the kitchen doorway staring at him with such a great, agitated intensity it was as if he had burst straight from a dream. Alarmed, Paul had asked if everything was all right at the farm, and Max had looked as if he hadn't known what he was talking about. Then he had sat while Paul made tea and looked into his mug as if waiting for something. Eventually he had burst out: 'I'm going flying, want to come?'

It had taken Paul a moment to register that Max meant right then. For some reason he thought Max was on his way somewhere else. Max dropped his gaze and began to shuffle his feet around. Now some of the urgency had dissipated, he appeared uncomfortable, almost caught out. 'The conditions are pretty good,' he said, his gaze still tied to the floor. 'There'll be too much smoke from the fires later.'

Paul felt compelled to move quickly back to the bedroom to dress properly in warm clothes. Pulling on his jeans, he glanced over to the bed where Elise lay hunched in hot sleep, her back rising and falling in time to her breathing. Collecting a spare jumper from a pile of clothes on a chair, he wondered why they had not bothered to hang their things in the wardrobe or put them in drawers. Their bedroom had a temporary, newly arrived air with things spilling out of bags and suitcases; odd new things like straw hats and sun cream which somehow they never bothered to use. He found a clean pair of socks in one of the bags and balled them under his arm. His boots were kept in a wooden rack in the hallway.

Outside the bedroom door he paused, thinking he heard the bedclothes rustling. He imagined Elise sitting up, hair falling over her shoulders in frayed ropes. He loved waking up with her. Nothing would change if he could wake up with her. He wondered why he doubted it, why he felt a slight current of uncertainty, nothing too obvious, just a tiny breath of unease. Ever since he had arrived in Africa he'd felt it. It was almost as if someone were calling to him, but inaudibly, at a frequency he could not hear. His head swam as he bent down to pick up his boots from the hall.

Max had gone. For a moment Paul stood stunned, blinking in the early morning light. The birdsong was piercing. Shoving his boots under his arm, he went out to the garden in his socks and saw then with relief the jeep parked like a battered white ambulance under the shade of an acacia tree. A strange, quavering gratitude flooded through him as he leaned against the tree and put on his boots, pulling the laces as tight as they would go.

They drove to the airstrip between folds of mist that lay over the coffee fields in thick blue-white bundles. Each field appeared spaceless and timeless, inseparable from its neighbour. The mist softened brittle edges, filled in holes and scars so that the landscape seemed joined up and whole. The trees stood quietly, their dark shapes bulging slightly as if they were trying gently to break free.

They parked at the airstrip just as the sun was starting to burn through. The first thing they needed to do was to turn the plane round. Max ducked down immediately near the underbelly and removed the wooden blocks from under the plane's small wheels. Then he began to check all round the fuselage with his palms spread open, moving carefully and quietly over her body, bending his face to her. The condensation on the fuselage melted in tiny little rivers that criss-crossed over each other, mirroring the sweat that ran down the sides of Max's face, collecting in the grooves on his collar bone. The ground smelled hot and oily. Max completed one side and then went round the other, occasionally stopping to wipe his eyes. He never wore sunglasses and in the mornings his eyes leaked tears until they got used to the light.

When all the checks had been done, Max motioned Paul over to help push the plane round. They stood shoulder to shoulder with both their hands on the tail fin. The plane moved easily, like a well-oiled sliding door which made Paul think about his father's old woodshed back in Scotland. On the roller his father had used a thick grease with a hot-paint smell and texture of burned toffee. Paul remembered the rich pleasure of dipping his fingers into it, its pond-mud ooziness against his nails, the strong temptation to gobble up the entire pot of it in the oily darkness of the shed.

The small aeroplane seemed to be breathing in the sun. Paul tried to concentrate on moving her, but his thoughts kept slipping over one another. Scenes from the previous night played across his mind, shocking in their intimacy. He saw, or rather felt, Elise arching under him, her face flushed with what seemed to be ecstatic triumph. His own body pumping ferociously as if he were trying to leave it behind, his thoughts of Max, of *becoming* Max. His hands on her shoulders then her breasts, then an inexplicable and almost painful tingling in the soles of his feet. He felt the pressure of the room around him, heard the curtains flipping slightly in the night breeze, and the dull sound of the bed frame knocking against the wall; her final cry of surprise and relief and joy and something else, something he couldn't describe.

'Turn her a little bit to the left,' Max said as they slid the plane round, bumping awkwardly against each other. 'That's it, steady her right here.' He narrowed his eyes and glanced up at the sky. 'We need to get up before the fires start.'

They positioned *Juliet* at the edge of the runway with her nose pointing slightly upwards. The aeroplane put Paul in mind of a bendy old-fashioned toy, one of those wind-up planes made from coloured tin. Max checked the fuel levels and gave a few jerks on the wings and rudder. Then he tested the oil. The dipstick came out clean silver, the rim of greenish oil glistening in the sun, and at this he broke into a slow smile. 'She's in good shape, not bad at all.' He slapped the fuselage and grinned at Paul. 'OK?'

Paul gave him the thumbs up. He tried to climb up into the cockpit effortlessly, but his legs felt heavy from lack of sleep. He stepped on to a little ledge set in the wing before ducking down inside the door. The cockpit had a worn, oily smell. The seat covers heating up in the sun were bleached and torn in places, the webbing on the belts slack with age. Strapping himself in, Paul looked through the windscreen. The mist had completely cleared and now the sky spread out from the dirt runway in a luminous blue fan.

'We've got to get a move on.' Max slipped into his seat and snapped his belt shut. He flicked a couple of switches and twisted a lever on the roof.

Paul looked at the dials on the instrument panel. There weren't very many controls, less than he had in his old car back at home. He watched Max as he turned the ignition. There was something very definite and precise about the way he was moving, as if the cockpit were a part of his own body space.

The sky was a pure race of blue. Impossible to imagine it curdled by the clouds of Scotland, the grey friezes of winter, the shivering lilac dawns. Paul tried to remember what snow felt like and found he had trouble dredging it up. Maybe there were seasonal memories. One day when he had returned to Scotland perhaps he would try to remember this morning, this infinitely blue African morning.

The propeller blades jerked once and then gave a little choke. Max switched off the ignition and waited for a few seconds before trying again, listening intently as the starter motor struggled to fire. The engine coughed and stalled. 'Battery must be low,' he muttered. He unbuckled his belt and opened the cockpit door and then looked up at Paul. 'I'll see if I can start her from the ground.'

'What do I do?'

'Stay where you are.' He ducked his head and climbed down to the runway. Standing in front of the plane, he rested one hand on the propeller blade and straightened his shoulders. He looked calm and steady, like an athlete about to start a race. His cropped dark red hair accentuated the sharpness of his jaw and the curving line of his neck and shoulders. There was something absolutely unmistakable about Max, Paul thought. He couldn't explain it, but he felt that whenever he looked at Max it was as if he were seeing him for the very first time.

At the second attempt the propeller jerked into life with a sudden fast beating of wings. Max reappeared in the cockpit, a smear of grease across his cheek, a smell of sweat and petrol about his clothes. Grimly he buckled his belt and tried the ignition, making quick forward movements on the throttle. The plane jumped forward and began to prance lightly down the runway, cracking small stones and grit under her wheels. Then the engine began to gather speed, charging the cockpit with a rattling roar that vibrated all the small bones in Paul's body, filling his throat with a voluptuous swell. Looking out of his side window, he saw the earth fall away cleanly and the pattern of trees become smaller and less defined, merging into one shifting dark green mass, like tightly bunched heads of winter kale. Looking down at the landscape in miniature, it appeared deceptively clean and well organized, as if put together by an extremely efficient tiny army. The sky in comparison seemed uncontained, a wild, rippling mass that reminded Paul of the sea on a hot day. Leaning his head back in his seat, his thoughts drifted to Elise, who would be waking up now, rolling, turning and finding him gone. He wished he'd left a note.

Without any kind of preamble Max told Paul to take the controls. He didn't wait for a reply and when the plane suddenly toppled and dropped, he simply nudged her back into position and told Paul to put his hand on the elevator stick.

'I didn't think you meant it,' Paul said as he gripped the stick. He wanted to brush the sweat from his eyes but was afraid to move his hands.

Max opened up a map and spread it against the side window. 'Head for Broken Hill.'

The name struck a chord. 'Is that the place with the mine, where the skull was found?'

Max nodded and studied the map.

'How will I know the way?'

'Don't worry, it will be obvious.' Max flattened the map. 'Try to straighten your wings, your nose is pointing up too much.'

Paul pressed the stick forward and felt the nose swing down towards the undercarriage. The movement was alarming, like riding a bicycle down a steep hill without brakes.

'Relax your grip,' Max said. 'Think of the stick as a thin branch that will snap if you treat it harshly.'

Paul eased the stick back and felt the nose push up more gently this time.

'Now centralize your rudder. Don't look at the horizon, think only of moving the plane.'

Paul pressed lightly on the rudders and felt the plane straighten. He began to see that if he used the smallest touches the plane felt as if she were gliding through silk, but too much pressure caused her to topple alarmingly. He continued experimenting with the stick and rudders, pushing the plane up and down with feathery movements. Max returned to studying the map, his eyes occasionally flicking to the brown flat earth below. Paul felt a beat of disappointment. He wanted Max to take notice and comment on how well he was getting the hang of this flying.

Wasn't he a natural? Hadn't he just worked out how to do this on his own? But Max kept his attention on the mass of brown wrinkles spreading across the landscape.

Biting his lip Paul brought the stick round to the left and the plane lunged and dropped several feet. He gasped. It was as if a stone had fallen through his body and out through the underbelly down to the ground.

'Don't forget your wings,' Max said. 'Press your stick to the left and right without moving forwards or back. Try not to worry about where you're going, just get the feel of her, see how she's connected together.'

With mounting frustration Paul continued to fly his zigzag path. He was ready to give up and admit defeat when he felt a sudden lull. He loosened his grip on the elevator stick, this time barely holding it at all, just letting the tension rock against his hands. He relaxed his arms and legs, flexed his feet and felt the blood begin to push more smoothly through his body. He released the tension in his face, closed his eyes once briefly and then opened them. He had been sitting jutting forward with his chin stuck out, his mouth open, literally flying with his head, but now he made a conscious effort to relax and let his body guide him through the flight.

The pressure began to ease and the plane felt suddenly lighter in his hands, almost seeming to fly herself. Sensing something different, Max shifted beside him and seemed to urge him on silently. Paul pushed on the stick. His wings were perfectly straight and level, the sky no longer an ice rink with hidden treacherous pits, but a deeply reassuring lake. He was floating on milk. He was flying. A smile spread spontaneously across his face. He was flying a plane across the sky and he had mastered it without proper instruction. A sweet feeling of achievement swelled inside him, and he allowed himself a whoop of joy.

Max folded the map and looked over at him. 'Flying the aircraft is easy. What you need to do is find your own position. Sit back, straighten up and bank her round 180 degrees.'

'What?'

'You can do it. Use your instrument.' Max tapped the turn and bank indicator dial with his finger. 'Watch the needle.'

Paul shifted the elevator stick and felt the plane fall away from him.

'Don't resist it, look overboard,' Max's voice encouraged.

But something in him felt stuck and locked in position on the high side, as if an iron rod had been pushed up his back.

'Right, level her up. Now bank again, the other way, and this time *look down.*'

He followed Max's instructions. This time the plane rolled and cautiously he released the tension in his neck and allowed himself to follow the movement. The sudden bright appearance of the ground made his stomach lurch.

'Keep her coming, that's it, easy now, easy.' Max leaned with him and the plane slid gracefully round, the blue and white blade of her wing slipping cleanly through the air.

Looking down, Paul saw that they were flying over some kind of industrial area. Great metal pylons had been sunk in the ground, some pitching under their weight so that they leaned almost horizontal while others straddled open pits and craters. A pall of coppery dust hung over the workings and sheds and row upon row of tiny tin-roofed shelters that Paul guessed was the accommodation for the workers. Even from the air it looked bleak, a dry, African version of the gulag.

'That's Broken Hill Mine,' Max said. 'Do you want to drop down for a closer look?'

Paul shifted the stick and felt the plane fall. Now he could see the mine more clearly, including a row of workers, coloured scarves wrapped around their heads, sitting against a shed. One or two raised hands as he flew round in wide circle, the shadow of the plane skimming across the broken ground.

He had first heard the name Broken Hill on the eve of his wedding and now just five months later he was flying over the place. It seemed incredible, an illusion of some kind. Paul thought back to the night at the Scottish hotel when Elise's father had told them the story of Broken Hill, his long legs stretched by the fire, eyes brightly lit as he talked about the skull that had been found deep in the mine in 1921 belonging to one of the oldest human beings ever to have lived and his own flight there thirty years later as an anthropology student. He had talked to them about his excitement at seeing the cave that had once been filled with animal bones. It marked the beginning of a journey for Elise's father, a long enquiry towards discovering the moment humanity came into being.

Circling the plane around Broken Hill, Paul imagined the miners working by candlelight, digging with wide shovels until they found the skull which – he remembered this detail quite clearly – had been covered in a crust of stalagmite, like a beautiful filigree stone carving. The rest of the skeleton had been found at the same time, but had been discarded and later thrown away by a mine official, who had attached little importance to the discovery. There was also the mystery of the bundle of skin found among the bones in the cave. The skin had over the years turned into an ore similar to gold.

He wondered what he would say to Elise when they returned, but thinking about her gave him an eerie kind of feeling and he rapidly switched his attention back to the plane. Max was saying that they should turn round and head back; they didn't have enough fuel to stay up much longer.

Paul banked and the mining town disappeared in the gathering dust. He was no longer worried about steering the plane. In a way it was as if he'd always known how to fly, but had never ventured into the place that knew before. Clouds in the shape of swordfish swam alongside his wings. He wished he could stay up in the sky for ever, supported by its blue depths. He imagined himself becoming weightless, a creature of air and light. He hadn't known the meaning of bliss before, but he felt close to it now, as if he'd been somehow rewarded by a higher being. Then the coffee fields came into view and Max took over the controls, landing the plane efficiently on her wheels, grunting as they hit the red dirt.

Max said he had some farm business that needed to be sorted out. He dropped Paul at the school on his way through and drove off quickly. Paul was glad of the time alone. So much had happened, he felt the need to catch up with himself. After drinking a full pint of water in the school kitchen, he spent the rest of the day absorbed in digging a garden plot where the children would be encouraged to grow maize and beans, or keep chickens and guinea fowl.

Raking the thin soil, he felt the afternoon sun lazy on his back. He had never gardened before. The plot around his parents' croft had seemed out of bounds. It was their space, clearly delineated, the potatoes and root vegetables belonging to his father, the herbs and fruit trees his mother. When he thought about them now, it seemed as if they had lived out their lives by dividing everything up between them. It was apparent in everything they did, all the small domestic details, from washing and eating to reading and sleeping. The few times he went into their bedroom – to do so was like stepping into a sacred place – he was struck by how tidy everything was; the table on his father's side of the bed held just a glass for water and a small blue travel alarm clock, the kind that snapped into a neat square when it was closed. On his mother's side there was a pile of library books by authors like Jean Plaidy and Catherine Cookson, the pages sweet as talcum powder, her reading glasses in a soft fawn pouch and a packet of mints. She preferred sucking on them to drinking water at night because it made her want to 'go' and she was worried about waking his father. The cover on the bed was apricot and made of a material his mother called candlewick. Pulled tight against the pillows it formed an indelible seal. He had never seen the bed open or unmade. It always had the same apricot impenetrability, like a perfectly iced cake. Many times he just stood at the entrance to his parents' room and stared at its smoothness. It was a perfect receptacle for an overwrought mind.

Walking back through the bush later, the first cicadas beginning to call, Paul decided he wouldn't tell Elise he had flown to

Broken Hill, not immediately anyway. Part of him felt guilty for not wanting to share it, but he didn't want her to think his adventure with Max had been planned. Telling her the truth – that Max had just turned up – seemed out of the question. He didn't know why he should be secretive. At the same time he felt intuitively that he needed to protect something. But whether this was himself or Elise, or even Max, he was not sure.

He arrived home just before dark. Elise was sitting on the veranda, curled up in a cane chair, a wool blanket covering her knees. She laid down her book as he approached and lifted her face, her expression all at once expectant and relieved. He sat down beside her. He wanted to hear about her day. It seemed important to him that he should know the details of where she had been, who she had talked to, what she had seen. It saved him from gushing his own news.

She told him about a village she had found a few miles away through the bush. The village had been abandoned, the huts left to collapse, and as she walked around she thought she'd heard men's voices and also a type of chanting that unnerved her. She had run all the way home and the experience had left her feeling in a strange mood, quite edgy and cold. She hugged the blanket around her knees and shuddered. 'I can't really explain, but there was a kind of creepy atmosphere about the place.'

Paul thought about the witch doctor. Max's security guard had been going to see him regularly and taking him money. But he hadn't gathered any more information about the children or the so-called soul thieves.

'You shouldn't walk about the bush alone. It's too risky, you know that.' He reached for her arm, but she withdrew from him. He looked into the garden.

'You seem odd,' she said after a while.

'Do I, in what way?'

'I don't know, like you have something to tell me.'

'There's nothing, go on about what happened . . .' He tailed off, uneasy under her gaze.

'There is something,' she said flatly. 'After the village I went to the school to find you. Then when I came back Joshua told me you had gone *flying* with Max.'

He didn't know what to say.

'Well, come on, tell me about it,' she said.

'I need a beer first,' he said, his throat suddenly dry. He went to the kitchen, took a bottle of Castle from the fridge and opened it, ripping his thumb against the sharp edge of the cap. Leaning against the sink, he took a gulp of beer and looked out of the kitchen window where the sun was slipping down below the horizon. He watched it until it was completely out of sight. This took less than a minute and there was no sunset or afterglow. In Africa, the sun was a great self-contained drama, a flaming disc that simply rose and fell.

Feeling somehow chastened, he returned to the veranda and momentarily put his hand on Elise's shoulder as he passed her chair. She shrugged minutely and then brought her hand up to curl around his. He felt suspended, caught between relief and a real feeling of pain that seemed to be advancing on him from some distance. He thought that maybe it was the flying that had made him more attuned to the slightest shifts in pressure. He sat down, drank some of his beer and looked out across the darkening bush. 'It was easier than I thought,' he told her.

'So, will you go again?' The slight edge in her voice made him careful over his response.

'I don't know, maybe if Max has time.'

She looked away so that he could not see her expression. The night sounds of the bush suddenly rose into an intense pitch of electric noise. He took another sip of his beer, feeling the flat fizz against his teeth. For the first time since they had met he could think of nothing to say to her.

They sat in silence. She picked at the wool fibres on the blanket. He kept his hand around his beer bottle, every now and again flexing his grip. The silence grew between them, unnerving him so much that he began, perversely, to tell her in rush everything about the flight, including the view of Broken Hill.

'I thought of you all the way there and back. You should have come with us, of course. Max wanted to take both of us, I could tell, but I didn't want to wake you so early.' He finished a little breathlessly and sat with his beer close to his chest, amazed at himself.

She shifted beside him and then quickly reached for his beer and took a long swig. Her hair swung across her face. 'I'm surprised that you could see so much from the air.'

'Actually the dust was pretty bad. We didn't really hang around. We only flipped there and back. Maybe we'll ask Max if we can all go again soon and take a proper look. He's coming round for supper later if that's all right?' He did not look at her. There was a collapsed feeling in the pit of his stomach and a fluttery sensation under his tongue.

'He's coming to eat here?' She got up, leaving a cool space behind her. He held on to his beer bottle tightly. 'I need to see Joshua then about the meal.'

'It's only one extra. I'm sure it won't make any difference.'

But she had gone. He sat with his beer for a while then he got up and took another from the fridge. Joshua, who was peeling potatoes at the sink, looked at him and nodded. His five-year-old son Kennedy sat on the floor cleaning a pair of Paul's shoes with a rag. Paul bent down. 'Please, don't let him do that. I don't want him to do that.' He picked up the shoes and went to the bedroom. From the bathroom came the sound of the shower turned on as hard as it would go.

Max arrived later wearing a fresh white shirt that accentuated the marine light in his eyes. He had slicked his hair back and his skin smelled of some kind of citrus cologne. The dog was left in the jeep. Paul saw him waiting with his paws up on the steering wheel, turning his head from left to right, rolling the whites of his eyes.

'Oh, you must bring him in,' Elise said.

But Max shook his head and said that the dog would only mess up the place. Paul thought this odd because Lucky was perfectly polite in company and would have lain down under the table all evening with his head on his master's foot. But it was clear that Max wanted to create an impression of some sort.

They took their places a little awkwardly in the small dining room where the table had been laid with old glazed china, heavy silver, a little tarnished on the handles, and thick white napkins, slightly speckled with damp. Half a dozen vegetable dishes rested on cork mats around a joint of beef that sat on a large oval platter, oozing scarlet juice. Elise set a gravy boat down on the table and lit two candles stuck at angles in an elaborate twisted silver holder. 'The power's been off again so the meat's underdone,' she said, burning her fingers on the match. She blew on her fingertips and waved them.

Max leaned towards the meat. He pushed up his sleeves. 'I'll carve, shall I?'

'Go ahead.' Elise looked at the table before she sat down. Her face was hot. She had put on a pale apricot dress. In the candlelight it was alluringly translucent, showing the dark points of her breasts. Her hair was still wet at the ends and dripped into the thin fabric. She flipped it back out of the way and started serving vegetables. 'Come on, Paul, help.' She handed him a heavy serving spoon. 'You do the carrots and potatoes.'

He spooned out vegetables on to three wide plates while Max carved thin slices of almost raw meat and lifted them with the knife, blood dripping in a thin, watery stream. A piled plate was pushed towards him. Paul felt his stomach turn.

They ate for a while in silence, knives scraping dully against plates. Max sat between them with his back to the door. He had placed his napkin too far from his lap and it looked white and small spread across his powerful knees. Max cut a neat piece of meat and mixed it with the gravy on his plate. He ate smoothly in a few bites and laid down his knife and fork while he chewed, taking his time. There was no greed in him, Paul thought, no need to reach over and take more, or add salt or anything at all to his plate. Max ate like a lion, cleanly and efficiently.

Elise pushed her still full plate away from her. She took a sip of water and wiped her mouth with her napkin. She glanced towards Max's dark head bowed over his plate. 'Paul has told me all about his flying lesson this morning. Did he really fly without instruction?'

Max lifted his head and looked at her. He chewed for a while and thought. 'I didn't need to teach him. He's a natural,' he said, his eyes clear and steady.

'I'm certainly not,' Paul said. But the compliment had pleased him. He glanced at Elise, hoping for some confirmation, but she was looking at Max, staring at him with a kind of awe. 'I'd like another try, though. I mean all of us should go up. Perhaps we could spend the day at Broken Hill.' He glanced at Max. 'You know about Elise's connection with the area?'

Max softened his neck as he looked at Elise. 'When was your father here?'

Elise put her hands on the table in front of her, making a delicate bridge with her fingers, which glowed in the candlelight. Paul noticed the way her face was lit; it was almost as if the three of them were sitting in a painting. Her skin was oiled by the heat and her eyes looked soft as if about to brim over. 'He came in 1951 as a student anthropologist,' Elise told him. 'He's particularly interested in Broken Hill Man. He's writing a book about him. He thinks he's the father of mankind.'

'That's interesting.' Max raised one eyebrow. He looked a little uncomfortable, Paul thought. Perhaps he was worried she was about to start talking over his head.

'When some miners dynamited the area in the 1920s they found a cave filled with bones, animals as well as humans. Dad thinks there was an entire skeleton, but it was lost or broken into pieces. All that's left is the skull and that lives in the Natural History Museum now. Actually Dad used to live there, too.'

'In the museum?' Max asked, his gaze fully on her.

'Yes, he had to stay there for a while, after he split with my mother. He slept in the herbarium.'

'You didn't tell me that.' Paul touched his hand on her wrist and leaned towards her. 'By the way, you look beautiful.'

There was a sudden lull. Paul picked up his knife and fork and rearranged them on his plate. He noticed a fly buzzing around the underdone meat.

Elise lifted the carving knife and gestured at Max. 'Please, have some more.'

'No, thank you.' Max took his still spotless napkin from his knees. He looked at it as if he didn't know quite what to do with it and then scrunched it up and placed it on the table where Paul watched it slowly bloom flat again.

'I'll get pudding.' Elise scraped back her chair and went out to the kitchen.

Paul looked at Max who glanced down at his boots under the table. 'I need to go and check on the dog.' His voice was hoarse. He got up quickly, knocking his hip against the table, sending a trapeze of shadows swinging about the room. A candle tumbled out of its holder, spilling wax across the tablecloth. The two men looked at each other in the dim room. Paul felt a breeze waft across the back of his neck. He wanted to follow Max, but something kept his fingers glued to the edge of the table, something he could not fight. He nodded and leaned forward to pick at the spilled wax. He heard Max go into the kitchen and Elise say something in a higher voice than usual. Then Max said something in a lower voice than usual. Then there was a pause. Then both Max and Elise said something at the same time and they both spoke very quickly. Then he heard the outside door slam and then a long silence.

He picked every piece of wax from the tablecloth, rolling it between his fingers into a warm ball. The room felt airless, but somehow it seemed impossible to leave his seat and open a window. The dining room faced the garden. The drive where Max had parked was on the other side of the house.

They returned, Elise first, carrying a bottle of champagne and three glasses. 'I think your maiden flight deserves celebration,' she said lightly, putting the bottle down on the table. 'Max is just coming. We took Lucky the leftovers.'

Paul wondered why she was speaking so fast as if she suddenly didn't have enough breath. He looked at the champagne bottle; the foil had gone from around the top and the cork looked poised to explode. 'Where did you find that?'

'There's a stash in a cupboard at the back of the larder, lots of old dusty bottles. I found it when I was cooking, but I wanted to save it as a surprise.' She paused as Max came into the dining room.

'Go on, Max, open it.' There was a slight catch in her voice as she sat down.

'Let me,' Paul said, and reached for the bottle before Max could reply. He felt shaky and needed to do something with his hands. Max watched while Paul twisted the cork and then let it pop towards the ceiling. It came out with a gunshot crack that made all three of them jump. A yellow, urinous fizz bubbled all over the table.

'What shall we drink to?' Elise's face was flushed and the hand that held her glass not quite steady.

'To flight,' said Paul, looking at her and Max. 'And friendship,' he added.

'To flight and friendship,' said Max evenly.

'What about love?' Elise said. 'We must drink to love.'

'To flight, friendship and love.' They all said it together and then laughed.

Paul took a sip. The champagne was dry and slightly acid on his tongue. He reached for Elise and held her arm. She kissed him swiftly on the neck and retrieved her arm from his grasp. He wanted to grab it back. What was the matter with him? Inside he felt contorted and wrong as if all his organs had shifted slightly out of place. He took another sip of champagne and swallowed against the burning in his stomach.

They finished the bottle and Elise went to get another. When she came back Max told them that Marsden, the old wing commander, had drunk champagne every night. One of the men in his squadron had become a wine merchant after leaving the air force and every Christmas had sent the old boy a case of Dom Pérignon. The cases had kept coming out to Africa long after the doctor had died. Max had tried giving bottles to his servants, but none of the Africans liked champagne. So he simply stashed them in a cupboard and forgot about them.

'But don't you ever want to open a bottle yourself?' Elise asked, her eyes shining at the thought.

'What for?' Max seemed genuinely puzzled and a little embarrassed.

'Well,' Elise said. 'I know I wouldn't be able to keep so many bottles in the house without raiding them. I'd make an excuse to celebrate every day! Isn't it strange, my father knowing the wing commander?'

'Everyone knew him,' Max said. He looked down at his knuckles resting on the table. 'He was the missionary here.'

Elise looked at him intently. 'Do you believe in anything, Max?'

He raised his blue eyes, gently uncurled a fist and made a slight movement with his head.

'I don't think Max wants to talk about religion,' Paul cut in.

'Sorry. You can tell me to mind my own business.' Elise took a quick gulp of champagne and some of it dribbled down her chin.

Max brought his glass up to his mouth and looked at her steadily.

'What made you buy *Hotel Juliet*?' Paul asked, to change the subject.

'I didn't really buy her. The doctor wanted to pass her on before he died. He sold her to me for very little, but I had to agree to do something for him in return.' Max swallowed nervously and reached for his glass.

'He set you a condition?' Elise asked, captivated. She leaned forward across the table, candlelight spilling down her arms.

'I suppose it was a condition,' Max said. 'He said I was to use the money I should have paid for the plane to set up a school.'

'He must have been a very generous man,' Elise said, looking down into her glass.

'He was.' Max glanced towards the dark window.

'You didn't tell me that's why we were building the school,' Paul said. He felt quiet as if he'd just understood something.

'It's like my father,' Elise said, looking intently at Paul. 'You know, the condition.'

'Yes.' Paul addressed Max: 'Her old man wouldn't let us get married unless we promised to travel. That's how we ended up here. It was a wedding present.'

'A wedding present.' Max looked at both of them. 'I'm sorry, I didn't realize you were . . . you had just married.'

'You mean it seems like we've been together years?' Elise drained her champagne and poured another glass. She looked over at Paul and then reached over and kissed him on the tip of his nose.

'I should go,' Max said and stood up abruptly.

'Oh,' Elise cried. 'Please, don't go yet . . .' She looked at the table. 'I forgot the dessert; we were going to have pears, chocolate and cream.' A flutter of distress passed across her face. 'It won't take a minute to throw together.'

But Max muttered an apology and remained standing, his eyes on the window. Paul rose from his seat. 'Come round tomorrow, as early as you like.'

Max gave a gruff nod in reply.

Glancing at Elise, Paul added, 'I'll walk out with Max.' Her eyes flickered and he thought she was going to say something, but she began stacking the plates and scraping cold, uneaten vegetables on to the bloody meat platter. He watched her for a moment. 'Leave it for Joshua.'

'No.' Her head was bent, her face hot. 'We should clear up, at least. Go on, go with Max. It doesn't matter about dessert. We can eat it for lunch tomorrow.'

Max thanked her for the meal, a little too formally Paul thought, his voice tight. They went out to the kitchen. The floor felt slippery underfoot.

After the heat of the house, the air outside felt cool and still. They stood under the trees for a moment, somewhat reluctant to close the night, Paul thought. He looked up at the stars, the dusty brightness scattered between the big pointing constellations. There were a couple of big single stars, one an icy blue, the other a gold that he guessed could be planets. He could look them up. He was sure he'd seen a book on astronomy in the wing commander's bookshelf.

Max jiggled his keys and let out a sigh. 'See you early tomorrow, then,' he said and strode off towards the jeep.

Paul watched him go, his shoulders seeming too broad for the white cotton shirt which had been carefully ironed. There were two deep diagonal creases across the back of the shirt, and oddly a dark patch, a smudge of green, as if he'd leaned against the bark of a tree. Paul swung his gaze back up towards the sky. Maybe he should go and find the star book. It would be interesting to see if he could decipher other shapes and patterns, the less familiar ones. He started to walk back to the house, but then could not stop himself from glancing back towards the jeep where the dog was jumping up and down in delirious excitement as Max slipped into the driving seat. Seeing Paul's look, Max raised his hand in farewell, a grim, set expression on his face. Paul felt something shift inside him as he lifted his hand in return, and then a jolt as he realized in that moment that he loved Max. It was a simple feeling. As pure and ancient as starlight. He would do anything for Max, lay down his life for him if need be. He stood at the top of the drive not daring to breathe, watching the jeep pull away, the tail lights glowing red as they bounced down the track and out of sight.

Inside, he found Elise at the kitchen sink staring out of the window at the retreating jeep. She jumped a little when she saw him as if she had been startled from a dream and then said that she was going to take a walk outside to clear her head.

Paul went to the small sitting room and sat at the old wooden desk. The wicker chair was worn into the shape of the person who had used it day after day, year after year, its arms scratched and eaten in places by termites. The desk top was scarred with black rings and plate marks suggesting that the user, and this must have been the wing commander, sometimes ate there. Sitting at the desk, breathing in its intimate history, Paul felt comforted. The desk was just the right size and height for him. If he'd had to choose a desk for himself, he would have wanted one just like this one, not too big or intimidating, or too small to feel cramped, but somewhere to slide behind whenever you wanted to know something, or work something out. A desk, he decided, should be somewhere to come in times of confusion or change. A desk such as this had a feeling of sanctuary, and that is what he needed now: to be safe and contained within something solid.

Reaching to one side, he found he was within touching distance of a low bookshelf. He put his hand out. He would pick out whatever book his fingers touched first, and what he would find there would help him; it had worked before in the library at college. His fingers settled on slim blue hardback, which he drew on to the desk and opened.

(ii) Intrinsic Variables

The second class of variable stars is the class of intrinsic variables. Here we have to deal with a single star in each case, which, for reasons not at all well understood, varies its light output. The reason is to be sought in the structure of such a star, leading to a situation in which the atomic energy output at its centre, and the mutual gravitation of its parts are not in perfect balance. Hence, at some times there is too great an output of radiation, leading to the star's puffing itself up to a large radius. This is followed by a period of collapse, when the star contracts in on itself, pushing up the pressure and temperature at its centre, and stimulating once more an increased output of energy . . .

He closed the book and went to the dining room. The disordered table with its scrunched napkins and snuffed candles looked remote as if the meal there had taken place years previously instead of a mere hour ago. He looked at Max's chair, pulled out slightly further than the rest. The champagne bottle with its cracked foil collar was still half full. He poured himself a glass and drank it down. He couldn't remember the last time he had drunk champagne. He'd missed the celebration on New Year's Eve, the night he met Elise, the night she stole into his car, mere months ago. He thought about the deer on the road, the warmth of it against his shoe as he pushed it on to the verge, the eyelashes speckled with snow. He drank another glass of champagne. He must not look back, it was better to look forward, to stay in the present. The school was important now. It was what they had come for and they had to see it through. He drained his glass. He must not forget what was important.

Leaving the dining room, Paul felt calm. He went outside and found Elise in the garden looking up at the sky. 'It's all right,' he said, taking her in his arms. 'It will be all right.'

They stood in the cool thin air of the garden listening to the vibrations of the night, the singing cicadas, frogs and night insects. He caught the faint green scent of the white flowers clustered on the yesterday, today and tomorrow plant drifting across the lawn, clear as light. He looked up into the dusty mass of the stars. This is the beginning, he thought, the beginning of everything. Grasses and trees rustled in the wind and from some-where deep inside the bush came the sound of beating drums.

Max walked towards the clearing. Behind him Paul and Elise fol-lowed; he could hear them talking together softly, but could not work out what they were saying. As they reached the party, a group of dancers and drummers shifted slightly under the trees. They wore muted, ragged costumes and their eyes shone from their faces like polished stones. Max recognized some of them. They were farm labourers mostly, including one or two coffee pickers from his farm. He knew they would have been sitting under the trees for hours without food or water, patiently waiting for the guests to arrive. It was one of the characteristics he most admired in the Africans: the ability to wait without complaint, sometimes for days on end.

Elise gave a small gasp and said something to Paul, and it made Max jump, hearing her voice cut into the dark. She had a distinctive way of speaking, slightly through her nose, which made her sound a little blocked up. When she was animated she would breathe in gusts and gasps, and rush over her words. It was like listening to a stream tumble over stones. Now she was laughing. He felt a shivering sensation shimmer down his back.

It had been like this since the dinner. Every word she spoke, every movement she made affected him physically and he was finding it difficult to be near her in case he gave himself away. He could feel her now walking behind him, her long thighs flexing under the red *chitenge* she had chosen for the party. The African style suited her, made her seem taller and more relaxed. He imagined the air brushing the silky blonde hairs on her arms, the sense of coolness on the back of her neck and around her ears. If he let himself fall fully into that night, he could feel again the strange melting softness of her lips, and hear the catch of surprise at her throat as he held her under the tree, leaves and stars blurring together in a shifting silvery canopy over their heads. His heartbeat had sounded so loud it was as if it had jumped from his body.

'Oh, look,' Elise said. 'The drummers are warming up.' He followed her voice. A group of old men stood holding the pale, stretched skins of their drums in front of a spitting fire. The firelight lit up their faces, showing sunken eyes, lines and broken-down mouths, some toothless. One old man with long straight legs, like two very smooth black branches, seemed to give permission to the others to start. Following his lead, they squatted down and arranged their drums between their knees, and then at another invisible sign began to beat out a rhythm, hitting the drum with the edge of their palms, slicing slowly and then building up a rippling sound. No matter how many times Max heard the drums he always felt a thrill when they first began; their sound was so proud and fearless, so definite. The drums were the only noise that could silence thought, and for that Max was now grateful.

He led them to a quiet patch and they sat down on the rugs they had brought. Max stood behind them with his arms folded. He looked around the clearing. About twenty or thirty people were sitting down, mostly white farming couples, some with children asleep across laps. He recognized Baxter, his children in a blond bundle beside him, and waved to him. Baxter lifted a stubby beer bottle in reply. Other farm workers greeted him with nods and the slight, subtle gestures he knew so well. He felt a sense of gratitude as he stood watching the last smears of pink light dissolve into the trees, and allowed himself to shift forward slightly so that his foot was just touching the edge of the blanket where Paul and Elise sat with their arms wrapped not around each other, but their knees, hugging themselves against the breeze.

There was a lull as the birds quietened and then the dance started without any announcement. One or two women got up from under the trees and came forward on to the wooden boards that had been placed on the ground as a kind of rough dance floor. They moved around each other at walking pace, swaying their hips in a rocking movement, gradually working into the rhythm. The drummers beat their instruments, bobbing their heads to keep time. More dancers slipped in from the trees, their drab costumes swishing with the sound of dried beans and leaves. They moved almost sullenly, planting their feet on the boards in short, squatting movements, eyeing each other warily. Max felt the hairs rise on his arms. In front of him Elise shuddered. The dancers came closer, wiggling their hips, gesturing at the audience to come and join them. The leader was an old woman wound into a black and yellow *chitenge* like a wizened wasp. The other dancers kept close to her, mirroring her movements, buzzing around her, offering her protection. A huge global moon heaved into the sky, emitting a stream of pale light that gave the dancers a slightly strobing effect as they bent and twisted arms and legs that seemed to be made out of very fine tin. Elise grew restless on the blanket, wriggling her feet in time to the drum beat and then in one fluid movement she stood up and kicked off her sandals. At the dance floor she looked back at him and he stumbled, snagging the rug slightly with his foot, generating a grunt from Paul and a glance of such happiness it made Max feel as if he had just been shot in the stomach.

They watched Elise dancing. She moved as if saturated, a full, soft look on her face that made Max want to moan with joy. Paul sat up on his haunches, tapping out the rhythm on his knees, rocking his shoulders. Max saw that he wanted to get up and join her, but there were no men on the floor, only the women with their strange, arcing movements, their rolling hips and long fingers, their mixture of spikiness and softness that intrigued and demanded to be looked at. As if sensing his thoughts, Elise came up to the edge of the boards and swayed there for a moment, her face perilous in the moonlight. Her lips parted and he heard a noise escape him. She moved to the other side of the floor and he lost sight of her for a moment. On the blanket Paul glanced at him and drew his knees up more tightly to his chest.

The drumming changed to a slower beat and the women gathered into a wide circle. Elise stepped off the boards and stood watching from under the trees as a dark shape moved into the centre of the floor. It wore a beaked mask and layers of ripped brown rags which hung in tattered wings from each arm. At the sound of the drum it began to leap and twist in the air, shaking its malevolent head, stamping its loosely bound feet. Each time it landed it would hiss and swing its beak viciously around the heads in the crowd as if it wanted to slice everyone to pieces. Max felt his body grow cold. Watching the creature, he felt as if his deepest fear had become manifest and was standing before him, taunting him with its filthy rags, its voiceless hiss and eyeless stare. The creature was everything he dreaded. It was all the harm that could ever happen to him. He wanted to turn away, but some primitive part of him understood that he would dream of the terrible image for ever if he did not see it dance away. He had to stay and watch until it had gone.

The drumming picked up speed and a shrill whistling began. The women dancers moved back on to the floor, although Elise remained where she was on the other side, understanding perhaps that she had to witness the display rather than take part in it. The women dancers moved around the creature, tentatively at first, as if anticipating a strike. They kept their faces turned away from the centre, but used their bodies to make gestures, thrusting with their hips in strong, wide movements, shimmying backwards when the creature lashed out with its winged arm or hissed too loudly or pointed with its beak. The drum beat gave the women courage and they circled closer, dancing with stronger movements as the creature hissed like a swan protecting its young. At one point it drew out a seed rattle from under its cloaked wing and began shaking it at the women who warded it off with sinuous thrusts and turns. Then the creature gave a cry, a piercing sound that made Max think of a rat caught in a trap, and began to step backwards. The women tightened their circle until they had the creature surrounded. Gradually they pushed it into a corner, nudging it with their bodies while it cowered and covered its eyes, trembling under their capture. Exulting with long ululations, the women pushed the creature off the boards and into the shadows where it gave one last desperate hiss before surrendering in a shrug of ruffled rags. At this the tension burst and the crowd broke into wild cheers. Elise was pulled on to the floor again by the old wasp woman and a feeling of relief poured over Max as she looked at them and waved.

'I'll go and get us some beers,' Paul said. 'I think we need a drink after all that.' He got up, leaving Max to watch Elise dancing with the African women crowded around her. She was smiling now and laughing and he felt himself relax. From the trestle tables Paul gave a wave, lifting a plate to ask if Max wanted food. He shook his head and looked at Elise who had noticed the exchange and mouthed, 'Not yet,' at him.

Paul returned with three beers pressed against his chest. 'There you go.' He handed a bottle to Max who took it gratefully. Then he glanced over at Elise. 'It's good to see her so happy for a change.' Paul watched her swing her bottom as she tried to mimic the African style of dancing. 'She needed this.'

'I guess so.' Max sipped his beer, but had difficulty swallowing. Elise was looking over at them. Paul held up a beer bottle and, breaking free from the spell of the dance, she came over to join them, wiping her forehead and fanning her chest.

'God, I am so hot I could self-immolate.' She took the beer bottle from Paul and shoved it roughly into her mouth and drank. Max turned his head away from her. He felt off-balance and, oddly, empty, as if his own body had been somehow stolen from him and mixed up with hers.

Paul went to fetch food and they were left alone for a moment. He looked up at the sky where the first stars were being shaken into position as if from a giant salt shaker. The moon almost seemed to give way, becoming duller and less compelling. He thought about saying something about the stars to Elise, but all his words felt dammed up somewhere around his chest. There was something about her quickness, the way she would look at him as if she knew everything that was going to happen, that deeply unnerved him. He directed his gaze towards the trestle tables of food where Paul had stopped to talk to a glossy African, with pillows of flesh straining at the sides of his denim suit. Beside him Elise watched the conversation too, the breeze slightly ruffling her hair so that her expression was obscured.

'That's the village chief,' Max said.

'Really?' She laughed and then turned her eyes on him. 'But I'm disappointed . . .' He felt a rush, a bolt of something leap inside him. 'What about paint and where are his beads?'

The chief gave a rich laugh that seemed to rattle every leaf on the trees and swatted Paul on the back with a plump black hand. Paul bent double under the blows and came up a little red-faced.

'He heard you,' Max said.

She smiled into his eyes and the feeling that was lurching inside him suddenly broke into pieces. Her irises had a speckled silvery quality and her lashes were a soft tawny colour. 'Take me flying now,' she burst out. 'I want to go up in the stars.'

Panic skidded through him and he felt he might collapse from shock.

She dropped her eyes and scraped at the ground with her toe. 'It's OK,' she murmured. 'I know you can't. It was just a thought, a mad thought, forget I said anything.' She looked round at Paul who was still talking to the chief, holding plates of food he was supposed to be bringing back for them. She sighed and rubbed at the ground again. Her feet were long and clean, naked-looking with the nails smooth and trimmed.

Conversations rolled around them, occasionally breaking the surface. He thought he heard Joe Baxter's voice saying something about fencing and a woman remark with a disbelieving laugh: 'Can you imagine anyone wanting to steal an orchid?'

'All right,' Max heard himself say next. 'I'll take you up.'

She whirled round and gave him a look that was almost hostile in its intensity. 'What about Paul?'

He gasped, wondering what he had begun. But when he spoke his voice was steady. 'We'll need him to drive the jeep to the runway.' His head felt clear and still. 'We can't land without lights.' He looked her full in the face and she met his gaze, the glittery sharpness of her eyes seeming to slice right through him.

'I'll go and tell him,' she said and went over to the trestle tables. Paul greeted her with obvious delight and put his arm out, but she didn't allow him to embrace her. The chief nodded at them benevolently as they talked. At one point, Paul looked over to where Max was standing, and it seemed to Max that Paul's face had turned paler, or maybe it was just the light from the stars which were now so tightly bundled into the sky there were barely any black patches left showing, as if the night had become a river filled with tiny flecks of torn paper.

She returned, full of bounce and smile, her hair hurled over one shoulder, the weight of it seeming almost too much for her at this moment. 'Max,' she said as she reached him. He didn't know how to respond. Some part of him was climbing out of the arrangement and remaining on the ground, but he was unable to articulate this to her.

'Ready, then?' A kind of toughness came over him. He would take her up just for a short spin; there would be no harm in it. In fact it might be a good thing because they would all have something in common. He knew Elise partly wanted to go flying with him right there and then because she was jealous of the time he'd taken Paul. If Max took her up tonight, they'd be equal. It didn't have to mean that he was coming between them.

The runway was only a short walk away through the trees. As they set off Paul gave them a cheery wave as if they were going on some errand he had managed to escape. Max shone his torch through the bush and led the way slowly.

The cockpit felt chilly. The windshield was already beaded with dew and he took a moment to clear it with the sleeve of his shirt. He tried not to look at her while he was making the pre-flight checks because he was aware that he might miss something if he did. She sat quietly in the co-pilot's seat looking out at the night. The weight of everything they were not saying pressed in on the cabin so that when he finally started the engine and pushed the plane into position he felt he was about to lift into the air with a heavy load. But when they got airborne something shifted. She reached over and took his hand, lacing her fingers through his, and that was the way he flew, with one hand on the elevator column, climbing steadily, and the other clasped in such a feeling of strange, pulsing strength it was as if he could feel her actual heartbeat through his fingertips. The thought that came to him as he pushed *Juliet* up through the smooth black sky was that this was life as he had never known it. This was *life* suddenly turned inside out, all the sensitive workings revealed, the innerness of things that he had felt but never held, exposed here now in his own hand.

The humming of the engine was the only sound as they flew away from the bush and into the sky where dark purple clouds formed mysterious dunes, shimmering at their moonlight-drenched peaks. The clouds seemed to seal them from the imperfect world, which they occasionally glimpsed below in the shape of two tiny points of yellow light winking insistently up from the runway. Max pushed the plane higher, risking turbulence to escape the lights, and they skimmed above the clouds for a moment until they reached the realm of stars, each one suspended in its own pool of immaculate black, as if underneath the sky, hidden in the clouds, there were thousands of tiny silver knives all poised to split open a great canopy of stretched silk. Elise gave a little cry and gripped his hand tighter as they flew across them, seeming to scatter them with their wings. Now in every direction there were stars flickering like little beacons, bleeding and melting and colliding against each other in a chain reaction of stars lighting stars, blue, white, violet and gold, colours he had never seen before, even green and pink. Next to him, Elise started crying and he told her then what he had thought about when they were under the tree the night of the dinner party. After he spoke she cried harder and the stars had seemed to fly faster then, coming in at the windshield like a great glittering blizzard.

They flew on, Max wrapped in joy. The feeling was growing in him, pouring into every parched membrane, every yearning cell and fibre. He could barely look at her for fear that she would see how much it meant just simply to be near her. The touch of her hand felt strange, but also familiar as if she were part of the sky landscape he was navigating himself by touch.

There was little wind. He pushed the plane up, gliding on his wings. The blackness slipped past the cockpit. The tiny space felt warm, everything was within his reach. He looked at the dials on the instrument panel glowing green and set the tail trim. She followed his movements and he told her to put her hand on the elevator column so that she could bring the plane down with him. Her face quivered with pleasure as she took the controls. Her touch was light and secure and he let her fly the plane for a while on her own, smiling at her gasps.

'It's nothing like I thought it would be. It's strange, almost like swimming,' she said. 'It's wonderful.' She turned her face to him then, lifting her chin. He wanted to kiss her, but knew that he had to concentrate on his descent.

'We have to come down, now,' he said.

'I know,' she said quietly. She removed her hand from his and folded it in her lap.

The oncoming world seemed remote as Max flew in lower, keeping his approach flat, wheels just brushing the expanse of hooded bush; the coffee fields seemed dark, the tracks pale in the faraway moonlight, the galvanized metal of houses and farms gleaming a dull silver, verandas glinting with small yellow lamps. When eventually the wheels hit the ground it felt almost temporary until he looked up and saw the heart-stilling lights of the jeep swing into sight.

'Well, that's it then,' Elise said as they glided to a halt. She released the catch on her safety belt and sat for a while staring straight ahead. Her breathing sounded thick to Max, as if she had a cold. He wanted to take her hand again, but couldn't. The feeling of warmth and joy was now draining out of him, as if a hole had been opened in his side with an ice pick. He climbed out of the cockpit.

Paul greeted him with a slap on the back, his voice momentarily unfamiliar, brighter and sharper than Max recalled. He asked about their flight and Max said it had gone well. He shrugged a few times and then Elise came down from the cockpit and after the two of them had hugged, muffled in each other's shoulder for longer than Max thought he could bear, Paul offered to push the plane around. Sliding her into the hanger, Paul made a joke about Max getting someone else to do the donkey work next time and glanced back at Elise who was standing with her arms folded, a frozen look on her face. Paul came out of the hanger and said something about coffee and warming up at the house, but Max told him he needed to go home to sleep. On the way back Max stopped the jeep just before the farm and got out and craned his head towards the soft black sky. The stars seemed distant and incomprehensible. Tiny points of white light. He climbed back into the jeep and, resting his head on the steering wheel, drew a deep ragged breath.

13

SPINNING

Dislike of spinning is no disgrace, therefore do not prolong a spin any longer than is necessary. Instruct the pupil to go into a spin each way and to recover without assistance.

Zambia, 1996

Memory wakes early and lies with her eyes closed, absorbing the sounds of the morning, the intimate drooling of wood pigeons from the garden outside, the soft boom of passing clouds and the rustle of acacia brushed by the wind, as if the trees are breathing, she thinks.

She pulls herself upright, shifting pillows under her back so that she can look about the room and watch the patterns of light play across the walls. In London she sometimes used to do this early in the morning and it always made her feel good for the rest of the day, sort of right with herself and settled in her body. It only worked, though, if she was alone.

A sound of steady snoring comes from the floor beside her and she smiles because this morning she is definitely not alone. Kennedy is asleep. She'd asked him to stay and he had sat quietly in a chair as she lay on the bed wrenched with tears, for hours it seemed. He didn't speak; he just kept looking at her as if she were the saddest person alive. She had tried to tell him to go, but he had ignored her and simply closed his eyes, waiting for her to finish what she needed to do. She had felt that she was unearthing some kind of deep, buried grief, triggered by finding the photo of

Paul Cougan, actually seeing what he looked like after all those years of imagining him – tall, blond and rugged, except he was none of these things. She had got him wrong and coming across him in reality had jolted her to her core. Strangely, he was in fact younger than she was now. In the photograph he must have been only around twenty. She had never admitted this before, but for a while when she was very young, she had thought of Paul as some kind of angel. The strange, jammed-up grief she felt perhaps had something to do with finding out that he was real after all.

Kennedy, strangely, miraculously, had understood. He'd sat in his chair, his long face gentle in the dark. He had let her open her heart without any thought of himself, listening to her without interruption, occasionally shaking his head as she spilled rivers of stuff that meant nothing to him.

She looks at his body folded on the floor. His naked knees and elbows are a pale dusty blue. His feet point neatly towards her, the toes arranged in perfect symmetry. He has on a pair of faded orange shorts and a green army vest, which for a moment reminds her of the bee-stung boy lying on the floor in Max's office. She wonders whether he survived.

Sensing her scrutiny, Kennedy opens his eyes and sits up, rubbing at his temple, rolling his neck from side to side, quite unconsciously pushing his body into its proper place. Seeing her stare he grins at her and then yawns, showing pale gums and slightly discoloured teeth. Rolling his head back against the wall, he lazes contentedly, his eyelids half closed as he watches her. She cannot help thinking that this would never have happened with Adam. He needed – she stalls for a moment, trying to remember just what it was Adam needed; there were so many demands for encouragement, or compliments or caresses, all the little strokes and licks of intimate living, that it was difficult to define exactly what this amounted to. Perhaps it was simply confirmation, a way of knowing that he mattered. It was impossible for him just to *be* with her. If she started talking about something that *mattered* to her, he wasn't able to take it, almost as if he were embarrassed by it. A strangely fearful look would come over him and she would check what she was saying. More often than not they ended up talking about work.

There are some people who don't let you think, who stop all your ideas from breathing, who kind of anaesthetize you to the truth, and these are the kind of people she had loved. Adam didn't want to talk about what was missing between them. He wanted to talk about what they could do to make things better. During these interminable talks, she would feel her body deflate, the life go down in her, until she became a dismayed weight on the bed.

Sometimes after sex she would fall into vivid dreams. In one memorable dream she was being carried over the back of someone's shoulder through a forest that seemed to be on fire. She always woke just as she was being dropped. In another dream she was visited by a chameleon creature with wrinkled browny-pink skin and blue eyes, who claimed to know all the secrets of the human heart. The creature was about the size of her hand and sat on her slate kitchen counter, swinging little pink legs with tiny webbed feet. It told her love would always remain out of her grasp until she found out who she was. When she asked how she could find out, the creature changed colour, from pink to blue and then melted into the slate.

Kennedy bursts into low laughter and she looks at him, startled, suddenly guilty for her drifting thoughts. He gets up and sits on the side of the bed, picking up her hand and stroking it. His skin smells of warm mushrooms and she has to resist an urge to put her arms around him and bury her face in his scent. He strokes her arm absently and she wonders what language is passing through his mind. What thoughts does he carry with him all the time? He reaches over her and lifts the curtain, pulling it back from the window so that daylight bounces into the room.

At breakfast he talks for a moment with Joshua in the kitchen. Sipping her coffee, she listens to the African language with its strange bitten-off rhythms that for some reason remind her of clockwork. Every now and again an English word or phrase breaks free from the bubble of conversation: 'Yes, tomorrow.' 'Actually, no.' Once she hears her own name spoken, and it startles her. She hadn't realized how African it sounds.

Joshua comes into the dining room and begins to clear away plates and cutlery, brushing the table with a coarse cloth, bending low, a pouch of loose skin wobbling on his neck. Afterwards he wipes the unused cutlery clean on a cloth pushed into the waistband of his trousers, holding each fork, knife and spoon up to the light to check for smears. He then replaces the cutlery in a box lined with blue velvet, which gives off a slight sour-cheese smell, snaps it shut and finally sweeps the floor. He uses a short palm broom, his eyes gentle and patient as he moves back and forth, his brush finding fallen insects, dried leaves and dust which he pushes on to a torn piece of fruit box to be shaken off outside.

In another world, he would be perhaps an architect, or graphic designer. Even a photographer; there were plenty she knew who showed the same interest in the patterning of things, the rigorous attention to detail, but in her world they were generally mocked for it. Irony, she thinks, cuts off integrity, never gives it the slightest chance.

Her world. The idea startles her. She had come to Africa, she supposed, to find out what the next thing was, but every day she saw something that mocked every sensibility, every belief or value she had. So far, Africa had brought her up short. London might seem trite in comparison: *up its own arse*, in its own language, but at least it was intelligible. At least it *had* an identity. Africa seemed so loose and unformed, a shapeless sort of place without any real boundaries. Each time she thought she had understood just one tiny thing it slipped from her grasp. If she were to sum up her experience so far it would be this feeling of having to keep on starting all over again.

Joshua finishes clearing the table. 'How is your headache?' he asks, looking at her, putting his head to one side in a gesture of infinite sympathy.

'My headache?' She doesn't remember mentioning a headache, but he clearly does. 'Much better, I'm feeling much better now.'

'Ah, that's a good idea.' Joshua takes another long look at her and then warmly pats her on the shoulder. She pours another cup of coffee and takes it with her out into the garden with a book. In the heat the new pages give off a faint smell of roast chicken. After a few pages she gives up. The novel is set in Texas and would be the kind of thing she'd devour on the tube in a couple of mornings, but here, her habits have changed. She realizes that she doesn't want to read someone else's story; she has an odd compulsion to write.

Going back into the house she finds paper in the desk drawer: heavy cream letter-writing paper with a watermark of an eagle, outstretched wings spreading across the centre of each page. In the top left-hand corner a name has been stamped with one of those old-fashioned ink pads: Wing Commander Peter Marsden. With a feeling of trepidation she writes her own name underneath it and then the date.

Dear Elise,

I'm sorry I haven't been in touch except to say where I am, but I've needed to be on my own with this because I feel . . .

Dear Elise,

Don't worry. I'm all right. I just needed some time on my own. I hope you are well and that work is . . .

Dear Elise,

I'm sitting here in a garden you must have known. There's a slight breeze and a smell of dry nuts. You never told me that even the air smells different in Africa. You never told me about the way the light comes through the trees, or the way that everything creaks and sways the whole time in the wind which never stops, not even at night, or the birds, so many birds, why did you never tell me their names? Why didn't you buy me books about Africa? You could have shown me where I came from in the atlas. You could have told me stories. Why didn't

you? Joshua made me breakfast this morning. You remember Joshua,
the old cook? He's still here, twenty years on, and his son, Kennedy,
perhaps you don't remember him? Well, he is here, too. Why did you
never describe the people here, the conversations you had, the parties
and dinners you went to? Why didn't you show me photographs? You
must have taken some. Being here now, I realize what I do not know,
what was kept from me. It's like my early life was a secret you refused
to share. You kept my memories from me. You never even talked to me
about the school you built, never described what it looked like. I was
here once, I was part of this. I woke and smelled this smell, listened to
the wind in the trees, felt the ground under my bare feet, the sun on my
arms and face. I washed in water from here, it ran into my pores. You
stole all this from me . . .

She writes, not forming phrases consciously, just putting down
whatever comes into her mind. As she writes she becomes aware
of how much anger she feels, how cut off from herself she has
been, but there's also a creeping fear and eventually she stops,
convinced that someone is calling her name.

Kennedy steps lightly across the grass and lifts his hand as she
looks up. Seeing him, she feels a rush of gratitude. He has
changed into his favourite rainbow pants and orange T-shirt. His
skin is still damp from the shower.

'Hi,' he says as he reaches her.

She drops her gaze into her lap where the writing pad rests
lightly across her knees. Her handwriting looks rushed, the
letters sloping backwards, almost lying down on their sides. Left-
handed letters, gawky writing Adam had called it, and there had
been the usual cack-handed jokes at school. Years later, at university, she remembers being utterly disturbed by a lecturer whose
comment about 'those of a sinister disposition' had obviously
been directed towards her. Discovering the keyboard had been a
liberating experience. She can still remember her first typewrit-
ten page, the quiet joy of it; the fact that it was completely neutral
made it all the more personal to her. Typed words contained

secrets that handwriting shouted out loud. Type was almost a code for Memory.

She even typed a diary on her first Amstrad, hiding it from Elise in cryptically named files. The diary was never printed out, but read late at night, its green glow comforting as she sat in her bedroom alone. Her thoughts then were mostly of rage and revenge. How to run away and become who she really was. She planned adventures for herself, invented new identities, saw herself elsewhere. One day she would get away and become clear. What happened was that she ended up needing to do things – earn money, for example, to pay off her student debts – and the life she was waiting to lead never quite happened, never quite opened out. Instead, everything had started to move inwards so that she had felt pinned in one place, as if someone had jabbed the spoke of an umbrella in her stomach and pushed her against a wall. Sitting in her office sometimes after everyone else had gone home, she would turn on her screen again and type out her name, the African version, just to see how it looked without anyone making a comment. MEMORY EDNA YAMBA.

Kennedy kneels down in the grass next to her and glances at the pages in her lap. 'You're writing a letter?'

'Yes, to my mother, except she's not really my mother. I'm trying to get her to understand why I've come.'

He strokes her arm. His fingers feel smooth and dry. 'Do you want to see your village?'

'My *village*?' she can barely speak.

'Yes, your village, the place where you were born. My father has told me where to find it. I asked him about it this morning.'

She can hardly breathe. She looks into his eyes and the darkness there makes her feel safe. He smiles at her, his teeth bright and smelling of something minty as he moves in closer and then takes her completely by surprise by kissing her on her forehead.

Startled, she pulls away and he bows his head. She tells him to wait for a moment and then, gathering up her books and writing paper, runs back inside the house. Joshua pauses in sweeping the

247

hallway and greets her as if she has been away on some long trip, clasping her hands in his and looking into her face. Eventually he releases her and returns to his sweeping with a wry smile. She feels as if a dozen small birds have been freed inside her chest as she rushes around packing a few essentials: camera bag, water, tissues, sunglasses. She shoves the half-written letters into an envelope on which she hurriedly writes out Elise's London address, and then zips them up in the side pocket of her camera bag. Glancing in the mirror she is surprised to see how fresh she looks despite lack of sleep.

They walk down the bush track. Waterfalls of dust and tiny gold insects tumble down from trees so outsized they seem to have raised the roof space over the world. Some of the leaves are the size of straw hats. She considers stopping to photograph them, but Kennedy, who insisted on carrying the camera bag, is striding ahead determinedly, head down, keeping his eye out for snakes.

After a mile of fast walking, they come to a village. A dozen dilapidated huts patched with feed bags and bits of torn cardboard squat in a clearing. A stale smell emanates from the ground which is blackened from so many stomped-on fires. The place feels like somewhere that had once been a village, until the people living there had lost interest. She feels no flicker of recognition and she wonders whether he has brought her to the right place.

A boy sitting under a shade of woven matting lifts his hand almost as if they are expected. He wears a pink shower cap on his shorn black head and sticks out the tip of his tongue. Kennedy greets him in English, which surprises her. The boy's eyes have a loose, shot look, and his wasted limbs dangle from his body, making him appear all head. At the sound of voices other children come out from huts and from under mats and plastic sheets, shuffling forward on bare dusted feet.

'Where are all the adults?' she wonders.

'At work,' Kennedy says quietly. In his eyes she detects the merest hint of tension.

'Of course.' She fiddles with her camera bag. It seems obscene to ask him to take a photograph of her near the huts. The smallest children stagger forward, grotty pastel leggings sagging between their knees, noses dripping with clouded snot. They wait expectantly. Kennedy instinctively crouches down to their level, his movements soft and inviting. Shyly clutching hands, a pair of girls, wearing party dresses several sizes too big with ripped flounces and ribbons, move forward an inch across the dirt and then stop; they look directly at her unblinking, four triangles of sunlight illuminating their cheeks. Memory finds their stillness unnerving; it's as if she were being observed by a pair of knowing stones.

The children shift position and acting on some silent communication others come forward, quickly arranging themselves as if for a school picture, preening their filthy rags like young starlets, dirty faces glowing from the unaccustomed attention. Their pride is agonizing, but she doesn't stop until she has photographed every child in the village. It seems essential somehow for her to do this.

When finally she runs out of film she looks around for Kennedy and sees that he has been watching with his back upright against a slender tree. He waves lazily. The group of children begin to disperse all except for one boy, younger than the rest, who toddles against the flow of the crowd, his blunt face set in an attitude of determined desperation, pushing the others out of the way with his solid little fists. At last he stands before her, thrusting out his plump starved stomach like a grotesque balloon. A beat of panic shoots through her as she realizes she hasn't got any more film. He continues standing before her, his fists gripping the sides of his shorts that were once green Lycra, but long since degraded into soiled nylon threads. Flies crawl around his eyes and at the corners of his mouth, glistening like caviar. She takes a pretend picture and then drops her camera on to her knee, indicating that she is finished. He continues to stand in front of her, his posture insistent, almost ruthless. She lifts the camera, but something about his expression makes her hesitate before fooling him again. He is staring at her with such shocking intensity, it's almost as if he can read her every thought.

Then something happens, a sort of flicker across his face, so subtle she could easily have imagined it, momentarily transforming him from a child to an old man. It lasts only seconds. When she draws her camera bag closer, it comes back, settling in his eyes, a dark kind of energy that seems to acknowledge the fact that he must live at a faster rate than ordinary people – that he must learn how to be a man before it is properly time. Memory scrabbles around in the side pockets of her bag. Her fingers close on a bunch of letters and there squashed into a corner is a forgotten film canister. The boy's eyes lift slightly as she fits the film into the camera and then takes his picture for real. The other children, sensitive to a change in mood, watch him as he thrusts his broad face up, smiling roundly as he is truly photographed.

When it is done the boy wanders over to the group without looking back. Kennedy gets up from his tree and joins her. He puts his hand on her arm and stands for a moment looking at her, his eyes troubled.

'I guess I'm finding it a bit emotional, suddenly coming here.'

'Are you remembering what it was like?'

'No. It's more than that.'

She wants to walk away and never come back, but finds herself agreeing to be shown round by the older boy in the shower cap. They wander around the huts in silence, poking at the odd flaps of plastic to see inside. A quiet feeling comes over her as Kennedy gently steers her away from the more dilapidated huts, trying to make the village seem less painful. The boy says he wants to show them inside his own hut.

Grinning and talking to himself, he leads them into a pungent hut that feels like a hot cave. A few possessions are hung about the mud walls and these he shows off proudly: a mousetrap displayed as a piece of art, wire workings intricate as clockwork;

flattened boxes of Omo and Daz turned into posters; and a broken fluorescent light tied to a rafter with pink string. The most treasured object he saves until last, delivered with an embarrassed shuffle: a scuffed wooden cabinet filled with plastic cups, preciously arranged in order of size like the best kind of lead crystal. He wants her to photograph it, but she shakes her head and mutters something about it being too dark. Coming out of the hut, the glare outside is so blinding she has to bring her arm up to shield her eyes.

The children insist on one last group shot, draping themselves over each other in loose poses with the close ferocity of a large family and she wonders whether she had lived this way too, without adults, in ragged clothes. She feels no disappointment at not being able to remember, only a sense of loss as if she has arrived too late.

Tracking back through the bush, the trees give off a subdued blue light. Kennedy walks quietly beside her, head down, lost in some thought, every now and then bending to pluck a strand of elephant grass to chew on. She feels a deep tiredness, an urge to sleep for days; all her limbs feel heavy and it is an effort to keep going. Kennedy waits for her at the top of the track and when she passes gives her shoulder a squeeze. They reach the house, windows glowing orange, smoke curling from the fire Joshua must have lit, the lawn tidy under moonlight. Kennedy takes her arm. 'Memory, you are a very beautiful friend.'

She doesn't know what to say. He smiles at her. The way he is looking at her makes her think of the word 'fond'. She likes the way the word sounds in her head, its simple resonance. She wonders why it is so often used disparagingly. She says it to him now.

'Kennedy, I am so incredibly fond of you.'

'That's good.' He strokes her shoulder. 'We should always be good friends.'

'We will. Thank you for today, for taking me to the village.'

'You are not so sad tonight?'

'No, I'm not feeling sad, just tired.' She puts her arms around his neck and breathes in his warmth. 'Go home, I'll be all right.'

'You sure?' He looks her up and down. 'I could sleep on the floor.'

'I'll be fine, really.'

He steps back from her. His rainbow pants are covered with a thin coating of dust and seem somehow defeated.

'Come for breakfast tomorrow,' she adds.

His face splits in the darkness, a beat of brilliance that she carries with her into the dark house where supper waits on the kitchen table, plates covered with a white cloth, and next to them, anticipating power failure, a candle stub on a saucer and small box of matches. She lights the candle then sits down to unwrap her solitary supper of cold lamb, potatoes and bitter relish. Drawn by the light, dragonflies drift in from outside and dance against the surfaces, touching the fridge and light casings with huge silver wings. Their shadows appear like Chinese fighting kites swooping about the kitchen.

Walking into her bedroom, the saucer of candle wax warm under her palm, she considers what preparations the village children might be making for bed and realizes that what she has come to regard as essential is for them unimaginable. She washes her face and makes sure that she does not leave the tap running. Slipping between cold cotton sheets, she tries to imagine how it would be to sleep every night on the ground with the smell of earth and smoke, the sounds of others close by, and finds it oddly comforting. But then just as she is drifting into sleep she wakes with a start, a strong yeasty smell filling her nostrils, heart hammering with unknown panic. She lies straight and tries to calm her breathing, wondering where the smell comes from and why it seems so familiar.

The next afternoon while Kennedy is sleeping off lunch, she leaves a note sellotaped to the fridge: *Gone walking, love Memory xxx*. She hesitates over the kisses, wondering whether they might be misconstrued, but decides it would look worse to cross them out. The garden is hot and still, the trees give off a sweet, resinous scent and under her feet the grass is warm and crisp. Wood doves call from shady branches and in the distance she can hear the low chugging of the bird that reminds her of a car making its way slowly down a hill. The sun stings her shoulders.

She arrives at a clearing. From here she can see the coffee farm with its silver metal roof and fresh green lawn. It looks tranquil, the neat hedges of coffee plant laid out on both sides of the house in two symmetrical halves like two open palms or leaves of a book. The house itself, a yellow-brown building surrounded by a peeling white veranda, appears empty even from this distance.

The veranda door is open, but Max is not at home, at work, she guesses. The kitchen and sitting room are open-plan and furnished in varnished caramel wicker, the cushions on the sofa scratched and torn, the white stuffing showing. At the window a pair of heavy beige curtains with dark brown stitching alternating in vertical lines and circles hang precariously on too few hooks. The only other feature is a low glass table strewn with farming magazines, a coffee mug with a chipped lip and a scrawl of dried orange peel. She walks around tentatively, wondering why she has come. The place smells flat and airless, as if the person who comes here spends as little time as possible in its rooms. Draped on the arm of a wicker chair is a single grey cotton sock. She keeps her arms folded to avoid touching anything.

There are no pictures on the walls, no photographs, no *evidence*, nothing other than the slightly stale things of a man who has lived for many years alone. Except she now had something else. A few days ago Kennedy had gone to check with Civil Aviation in Lusaka. It was surprisingly easy, he said. The records of all accidents were stored in box files and the attendant had handed over the lot. Kennedy had quickly discovered that during 1972, the year of the Cougan crash, a plane had gone down, but on the east wing of the country in the Marungu Mountains close to the border in Zaire. According to the report, which Kennedy had accidentally put in his bag to take home for her, the cause was 'unknown'. The pilot was Swedish, aged thirty-seven, a doctor. She had read the report perhaps a thousand times, and then put it in an envelope and left it beside her bed. She was too frightened to carry it around in case Max sensed she had it.

The confirmation that the plane crash was a lie did not shock her. She felt mostly disappointed, a vague sense of being pushed into a place she didn't want to go. The feeling had not persisted; she had always known that it was covering up something else, but now she found that she did not want to know what that really was. It was strange, but the closer she came to the truth, the less she wanted to confront it.

Now wandering through Max's meagre rooms she is struck by a sudden urge to *know*. She lifts covers and rugs, opens cupboards and drawers, scrabbles under vests and shorts, rakes between shirts hanging with amputated arms and digs into the pocket of a dark suit. She realizes she is looking for a single key that will open up all the closed doors. She finds folds of money and a programme from a flying show tucked under some T-shirts, nibbled around the neck. All his clothes have a limp, well-used quality, a *fondness* even. She replaces them carefully, suddenly anxious at the sound of the screen door banging outside.

She feels safer out on the veranda where she might be expected to wait if she really had come round to talk. The sky burns. Across the lawn a sprinkler spurts nervous jets of water, hissing on its axis. On its next turn she sees a blurred figure coming towards her, grey head bent, a decayed root where the left leg should be. The arms leaning on his crutches are at once elegant and awkward, like crumpled wings. He draws closer, his crutches making a sandpapery rasping against the ground. She can hear the hoarseness of his breath and see the determination in his eyes. She leans against one of the veranda posts for support. She will not bolt. She will stay and wait. All around the outside of the house the air is filled with tiny golden flies, swirling into a frantic dance.

Max steps into the insect storm, wipes the sweat from his brow and blinks. 'Memory,' he says, glancing back over his shoulder as if he had forgotten something. 'I didn't know you were coming.'

She feels her stomach tighten. 'I want to ask you about Paul Cougan.'

He collapses slightly on his crutches and looks up at her, eyes the colour of twilight. She feels him gather himself for a moment and then he leans on his crutches and lurches on to the veranda. He sways precariously and she has to resist reaching out to save him. Righting himself, he turns with little hopping movements and rests his hand on the back of a cane chair. His breathing is laboured and his face is running with sweat. 'Sit down,' he says. 'I'll go and find us something to drink.'

She leans back into her seat, feeling the cane press against her spine. Max heaves himself into the kitchen and she hears him open the fridge. The sound of glass shattering on the floor makes her jump. Over on the lawn the sprinkler twists and turns, spinning water in rainbow arcs, almost enjoying a dance with itself. The borders under the veranda are heavy with fragrant plants: hibiscus, orchid, lilies and frangipani, lushly incongruous against the starkness of the house. She hears Max sweeping up the glass and pouring the shards into the bin. Then he opens the fridge again and she hears the slight clunk of two bottles. The fridge door closes with a sigh. Her stomach tightens again as he begins his slow shuffling walk back outside.

He makes his way on to the veranda, carrying two bottles of Coke, holding them loosely by the necks as if he were carrying a pair of newly slaughtered chickens. He puts her bottle on a low table near her elbow and keeps hold of his own, hugging it awkwardly against his stomach as he manoeuvres himself down into his chair. When he is finally seated he uses his hand to shift his damaged leg quickly into position. He takes several rapid sips of his drink and then wipes his mouth. Then he leans forward, eyes downcast, his gaze fixed on a sunlit square of wooden floorboard just in front of his foot. 'What do you want to know?' He twists his Coke bottle round, his fingers nervously rubbing at the raised pattern on the glass.

'Everything. I want to know everything you can tell me about Paul Cougan.' Even to her, the words sound breathless and sharp, thrilling almost.

Max glances at the lawn, his eyes steady as he takes in its perfect symmetry, spoiled only by little dark pools of fallen fruit. He looks around the borders, where the dahlias and sunflowers are in full bloom, bursting with indignant colour. He nods and then looks at her, taking her aback with the blueness of his gaze. She feels her heart rise and begin to pound, her palms grow clammy as she realizes the enormity of what she is asking. She feels ashamed as if she has disturbed something delicate, but also curious because his look is telling her that there is more to this than she thought.

'Paul.' Max says his name and closes his eyes. His breath rises and falls. His lids flutter as if something is trapped underneath them. Then he opens his eyes, which now seem dull. 'I'm sorry,' Max says. 'I can't.' His voice drops. 'I don't know how to.' He looks away into the distance. 'Maybe you could help me.'

Memory swallows, not sure how to proceed. She hadn't realized how difficult this would be. 'What should I do?'

'Ask questions,' Max says, his voice husky. 'Ask me questions and I will try to answer. It will be easier than . . .'

'OK.' She wonders whether it would be better not to pursue it at all. She could just go, spare him the ordeal of having to drag his memory back more than twenty years. Her throat tightens as she looks at Max sitting with his head bowed. She listens to his breathing for a moment and feels a breeze flutter against her face, like moth wings. Something tiny leaps inside her, a beat of hope, and then suddenly resolved, she directs all her strength towards him. She must not falter now. She must know the truth. 'Tell me how Paul Cougan died . . . I know it's difficult, but I need to know; it's the reason I'm here.'

Max lifts his head and looks at her. His eyes are watery, the rims blood sore. He blinks and chews, his bristly chin moving stiffly. 'I always thought you might come back,' he says, keeping his eyes on the lawn where water is leaping in loose, playful arcs. 'I always knew this would happen. It was just a question of being prepared for it, but as you can see I'm not.' He pulls his gaze from the lawn and looks down at his thighs.

'Well, neither am I.' She tries to keep her tone light to encourage him, but he keeps his head turned away from her, his eyes fixed on the horizon.

She hugs her arms and leans towards him. 'Max, there's something I need to say to you: I need you to know how it has felt for me all these years, how odd it has been having someone's name and not knowing who that person is. Can you imagine how strange it is being called by a name that has nothing to do with you? It feels like every time my name is used, it is asking a question – a question I can't answer. I've been called *Cougan* for as long as I can remember. I don't have any memories of any other time, do you realize that? And because I am a *Cougan*, I need to know. I need to know who Paul Cougan is because he is what I have become. Does that make any sense to you at all?'

Max sits breathing for a long moment, his eyes still trained on the horizon where the flat red disc of the sun is beginning to soften. He bows his head and nods several times. 'I have thought about you over the years,' he says. 'I always wondered what you would end up doing.'

'But I can't go back until I know what happened here. You need to tell me, Max. I can't wait any longer. I need to know something about this man I've never met.'

Max looks directly at her. 'You did meet him.'

'What?' She is surprised to find hot tears on her cheeks.

Max sits completely still. Only the air is moving, swarming with the tiny golden flies, meeting and separating over and over again in a delirious nimbus. Then he makes a sound that is partly a gasp, partly a sigh and swings his head from side to side. As if floating on water, the flies disperse. 'He saved your life,' he says. He looks down at his broken knee.

She wants to hit him. She wants to get up from her chair and swipe her hand across his face. Then she is sobbing, kneading her fists into her lap. He reaches over and offers his hand and she takes it, clinging on to it, pressing against his bent knuckles with her fingers until the knots inside her release their tension.

'Tell me,' she finally breathes. 'Just tell me.' Max drops her hand and turns his face away from her and back towards the horizon, streaked with feathered lines of pink and apricot and violet. He lets his eyes melt against the cooling sky, and then he begins to speak.

14

INSTRUMENT FLYING: GENERAL REMARKS

It is through his eyes that a pilot largely obtains his sense of balance and position. Remove either his sight or ability to see outside objects and his sensory powers disappear, often producing sensations completely the reverse to the fact.

Zambia, 1972

Max let Elise take the elevator column. The morning had been turbulent, but now the sky was clear and carried a soft lifting wind. She took over the controls smoothly, impressing him with her confidence. She was a natural flier, her approach calm and intelligent. She flicked her eyes across the dials, checking their speed and altitude. She had tied her hair back from her face, which showed her ears and the line of her neck. Her earlobes were tiny, two soft downy pads, which were now flushed with the heat. When the sun came up it was always blinding in the cockpit. He could see the start of a tear, like a single raindrop, in the corner of her left eye.

'Max, I need to make a medium turn, but I'm worried about skidding out.' Her eyes were steady, fixed on the horizon.

'Push your stick slightly forward, now a little top rudder, not too much.' Her thighs shifted under the thin cotton of her skirt as she pressed her feet on the rudder. She normally wore jeans, but now it was coming up to the dry season she said they were too hot and restrictive for flying. She shifted in her seat and corrected the plane, shooting him a glance that made him exhale sharply.

'Now, keep a look-out for other aircraft and start to make your landing approach.'

She leaned forward excitedly. 'We're nearly there! I can see the wind sock.'

'Right, keep away from the boundary and fly to the downwind side. That's it, you're doing great.' He watched a smile hover over her lips.

'When do I start to close the throttle?'

'Wait until you're within gliding distance; right, that's it, about now.' She began to shut the engine down. He could hear the wind lift the wings, rattling the flaps, which gave a slight whine. The plane began to rock. He leaned forward. This was her third landing and he wanted her to get it right. 'Set your tail trim, watch the ground. Your position is correct, now turn head into wind, good. Lower your flaps. You're drifting, well done, well corrected, centralize, check glide, ease your stick back.'

'Max, I'm dropping too fast . . .' He could see the tension in her neck.

'No, you're fine, back with the stick, more, more.'

'I'm not straight . . .' Her voice rose. Her teeth were set. He considered taking over, but they were so close. A little fast, but so close.

'Ease your stick right back. You're going to land.'

'I'm not!' Her lips flinched back.

The plane bounced down on her three points, sending a jolt through him. 'Right, keep her straight, retract your flaps and come to a standstill.'

'I didn't think I was going to do it.' Her eyes gleamed as she taxied across the aerodrome, wheels crackling over the red grit surface. He swallowed and looked at the sky thick with orange dust.

Just before they climbed down she glanced at him. Her hair clung damply to her forehead and two slender rivers of sweat ran down her neck and seeped into the deep V of her T-shirt. He peeled his gaze away from her and looked down from the side window where the hard-baked earth was just visible, like brittle pie pastry, all cracked around the edges. He wanted to tell her how well she had landed, but somehow he couldn't.

The air felt hot around his eye sockets as they walked across the aerodrome and filled in the paperwork at the pilot desk. He kept his hand curled around the paper as he wrote because he didn't want her see how awkward he found it.

They took a taxi into town where Max bought animal feed for the farm. While he was paying, peeling notes from a sour wad of kwacha, Elisa walked around the cool shed where maize poured from a huge funnel with a sound like the sea washing over pebbles. Max watched her bending over seed boxes, her hair rippling forward, as she picked out packets he would never have considered: sunflower, dahlia and peony. She brought the flower seeds up to the African attendant and made to pay, but Max gave him the rest of the money. Smiling, Elise put the packets into the pocket of her skirt. They walked out into the sun again and Max could see the cloudy rosette of a peony bobbing against her hip.

He had not taken anyone to the town house before. As he unlocked the door, using the key Marsden had given him, for it had once been his house, bought for his retirement, but never used, he wondered what he was opening up. The familiar smell of animal and dust prickled his nostrils as they went in. He heard her breathing behind him. She went straight to the mezzanine and stood looking into the eyes of the lion. The trophy had been given to Marsden by an Italian whose life he had saved after a shooting accident in the Rift Valley. Marsden had told Max the story one night as they drank champagne on his veranda. The Italian had been showing off for a woman when the gun went off and caught him in the foot. He would have bled to death had Marsden not stopped the wound with a sleeve ripped from his safari shirt. Most of the trophies were gifts to the wing commander for other acts of generosity, but some animals Max had shot himself during a couple of lean years on the farm when he had taken on a job as a guide for a private game reserve.

He watched Elise run her eyes over the display. He had seen the trophies so many times that they just seemed part of the furniture, but seeing her expression, a mixture of dismay and awe, he wondered whether she thought he had brought her here to show off, like the Italian.

'I didn't shoot them all,' he said watching her face. 'I used to take parties to game reserves and because some of these people had never learned to fire a rifle properly, they made mistakes.'

'So you put the animals down?' She lifted her head towards a fine young antelope.

'Yes.'

She turned away from the trophies and went into the front room. She sat down in one of the red leather chairs near the fire which had never been lit. He took the other chair and faced her.

She shuddered. 'What will you do with this place, Max?'

'I don't know. Marsden was saving it for his retirement, maybe I should save it for mine.'

'I can't see you ever living here. Too many ghosts.'

'Where will you live, Elise?' The words shook as he said them.

Her eyes were downcast. 'I'm trying to ignore what I feel, but it isn't working. I'm living in my mind and that means I'm living with you.'

'Don't . . .'

'I can't go back, not to the way I was.'

'I'm not asking you for anything.'

She lifted her eyes and looked him full in the face. Her voice snagged. 'I know, Max. I know you're not.'

He dragged his chair closer to hers and took both her hands. They sat with their knees pressed together. He could not look at her. He could only feel her through his closed eyes, holding him. He knew that if he spoke, if he really let her know what he felt, it would mean the end of solitude – and that he couldn't live with. Solitude had been the one certainty in his life, the one comfort. It had made him who he was. If he let go of solitude he would become nothing. Holding her, he told her that he wanted to take her to the Broken Hill Mine for their last flight.

They took off one hot afternoon. At lunch she'd been unable to eat much and Paul had asked whether she felt unwell. He had been sick with food poisoning himself, which had stopped him going to the school. It occupied most of his time, now. Even though he had continued his flying lessons and still intended to take his pilot's exams with her after they had both flown solo, she knew that he had lost his enthusiasm for it. The school was more important to him and he went early every morning to teach a reading and writing class. In the afternoons, while she flew with Max, he helped the children with their garden and had planted the seeds they had bought.

Juliet's engine thrummed steadily as she climbed away from the farm with its orderly rows of green coffee plant and into a sky so clean it made her heart expand. Max was quiet beside her, his big knees stilled from their usual restless rocking. The tremor had started after they had visited the town house, affecting both knees, but worst in the left. It was so severe sometimes that Max could not rudder and she had to fly on her own.

On the dashboard there was a printed instruction, white on black: *Acrobatic manoeuvres are limited to the following. Spins (flaps up). Steep turns 129 mph. Lazy eights. Chandelles.* She imagined for a moment taking the plane and spinning her upside down and then brushed the thought from her mind.

They flew over villages, huts dainty against the hard flat earth, great stretches of deep forest and swampland where birds waded on wire-thin legs. A flock of flamingos scattered as their shadow flitted across one reach of water, filling the air with a luminous beating of wings and dry, panicked cries.

The mine was in rocky country. Pits and craters showed up as dark pools in the broken-up landscape which was busy with tiny workers pushing wheelbarrows and carrying shovels. She began to prepare for descent. She thought she would go as low as she could and make a few circuits, but then Max leaned forward and told her to signal for landing.

'What, here?' The uneven ground lurched towards her.

'Go on a bit, you'll see the strip.'

She eased back on the stick and straightened her wings. The ground bumped past and then over a rocky ridge she saw a darker patch of red dirt with a torn windsock flapping in the breeze. She eased *Juliet* into position and came down lightly on her wheels.

They listened to the plane chinking as she cooled down. Max sighed and rubbed his face. He hadn't shaved, she noticed, and there were shadows under his eyes which had a hooded look. Glancing away from him, she reached under the dashboard for the black notebook with the elastic strap in which she recorded all her hours. She had clocked up enough almost to qualify as a pilot, all her lessons named and numbered in her secret diary of flight along with manoeuvres completed and areas still to be worked on. Elise read her little notes. She had studied some of the passages from *The Complete Flying Course*: low flying, steep turns, side-slipping, night flying, and had come to know them all by heart. She now understood the effects of slipstream, staying in and maintaining bank; she had mastered spinning, slow landings, fast landings and landing in a strong wind. The only lesson she had not completed was solo flight.

They climbed out. A flock of tiny gold birds took off from the edge of the strip, rising in unison like a small cyclone, spinning into the distance, a ribbon wrapped tightly around an invisible maypole. Their shadows touched at the shoulder and hip as they walked across to the mine.

One of the workers told them where to find the cave, pointing with his thin black arm to an area of jagged rock. They had to bend low to enter and walk through a tunnel. Carrying a torch, Max went first and she kept close to his back, watching his neck. The walls were clammy and the sudden chill on her chest made her cough.

'All right?' Max looked at her, his eyes blinking in the torch-light. 'We can go up again.'

'No. I want to see.' She tried to push down her fear. The surface underfoot felt soft and gritty. She wondered whether she was walking on the remains of the dead.

They came to an open area with an arched ceiling. She guessed this was the bone cave. Max shone his torch around, picking out the salt crystal sparkle of stalactites hanging in a great ragged curtain from the roof. More cone-shaped masses erupted from the cave floor, rising up to meet the suspended rock icicles, some fused together; the cream, brown and red colours reminded her of slabs of meat on a butcher's counter. The only sound came from their breathing and the regular drip of water that resounded through the cave like a pulse. Her father had said Broken Hill Man had been helped as he lay dying from the abscess in his jaw. She wondered whether the cave with its strange, anatomical rock formations had been his safe place, the place where no other being, animal or human, could harm him. Perhaps this was the place where he had come to be loved, where he had felt the touch of another and known that he was not going to die alone. Perhaps this was the place where love was born in the deep heart of the earth. Max's torch caught the stalagmites and stalactites and she pointed out to him which were which, pleased that she had remembered this detail from her father. She imagined him here in the cave, with his notebook and rucksack, his bony student eagerness and quickening eyes and felt a pull of sadness that felt like homesickness.

Needing air, she left the cave first, Max following behind her, treading carefully over the surface, moving the grit with the toe of his boot as if looking for more bones. Back on the landing strip, he made the pre-flight checks, running his hands over *Juliet*'s flank, testing her flaps and propeller with his fingers, his expression intense. The breeze lifted the hairs on his arms and chest as he held the dipstick up to the light to check the oil. He swallowed when he caught her gaze and looked off into the distance where the sky had taken on a dull metal colour.

When they had strapped themselves in again, she asked him to pilot. She leaned back in the seat as he took off, arms straight on the column. His knees were quieter now that he had something to focus on and the tension in his jaw had relaxed. She looked down over Broken Hill and again thought about the creature, imagining it drawn into a foetal position in the cave, its animal back breathing shallowly against the pain in its jaw; the helper, perhaps a female sitting on its haunches in the dark, listening to the slow drip of water echo through its brain. She would have liked to have asked her father whether he thought Broken Hill Man and his helper had minds or souls. Maybe they were creatures of pure instinct, a bundle of action and reactions, the need to survive creating their bond. Maybe love was a simple urge to live. She felt a pressure behind her eyes and kept her gaze fixed on the sky. Beside her Max shifted and then with a swift almost rough action pulled her hand into his and held onto it as if it were the most vital thing he had ever touched. She heard herself gasp and then the words began to tumble from her, words she promised herself she wouldn't say. Words of need, of survival, of love.

When they got into the jeep it was dark. They had not stayed away so long before. Max drove quickly down the track, following the smooth grooves along the sides, avoiding the holes in the centre. The trees swayed overhead, bending in the wind, the moon racing between feathered branches. Every now and then a pale owl swooped across the headlights.

He held on to the steering wheel tightly and tried not to look at her face which was drawn and still. Flying back from Broken Hill he had seen an orange glow that signalled the start of bush fire and now he wanted to check where it was. The jeep bucked in and out of a deep hole and slammed back onto the dirt. He saw her jump with pain as her temple caught against the door jamb. He forced himself not to reach over to her. Driving more carefully, he felt as if all the air had been squeezed from his lungs.

'Why?' She said into the dark. 'Why are we doing this? What if this is important?'

'It is.' He kept his eyes on the road.

'If we do nothing, Max, we might regret it for the rest of our lives.'

He gripped the wheel. 'We will regret it whatever we do.'

'You can't know that, how can you know that?'

Max pushed the jeep on a little faster. The stars were blurry lights in the trees ahead and he shoved his hand across his eyes to clear them. Now he could smell and taste smoke. Elise began to say something and stopped abruptly. Up ahead a flaming branch was falling in slow motion across the track with the splitting sound of an axe being driven into dry wood.

The first rings of fire looked strangely cheering as if someone had taken the trouble to light the way by shining torches in the spaces between the trees. Max drove on, keeping his eye out for falling branches. Inside the bush he could see more rings of fire, feeding on oxygen, multiplying until there were rings overlapping rings, each one encircling a blackened stump. It took him a moment to register that the small fires were dancing around burned down trees, and that the whole bush was in flames.

Hurling the jeep around a corner, he reached his coffee fields and there opened up a whole stretch alight, dangerously low and flickering. There were twenty or so fires fanning across the landscape with a terrible internal light. Sparks soared on sails of smoke and the air was filled with an ecstatic crackling as whole sheds and barns were eaten by the flames. The main house, however, was just off the route the fire seemed to be taking, and sat untouched, its white veranda looking oddly innocent and peaceful in the midst of the yellow inferno. Arms braced on the steering wheel Max sat motionless. Smoke sneaked its way under a gap in the window, making Elise cough and gag. She turned to him with streaming eyes. 'Max, I'm frightened.'

Her fear activated him. Pushing the jeep into reverse he drove as hard as could to a position he thought safe. Then he shouted at her to stay where she was. He got out. The smoke swarmed into his throat, making him bend double. The sky reared with flames and seemed to engulf him. Holding his stomach he ran towards his fields where streams of workers were hurling buckets at the flames. He caught sight of someone, a man sprinting as hard as he could, legs pumping, green shirt billowing at his back. He headed towards Max, chest heaving from effort, face drenched in sweat, his eyes wild. Max saw that it was his security guard Geoff Seven.

'Sir.' The guard stood breathlessly to attention. 'Sir.' He swallowed; his lips trembled. 'Sir, the fire has taken the school.' He waved his arm back towards the plume of smoke.

Max ran back towards the jeep where she sat white-faced, watching the flames.

'What's happening, have you lost your fields?'

He shook his head and wrenched the jeep backward over the rough ground. He drove straight into a storm of smoke. It poured through every gap and crevice, filling the jeep interior with a stinging, acrid haze. Elise screamed and flung herself against her seat as the smoke thickened around them, closing in on their throats. Outside great plumes of fire rose in huge almost joyous columns against the sky, cackling and cracking, shooting jagged fountains of sparks in great arcs, like long lines of frayed burning rope. The bush looked like the aftermath of an explosion with trees twisted across tracks and blazing huts, thatched roofs burning with a terrible clear brightness.

They reached the school and climbed out. The first sound Max heard was a frenzied high barking and then he saw his dog Lucky yapping at the flames, yellow jaws working mechanically, the whites of his eyes rolling as branches fringed with flame fell across his path. Seeing his master he barked even more furiously, his instinct to guard driven mad. The school was completely alight, the great wooden A-shaped beams wreathed in vicious licks of blue and tangerine as they were eaten to their core. Max watched one beam break in the middle, splintering into two jagged arms that flared grotesquely before falling into a heap of smouldering charcoal. The thatched roof was gone, except for the thicker edges, which spat streams of sparks. The windows were being sculpted into crude new shapes by licks of orange. Planks of timber that had required the strength of four men to carry were gobbled in seconds. Around the perimeter, smaller bonfires flared in the wind, flames flying free in the sky like comets with bright tails.

'Keep back,' he yelled as Elise rushed forward. Ignoring him, she plunged further and without thinking he lunged at her like a lion about to bring down a gazelle. Grabbing her arm, he flung her to the ground and then ploughed on ahead. When he glanced back, he saw her sit up and rub her arm and ankle, her face contorted. He ran across to a group of Africans who had formed a human chain around the school, passing buckets and cans of water, bare chests slick with sweat. He joined them, bracing his feet, taking the next can of water in his arms, holding it up so he wouldn't slip, feeling it slosh against his shirt, which he ripped off before the next pail reached him. More men joined the chain and the pails came faster, the men in front hurling them at the fire with greater force as if the effort might drive the flames back. Near the top of the chain he saw the red bullock shape of Joe Baxter, stripped to the waist, trying to put out rebel fire rings on the ground with his boots, temper at boiling point as he kicked and stamped. Further down the line was the boyish frame of Paul, in a white vest streaked with black, his face haggard and grey. Noticing Max, he wearily lifted his hand before taking his next bucket and pouring it uselessly at the fire; the school was going down like a sinking ship and all the buckets and containers seemed empty gestures of rescue.

Realizing they had been defeated, the men stood and watched as a large section of the roof fell in slow motion, brazenly taking the entire rear wall which collapsed like a giant flaring picture frame. Then there was nothing but a mound of smoking ash around which they all stood, wiping away tears from the smoke.

The only sound was Lucky who continued to bark, his voice never giving up its insane optimism.

The kitchen smelled of burning. They sat at the table around a candle stub, which cast a dirty light. Electricity surged around the house, intermittently turning on the refrigerator and flickering lights. The wind stormed outside, banging the gate. No one made eye contact. It was as if they were all suddenly at war with one another. A strong smell of charcoal rose from the dog cowering under the table at Max's feet. Every now and then he gave an anxious yelp.

'Shut up, Lucky,' Paul said dully. 'It's over.'

Elise sighed and rubbed at a black patch on her arm. Her hair was grey with smoke. She caught Max looking at her and flinched.

Lucky yipped, his tail twitching under the table. 'Come here,' Max said and pulled the dog's head tenderly on to his knees and kneaded the fat ruff of fur around his neck. The fridge chimed and gurgled, making them all jump for a second or two and then the light died. Elise scraped her fingernail in the oozing warm wax around the candle stub.

Paul rose from his seat. 'I'll go and look for more candles, there might be some in the dining room.' He sounded weary, his voice strained from the smoke. His face and arms were thick with grime and his clothes seemed to sit on him heavily.

Elise watched him go, her eyes listless across the table. He wanted to reach and hold her, tell her he was sorry.

Paul returned and lit a candle, his hand shaking slightly as he blew on the match. Max knew he ought to go back to the farm, but he did not have enough strength to make the journey across the bush. Out of the corner of his eye, he watched Paul put his head down on the table and groan. 'I can't believe it.' His voice was muffled by his arms. 'All that work.' He lifted his face and looked at Max. 'I can't believe it's all been for nothing.'

Elise reached forward and picked at the candle wax on the table, her own expression hidden in her hair. She didn't try to comfort Paul, Max noticed. Perhaps she realized that he was beyond comforting.

They sat in the silence, the only sound the breathing whine of the dog who was now asleep, his head resting on Max's foot. Max felt a sense of despair fall over them. He could almost touch it, rub it between his fingers like fine net. He searched his mind for something to push it away, to stop things closing over.

Paul spoke first: 'What will you do, Max? How much have you lost?'

'Hardly anything.' It was true, his farm had escaped the worst of it. There had been other years when his entire crop had been wiped out. 'It's a setback,' Max said. 'That's all. You get used to fire living in the bush; we can rebuild.' At the note of hope in his voice, Lucky lifted his muzzle and pushed his nose between Max's knees. He stroked the narrow bones on the dog's yellow head. He felt calm and in control. It could be done; they could rebuild the school; it all depended on time, on how much longer they were prepared to stay.

Paul's brow was knitted. 'But it took us weeks. It would be like starting again.'

'That's what we'll do. That's what we have to do. We can start after the rains.' Max felt excitement lap in his belly. If they stayed – just the thought was enough to give him encouragement.

Elise gave him an intense look from under her hair, which she was combing out with her fingers, teasing it apart strand by strand. 'We can't stay.'

Paul sat up straight. He was staring at Max with a thoughtful look in his eyes. 'We could,' he said slowly, looking at Max as though he were testing him for truth. 'What's stopping us?'

'Our college courses,' Elise said, dropping her hair and flicking it back over her shoulder where Max noticed the beginnings of a bruise. 'Only our futures.' Her voice cracked and he saw Paul glance at her with concern. 'We can't stay. It would be irresponsible.'

Paul directed a steady, clear look at Max. 'Our future could be here. Maybe this is what it takes for us to realize it. This could be what we need.'

Elise stood up, hair flying around her. 'We have to go home.'

Tears streamed unchecked down her cheeks and he saw Paul's look of alarm. Paul reached for her arm, but she shook him off passionately and walked to the window where she stood with her back turned to them both. Max felt as if a ball of indigestible fibre had lodged in his throat. He looked at her shoulders heaving slightly in the soft candlelight and pushed his fist against his chest to stem the pain right in the centre of his breastbone.

'We shouldn't decide tonight,' he said, trying to keep his voice steady.

'Max is right,' said Paul, his face tight. 'It is a setback not a tragedy.'

Elise remained where she was, looking out on to the starless night. Max stared after her, every part of him longing to go up and take her in his arms. He knew that Paul was feeling the same and for a moment he felt an understanding flicker between them. She would listen to Paul later, Max thought. She would let Paul persuade her that they should stay. He stood up, scraping his chair more roughly than he intended and announced that he was going.

The dog followed him, clicking across the floor on his claws, tail held high, as if setting off on an adventure. He tried not to look at Elise as he passed the window. The jeep smelled of smoke as he climbed in. He turned the key in the ignition and felt it jerk against his hand. The engine was dead. Now he remembered: they had left the headlights on when they got back to the house because it had been too dark to cross the garden. Paul had tried his torch and found it dead. Max rested his head on the wheel and thought of the cave; the feel of cold ancient rock and the smell of deep water seemed to pull at him with a magnetic force. Anxious to get home, Lucky whined from the back seat.

After a moment Max got out and returned to the house. He thought that they would have realized his battery was dead and would be waiting for him. But the kitchen was in darkness, a whiff of candle smoke indicating that they had taken the lighted saucer with them. He sat down at the kitchen table and gave the dog a moment to arrange himself at his feet, watching him circle a few times as he tried to find a comfortable spot. He wondered whether they had gone straight to bed and the thought tightened his chest.

He put his head down on the kitchen table and tried to sleep, but he couldn't shake off images of fire: flames travelling across fields in low flickering tongues, igniting everything they touched; trees falling in great showers of sparks, roofs collapsing, tiny desks and chairs eaten up. The school falling like a deck of cards. How easily it had gone. Now Max felt the full force of the loss. They had put everything they had into the school. Every day they had added something new, a door, or window frame, a coat of paint. Even the small garden that Paul had made had been burned, the little buried seeds scorched before they had time to make their way up through the soil. He had thought that they could rebuild, but now he didn't feel so sure. The work would take months and he didn't know if Elise would give them that time. She was the one who would now decide for all of them. It made Max feel afraid.

Doubt collecting in the pit of his stomach, he got up from the table and paced around the kitchen, pausing every now and then to listen for voices. At one point he thought he heard her murmur his name and it almost made him go to her, but he managed to keep a hold of himself. He walked around until he felt calmer. Then he sat in the dark with his dog at his feet and waited.

15

INVERTED FLIGHT

A particularly careful survey of the sky should be made before inverting, as then the outlook is very poor. When inverted, the feet tend to leave the rudder bar and a conscious effort must be made to keep them in position.

Zambia, 1972

Paul reached the clearing. Stripped of its filter of leaves the sky was cruelly blue, marked only by smudged ribbons of smoke streaming from the smouldering remains on the ground. What could be salvaged from the school had been dragged outside. A blackboard leaned against a tree, chalked with names of children: *Darius Love; Martin Lupenga; Cherry Munkumpo; Memory Edna Yamba.* Paul stared longest at the last name on the list. It was hard to believe that he'd seen her just the day before, in the high-beamed classroom where the light shot down in gold arrows. She had sat at the front as usual, swinging her legs, her bare toes clenched around the rungs of her stool. He remembered how she concentrated, squinting to read the letters of her name. He had wondered whether she needed glasses, she sat so close to the board, but she seemed to have no trouble learning, or remembering, and was able to write out her name after he had rubbed the letters away.

He kicked at the soft mushroomy ash with his boot. He couldn't believe it had gone. The rows of desks, the stools, the blackboard and cartons of pens, the stack of white paper; the glossy faces looking at him were still vivid and fresh in his mind. It was as if they had all somehow been lifted off and carried away by the wind, and were still somewhere in the atmosphere waiting to return. Looking around at the smoking debris, he saw that there was nothing left of the structure: not a single doorway or window frame. Of the furnishings there were just a few desks that had been rescued and stood in a huddle, all facing different directions. He went over to one and lifted a blackened lid. Inside the wood was clean and blond, miraculously unscorched; there were even a few pencil shavings nestling in one corner in perfect, untouched curls. He stirred his fingers through them, smelling the new-paint smell of the wood and then let the lid drop with a crash that resounded over the bush, but flatly because there was nothing to be stirred or startled. All the birds, it seemed, had flown.

He paced around, treading carefully, lifting his boots high through the smoking damage, keeping his gaze low for anything he might salvage. Pacing made him feel better, as if he were doing something positive, or even useful. He went round a few times and then out of the corner of his eye noticed something unexpected. Across the entire charred bush floor, small, waxy shoots with tiny pink flowers were already thrusting their way up through the blackness. He bent down to inspect them closer; they were like nothing he had ever seen before, blooms so tiny and perfect and exotic and strange they looked almost manufactured. He straightened up, his head swimming. The air around him felt thin and exhausted and the strong liquorice smell of charred wood made his eyes prickle with tears. The place felt tightly squeezed, and curiously fragile. He wiped his eyes with the back of his hand and wished he had brought some water to drink.

A snapping of dry twigs made him whirl round. At the edge of what had been the vegetable plot stood a boy of around three years old, dressed in tattered blue shorts, his legs bowed so that the gap between them made the shape of an egg. He was looking down at the ruined garden with a mournful expression. Noticing

Paul, he took a few steps backward and placed his hands on his hips, rocking slightly backwards and forwards in a posture he had possibly seen adults take when they disapproved of something or wanted to show that they were serious. Paul shrugged his shoulders at him and pointed at the desks. The boy's face never flickered, instead it retained a glassy concentration as he rocked over the burned-out garden. Then he began to moan, a low bellowing like a calf that had been separated from its mother. The sound drew other children, who arrived with red exercise books tucked under their arms, ready to work. The older ones looked around coolly, one or two even smiling as they stepped through the broken pieces of their school. Some, however, seemed angry and kicked at the hot piles of ash with bare feet. 'We're going to rebuild,' he told them. 'After the rains, you'll have a new school.'

The children looked at him with interest. Sensing time to be filled, a couple of boys took out spools of knitting and slipped into a trance. Others just stood, wobbling slightly, bloated bellies thrust out. There was something almost comical about them, he thought. With their big hungry eyes they resembled nothing so much as doleful brown penguins that had arrived at their usual fishing ground only to find it had been dynamite-blasted out of existence.

'Why don't you go back to your villages and wait for this to be cleared?' he asked. But his question sounded ridiculous to the children who bunched closer together and looked at him with inconsolable eyes. Most of them, he knew, did not have parents. Instead they were looked after by older sisters or aunts, or even grandparents. He didn't think there was one child in the school who had not experienced the death of someone close. Out here, losing two parents was nothing sensational.

Paul watched as a toddler picked up a piece of bark and put it in his mouth. Another boy began throwing stones at the smouldering patches. He tried to explain about the rebuilding with gestures and mime, realizing too late that he was acting out a builder using bricks. The children regarded him with delight as if he were a magician putting on a special show. Aware of the futility of his act he stopped and perched on a desk. Looking over them, he saw that most of his class had come, except Thomas, a four-year-old with crooked teeth, Cherry, a quiet girl who sometimes went into fits, and Memory. He counted again just to make sure and the children looked at him expectantly. 'Does anyone know where Memory is?'

The children looked at him blankly.

'Memory,' he repeated. 'Have any of you seen her today?'

The boy in the tattered shorts who was called Rudinka shouted out his syllables, nodding his rough head vigorously: 'RU – DIN – KA,' and the other children laughed as the name bounced around the smoking bush. It seemed to cut through the gloom and lift everyone's spirits for a moment or two.

Paul laughed with them, but his mind was on Memory. It was unlike her not to turn up. She was normally the first to arrive and often helped set out paper and pens. Maybe, he thought, her village was close enough to the fire for her to realize what had happened. She might have come earlier. 'Go home,' he said to Rudinka. 'There's nothing here now.'

The boy looked at him closely. Paul tried to stand his ground. 'No school.' He flapped his hand at him, but Rudinka stayed where he was, staring straight into his face, disappointment and confusion clouding his eyes. 'I'm sorry,' Paul said, looking at the sad little boy. 'I really wish there was something I could do.'

Sensing the show was over, the other children began to disperse, balling up their knitting and linking hands. Rudinka remained. He stared at Paul, muttering in his own language, holding out a piece of burned bark in his hand.

Paul found his insistence disturbing. 'Go on, get lost.'

In response, the boy thrust his face upward, rolling his eyes so that only the whites showed. His mouth went slack and for a moment Paul felt afraid that he was about to go into a fit. Then he relaxed his expression and gave Paul a look of absolute conviction.

'What?' Paul said, looking at him. 'What do you want?'

Rudinka dropped his eyes and began to move off slowly, rounding his shoulders, trying to make himself as small as possible. Puzzled, Paul watched him trail away on his bendy legs until he was just a little brown egg shape hobbling through the smoke.

The sound of a large vehicle crashing through the undergrowth diverted his attention. Cutting across the bush, stripping and breaking branches in its wake, was a bright yellow tractor. Sides heaving, it churned its way right up to the edge of the burned-out site. Inside the cabin was Joe Baxter, dressed in a sparkling clean white vest, his blond hair slicked back. His squeaky cleanness seemed almost a statement of defiance, as if by insisting on neatness he was declaring to the bush his commitment to man-made order. There was something indestructible about Joe Baxter, Paul thought, as the tractor came to a wrenching halt; something whole and good.

'Fucking mess, isn't it?' Baxter said as Paul climbed up into the cabin. 'Always gives you a shock, the morning after, the way everything just looks so mangled, like a pile-up.'

Paul was surprised. Baxter must have seen hundreds of bush fires in his time, but he seemed genuinely upset.

'Ow.'

'Mind your head.' Baxter shoved the tractor forward, branches snapping like dry bones under the smothering wheels. The cab smelled new. In fact, the entire vehicle had a kind of stiffness about it; the paint was too shiny and the wheels too big and black for daily use. Paul wondered whether Baxter might even have been saving it just for the occasion. He was certainly enjoying romping it across the bush, hand lightly at the wheel, eyes narrowed against the sun, like the proud captain of an exuberant boat.

They surged ahead. Paul hung on to a strap and tried to stop himself from sliding forward on the slippery seats. Baxter pressed a lever, releasing a heavy metal trough, which came thumping down, flattening branches and cracking against small stones and flints. The trough began to shove a still smouldering branch across the bush floor, trailing bindings of thin rope-like ivy. Baxter pressed another lever and the trough scooped up the branch in its maw, swinging it round, the straggling ivy tails seeming to Paul like some kind of blackened intestine hanging down from a severed body part. Baxter put the tractor into reverse and dropped the branch on to a patch of scorched ground where it steamed and smoked. He then repeated the operation with another limb that had been burned from root to tip, working his mouth, his expression fixed in a look of deep disgust as if he believed the fire had been sent to insult him personally.

'There's a rumour that some kids were taken last night,' Baxter spat out as he pushed the tractor on.

Paul's teeth were on edge from being thrown about. 'What?'

'Witchcraft business.' Baxter yanked at the steering wheel and worked his thick freckled legs on the clutch and brake. Bristles of white hair sprawled all over his skin and he reminded Paul of a prize-winning pig he had once seen at an agricultural show. 'You've heard about it, I guess?'

Paul felt as if he had been punched in the throat. 'How many children, do you have their names?' For some reason Rudinka's beaming face came into his mind, which was illogical, considering Paul had only just seen him.

Baxter drummed his fingers on the steering wheel. 'Don't know. Got it from my houseboy this morning. He said three went missing from a village up near the airstrip. They grabbed them while everyone was up here with the fire. Wouldn't surprise me if they hadn't started it deliberately. Bastards,' Baxter snarled. 'No better than animals. I'd say a snake is more honest than a *muntu*. Isn't that right?'

Paul ignored the comment. His hands had gone cold with fear. 'The village nearest the airstrip, you say?'

'Yeah, that's what he said.' Baxter wrenched the gear lever forward and shoved the tractor over a pile of smoking planks. His face was purple, his small eyes twisted with rage. 'Fucking thieving opportunists, the lot of them.' He punched the steering wheel, lurching the tractor to one side.

Paul grabbed at his seat, a sick feeling in the pit of his stomach as Baxter continued: 'You know what they do? They take the kids to the graveyard and literally terrify the life out of them. They tie them up, blindfold them, do all sorts of voodoo on them; cut them, put chilli in their eyes. When these kids come back, they can't speak. I've seen perfectly normal kids become like zombies, some of them never talk again. I don't believe in witchcraft, but the damage is real all right. You can't ignore it. Some of the farmers here just think it's some kind of joke, but you can't laugh at it. It's more than superstition, it's a kind of business. During the rains last year, one boy they bewitched went down to the creek and sank into the mud. Right up to here.' Baxter made a slicing motion with his hand against his belly. 'Poor little bastard got stuck. He couldn't cry for help because his voice had gone. Croc got him.'

Paul was silent. In his mind he saw a boy twisting to free himself from a bank of mud, his mouth open in a scream, but making no sound. 'Put me down,' he said to Baxter. 'I need to get back.'

As soon as his feet touched the ground, Paul ran. He ran as he had never run before, pumping his arms and legs, smashing his feet on to the still smoking ground, trying to propel himself as fast as he could. The sun pounded down. His head cracked with pain, his muscles, unused to being pushed at speed, expanded slowly. He felt as if he were running in a dream, his mind was racing on; his mind knew everything, but his body was slow to catch up and was holding him back, weighing him down, making him feel as if he were lifting his legs through glue or sticky yellow paint.

When he reached the garden gate, he stopped. Light spots swam before his eyes and he took a few deep breaths to calm the pounding in his ears. His stomach contracted; he felt like vomiting, all his balance seemed to have gone and he found he had to clutch on to the gate for support. When he lifted his head again he saw that Max's jeep was still parked in the drive. Then a familiar shape stepped out from under the trees. It was the security guard from Max's farm, who looked as if he had been waiting for him.

'Please, wait a moment, sir,' the guard said and put his hand on Paul's arm. 'Don't go in yet.'

Something rose up in him and burst. Unable to hold it down any longer he turned his face from the anxious eyes of the guard and spewed up all over the grass.

Some time during the night someone had draped a blanket around Max's shoulders to ward off the chill from the kitchen window. Now light was streaming in, making patterns on the floor and something warm was brushing his neck. He brought his hand round and felt his fingers caught. Lifting his head he saw her face, half hidden in her hair which still smelled of smoke. She was smiling, her eyes glowing with a lovely, liquid closeness. He felt his breathing quicken, his chest tighten and his stomach tip over itself as she wound her arms around him.

'We're alone.' Her lips were hot by his ear, unbearably close. She eased her fingers down his chest, lightly rubbing his shirt. He felt his thighs thud with shock. At the same time his senses seemed to lighten and become more delicate as if some kind of insulating layer was gently being torn from his body. He pulled her arms and somehow drew her to him. She was loose and warm, strong and soft at the same time, like a young animal. She lifted her face. Her mouth was a little chapped and sore, the bridge of her nose sunburned. She seemed almost too real. He closed his eyes and briefly heard the birds chattering in the garden outside. Then he kissed her. She brought her hands up around the back of his head and pulled him closer. He tasted her saliva and felt her breath in his nostrils. His knees shook as he stood up; the shock of moving against another making them buckle. The chair fell and broke its back on the stone floor, but he did not pause.

The blanket dropped from his shoulders and puddled around his feet as he met her fully, his arms around the top of her back, where he felt the fluid movement of her shoulder planes. He smelled the burning forest in her hair, which he lifted with his hand as they stood kissing, his feet meeting her feet, bare toes curling to greet one another. It was enough; it was more than he could bear. It was everything just to hold her, to feel her around him. An exquisite feeling swelled in his throat, in his chest, in his hands as he breathed her in. He felt suffused with grace; all his years of longing seemed to dissolve in the moment. But he didn't want her to see how it was and abruptly pulled away.

'Max?' She took his head in both hands. 'Don't – why are you crying?' Her eyes were wide and childlike.

Ashamed, he turned his head away.

She put her palm on his cheek and swiftly pulled her dress over her head. He closed his eyes at the sight of her breasts and felt her fingers rub his face, nibble at his mouth. He tasted her fingertip, salty and sweet, and then, tremulously, ran his hand down her neck. Excitement swelled in him as she undressed him, caressing him, agonizing him, pulling him closer, teasing his nerve endings to a point of blinding whiteness. She guided him, showed him what to do and he forgot that he did not know. He remembered everything. He embraced her. He wanted to tell her that he knew her. That she was inside him already, but he couldn't speak because he was crying. He took her in a state of profound grief and longing, moaning, his hands fluttering around her back as he carried her with him. He felt her legs tighten around his waist. He was deep within her, and it felt as if he were inside himself, as though he were touching the most extreme points of his own body, points he had not known about before. Now his grief dissolved and he felt ecstasy. He carried her around the kitchen in a glorious, voluptuous embrace. He felt as if he were lifting aloft the entire load of his life; all his dreams and hidden hopes, everything that he had ever thought about he was now holding in his arms. In a moment of condensed silver light, he came, swiftly and brilliantly. He shouted. She clung to his body and laid her head against his chest as she slipped slowly down him. Then the light split from silver into white as the door burst open bringing with it a dark shape, and a pair of brown eyes that widened and rapidly dropped to the floor.

'Sir,' Geoff Seven mumbled, his gaze fixed on their pool of clothes. 'Sir, there are children missing from one of the villages.'

A space opened like a wedge of ice as Elise slipped from him and ran from the kitchen. The green and yellow of the guard's uniform appeared accusing, its occupant clearly unsettled, eyes skittering from surface to surface, his lips trembling with emotion. Max tried to frame an explanation in his mind, but he was too stunned. He felt as if he had just emerged from a car crash. Bending down, he picked up the blanket and quickly pulled it over his naked body, where it hung in heavy crumpled folds that gave off smoke fumes and a sour sweet smell. 'Please,' he said to the guard. 'Wait for me outside.'

'Sir.' With lowered eyes his guard left the kitchen, leaving the door slightly open, letting in the brittle sound of birds.

He dressed quickly and went to find her. She was pulling on a white shirt and jeans, her hair in tangles. He saw that she was crying. She shoved her hand across her eyes when she saw him and just looked at him for a moment. He felt something in him stall. He didn't know what to say to her. The bedroom felt hot and airless. He noticed a man's watch sitting on the table next to the bed, the leather strap slightly frayed near the buckle. Paul must have gone through the kitchen when he left. Max wondered why he had not woken him. There was also a photograph on the bedside table, showing the two of them outside somewhere near some dark green pines, looking white and cold. Elise began to yank a brush through her hair. 'Look, you'd better go before he comes back.'

He swallowed. She seemed to be dismissing him and it felt wrong. If only he could reassure her.

'For God's sake, Max, just go.'

He stood in the doorway for a moment longer, watching her pull on her shoes, everything about her now turned against him. He went back through the kitchen and then out into the garden where the light cut through the trees in clear slashes. A hot wind was lifting piles of giant crackling leaves and hurling them all over the place. A quick movement over at the gate caught his eye and he remembered the guard. In shock, Max saw that he was standing over Paul who seemed to be doubled up in pain. Noticing Max, the guard flinched and moved slightly closer to Paul, resting his hand on his back for a moment. Paul was bent double, kneading his fists into his thighs as he tried to catch his breath.

Max closed his eyes and then began to walk towards them.

Paul's face was sickly, his breathing clogged, his eyes sore. 'Max, God . . .' he said as a wave of vomiting rolled through him. 'I'm all right, I just' – he swallowed and gasped – 'ran back from Baxter . . . some kids have been taken' – he took another breath and waited for the spasm to pass – 'from the village near the airstrip.' He looked up and smiled. 'God, Max, you look terrible, worse than I feel.'

The urge to confess everything was almost overwhelming, but somehow Max stopped himself. He turned to the guard. He would have to sack him, perhaps not today, but soon. Max understood how it would be: the looks and underhand comments, the slight challenges, the whispers among the other workers. The rumours would quickly spread to his farm among his pickers who would lose respect for him. In one moment Max had undermined all the authority he had built up. In a single moment, he had changed his entire life, but it was too much to think about. He needed to focus. He looked closely at the guard. 'Can you take us in?'

Geoff Seven glanced over his shoulder as if he expected someone to be listening. 'Yes, sir, but it is dangerous.'

Max held the guard's gaze. 'Are you too frightened?'

The guard's eyes glistened with panic. 'Sir, you don't know about these people. They are evil.'

Max remained steady. 'I don't believe in witchcraft. It can't harm me.'

'Sir,' the guard said. 'It does not matter if you believe or not. They will kill you.'

'Are you a Christian?' Max asked.

'Yes, sir, Jehovah's Witness.'

Max's mind sprang back to the kitchen and quickly he pushed the image away. 'Then you must allow God to protect you.'

'Sir . . .'

'Come on, let's go.'

The security guard bowed his head. 'I will show you the old camp, this is where they sometimes meet.' He paused. 'Sir, you will need to bring your gun.'

Max looked at him for a minute. The panic had gone and now he seemed calm. Perhaps Max could trust him. He certainly needed him. Getting through the deep bush interior with its network of secret villages and drinking dens would be impossible without him. He nodded at the guard. 'We'll stop at my farm on the way.'

The camp smelled of dust and dry dung. They walked around quietly, the sun hot on their backs, tired from the long, jolting drive across tracks of hard dried earth. There had been moments when Max thought the jeep wouldn't make it, the ground was so steep and crumbly, but he had pushed on, driving, it seemed, with every muscle in his body. Now he ached for a rest and a cool drink of water.

Paul seemed exhausted too, his face strained as he followed the security guard around the camp which consisted of a dozen or so mud huts with pock-marked walls and roofs of grey, dead straw. Occasionally they pushed open doors, releasing dark, forgotten odours. In some of the huts clothes were still hung on twine strung between the mud walls. A toddler's woollen boot had been left behind in one, ribbons steeped in dirt. The place felt abandoned, cut off from any kind of human activity or occupation. 'It feels like everyone's died,' Paul said, his eyes bloodshot as he stared at the grim scene.

'When the chief lived here it was different,' the guard said. 'He was a very famous chief.' He stopped by a clearing where a platform had been built from wooden planks. 'This is where they used to have meetings.' His eyes swept around the platform and then looked across to the huts. 'Everybody used to come and listen to this chief, but then he got sick. He had nightmares and fits. Nobody could help him, and so many of his people tried. He asked his people to find him a witch doctor and they found out the name of a young herbalist. The chief was very generous and paid for him to come and live in this village.'

Max stopped. 'What was his name?'

The guard lifted his eyes. 'Christian Tambo.'

Max felt a prickle across the back of his neck.

Paul was looking at him, his brow furrowed. Some colour had come back into his face, but he still seemed tired around the eyes. 'Is that our man?'

Max nodded. He looked at his guard. 'Tambo lived here?'

'For a short time until he persuaded the chief to pay to have a special clinic built in another area, closer to his own people. Tambo moved to the clinic with the chief and looked after him with his herbal medicines. The chief was very sick. No one saw him for weeks. Everyone thought he had died, but he had been moved to the new place.'

'Then other people moved in here?' Paul asked.

'Yes.' The guard's voice was serious. 'The wizards and black herbalists took over. They thought that because it was the chief's old place it would bring them good luck.'

'What happened to the chief?' Paul asked. 'Was he cured?'

'Afterwards he went to live in the town. He gave the clinic to the witch doctor and said he could continue his business from there. Tambo started making a lot of money and the people at this camp became jealous of him and tried to poison him. He has told me they have sent wizards and spirits to kill him and that it is now too dangerous for me to visit his camp. I have not been there for some time.' He bowed his head guiltily.

Max was silent. An image of Tambo smoking a cigarette flickered across his mind.

'What about the other herbalists, what do you call them, the wizards?' Paul asked.

The guard's eyes flickered. 'They are very bad people. They started taking children soon after the chief left. There was one very old man among them who used to live at the Catholic Mission. It was known that he had captured a young girl and tried to take her spirit to bring him luck in business. When the people at the mission found out what he was doing they asked him to leave.'

'What happened to the girl?' Paul asked.

'She survived. I have not seen her myself, but other people have said that she is OK and that she is going to school.'

Paul looked at the guard intently. 'Baxter told me that children have died from fright. Is that true?'

The guard exhaled and slumped his shoulders, his eyes full and black. 'Yes, I think it is true. These people want so much they do not care. To them, a child is nothing.'

Exhausted by the heat, they rested in a pool of shade for a moment, and drank some water from the guard's plastic container. They closed their eyes as they drank and each one of them wiped the top of the bottle before he passed it on. Max shifted the gun across his shoulder, wondering why he had brought it because it was clear that whatever danger had been there had gone. The herbalists must have moved on somewhere else. The ground felt warm and seemed to suck at him, pulling him into sleep. He tried to fight it; they needed to work out a plan to find the children, but his head felt woozy, his limbs loose and heavy. He felt almost drunk. All his energy seemed to have drained out of him to be replaced by a dreadful inertia. Leaning his head back against a warm mud wall, he felt as if everything he cared about no longer mattered. All he wanted to do was sleep.

'This place sucks the life out of you,' Paul said, fanning his shirt, trying to direct some cool air over his body.

Next to him the security guard squatted on his haunches, the gold buttons on his uniform shining dully in the afternoon sun, the acid yellow braid like two thick caterpillars sleeping on his shoulder. He glanced at them, his eyes glazed. 'We should go somewhere else,' he said thickly.

Paul stood up and stretched his arms, trying to invigorate his body. Max caught the smell of his sweat, lighter and less pungent than his own. Geoff Seven unfolded himself and stood up, swaying slightly, one hand shading his eyes, as he looked around the camp. He appeared as if he had just woken from a drugged sleep. Next to him, Paul also seemed unsteady on his feet, as if one slight push would send him over backwards. A beat of alarm pulsed in Max's chest. With a great effort he heaved his body up and stood in the heat. His balance felt suddenly out of true. Even though it was by now late afternoon the temperature had not dropped; the place seemed stuck, caught in a time of its own. Max wanted to get away from it, but some strange kind of magnetism held him, almost glued him to the spot. Idly he noticed that Paul had gone over to one of the huts.

A sharp cry jolted Max out of his torpor. He ran over to the hut where Paul was standing, his face grey, in his hand a dirty green T-shirt and a red exercise book.

'She was here, this is hers.' Paul held the T-shirt out to them. His eyes were stricken as he flicked through the exercise book, pages filled with sums and names of rivers, which he was now scanning as if they might contain a message.

Ignoring the guard's warning, Max ducked inside the hut. The stale smoky dampness of the walls seemed to close in on him, causing him to lose perspective and scrape his shoulder on their gritty surface. Fear pricked him as he used his rifle to check the corners of the hut, jabbing its muzzle into the dark, soft earth. Nothing came to the surface. The hut was entirely empty expect for the stale smell and enervating presence. He backed out into the light where Paul stood, bunching and twisting the T-shirt in his hands, an agonized look in his eyes.

Geoff Seven went with Paul to check the other huts. Max recovered his breath under a tree, trying to fight off the creeping sleepiness the place seemed to bring on. He sat down in the shade for a moment and wrapped his arms around his legs and tried to stretch the muscles across his back and shoulders, which were still aching from the way he'd slept at the table. His mind began to swim with thoughts of Elise; her touch on the back of his neck lingered so indelibly it was as if her hand were still there, resting lightly on his skin. Just thinking about it made him feel complete. He glanced over towards the huts. The security guard had gone inside the largest hut leaving Paul outside. Then there came a muffled shout, propelling Max across the dirt with the speed of a stone leaving a catapult.

The guard stood breathing heavily, his face bathed in sweat, his eyes showing their whites. Max made a move to duck inside, but Geoff put his hand out and swallowed as he tried to catch his breath. 'Sir, you mustn't go in, there's bad in there.'

'What are you saying?' Max raced through the possibilities in his mind.

'It's bad,' Geoff repeated.

Paul blanched and took a step forward. 'No, stay back,' Max said, holding the rifle in front of him. 'I'll go.'

He entered the hut, his eyes fluttering against the dark. It was bigger than the first, higher and rounder. At first he could see nothing. He felt for a wall and used it to guide him, avoiding the centre of the floor where a white cloth had been placed. An overpowering stench came from something nestling on the cloth, something dark which raised all the hairs on his arm as he approached. His eyes adjusted. He saw a few small white bones on the cloth surrounded by a pile of dirty white feathers. There were also some bundles of sticks, tied with vines, and the skin of a small antelope, stretched and curling at the edges, with tiny trussed hooves. The dark object lay in a small basket. He leaned over to take a closer look, covering his nostrils with his hand. The object was shaped like a turd and seemed to emanate badness. It acted on him, pulling him towards it, dizzying him with its ripe, human smell. Feeling his stomach heave and turn, his eyes water, Max ducked out of the hut.

For a moment he was unable to speak and stood with his knees braced, gulping clean, uncontaminated air. His body convulsed with the strongest sense of revulsion he had ever experienced. The other men stared at him. Eventually he drew his palm across his face, breathing deeply, catching a ghostly scent, a lingering smoky tang. 'There's some voodoo in there, stinks like a dead cat.'

Geoff Seven swallowed. The corners of his mouth were flecked white with dried saliva and his eyes were two small points of light. 'You didn't touch it?'

'No.' Max screwed up his face. 'The smell is enough to make you sick for a week.'

'You must not touch it.' Geoff's eyes swivelled over the two men. 'You must not.'

'What would it do to us?' Paul asked, looking at Geoff. 'What would happen if I touched it?'

The security guard shook his head. 'You should not think about it even. Don't let it come near you.'

'Why? What are they going to use it for?' Paul persisted.

'I don't know,' Geoff said, his face suddenly closed.

Max recognized the look. It was how his coffee pickers some-times looked whenever there was talk of black magic. Some were so superstitious they would not discuss what happened in their villages at night. It was too risky and might summon the dark forces they were so afraid of.

'But they might come back to claim it,' Paul said. 'Perhaps we should hide out in the huts and wait for them. We could surprise them, force them to hand over the children.'

'They won't come back,' Geoff Seven said. 'Not now.'

'Where have they gone?' Paul asked.

'You can't find them in the daytime,' Geoff said, his eyes wide. 'They have protection. We must wait until the night when they become drunk. That is the best time to catch them.'

'What about the children, Geoff?' Max asked.

'Sir, the children will be sleeping. They give them medicine to make them sleep.'

Paul paced up and down, his forehead knitted with concern. 'I think we should try to track them down, now.' He looked at Max for support. 'Get them while we can.'

'No, Geoff's right. It could take a whole day of searching the bush for them. We should wait until later. The drinking dens are easier to find.'

Paul picked at some loose straws on a hut, disappointment showing in his eyes.

'Go back with Geoff and get some rest,' Max said. 'You'll need your strength for later. I want to take a closer look around.'

'I'm staying,' Paul said. He looked at the little girl's T-shirt. 'I want to find her.'

Watching him, Max felt constricted. He realized he envied Paul because quite simply he was free to love another human being in a way that he could not. 'Geoff will take you back,' Max said.

The security guard stiffened as if he had been caught thinking aloud. He looked at Paul.

'I'm staying.' Paul walked off a few paces, clutching the T-shirt.

Max felt a jolt of fear. 'Elise shouldn't be left on her own,' he said, hating himself.

Paul gave him a swift glance. Geoff Seven stood between them, a muscle twitching high on his polished temple. Overhead the sky was still and clear, perfectly brilliantly blue.

'She was in a state of shock this morning, went a bit wild and I had to calm her down,' Max continued, avoiding the brown pools of the security guard's eyes. 'You ought to get back and be with her.'

'Wild?' Paul looked at him with alarm. 'That doesn't sound like Elise.'

A putrid smell from the voodoo drifted from the hut. Max swallowed. 'When she woke and found you'd gone, she thought she'd lost you in the fire. She was terrified, shaking and crying. I had to hold her to calm her down.'

Paul met his eyes. Max felt his insides churn and bubble as if his viscera were in revolt and about to betray him. He thought he tasted blood in his saliva.

'I needed to go to the school,' Paul said quietly. His face was pale. 'I thought she'd be all right. You were there . . . I didn't want to wake you.' He looked at Max and then at the security guard who shifted between them and cleared his throat.

'It was probably just shock because of the fire, but you'd better get back, just in case.' Each word was bound in barbed wire. Sweat trickled slowly down Max's back in the space between his shoulder blades. It felt as though a cold snake were working its way down the length of his body. The security guard rested his eyes on Max for a moment and then looked away, pursing his lips.

'I couldn't sleep.' Paul's face was pinched with guilt. 'I just kept thinking about the school, everything we'd put in. I had to go and see if it was real.'

Max nodded. Paul clenched and unclenched his fists. His hair had fallen forward into his eyes and he shoved it away abruptly, giving Max a sudden, piercing look. He seemed on the brink of saying something, but Geoff Seven stepped between them, shoulders braced.

'Sir,' he said, looking carefully at Max. 'It is getting late and we should start to go back.'

Paul chewed at the inside of his mouth and then, glancing at the T-shirt in his hand as if he had never seen it before, scrunched it into a ball, and threw it underarm towards Max. 'Here, you'd better have this. She might need it.'

Holding the T-shirt close to him, Max watched them go. They were about the same height, but the guard was heavier in build, his shirt puffed out around his waist where he had fastened the black leather belt of his trousers too tightly. Paul's outline was slender; in his light brown vest and worn working trousers, he seemed to blend with the bush, his brown hair like the soft plumage of a young thrush. At the edge of the camp the guard turned and gave Max a long solemn look. Then, as if he had made up his mind about something, he turned and walked on a little faster towards the slippery light of the trees.

After they had gone Max took out his pocket knife and cut down a slim branch and stripped it of leaves. He sharpened the end into a point and holding the stick in front of him like a spear went back inside the hut. The voodoo smell filled his mouth and nose, making his gorge rise. Retching and sweating against the poisonous fumes, he steeled himself and swiftly stabbed down into the basket. The voodoo stuck to his spear in a lump of black tar and when he carried it out into daylight he saw that it was covered in fibres of what appeared to be burned human hair. He pulled a piece of plastic sheeting from one of the huts and rolled the voodoo inside it before securing it with a length of vine. Then he balanced the stick on his shoulder, alongside his gun, and set off across the bush.

Many times he lost his way, caught in swaying seas of elephant grass that screened the tracks. Looking ahead, all he could see was a shifting gold wave that rippled and changed direction with the wind. As he waded through, pushing the grass aside with his hands, he disturbed huge ants with white wings. A flock of birds startled him, whirling up from the hidden, hissing depths in a nervous twittering, circling the sky in gold chains that kept breaking and coming together again before swooping down on distant crests of more grass. The wind blew in hot, dry gusts, rasping the bones on his face. He felt as if his skin were being rubbed all over with glass paper. He still hadn't regained his balance properly and constantly tripped as he stubbed his toe on rocks and boulders buried in the grass. Up ahead branches crackled in the high trees with a sound like dry newspaper, setting his heart flipping, tensing all his muscles. Holding his spear, he felt as if he were being pushed blindfolded into a booby-trapped room.

Stopping to rest under a tree, he was parched with thirst and wished he had brought more water. A black snake, twice the length of his body, slithered drily across his path, its yellow eye fixed on the toe of his walking boot. Heart thumping, his finger moved towards the trigger of his gun. He was close enough to put a hole in the snake's snub-shaped head, and he imagined it recoiling from the shock, its yellow eyes stunned. But he let it slip by him, watching it drag its body like a well-used rope, leaving an elegant curving imprint in the sand.

He kept walking, the grass whispering edgily. The sun prickled his arms and flies buzzed his nose and mouth, craving moisture, the dry ticking of wings sucking at his nerves. He hurried on. After a while the dry grass parted, revealing an expanse of wood with arching trees forming a high green canopy. He had to put his head right back to see the crowns. For some reason the green grandeur filled him with fear. He considered turning back; his journey was loaded with menacing possibility, the sense of peace and order he usually felt deep in the bush interior had dissolved. Now every tree appeared to him a threat; every bush and clump of grass twitched with menace. He kept stopping and whirling round, convinced that he was being watched, or followed, his sweat-soaked neck certain of it. He expected a stab between his shoulder blades at any moment, a hand around his throat. Raising his spear, he turned round and even called out, so pervasive was the presence. But the bush breathed innocence, the trees bending sinuously in the wind. He spat at the flies around his mouth and shifted his rifle. His shoulder was tired and the fumes coming off the stick were making him lose his judgement.

Max had spent long enough living in the bush to know how powerful dark forces were. He knew people died. He had even lost a houseboy five years back to witchcraft, a victim of a magic aeroplane filled with evil spirits that had crash-landed near his hut and killed him. The boy had been found, limp, his body unmarked. Max had gone to the funeral and watched the Church people, dressed in white robes, carry him away to a holy place. Max had believed in the fear, but not the magic. By not believing in witchcraft he thought he was immune to its terror. Now he was not so

sure. He felt a sense of danger so acute it was as if some manifest-
ation of darkness were imminent. He had drawn black magic to
him by disturbing the natural order of things. By loving Elise and
betraying Paul he was pursuing chaos. It made the very air dangerous. He could feel it all around him. It was as if evil had broken
out of some shell and was pouring across the ground towards him.
He broke into a run.

Thin wisps of blue smoke rose through the trees. Drenched in
sweat and fighting nausea, Max shifted his spear. In the early
dusk the settlement seemed peaceful. A few white chickens
scratching in the dirt cocked their heads to register his arrival.
He stepped forward. A low thrumming caught his attention. It
came from the largest of the huts, and as he got closer he saw
what it was – a new generator throbbing against the side of the
hut. He walked over and used the barrel of his gun to push the
door open.

The witch doctor was lying on a mattress, jeans slack at his
waist, a stack of empty beer bottles at his side, his mouth open in
a loose and foolish grin, which shut like a clam when he saw his
visitor.

In one swift glance, Max understood what had been happening
to the money he'd been sending weekly; the money he'd been
paying to the witch doctor to keep him informed about the soul
thieves in the rival camp. A television flickered luridly a few
inches from the witch doctor's face, cartoon animals chasing each
other across a bridge slowly collapsing from the middle.

'Hey, sit down,' the witch doctor said and reached for his beer.
In the afternoon gloom his skin had an amber cast and his hand
shook as he fumbled with the bottle cap.

Max was at the television in a single stride. When it tipped
over under pressure from his boot, it made a tinkling music box
sound, blaring full volume for a second before it died. The witch
doctor jumped up, dismay crumpling his face, bringing with it a
slow realization that Max had not come to pay him a few more
kwacha for his services. He blinked and then backed away from

the television, slowly putting his hands in the air, bending his back towards the wall. His eyes narrowed rapidly as a stick with some terror on its end came towards him.

'You are now going to tell me,' Max said deliberately, punctuating each word with a thrust on the spear, 'exactly what this piece of shit means.'

The witch doctor collapsed slowly down the wall until he was on his haunches, his arms drawn around his knees, his neck hunched into his shoulders. His eyes flickered towards the spear and his lips began to tremble. He unlocked his arms and still on his knees quivered across towards Max, fingers scrabbling at the dirty rug laid across the hut floor. He would have licked the white man's boots had Max not suddenly stamped on the ground with all the force he had.

'Please don't kill me,' the witch doctor said. Then he brought his arms over his head and flinched as Max started kicking the fallen television to pieces.

Elise was lying on her back in the garden, a book across her chest. Paul sank down on the grass next to her. The drive across the bush had left him dizzy. Sun spots swam before his eyes and points of pain throbbed in his temple. As he ran into the house, he half expected her to be gone, a note left on the kitchen table. Finding her in the garden had come as a shock and relief. Now he felt foolish and slightly ashamed of doubting her. Her shirt had ridden up under her breasts, exposing the vulnerable swell of her stomach. 'What's happened?' she asked, sitting up and looking at him.

'I had to came back.' He sat facing her, his knees crossed, the tip of his foot just lightly touching her calf. Her skin was hot and she gave off a smell like fresh biscuits.

'Where's Max?' She drew up her knees so that he couldn't see her face.

'Still out there, looking for the children. I came back because Max told me about this morning.'

She lifted her head, her face rigid, pale lips quivering. '*He told you,*' she said in a half-whisper and then covered her face with her hands.

'It's all right,' he said. 'I understand.'

She kept her face covered. He stroked her shoulder. 'Elise, it's OK, I'm here. I'm not going to leave you.'

She looked at him then, an intense glare as if trying to read his soul. He reached for her hand, but she twisted away from him and looked out across the garden where the birds called regardless. 'I love you,' she said after a while.

'I know,' he said soothingly.

She turned towards him and flicked her hair back. She was flushed and her eyes had a glittery brightness. He recalled Max's words: '*She went a bit wild.*' It struck Paul that there was something different about her, something a little bit edgy, as if she could explode into either anger or tears at the slightest comment. He felt guilty as he imagined what kind of day she might have had, waiting in the garden on her own while he and Max had gone in search of the soul thieves. He hadn't given a thought to how anxious she might have felt, not knowing where he was. He hadn't even taken the time to come in and tell her where he was going after he'd got back from the school. If Max hadn't said anything, he wouldn't have known what she had been feeling. What kind of husband did that make him? She was supposed to be the person he cared about most, but he had neglected her. Since they'd arrived in Africa, he had put her second; his own need to build the school and then set it up had taken priority over her. Max had looked after her better than he had, taking her flying, giving her lessons, including her. Max had known what she needed, but why hadn't he? Why hadn't he taken her into consideration more? Was it because she hadn't asked him to? She had never said to him that she was fed up with being left on her own. She'd also never said that she wanted him to be with her more, and Paul now realized that he had needed that. He had needed her to say something, too. He wished he could give her back some of the time he'd taken from her. He put his arm around her and felt her collapse slightly into him. 'Everything's going to be fine,' he said.

She pulled away from him and looked into his face. It was a look of absolute anguish that made him feel strange, as if the speed of gravity had suddenly increased, making everything spin faster for a moment.

He pulled her close and kissed her very softly as if she were a child that he didn't want to harm in any way and he felt her slump against him. It made him wonder about Memory and what kind of place had she been taken to. There was a part of him that was tugging to be free, running across the bush, running off this sense that something was about to happen. Something he knew but didn't yet understand.

16

IF YOUR GLIDE HAS BEEN TOO FAST

You will find that when close to the ground, not only is the stick more sensitive, but back pressure increases your height. As your speed declines, apply very gentle pressure. The chances are you will make a wheel landing.

Zambia, 1972

Paul slipped carefully out of bed. Leaving Elise shrouded in mosquito net behind him, he bundled up his clothes and went out into the hall, shivering as his feet touched the stone floor. He dressed, first pulling on a dark green university sweatshirt and then an old-fashioned pair of black trousers that belonged to a dress suit. He hesitated as he fastened the small brass hooks on the waistband, wondering whether the trousers would restrict him; he expected he might have to run, but they were the only dark pair he owned. He pulled on his socks, holding on to the wall for support, balancing on one leg, and then laced up his running shoes.

He went into the kitchen and lit a candle, carrying it on a saucer to the pantry where he had hidden a small pocket mirror. Closing the door behind him, he propped it up against a honey jar and angled the candle near it. The sealed pantry had a hot, yeasty smell, the shelves lined with crusty old packets and jars, lids giving off a fool's gold gleam in the low light. A fat moth, wings the colour of burned caramel, fluttered among a shelf of dry paper bags before touching down on a sack of rice. Paul moved the mirror closer to the light and studied his face. His skin looked like wax, his eyes dark, unblinking pools, and some sort of static was making his hair stand on end. He tried to swallow down his fear. He needed to slow his pulse which was beating so fast he could have just finished a race. Taking deep breaths he went back out into the kitchen.

The fridge light shone a buttery yellow when he opened the door. Cold shivered up his arms as he reached into the back and drew out a small folded plastic bag. It was slimy and hard and cold against his hand as he returned to the pantry with it. When he tipped it into a dish it slipped from the plastic like bloody afterbirth. He hesitated before dipping his hand into the thin red pool mainly because of the smell, a mixture of fish and sulphur and the sour mould that grows on damp windowsills. He looked at the neck giblets coiled in the base of the dish, a small bruised penis ripped out at its root, and shuddered. Perhaps he needn't take such precautions, his dark clothes would surely be enough. If he stayed close to the trees he wouldn't be seen. But then another kind of fear overtook him and, tilting his head as if he were about to start shaving, he dipped his fingers into the offensive dish and began to colour his face with chicken blood.

Paul peered at his candlelight reflection. The blood was drying on his face in wide brown stripes. He rubbed some across his forehead and then, realizing that his hands would be visible, used the rest of the stain on his knuckles and fingers. His hands looked gruesome, as if he'd just committed murder, his fingernails yellow and sticky. He went out to the kitchen. The moon hung bloated in the window above the sink. He put the dish on the draining board, pausing at a sound from the hall, a slight rustle that jittered his fingers, nearly making him lose the dish as he tipped the grisly remains down the sink. If Elise got up, how would he explain? What possible explanation could he have for getting up in the middle of the night and covering his face with foul-smelling slime? The noise in the hall stopped. Maybe it was just dry leaves skittering across the flagstones. The wind sounded as if it were getting up outside and it made him anxious to be out before he was discovered. He was too frightened to rinse the blood from the bottom of the sink and covered it over with a cloth. He knew Joshua would find it later and clear it away without comment.

Outside, the wind surged in great gusts, rocking trees and shaking bushes. It seemed to be rolling in from a distance. It tugged at his hair and blew up under his sweatshirt, ballooning it out in front, unbalancing him. He stood for a moment and caught his breath, looking up at the clouds racing across the moon, the sky darkening and then lightening, as though a big yellow searchlight were being trained across the bush illuminating every step he was about to take.

He crossed the lawn, the grass crisp under his feet, the nervous light swinging and dipping and looping around him. He kept his eyes on the track and tried to ignore the sense that someone was standing at the kitchen window watching him go.

The blackness closed around him as he walked deeper into the bush interior, ducking his head against overhanging branches that tugged at his clothes and hair, spiking him with unseen thorns. The wind soared, buffeting his eyes and ears. He jumped at every crack, every snap, his senses so brittle it was as though something inside him were about to break.

He chose the bush path that looked least dark and stayed in the middle of the track so that he could watch both sides. He had walked along this track many times before, but never at night and it appeared different, not exactly changed, but somehow clearer and more defined, as if he were seeing it in its own time. Great limbs and heavy branches were precisely outlined against the sky in shapes that seemed oddly familiar as if he had known these trees all his life, as if they had been part of his childhood. He looked up at their dense black and purple crowns, swaying in the wind, the underside of the leaves flashing silver, trunks glowing pale in the moonlight, and felt a kind of relief.

The old grey trees remained motionless, heavy boughs folded into one another in a private embrace. The bush was alive with twitterings, scrapings and twitches from a hundred unseen creatures whose eyes he guessed were watching him. But he did not feel afraid. He felt a kind of awed calm as if he were being given a glimpse of the world in another state, a freer, more distinct reality.

He speeded up, looking out now for the rough piles of stones that acted like signposts across the bush. An image of Memory came into his mind. She was standing quite still with her hands on her hips and she seemed to be waiting for something. Since discovering that she was missing he hadn't wanted to think about where she was being kept, or what had been done to her. He hadn't let his imagination dwell on her capture. He had simply planned how he might save her. Even though he knew that she was in danger, she would not give in to the kidnappers. If they tried to frighten her, he felt sure that she would put up a fight. All he had to do was find her.

He pushed on; his body felt light and capable, his feet warm and flexible. He did not doubt that he would find her. She was waiting for him, he was convinced of it. It was clear to him that he had been chosen; Memory had singled him out, knowing that she would need him one day. He was *meant* to save her. This was what he had come for. A soft thrilling feeling came over him, bringing with it a sense of true understanding. There was something he had always known; something strange, nameless and secret, and tonight it was leading him, encouraging him, giving him a sense of rightness and purpose. It made him feel almost drunk, as if he had taken some of the essence of the very stuff of the universe. His ordinary self, the part of him that was weak and needy, had faded into a tiny distant being, a memory, a dream. His body tingled. He felt alive, more alive than ever, his blood and heart and lungs filled with a strange kind of power. He was prepared. He had no needs or desires; no urge to be anywhere other than where he was. He felt satisfied. How simple and complete everything seemed; there was nothing superfluous in the forest; everything was in its right place. The night felt abundant. If he could pull down the sky and wrap it around his body it would feel as warm as cashmere.

Sooner than he anticipated he found the stones, the primitive pile of flat red pebbles balanced precariously one on top of the other. He rested his hand on the signpost for a moment. In the distance he could hear laughter, and between the trees he caught a glimpse of flames and smelled smoke. He stepped forward.

Max cut the engine. 'We'll go on foot from here,' he said into the dark. Next to him, Geoff Seven moved into action, reaching for one of the two hunting guns resting in the footwell, his eyes glittering. He opened his door and a gust of wind rocked the jeep, jolting them, causing them to suck in their cheeks and wait for a moment.

'Have you ever fired a hunting rifle?' Max asked. Geoff Seven shook his head, his hand still on the door, which the wind was trying to rip off the side of the jeep. His forehead was shiny in the darkness and beaded with a rash of small hard blisters. He was breathing with his mouth open. 'I'll show you what to do,' Max said as he climbed out.

He picked up his own rifle and slid it against his shoulder, feeling his body align itself to the familiar density of gunmetal. The security guard watched, his shoulders thrust forward, his mouth slightly open, his lips parted, showing the raw pink of his tongue. Max lifted the rifle and looked down the barrel. The metal had a warm, oily smell.

He aimed his sights at the branch of a mupane tree, training his gaze on a cluster of leaves. It was years since he had hunted, but now with a gun back on his shoulder he felt instantly prepared. A quiet, watchful sense came over him. The moon shone sullenly above the trees. The wind had dropped and Max saw there was little cloud. The conditions were not ideal. They would just have to stay very low.

Geoff took his gun and looked down the barrel, his face flat and serious as he concentrated, breathing shallowly. 'The recoil on these things can dislocate your shoulder,' Max said. 'Use your arm, like this.' He lifted his gun and demonstrated. Geoff copied his movements, brow knitted. Max nodded. He had once shot a wounded elephant with the rifle the security guard was handling so gingerly. The twin bullets had blown the narrow, bony top of the animal's head clean off. Afterwards, a neat grey skullcap of skin had hung from the branch of a eucalyptus tree, blood dripping drop by drop. The rest of the elephant had been untouched and lay on the ground, its great side heaving, colossal feet twitching in spasm. From the trunk had come a sound like a whale blowing air. He had raised his gun a second time, but the paying hunter had stepped in and said he wanted to finish it off. It was the last time Max had taken a party hunting.

They set off through the trees, the security guard taking the lead, lifting his feet high to dampen their sound. The moon flickered behind racing clouds, visible one moment, hidden the next and the trees bent over at their tops and became tangled together with a sound like dried beans shaken in paper. Max thought about the witch doctor crawling on his hands and knees, picking up crystal pieces of his television, mourning them as if they were shards of diamond. At first he had denied knowledge of the soul thieves. They had moved on to another region, he said. Max needed to pay him more so that he could use his disciples to find out where they were. He had been sick; he needed more money for medicine so that he could cure himself. With another jab from the noxious stick, Max had forced Tambo on to his feet. 'Tell me how to find them.'

The young witch doctor had looked at him, eyes narrowed. He described an area but warned Max not to go there alone. 'They will use their power against you, they will make you sick,' he said.

It was clear to Max that the witch doctor was lying. He wondered how long Tambo had been handing his money over to the soul thieves and whether the television had been some sort of reward. He pushed the witch doctor on to the floor and shoved the stick into his neck. 'If you are lying this time, I will come back and shoot you.'

Later after returning to his farm and collecting another rifle, he had walked over to his security guard's quarters. It was dark. The guard was preparing to eat a meal with his wife at a small table behind a thin curtain. Max had hesitated, his stomach growling; he had been unable to eat all day. He heard Geoff say prayers with his wife and then went to wait in the jeep parked outside the concrete quarters, listening to the wind build up in the trees.

Up ahead Geoff Seven stopped, one foot lifted from the ground in the manner of a gun dog. From the angle of his back and neck, Max could tell that he had seen something. He strained his eyes, trying to catch a glimpse of whatever had caught the guard's attention, but the surrounding bush had a woollen density, soft and thick and impenetrable. Geoff Seven tilted his head back slightly. He seemed to be listening to something. Then Max heard it, a faint thrumming of drums, a soft cushiony sound that he could have easily mistaken for his own heartbeat.

They walked on, more cautiously now, stopping every five paces or so to peer through the trees for signs of light. Max released the safety catch on his rifle. Hearing the click, Geoff Seven jumped and whirled round, his face taut with fear. Max showed the guard the underside of both palms and watched him relax, but he realized how stupid he'd been to take the catch off without warning. The guard had entered a state Max knew well, a state of total awareness in which the senses – sight, hearing, smell, touch, even the taste of the air – were working together at their most refined and alert. It was the ideal condition of the hunter. It made him super-sensitive, attuned to the slightest changes in temperature, wind direction, scent or softness of the ground, the adjustments being made not consciously but instinctively as he drew closer to his prey.

Max remembered spending a whole day hunting zebra, lying in the grass watching their movements, noticing how often they lifted their heads when they went to drink and the way they would take a few mouthfuls of grass and munch with their ears trained forward, eyes fixed on some invisible point on the horizon, so intently that all the other zebra around stopped and looked in the same direction. He had watched the mares keep their foals in line by using their necks, bumping them every now and then on their hind-quarters, drawing them in close for a moment. On that day he had developed a love for zebra; their dark-eyed, fringed wildness and polished stripes like markings on stone had absolutely thrilled him. He had stayed with them until dark, a great feeling of contentment coming over him as he listened to them feed and breathe. That night he understood something of what he had missed in his own life and he had left with the scent of their sweat clinging to him, his rifle limp across his shoulder.

The guard stopped dead. Max almost went into the back of him. Geoff's nostrils flared as he looked at the heap of red stones and broken bits of anthill piled up on top of one another like a rough totem pole. They had reached the track leading to the drinking den. 'Go on,' Max told him. 'But keep low.'

They crept forward, stopping to listen for voices or drumming. Geoff was trembling and kept wiping his face with his sleeve. At the next stop Max rested his hand on Geoff's shoulder, making the guard jump. 'You've got to take it easy.' The security guard nodded and swallowed. He shifted his rifle on his shoulder and made an effort to calm himself. Suddenly he stiffened. He pointed through the trees. Max looked, but could see nothing, only a melting blackness. Then it came: a prickling smell of smoke.

They crouched low in the sharp grass, heads so close they could feel the heat from the other's blood. From the den came a stench of rotting fruit. Max felt his shirt stick to his chest as he lay on his stomach, his rifle propped under his chin. The bush floor was alive with stinging red ants, but he didn't dare move. He watched the den. A group of six men sat around a fire, faces oily in the heat, legs outstretched, blue cartons of *shaky shaky* drink wedged between their knees. Gold sparks spiralled from the fire and drifted up towards the blue-black sky. The men seemed peaceful, almost subdued; it would be like picking off pheasants, Max thought.

Geoff Seven turned and swivelled his eyes, needing a sign as to what to do next. Max whispered that they should wait. He could hear the men around the fire talking in low voices. Occasionally one would get up, stretch languidly and fetch another carton of drink from a rickety shelter. Max looked up at the sky where the stars sprawled across the blackness in loops and odd misshapen squares and triangles. A shooting star streaked across the darkness in a spark of pure brilliance, like a champagne glass exploding. He thought of his flight to the stars with Elise and felt a thickness in his throat.

Max laid down his rifle. The easiest way would be to let the thieves round the fire fall into a drunken sleep. Then they could knock them unconscious with the rifle butts and move in to take the children. He looked at the men gathered groggily round the fire. The children were probably asleep in the huts. It wouldn't be that difficult to move around the back of the camp and creep in. They could lift the children out, carry them in their arms, without a sound, like phantoms or angels in the night. Maybe they could do this without knocking the men out; they would be unconscious with drink soon enough. All they needed to do was watch and wait.

The stick pressing into the back of his neck brought with it a lethal stink. Max felt his eyes water against the stench and then recognition, and then, simultaneously, fear. He reached for his gun and was knocked sideways with a blow to the head. Everything slowed down as a pair of feet in white plimsolls, rubber soles studded with little glittering flecks, stepped over him and moved towards the camp.

When Max lifted his head again the scene around the fire had changed and seemed to be taking place through a curtain of net.

He saw Geoff Seven walking towards the fire with his hands up, a figure behind him, wearing a white suit and fur hat, jabbing at him with Max's rifle. The men around the fire jumped into life, running about frantically, shouting and screaming at the guard who was being forced on to his knees. Max saw his mouth opening and closing, his eyes white with terror as his hands were wrenched behind his back.

Max staggered to his feet. His fingers found a warm, spongy patch on the back of his skull. His vision was blurred and nausea lurched through him. He grabbed the elbow of a tree to keep his balance and stood swaying, trying to clear the fog from his eyes. The men seemed to be lighting branches on the fire to make torches; he heard them chattering and screaming. They formed a circle around their captive and began to thrust their torches at him. Max shook his head and the red mist across his eyes cleared for a second. Then a bolt of energy surged through him and he broke into a run.

He crashed through the undergrowth, stumbling over roots and fallen branches. Termite mounds loomed up at him as he ran, keeping his back low, twisting around clumps of grass and snarled bushes. He could see Geoff's gun on the ground, partly hidden under an umbrella thorn, its oily muzzle pointing towards him. Inside the drinking den, the circle loosened. The men had lit fire branches and were waving them, faces violent with excitement. He caught another glimpse of Geoff Seven kneeling on the ground, his hands tied behind his back, his eyes closed, his lips muttering. Every now and then one of the men would take his fire branch and poke the guard in the side.

Max reached the bush and grabbed the gun, ripping his hand on the thorn that guarded it. He stood up and pointed the rifle towards the men with the torches and pulled the trigger.

Behind him someone fired, deflecting his own shot which slammed into a tree trunk. Max was caught in the back of the knee. He felt the bone spark and shatter. He smelled his own burning skin. Pain shivered in long tongues down his leg, and the sky was filled with bleeding lights. Blood poured into his boot. A second shot caught him in the same leg, felling him like a birch. He went down on both knees. Out of the blackness came a figure dressed in white who stood before him, head held to one side as if in sympathy for his predicament. Max rubbed his eyes, trying to clear his rapidly fading vision. The figure was familiar and wore a silver pendant around his neck. Max lurched forward as the figure fired again. He closed his eyes against what he knew would be point-blank death.

He was surprised that he could still hear, still smell and feel the ground under his soggy knees. If anything, his senses were sharper than when he had been alive. When he opened his eyes he was astonished to see stars in the sky, in the same achingly familiar constellations and realized that he was alive. He was crouched on the ground in his own body that shrieked with pain and across the dirt was his killer, white overalls flecked with blood, smashing the hunting rifle against the great weeping trunk of a mupundu tree.

Max hauled his upper body up; his leg was the texture of soft sponge and squelched when he moved it. The figure in white turned and pointed the muzzle of the gun straight towards his head. His eyes were moving sideways and his thighs were shaking. Max closed his eyes. He'd thought he'd been given another chance to live, but now he was going to die on his knees. He tried not to wait for the sound of the bullet leaving the rifle; he thought of the man in the bone cave surrounded by animal remains slipping slowly into unconsciousness and then he thought of clouds billowing under the belly of his small aeroplane and the warmth of her voice asking him something from the cockpit. As he prepared to die, he recognized that she was the end of longing. He had been aiming for her as long as he had lived. At last he knew that he had reached her.

The rifle jammed. With a sneering look at Max, the witch doctor dropped the gun and ran back towards the huts to join the men around the fire. Max raised his head. There was a racing sensation in his chest and back as if all his organs had speeded up. His left leg was on fire and when he rolled over to look at it he saw a mash of blackberry and treacle with strange white pieces like broken mushrooms floating inside the mess. Biting into his arm against the pain, he began to drag himself towards the huts on his belly.

Halfway he stopped, his face level with the ground, the rust smell of blood all around him. His vision was cloudy and kept fading in and out. Through a grey curtain he saw another tribal figure, dressed in black, face smeared with a red stain, come out of the trees and run towards a group of children who were crouching down against the wall of a hut with their hands over their ears. The children cried out when they saw him and huddled closer. The figure in black scooped up a child and carried her off towards the bush. The child, a girl, was shouting numbers in English; Max saw her eyes, wild with fear, her hands kneading the man's neck. Max rolled over and his fingers touched the jammed rifle. He dragged it towards him and lifted it to his chest, retching at the pain from his shattered leg. He took aim. He knew how many bullets were left and he had only one chance.

Max fired. The shot rang out clearly. The girl screamed, a terrible piercing screech. The figure in black went down neatly and the girl tumbled from him and rolled, landing like a gymnast on her feet. She stood for a moment looking at the man lying face down, the dark pocket of blood opening in his back: the sudden surprising whiteness of his neck. Then the men shouted from the fire and without looking back she fled, jiggering through the trees, her light T-shirt occasionally flickering, and then fading as she ran deeper into the bush. Max let the gun fall off his body, grunting as another wave of pain ripped through him, bringing the curtain down in front of his eyes.

The veranda is in darkness Max has not lit candles. Drained by his confession he puts his head in his hands, covering his eyes with his fingers, as if everything is too much to look at. Beyond the veranda the night insects give out their fragile sound and the air smells cool and sweet, like fresh cotton sheets. They have been talking for nearly four hours without moving and Memory is exhausted. She wonders whether she ought to leave. Now that Max has told her everything and she has imagined details he could not bring himself to reveal, she feels like an intruder into his private grief. But the thought of walking alone across the bush with the story fresh in her mind terrifies her. She wishes Kennedy would come. She has a sudden need to be close to him and feel real again.

Leaving her chair, she goes over to lean against the veranda rail and looks out towards the night. It's good feeling the air on her face, the breeze through her clothes. She searches for the moon. It is just visible, a delicate white crescent swinging in the dark velvet space between two acacia trees. She thinks how strange it is to have been finally given the truth. How odd to have the full story out in the open, but also how ordinary everything seems. She leans over the veranda and looks at the dark lawn, where the sprinkler is now silent. A gardener must have stopped it while they were talking. She had not noticed; she had sat entranced by the sound of Max's voice, which every now then had broken, once or twice halting for whole minutes at a time. There were moments when Memory had thought that he would not be able to continue, but each time he managed to recover by drawing on some source of strength that perhaps he had saved unconsciously for this occasion. He did not look at her as he spoke, but kept his gaze trained on the horizon, never faltering once from its line.

She closes her eyes and allows herself to feel once more. Paul Cougan is running across the bush under a racing moon, breathless, scared, but more alive than he had ever felt. He scoops her up, telling her that it will be all right, she needn't worry, he is here to take care of her, and she feels warm inside, even though on the outside she is cold and terrified. He starts to run and she puts her arms around his neck, clinging on tight, her face buried in his throat. He smells of sweat and raw chicken. She touches his rough, newly cut hair as he ducks to avoid a low-hanging branch. Her legs are wrapped around his waist and she can feel his heart pounding beneath the material of his sweatshirt. Then there's a loud crack, like a snapping branch, and she glances behind them thinking something is about to fall. Gunshot. She grabs his shoulder to warn him. She calls his name, *Paul!* But he doesn't hear her because something is making him stumble and lose his footing. She holds on to his sweatshirt, clutching it in her fingers, and they go down together, in a dive, in a whirl of leaves and smoke. She falls with him, wind roaring in her ears, but then just before he hits the ground she jumps and lands on her feet. She stands looking at him. He seems very far away, as if she is looking at him from the top of one the tallest mupane trees. He lies face down and she knows that he is not going to get up again because of the stain spreading like wings across his back. She edges away from him and begins to run wildly into the trees, which reach out to scratch her face and snare her hair, but she keeps running, knowing that if she stops her soul will be taken and she will die from fear because that was the last thing the white man said to her just before he went down, whispering it to her in a strange, hoarse voice: 'Run, Memory, run for your life.'

Then as if she has come up against a wall, the veranda swings back into focus. Taking a deep breath, she looks up at the pattern of stars. Finally she turns and faces Max. 'Thank you.'

He lifts his head; his eyes are red and sore as if he has been blinking grit. He stares at her for a long moment, and then in a rough, swift movement drags the side of his palm across his eyes. He nods at her and swallows, incapable of further speech. She looks into the bush. She hears a branch snap and jumps as a dark figure, head bent, emerges from the cover of trees and calls out her name.

Reaching the veranda, Kennedy stops and peers through the wooden bars at the two of them still in darkness, the smile in his eyes fading as he looks first at Memory and then at Max. 'A call came from England,' he says hesitantly. 'She said she would ring back.'

17

LANDING

Clear last obstacle. Flatten glide with engine. Close throttle. Hold stick if wheels touch first. Tail settles.

London, 1996

A swimming-pool clamour ripples through the museum. Elise hesitates a moment, unsure of what to do next. The place is not how she remembered it. The cool cathedral space with its painted ceiling and stone stairways now seems disobediently hot and frantic. A line of school children with rucksacks clinging to their backs shuffles past her. The teacher, a young woman, glances at Elise as she passes before turning to a young boy who is asking her a question, standing on tiptoe, his glossy face fringed by masses of tiny beaded braids. When he has his answer, the boy rejoins his friends, his eyes shining as he takes in the great hall with its dinosaur masters standing guard at the entrance, its sweeping stone steps leading up to balconies where skeleton monkeys fling themselves from wall to wall on invisible wire.

Finding herself staring at him, Elise looks away. She shifts her shoulder bag, squeezing it a little to check that she still has her mobile phone. Then she takes the plunge through the crowd and makes her way up to the herbarium where it is quieter. She sits down on a low stone seat and loosens her scarf to let the air circulate around her neck. From up here she has a fine view of the heavenly ceiling painted with plants and herbs, the names inscribed in gold leaf: *citrus bergamia, saccharum officinarum, pyrus indica*. The names have a distant familiarity like forgotten fragments of poetry or lost recipes. She remembers coming to the herbarium to meet her father after school. For some reason the place seemed to her like a hospital, with its rows of glass cases and quiet, old rooms. But maybe that was because it was where her father came to be healed after things started going wrong in his life. Eventually it became his sanctuary. He had enjoyed choosing exhibits as meeting points, making them more difficult to find as she grew older. The mineral hall had been one of his favourite places and as a child she had spent hours looking at the stones. The big solid haunches seemed to emanate sober waves, which acted on her turbulent stomach like a balm. At night when she couldn't sleep she would try to remember the names: beryl, aquamarine, chalcedony, limonite, topaz, rubellite, rose quartz, zircon, celestine.

Her visits to the museum had ended abruptly. Late one night while she sat doing her homework at the breakfast bar in the kitchen of their flat in London, her father had called. She remembers looking at the phone on the wall as it rang, and the tone, shrill and empty. Her mother had taken the call in the lounge where she had been watching television, lying full-length as she always did on the plump red sofa. Afterwards she had come into the kitchen and poured herself a drink from the green bottle in the fridge. She had taken a sip as she walked over to Elise, clinking the ice cubes against her teeth. Her fingers had felt freezing as she touched her shoulder, and her breath had smelled of Martini sours.

'Your father's lost his job,' she said, slurring the 's' in 'father's' and 'lost'. 'He's going back to Durham.' She had drunk the sour down in one and gasped, eyes watering. Then she had gone to the fridge and poured another, leaving Elise to make her own way to bed.

On the first day of her next school holiday, Elise went to the museum even though she knew he would not be there. No one even recognized her as she passed through the entrance. She had gone straight up to minerals, to the pyramid of calcite from Iceland moored in its display case like a broken piece of iceberg. Her breath misted the glass. The cuts all over the stone were called cleavage marks. Afterwards she had picked up her school bag and walked the length of Brompton Road, her coat open to the wind and rain.

Shrill voices float up from the crowd downstairs. Half an hour has passed. She must not worry. Her father was never punctual. He stumbled over time, fell into conversations with officials, bought coffee for strangers, found bookshops on his way to meetings; he lived his life as if it were one long unravelling adventure. She had missed all that when he went. He took it up to Durham and gave it away to others while she and her mother slept, or so it seemed in their small north London flat where the curtains were always drawn. Her father still phoned, but it was never the same. He didn't even sound the same. His voice too thick with cheerfulness.

She looks down the stairs at the crowds milling about, hoping to catch a glimpse of his head with its flop of grey hair falling down into his eyes, his stooped frame and slight scurrying walk as if he were trying to catch up with himself. The hall is still packed with school parties. Moving over to a window she checks her mobile phone. No messages have been left.

At the weekend when he'd called to say he was coming down for the day he had sounded excited. Would she meet him at the museum next to the— 'Dinosaurs?' she had interrupted, enjoying the lightness in his voice.

'Huh, funny. I'm not that prehistoric.'

'You are to me, Dad,' she teased. 'One of the great lost species, unique to the world. Who else would keep a kidney stone as a *paperweight*?'

'Call yourself a scientist? I've told you a hundred times, it's a gallstone.'

'Whatever it is, it's disgusting. How long are you coming down for? Can I put you up?'

There had been a pause in which she expected him to refuse. He usually came down in the morning and returned the same evening. His excuse for not staying in London was that the traffic kept him awake. In Durham, he slept long hours in his tall, quiet house, retiring after supper so that he could get up in the early hours to write.

'The meteorites,' he said gleefully. 'See if you can find them. I'll meet you there around noon, and I think I would like to stay the night, if that's all right?'

She glanced around the Highgate flat. She had bought the place to be close to her mother when things had got bad. There was only one bed. He would have it, and she would sleep next to him on a pile of bedding on the floor. 'That's fine,' she said, then, 'Dad, you sound different, has something happened?'

He laughed richly. 'I'm not going to be tempted into telling you over the phone. See you by the meteorites.' She had kept the phone close to her ear for a moment before putting it down.

The meteorites shine dully, swinging gently on invisible wire. Inside the glass case there are perhaps a dozen or so irregular pieces of space rock suspended like grey pieces of slate. The display room is dark and overheated and empty. Elise feels sleepy. Her legs are tired. Noon has long gone.

A young assistant comes over. 'I'm sorry, I'm going to have to ask you just to move slightly away from there.'

She realizes she has been leaning on the display case for support and apologizes in return.

The assistant's ears redden. He wears a badge with his name, Dominic. 'Thank you,' he says and walks away, leaving her in stifling silence.

She waits for a minute longer then goes downstairs. At the information desk an assistant slowly scans a scrawl of messages written haphazardly on an ink blotter. Elise notices her Natural History badge with its little motif that could be a tree, a leaf, a footprint, even a flame. 'No, he hasn't left a message,' the assistant says.

317

'He's coming from Durham.'

The assistant looks at Elise. A large pale woman with a sloping shelf of chest, she wants to be helpful. 'The train is probably late,' she says, smiling.

'You're probably right,' Elise says, softening, mimicking the woman's speech rhythms. 'I'll go back upstairs and wait.'

It is the time of year for lateness. November. Sometimes people were stuck on trains for hours. Perhaps he couldn't call because he was out of range. He probably wouldn't think of calling anyway. He was the kind of traveller who just stoically waited to arrive. He didn't mind delays. To him a delay was bonus free time when he could read or draft letters or simply retreat into his own mind to think. He had everything he wanted in life, he told her once, except time for free thought. When he retired from the university, he would make thinking the most important part of his day. He was designing a room, a garden house, especially to think in.

'Dad, it's me. I'm still here with the meteorites. Where are you? Call me please, on the mobile.'

She decides to leave another message at the university in case he's muddled the days. Then she calls his home. The housekeeper answers. 'No, he got on the train this morning. I drove him to the station myself. I expect there's been a delay. He was so looking forward to seeing you.'

'Thank you.' She does not know why she feels so grateful. Maybe it's simply the fact of talking to someone who has seen her father. It confirms almost that he still exists somewhere and has not vanished without reason. She stares at the ceiling; the stained-glass gold and blue colours of *pyrus indica* dissolve into a moody wash. *I was really looking forward to seeing you, too, Dad, because I also have some news. You know the chief executive job I was going for? Well, I got it. Apparently the conference sealed it. They really liked the paper I gave. It's going to be published in next month's* New Scientist. *Of course you can read it, I'll just print off a copy. Make yourself at home.* She imagines her father standing in her galley kitchen drinking tea; he didn't like coffee, said it made him nervy. She sees him looking around, taking in her life, her successful life that is somehow much smaller and more tightly bound than his. She offers to run him a bath, and goes to scatter warm towels on the floor and swish some pine-scented salts through the water. He can take his wine in there, and the newspaper if he likes. He smiles at her and frowns slightly. No, he'll wait if she doesn't mind, until he gets home. And the word hurts her, the word *home*. Because it makes her feel disconnected from him. They would stay in to eat, something expensive sealed in cardboard and plastic, which she would guiltily unwrap, her father nodding behind her at the ingenuity of a meal in a box, she wishing she had taken the trouble to cook properly. Later, in the bathroom she would see his wash bag, with its curious collection of soapy male things, and she would be overcome by tenderness.

The meteorite twists on its wire, a piece of dying star caught in its final moments. She makes a call on her mobile, to King's Cross Station, wondering why she hasn't thought of it before.

A distant version of Dvořák's New World Symphony plays as she waits on the line for assistance. She wonders why silence is so forbidden now and why it has taken three stages to reach someone to actually talk to. The symphony is interrupted by an operator who informs her that the train was on time.

'Are you sure?'

A tiny pause, in which hope leaps like a flame. 'Yes, I'm sure. Is there anything else I can do for you, madam?'

'No, nothing else, thank you.'

For some reason she imagines the train still waiting at King's Cross and, leaving the museum, she hails a cab outside. The interior upholstery has a faint singed-hair smell mixed with the sickly aroma of Kentucky Fried Chicken. The back of the seat sticks to her suit like Velcro. She tries not to think about her father, and instead looks out of the window at the snarl of red buses, taxis, motorcycles, bicycles, silver cars, push-chairs, skateboards and pedestrians that make up lunch-time London. The streets seem to be filled with people oblivious to danger. Mothers lean into the traffic while waiting to cross the road, skaters unflinchingly step into the paths of buses, cycle couriers weave in and out of cars, an old man pushes a supermarket trolley slowly up a hill, avoiding the pavement, his eyes white and blank.

Pushing through the knots of people gathered under the arrivals and departure boards at King's Cross, she almost expects to see her father waiting for her with an apologetic expression, some mix-up, so sorry: his scuffed leather travel bag on the ground next to him, looking punctured. Perhaps it will happen with him as it eventually happened to her mother, periods of forgetfulness, moments of disorientation, although for different reasons of course. Maybe it was inevitable. She glances at the passengers streaming down the platforms. Perhaps he had boarded the wrong train and was now in another part of the country trying to get through to her. She scans the crowds, her father's precise shape and bearing absolutely sharp in her mind. Her image of him is so utterly *real*, she cannot believe that he won't soon come walking towards her. After a while her face aches from looking. She begins to transpose her father's features on to any man of similar age or height, even walking towards one or two with a welcoming smile. Strangers start to look at her with puzzled expressions as she stares hard at every person, as if by merely looking forcefully enough she can extract what she needs to see.

The queue at the information desk stretches halfway across the station. She studies the shoulders of the man in front of her. His grey hair has been cut neatly and sits just above his collar, showing a pink line of skin and a single apricot-coloured mole. The station smells of bacon and coffee and urine. Piles of newspapers bound with twine are stacked in corners. A man selling the *Evening Standard* calls out to commuters, the falling cadence of his cry suddenly making her want to weep. The information line inches forward. Her knuckles ache with cold. She should go home. Her father might have caught a taxi. He could be waiting for her on the doorstep. But somehow she can't leave the line of people. There is a kind of comfort in waiting, a sort of basic human warmth. She won't go until she has spoken to someone face to face. She will know, then. She will *know*.

'I just want to check that the 9.35 arrived from Durham on time,' she tells the assistant, a young man with pale hands, white eyelashes and a name badge reading *Chris*.

He checks his computer and glances at her. 'It was on time.'

'My father was on the train and he didn't meet me when he was supposed to.'

'Perhaps he's gone somewhere else first? Shopping or something?' Chris looks over her shoulder at the next person in line.

'I don't think so, he wouldn't do that. He was coming to meet me. We had an arrangement to meet at the Natural History Museum.'

'Maybe he forgot? Have you checked the station?'

'I've been standing by the platform for an hour. If he was on the train, I would have seen him by now. I'm more than a little worried.'

Chris looks at her properly now. 'Would you tell me his name and I'll see if I can find out?'

Moments later she is offered a chair in a grey back room where irregularities are sorted out. She refuses to sit down. She looks at the faces of the two men, one craggy and deeply pitted, like a sharp piece of dumortierite, the other younger, smooth as opal. The older one tells her that he was the driver of the Durham train. He found her father still sitting in his seat after all the other passengers had left. At first he thought he was asleep and tried to wake him, but when he didn't come round he called an ambulance. He writes down the name of the hospital on a piece of paper and gives it to her. 'That's where they've taken him, love.'

She looks at the paper. The younger man offers her a cup of tea and she almost accepts, thinking how nice it would be to sit for a while in their overheated office and just absorb their concern. She thinks how odd it is that the most important times of one's life are so often shared with strangers. The station men offer to call her a cab. She thanks them and says she would prefer to walk.

The traffic parts for her as she crosses the road and into a flawless autumn afternoon. Amber shadows pool under the blue awnings of cafés, late sun glinting off the metal chairs arranged outside in ones and twos. She passes office furniture shops, windows stacked with black tubular arrangements, like oversized windpipes, and desks with their legs in the air. She walks up Gray's Inn Road, her feet shifting through ankle-deep pockets of drifted leaves. The inner city air has a rare clarity, a pure blueness that wraps itself over the skyline, making the buildings seem elegant. There are few people around and she feels as if the city has been opened just for her. It's almost as if she were being given a gift, a perfect afternoon and anyone looking at her might have thought that she was taking the long route back to her office, perhaps to clear her head after a pleasant lunch. She realizes that she has eaten nothing all day, but the idea of food is preposterous.

At the hospital she is taken into a yellow room and told that her father died of a heart attack on the train. She signs the death certificate after identifying his body. There's a moment when everyone withdraws and she sits with him for a while holding his cool hand, looking at the soft sunken veins under his skin, which has a blue whiteness and seems more naked than when he was alive. She brushes his eyebrows straight, but cannot look properly at his face because she keeps expecting him to speak. She looks instead at the sky through the sash window, which is open a fraction, a persistent breeze knocking the wood in its frame, vibrating the small clean ropes that sit there. She wonders why she isn't crying.

A nurse taps discreetly and then comes in with her father's things in a plastic bag. She holds the bag to her chest and does not look inside. The nurse smells of a young, fresh perfume. She tells Elise that there is something else that might belong to her father. It was found on the train. She'll just go and fetch it. 'Wait outside, if you'd prefer.'

Elise sits in the corridor, the Tesco bag between her feet. Yellow light spills across the floor, which is being slowly buffed by a man riding a polisher who waves as he passes like a prince on an elephant. She leans down and opens the bag. Her father's green diary rests on top of a pile of a carefully folded spare shirt, socks and underwear, still with their washing-powder sweetness. She pulls it out and turns to the current date. The day is a blank space. He hadn't even written in that he was coming to London. She flicks through the other pages. The day before he'd written: hair cut, 3 p.m. Turning back over the year, through October, September, August, July, June, May, April, March, February, January, she finds sprinkled notes, small shorthand reminders: teeth 1 p.m., lunch, LJR, eve drinks – Harry. Her name springs from a page in May, but nothing explains the entry and she cannot recall anything of significance. She cannot remember whether they even met in May. She puts the diary back into the bag. The other clothes folded less carefully at the bottom, she can't touch, certainly not his shoes, which feel heavy and cold, a thumbprint of scuffed leather sole visible through a tear in the plastic. Tying the handles of the plastic bag into a knot, she shoves it out of sight.

She looks up and down the corridor, which now gleams with polish, and sees a doctor come out of a room and wipe his face with a white towel. He goes over to a water dispenser and takes one of the small cone-shaped cups and fills it and drinks, the water glooping through the dispenser like a heart beating under water. He looks down the clean corridor for a moment before dropping his cup in the bin and going back to the room he came out of. Elise leans her head back against the wall. From under her seat comes the small ticking of her father's travel alarm clock.

She waits. There's a stack of magazines on a low table nearby, but it seems to her that blithely to read would be to commit an obscene act. She remembers her father saying that no one should ever do what he finds distasteful. He explained to her once that the Polynesian word *taboo* meant setting something apart from human contact. She had understood it years later when she began her training in biology and had to open the stomach of a rat. She had been forced then to overcome a deep-seated instinct not to harm the dead.

The young nurse returns, a serene look on her face, holding against her chest a large padded envelope. 'Here you are.' The nurse hands her the envelope which feels warm from her body.

'Thank you,' Elise says. Her head feels light, her eyesight blurred. The nurse asks if she needs anything. 'No, no, I'll be all right. Thank you – you've been very kind.' The words feel wrong, but she doesn't know what else to say. She picks up the bag and leaves the hospital.

She begins reading the manuscript on the train, hugging it close to her to stop the pages getting blown about. The train rattles, passing buildings of concrete and red brick, every one marked with the defiant alphabet of spray paint. She reads in short bursts, frequently putting the pages down in her lap to wipe her face. The window of the train reflects a younger version of herself, paler and less well-groomed.

She realizes as she turns the pages filled with descriptions of the first humans on earth how little she has understood of her father's life. How brilliant-hearted he was, how persevering. How lonely. His book took years of his life to complete, and now sitting with it on the train home, she feels a mixture of elation and the deepest sadness she has ever known. The image of a half-human creature in a cave nursing a weeping abscessed jaw, eyes dilated with pain becomes mingled in her mind with an image of a man wearing reading glasses slumped on a train 275,000 years later. Fields go by and houses, whole towns and landscapes. Places he travelled but never saw. People must have noticed him and assumed he was asleep. The manuscript had not been with his other things because it had been found under another seat where it had fallen, indicating that her father had been working on it at the moment he died. Someone, perhaps the train driver, had put the scattered pages in order again and bound the whole thing with a large elastic band. She reads the handwritten amendments and wonders whether these were his last words. *Early man identified his own welfare with that of others. Early man was ethical. Without honesty freedom is unsafe.* She stares out at the darkening city, and lets her imagination roam.

The dreams of the man in the cave featured great fire hunts where scores of antelope and elephant were driven into a circle of flames lit by the hunters. The animals were speared as they tried to escape from the smoke and heat; the wild chants and dances. Feasts and celebrations of hunts lasted days. Wherever there was food, people gathered. Food was the gift of life and it was shared. Food was also medicine. In his last days the creature in the cave had a helper, who came with roots, seeds and grubs. The helper stayed in the cave, squatting near the sick man, emitting occasional sounds so that the other would know he was not alone. The cave was hung with stalactites that dripped greasy water, each droplet falling with an echo that resounded around the slippery walls. A lion skull had been placed near the sick man as a symbol of strength along with a bundle of skin that had turned into gold ore. Squatting on the cold ground, the helper offered the creature sips of water, emitting grunts when the creature did not respond, sometimes putting a hand out to feel flesh in the dark beside him. As the slow poison from the abscess spread, the creature twitched into fever and infection, kicking and buckling his legs, screaming when the pain grew too much to bear. Then one night the fever cooled and the creature lay at peace, his fists relaxing for the first time in days, his jaw unclenched, and the helper slept the whole night through, dreaming of the great plains filled with rippling rivers of game. In the morning the helper came out into the sunlight where he stood for a moment with streaming eyes. After that he made his way back towards his tribe, passing antelope, feeding under the trees, who lifted their heads at his scent and scattered.

Dawn is breaking as Elise finishes her father's manuscript. Her legs have gone to sleep underneath her and she uncoils from the sofa, walks to the window and looks out across the city. A silver light rims the horizon and the sky is pinkish grey in between spiky trees that resemble upturned umbrellas with the covers ripped off. She looks across to a fire escape curving down from the block of flats opposite. There are terracotta pots on every one of the black iron steps and ivy has been trained to wind around the handrail. A watery light catches the windows. For years she's watched people moving in the flats, washing, cooking, hanging up clothes, and she has taken comfort from human proximity even though she's never known anyone by name. She always felt excluded from the neighbourhood, knowing that she never quite belonged. Now looking at the draped, anonymous windows, she feels a sense of gratitude. Clouds rimmed in pink start to drift across the sky. She remembers once flying through a cloud, holding her breath through the terrible muffled whiteness until she had come out the other side. Returning to the manuscript on the sofa, she gathers up the loose pages and slips the elastic band around it.

'My father's died.' There's no response at first and instantly she regrets calling.

'Oh, God, Elise.' His voice sounds young and drunk with sleep. 'I'm so sorry. Would you like me to come over?'

She considers the fact that he has to ask. 'No, I'm all right. I just wanted to tell someone close.'

'OK.' He pauses. She realizes that he doesn't understand. In his mind they aren't close. Of course not. They've only slept together once.

'Matthew, I'm sorry,' she says. 'Go back to sleep.'

He starts to say something, but she cuts him off.

Next she telephones the nursing home and endures a pause filled by Mozart. Her mother is having breakfast, the care nurse says, would she like to call back later? She asks the nurse to tell her mother that she will visit her that afternoon. 'I'm sorry,' the nurse says brightly. 'We are taking the girls shopping then.'

It takes her an hour to get through to Africa. The woman on duty at the plantation office doesn't know who Memory is, but says she will try to find Max and leave a message. It feels strange to say his name.

Leaving the flat, she walks down quiet early morning streets lined with glossy cars parked nose to nose on both sides of the road and enters the park. A few morning dog walkers with animals on extended leads stand about on the wet grass making eye contact not with each other but with rival pets. A couple of teenagers light a cigarette, cupping their hands around the lighter flame. An old drunk kicks at a beer can with his feet. The sky is filled with the cracking sound of jets, white trails marking perfect crosses into the blue, and she stands looking up at them, her throat exposed to the cold.

Walking across the grass to the ponds, she remembers how she used to take Memory to Parliament Hill. One of the first presents she bought her was a kite, shaped like a swallowtail butterfly with a long yellow tail.

The cold bites at her face as she walks across the park, the wet grass seeping into her shoes. A line from her father's manuscript comes into her mind. 'Without truth, nothing can live or breathe,' he had written. She thinks of how she had compromised Memory's freedom by not telling her the truth. Her legs feel heavy under her. She heads towards the hill, which looks fresh and green in the morning sun. Her father's story has set up a yearning in her, a need for bigger skies and space. She wants to see the whole of London spread out before her and think about her own crossroads. A little breathlessly she climbs the hill, her feet slipping on the grass, which stains her new shoes, but she doesn't even look down. Her hair blows back from her face and streaming eyes. Looking out across the city, she spreads her arms and lets the wind rock her.

18

STRAIGHT AND LEVEL FLYING

Final conclusion: Straight and level flying is the prevention of errors, so check tendencies before they grow by easy and gentle pressures on the controls and yet allow the aeroplane to fly itself as much as possible.

Zambia, 1996

Max stops the jeep at the airstrip. He points towards the slight rise of a hill shimmering in the afternoon heat. 'It's over there, right on top of the mound.' He juts his chin forward, lower lip trembling slightly. Memory follows his gaze. The hill is smaller than she imagined and more green.

'Are you coming with me?' She feels embarrassed to ask, but she doesn't know what he wants now that he has brought her here. She could help him climb the hill, standing by in case he fell. He has told her that he has never been to the top.

Max swallows. He stares into the blue distance. 'I'll wait for you here.' His shoulders heave slightly as he exhales a long, tight breath. She puts her hand on the door. 'Take your time,' Max adds. 'I'm not going anywhere.'

She climbs out of the jeep. The wind bounces off her face and ruffles her hair. She can sense him looking at her, hunched over the steering wheel, an unfathomable light in his blue eyes. Since the night of his confession a couple of weeks ago, being near him makes her ache. She feels as if she has both lost and gained something, but she isn't quite sure how it all fits together yet. She has an odd compulsion to be close to him, to feel what he is going through, to sit with him, so that she can absorb his thoughts and his memories.

Speaking his secret has weakened him, though. In the past few days he has not been eating or sleeping well and she feels partly responsible. He has been going to his farm every day, but in the evenings he has returned to be with her. Most nights they sit on the veranda and talk under the stars. There is still so much she would like to know, but she is learning to take things slowly. She understands that they both need time. So much has been stirred up they need to let everything settle down again.

Her thoughts about Elise are more complicated. She feels a sort of admiration for her and frustration, too, for not being brave enough to tell her the truth. She now sees why it was so difficult for her to be open about the past and she is trying not to blame her. Memory is trying to understand. When she looks at Max she feels close to the truth. Max now fills her heart. Just to see him sitting in his chair, his damaged body hanging heavy on him, like an old black leather harness, tells her everything she needs to know about forgiveness.

Memory walks across the runway. The hill swells gently against the sky, its slope the only curve in the rough, scrubby landscape. It looks like an old fort, stepped on its sides with tufts of wiry grass which act as footholds and handholds as she begins to climb.

At the top she stands and catches her breath for a moment. She looks down over the airstrip where she can see the blue and white wings of *Hotel Juliet*, her red landing light perched on her tail fin like a clown's nose. There is a slim dark figure near the plane and she wonders whether it is Kennedy, back from a flight to town. The thought comforts her as she begins her search, parting the thick, reedy grass until she finds what she is looking for.

The marker is small, no higher than her ankle, like a quiet war cross. She kneels down. The wood is unpainted and she can see tiny muted thumbprints in the grain, and the name bleached almost invisible. She puts her face close and squints at the letters. She can make out the P and part of the L, the G is intact and one stroke of the last N, but all the other letters have gone. One day the name will disappear completely. There will be nothing left to mark what happened except the memories of those involved and they will dissolve in time, too. But she is glad she has come. She sits for a while, watching the wind sift across the bare hill, the grasses moving like restless water in waves and eddies.

She stands up and brushes down her knees. Her movement disturbs something in the undergrowth and then she sees a young bushbuck skim over the tops of the grasses in a single graceful leap. The sight of the young, perfect animal with its glossy eyes, sharply defined ears and light fawn coat sits in her mind for a moment like a beautiful, luminous photograph. Turning her glance back to the cross, she sees that the grasses around it have already sprung back, hiding it, every seed head pointing immaculately in the same direction.

'Memory!' Her name comes sailing up, clean out of the sky. She starts to make her way back down the hill towards the runway. There are two figures down there and they are both looking up the hill towards her. A feeling comes over her in which she imagines the three of them united in some way. Perhaps they will continue what they have begun. Perhaps this is not the end, but the start of something.

She kneels in the grass right where she is and with her face lifted to the wind makes a promise to the man who died saving her that she will do everything she can to honour the name he gave her. She will make something of her life so that his life will not have been given in vain. She will try to be honest and she will try to be brave. She will try to become someone Paul Cougan would have been proud to know.

She opens her eyes. The wind sways the grasses, the sun is warm on her head, the sky rolls a soft blue around her and she feels that she has reached a point where she can, if not exactly rest, then at least continue without fear. Standing up, she wishes she had something to leave, but she has nothing; not a pen to write a note, not a single piece of jewellery or coin. Instead she takes a few stalks of grass, sprinkles the seeds over the ground and then watches them spiral up into the wind.

'*Memory!*' Kennedy's voice calls her from the airstrip.

'I'm here!' She waves down. Kennedy signals back, his arm dark against the shimmering sky. She knows he will be smiling, it's what the Africans do – they smile straight into your heart.

Later when they have returned to the farm Max gives her the key to his office. She makes the short walk alone across the gritty tracks between the coffee fields, now turning bronze under the falling sun. The air feels soft and musky on her bare arms. Birds flute in the twilight, and a few children come out of huts to watch her go past. An older boy, slingshot in hand, calls out and she smiles and greets him in his own language. He gives a little dance in reply. Something about him is familiar and she turns round and sees that it is Victor, the boy who was stung by bees, who is now grinning at her with a kind of wild brilliance.

She unlocks the office and, stepping carefully over the spot where Victor had twisted in pain, perches on the desk to make her telephone call. A heavy old typewriter rests near her hip on a shredded rubber pad. She rolls pieces of green rubber into small balls between her fingers as she waits to be connected. The line crackles and she imagines she can hear someone talking faintly in French. Eventually she is put through to London and hears the phone ringing, a twin-tone, duh, duh. Then a click and a voice she doesn't recognize. Memory asks for her own desk.

'I'm sorry, but she left some time ago.' The new receptionist sounds older than the usual husky-voiced candidates, even apologetic. 'Would you like to speak to her replacement?'

'I would, thanks.'

She waits. Her heart thumps. She feels an urge to disconnect, to leave things literally hanging in the air. It would be easier than having to explain. Then Adam comes on the line. 'Took your time, didn't you?' His voice sounds stretched. Behind it she can hear muffled traffic and the swooping sound of a siren.

She doesn't know how to respond. He cuts in again, his voice sharp. 'I suppose you're not coming back?'

She reminds herself to keep things light. 'There's nothing to come back for. You've got my job.' She reaches over and pushes down a key on the old typewriter – C – then another – O.

'I haven't got your fucking job. I'm just sitting at your desk, that's all.'

'I meant it as a joke.' She pushes down another key – U.

'Obviously you don't care.'

'Well, I do actually. Who has got my job?' The G is a little sticky and she has to press it twice.

A sigh. For a moment she thinks he's not going to respond, but then he fires back. 'Some American tart, used to work for AP. Look, what the fuck are you doing out there?'

'Thinking.' She's forgotten how aggressive swearing can be. She presses A.

'You sound a long way away.' His voice softens a notch. The siren noise winds up and then down and then fades mournfully. A new sound replaces it, the television giving out what must be the six o'clock news.

'I am.' She couldn't imagine being more remote. The feedbags on the floor, the smell of coffee beans, the yellow light glancing off the typewriter keys, the soaking silence. She feels wrapped inside another universe.

'What's it like out there?' Adam asks.

Quiet.' The N goes down, a tiny metal hammer.

Adam clears his throat. 'I have to know: have you met someone?'

She's about to say 'yes'; it would make things simpler, but somehow she wants to tell him the truth. 'No, it's kind of bigger than that.'

He laughs hollowly. 'Don't tell me you've discovered who you are. I think I might be sick. Hold on, I'm sure I put a brown paper bag in the drawer especially for this phone call.'

'Why do you have to scorn everything, Adam?'

'Here we go, we've only been on the phone for five minutes, I have to say, *for the first time in three months*, and already we're arguing.'

'We're not arguing; well, I'm not. I suppose I'm just trying to tell you that I'm happy.'

'Huh!'

'No, listen. Mock if you like, but I'm feeling for the first time that I'm who I'm supposed to be. I'm not anyone else's version of me. I'm not what someone else wants me to be.'

'Thanks,' says Adam bitterly. 'For reminding me. You'll never forgive me for that night, will you?'

'You're not listening. You relate everything to yourself. You never really loved me. You loved an ideal, something you created for yourself. It was never about me. It was all about you and what you wanted.'

'Have your say if it makes you feel better.'

'I'm trying to be honest.'

'It sounds to me as if you're trying to tell me I was a crap boyfriend.'

'Adam—'

'Look, Memory, if you wanted me to fuck off, you could have told me years ago. You were the one who hung on. You were the one who couldn't make up her mind. We were together five years. *Five fucking years . . .*'

'You make it sound like a sentence.'

'The thing is, Memory, I waited for you. All those years I waited for you to make up your mind about us. The truth is, when it came to the crunch, you just weren't brave enough. You just didn't have the guts to go the distance, so you bailed out. Ran away to Africa. What a joke. What a complete and utter fool you've made out of me.'

'There were things I had to find out.'

'And now you have, but you're not exactly coming home, asking me to forgive you and take you back, are you?'

'Is that what you expected?'

'I don't know any more. I don't know anything.' His voice sounds full. She imagines people looking at him as they clear their desks and fetch coats. Some will be standing under the TV pretending not to listen.

'Adam, I'm sorry,' she says. 'I'm not sorry for what I did, but I'm sorry for the way you feel.'

But he has gone. Slowly she replaces the receiver back in its cradle and sits for a moment in silence, looking at the dust rising in the light. That's it, she thinks. *That's it.* She slips off the desk and stands at the window. The coffee fields stretch to the horizon, milky with starry blooms. She remembers Max telling her that the blossom lasted only a couple of days, just long enough to be pollinated. She glances around the office and sees her name traced faintly on the typewriter roll. The desk is clean where she disturbed the dust. For some reason she picks up the receiver again and listens to it purr. Then she lets it drop and steps out into an early evening, palely scented with coffee blooms, tiny and vanishingly sweet.

London, January 1997

At Heathrow Elise steps from her taxi on to hard frozen tarmac and almost loses her footing on a patch of black ice. The lights of the cars are dirty yellow diagonals swinging through the freezing fog and the air has a clammy chill that tightens her chest and oddly makes her sweat. The taxi driver steadies her elbow. 'Careful, madam,' and then lifts her suitcase on to a trolley. She pays him, adding a generous tip into his outstretched palm, which has the slightly oily texture of chocolate marzipan. He lowers his eyes and wishes her 'Happy New Year.'

On the way to the airport he had told her that he was a Muslim and didn't celebrate Christmas. On Christmas Day he had worked then gone to the mosque to pray. His prayer beads dangled from the rear-view mirror, tiny pearls with an iridescent rainbow sheen. When he turned on the radio the sobbing voice of an Arabic singer had filled the cab. Elise had looked out on the roofs of Hounslow, some encrusted with lights and plastic reindeer, steeped in a fresh dusting of unexpected snow, and felt grateful that he had asked her no questions about her own Christmas.

Now she glances at his bright black eyes beaming at her from under a coarse wool skull cap and nods. 'Yes, Happy New Year to you, too.' Then, watching out for further patches of ice, pushes her trolley towards departures.

The airport is bursting with heat. Every few minutes, messages ring around the hall, announcing delays to flights and desk numbers to contact for further information. Many planes have been grounded due to the freezing conditions and hotel arrangements are being made for passengers. She wonders whether she will be able to leave. Somehow she can't imagine returning to her flat with its empty fridge and naked shelves; its stripped, cold rooms. She heads for a café and buys a latte, sitting at a metal table, warming her hands around the tall glass. A group of Pakistani youths in white chemises and silver gel trainers lounge on the table opposite, not talking, ears plugged into rhythms only they can hear. On the next table a mother sits with three children and a hectic pile of presents unravelling under cheap wrapping paper. The children whine and scrabble at the boxes with their sticky fingers and the mother plies them with glasses of Coke. 'Stop it, Nathan,' she keeps saying in a tired voice. 'Leave them alone.' On another table a man in his fifties with swept-back grey hair catches her eye and smiles minutely.

She listens to the messages. Most of the planes to Europe are being postponed for the night and all connecting flights to Edinburgh, Glasgow and Aberdeen have been cancelled. The radio news said that the snowfall in Scotland was the heaviest in twenty-five years, with some towns cut off by drifts the height of London double-deckers. She imagines the loch, the deep black loch where she swam twenty-five years ago, frozen to its core.

To take her mind off the delays, she pulls a novel from her bag: *Listing*, by a young American writer she has never heard of. Recommended by one of her work colleagues who said it was about a family whose lives were bent all out of shape. She wonders whether there is any family that is truly coherent, any group of people or organization that does not have its buckles, warps or contortions. Perhaps all families need to make their own shape, find their own pattern. She thinks how easy it is to become exhausted by the wrong kind of living. Unable to concentrate, she puts the novel face down on the table.

The man opposite is staring at her. There's something vaguely familiar about his hands, which toy with a pair of gold-rimmed reading glasses. She looks away. He gets up and walks over to her table and then she recognizes him.

'Richard.' She offers him her hand. He takes it and looks embarrassed.

'I knew it was you, but I'm afraid I've forgotten your name. I'm sorry.'

'It's Elise.' She fiddles with the spoon in her latte glass.

'Elise,' he repeats. 'Of course.'

He is immaculately dressed in a dark grey suit, but appears to have lost weight and the melancholy she first sensed around him has deepened and darkened. 'Sorry,' he says again. 'I can never remember names; it's an unforgivable habit.'

'Still mending broken hearts?'

Richard sniffs, but she can tell he's pleased that she's remembered. 'I'm on my way to a medical conference in Chicago,' he says. 'How about you, work or pleasure?'

'Both.' She hesitates. 'I'm flying to the Copperbelt to see my daughter and then I'm meeting malaria workers in Lusaka.'

Richard nods. His eyes are greeny grey, the colour of the English sea. Inexplicably, Elise feels a stab of love for the cold, awkward country she's about to leave.

Richard hands her a white business card. 'Good luck,' he says. 'Maybe, we could have lunch or something when you're back?'

'Maybe.' She offers her hand. 'Have a good trip to Chicago.'

He takes her hand and holds it for a second longer than is comfortable. 'I'll try.' Then he says her name: '*Elise*,' lingering over the consonants. 'You look wonderful, it is good to see you again.'

As she walks towards departures an intriguing feeling comes over her as if someone has just asked her a difficult question to which she knows the answer but can't quite put into words.

She zips her bag and drops it on to the metal rungs of the X-ray machine. A woman security officer calls out to passengers: 'Anyone got anything sharp? All sharp metal objects here, please.' Elise steps through the grey arch, on the side of which is a plastic bowl filled with keys, cigarette lighters, jewellery, watches and mobile phones. She unclasps her watch and puts it in the bowl with the rest. This divesting of the body of adornment and icons she thinks is almost ritualistic, a form of cleansing in preparation for a journey to another realm, another space and time. The passengers collect their X-rayed bags with a passive, good-natured humour and she moves on behind them to passport control where an African man glances at her boarding card, nods, and tells her, 'Gate 21, and it's on time.'

Settling in the business-class cabin of South African Airways, she pulls her pashmina around her shoulders and puts her head back in her seat. The captain announces they are stuck in a traffic jam and waiting for clearance, his voice flat, a little bored. The passengers lean against their headrests, each one enrobed with an immaculate white bib, and talk softly. She looks out of the window at the activity on the runway. The plane next door has just landed and she watches as workers check underneath the aircraft with torches. A pocket at the side of the grey landing corridor unfolds like a Japanese fan. Moments later a catering container rises on a hydraulic lift up to the other side of the nose. She observes how smooth the process is, how each small action glides noiselessly on to the next. She watches the outgoing crew and the incoming crew meet in the temporary connecting corridor and exchange a few words. Some touch hands and kiss. The two crews separate and the incoming party boards, the captain last, carrying a narrow black case. He hovers on the step for a moment, his attention caught by something, his face lit by the flashing orange lamp spinning on top of the catering truck. The truck leaves and the captain solemnly dips his head inside the aircraft.

Her plane begins to stir. She looks out of the little arched window at a rising pink dawn, the sky limpid and clear. The Boeing glides serenely down the runway, fuselage sparkling with frost, easing noiselessly past other aircraft beached together, tail fins jubilant with bright markings: a red maple leaf, a white kangaroo, a gold moon. How impossible it is to imagine a world without such exquisite engineering, she thinks. She remembers someone saying, perhaps her father, perhaps another professor, that flight is human transcendence, the moment when man flings himself from his own confined space, when he truly lets himself go.

The jet gathers speed down the runway, roughly, almost sexually. There's a soft tone, like someone striking a triangle, and then they are airborne, sliding up in a smooth perpendicular, beams of light bouncing off the icy wings. They climb over London. Everything down below is frozen, even parts of the Thames, the first time in years. There are people skating near the banks, children with home-made sledges, dogs chasing snowballs, small melting fires. The plane groans as it turns, stretching its fabric, flexing its deep muscle. Elise looks at the screws and rivets glittering on the wing and the enigmatic message there: No Step.

The plane levels out and climbs over suburbs laid like little lead fortifications on a white sheet. The suburbs give way to fields lined with poplar trees, casting shadows of folded summer parasols against the white powder snow. The sky slips over the iced fields in liquid bands of blue, violet and lavender. They climb higher, straight lines dissolving into curves as the irregular stitched pattern of fields slopes down to the sea and slips off the edge of the land. A pale blue mist blows across a layer of cloud and turns Britain into a floating island.

Now, for the first time in her life, Elise has no plan, no carefully worked-out agenda, no project to cling to, no timetable apart from her one meeting in Lusaka, and it is terrifying, like going into free-fall. It is also exciting; part of her leaps at the thought of seeing Africa again – of seeing Max.

One of the paradoxical things about getting older is that she had somehow expected to become stronger, but the more she discovers about life, the less certain she is of anything. She has more questions to ask herself now, more puzzles to work out, and of course more storms to weather.

The first letter had arrived almost a month ago now. Elise knew it by heart even though it pierced her right to the very centre of her being when she recalled it. Memory was angry and hurt. Mostly she wanted to know why it had been so difficult for Elise to be honest. Why hadn't she told the truth? The plane glides across a silent frozen Europe, and Elise pulls her shawl tightly around her shoulders. She understands how her lack of courage had betrayed Memory. What Elise had thought of as 'protection' was simply an excuse. How much easier it had been to lie than admit being weak. How much easier to cover up than admit mistakes. Memory's letter showed her this painfully. Elise had thought of ways to reply, even started one or two explanations, but in the end she knew that the most honest thing she could do was to go to Africa and face the truth.

She knows it will not be easy. There is so much she will have to confront. Since the letter, buried images from the past have been rising up in shocking detail. One image in particular haunts her: Paul crossing the grass in dark clothes, his head and face almost invisible except for a white streak on the back of his neck. Standing by the screen door, she watches him go. She has a sheet pulled up to her chest, and her feet are cold on the stone floor. She wants to call out to him, but lacks the courage to do it. She watches him run across the lawn and disappear into the bush. Then she goes back to bed. Sleep is impossible. She lies and thinks of Max, his smell, the feel of his hands, the heat of him. Through a gap in the curtain she can see the moon like a racing heartbeat in the bent trees over the house.

'Are you all right?' a hostess asks. 'Can I get you something?'

'Just some water, thanks.'

A mountain range appears below the clouds, piebald peaks overlapping in cones of light and dark, valleys of snow shining pure and unspoiled. The hostess returns with a small beaker of water. Elise takes a sip and dabs at her eyes with a tissue. 'Thank you,' she says to the hostess who smiles in sympathy.

'Have you left someone behind?' the hostess asks, eyeing the wedding ring on Elise's finger.

Elise nods silently.

The hostess takes the cup from her. 'Can I get you anything else?' She has an open face with wide-set hazelnut eyes.

'No, I'll be fine.' Elise turns towards the window.

'Try to get some sleep,' the hostess says, in her softly clipped South African accent. 'It will help you feel better.' With one last look, she moves off down the aisle.

Elise leans her head against the porthole window and lets her eyes rest in the redeeming sky. Her thoughts drift to the other letter in her bag, this one from an academic publisher inviting her to make an appointment to discuss her father's book. She had found the envelope on the mat yesterday evening and had read the letter in the hall, her briefcase on the floor, the door still open, cold air breezing about her ankles. It was short, to the point: 'We believe this could be an important work, do make an appointment to discuss this further.' She had wanted to call the publisher, but it had been too late, and she had to leave at four o'clock the next morning to catch her flight to Johannesburg and then Lusaka. She had thought it was a bad omen, the letter arriving just when she was unable to respond, but now thinking about it, there is no reason why she can't write to them from Africa. She finds a blank page in her diary and writes the single word: *Crossroads*.

Max leans forward from the back of the plane, so close Memory can smell the coffee on his breath. 'One more circuit and then we need to come down,' he tells Kennedy, his voice shaky.

Kennedy eases the plane into a bank and then prepares for landing, his knuckles solid on the steering column, shoulders braced. He seems pleased at something today, some joy he can barely keep to himself. His narrow face brims with it and his fingers dance on the dashboard. Memory thinks about her request to Elise to bring extra packages of anti-malarial drugs. The latest attack has left Kennedy thinner than ever and she worries that he may not be able to survive another. Just thinking about it makes her throat swell and she looks out of the window at the brown grasses rippling in the breeze. Kennedy glances at her: 'Why don't you bring her down?'

'You're not suggesting I land?' she asks.

'Why not?' Kennedy smirks. 'You said you wanted to learn.'

'But *now*? Surely it's not the right time?'

Max grunts from the back. 'Go on, if we're all going to die, it might as well be here.'

'Charming,' she says, taking hold of the controls. The plane tugs under her hands. Down below she can see cars and houses buried under a carpet of red dust and the line of the Great North Road pushing across the country like a twisting, red river. She feels something in her stretch as she flies the plane towards a wide slab of dark tarmac, like a four-lane motorway. Kennedy takes the second column and together they bring the plane down lower, engine thrumming, wheels delicately reaching for the ground.

Heat shimmers in oily wreaths around berthed planes the size of dinosaurs. 'I did it.' She feels dazed.

'Not bad for someone who swore they hated flying,' Max says as they climb out into a heat so dazzling and filled with fumes it makes their eyeballs burn. He gestures to a bank of small planes. 'We need to push her over there.'

'Wait a second.' Kennedy scurries back up to the cockpit and comes down with an old black book. He hands it to her and tells her to record her first flight. She turns over the dry pages aware that Max is watching her. She reads the descriptions: *Night flight to Broken Hill, 14 July 1972; Landless Corner, morning 16 July; Kitwe, afternoon 18 July; Kafue River, morning 20 July; Broken Hill, afternoon 22 July 1972.* The entries are neatly recorded in blue ink, records of short flights, some no longer than twenty minutes; Elise's handwriting rounder and looser than the precise version Memory had grown up with. She reads every entry, every small detail, every date and time and sees how little it adds up to, a few hours, not even a whole day if all the hours are placed together end to end, but still time enough to change the direction of a life; still time enough to set in motion a series of small shifts that end with a man lying face down under a tree with a little girl standing over him watching the blood stain into his sweatshirt. The last entry in the log book reads: *Broken Hill, day 5 August 1972,* and is in a writing she doesn't recognize, but assumes belongs to Max. He exhales and shifts his balance on his crutches. Memory writes her name underneath the last entry, and then the date. Planes tremble overhead, new jet streams scribbling out old ones. Max watches her close the book. He nods at her slightly and then turns towards the runway where a South African Airways Boeing 747 is just coming in to land.

Shielding their eyes against the glare, they watch the Boeing shimmer down the runway in waves of rippling heat. The nose, white as a swan's neck, glides purposefully towards them. The air is loaded with the soft afterglow of flight, the sense of something fragile come safely to berth. For a moment they look at each other, and then with Max leading the way on his crutches, they walk towards the plane where a slim blonde woman waits at the top of the steps, one hand lightly holding the safety rail.

ACKNOWLEDGEMENTS

Thank you to Michael Huntingford for starting me off on this journey in the first place. This novel could not have existed without his huge generosity and enlightened decision to leave London for a remote coffee plantation in Zambia. In Africa, I was generously looked after by Kathy and Patrick Tobin on so many occasions and I will never forget the evenings spent with Denis and Toni in their house at Munkumpo overlooking the lake. There were many others who helped me feel welcome and who told the most wonderful stories, some of which found their way into this book. Thanks are due to flying instructor Geoff Robinson, who couldn't have known what he had begun when he calmly suggested I flew *Hotel Juliet*. *The Complete Flying Course* by N. Roy Harben, published by C. Arthur Pearson (London, 1939), helped fill in all the gaps later. This illuminating gem is now the single book I would save if my house were burning down. I am also grateful to Robert Kruszynski at the Natural History Museum for taking Broken Hill Man from his box and allowing me to touch the skull of one of the oldest humans ever found. The notes he sent later were invaluable. Much light was shed on the subject of malaria thanks to Ellen Ruppel Shell's lengthy article in the August 1997 issue of *Atlantic Monthly*. I also made use of a 1958 edition of *Teach Yourself Astronomy* by David S. Evans published by the English Universities Press. Warmest thanks to Sam Boyce for her unfailing enthusiasm for this project, my wonderful agent Maggie McKernan and my wise editor Kate Parkin at John Murray whose many suggestions have helped to make this a better book. I am also grateful to Roy Pike,

Headmaster at Torquay Boys' Grammar School, for his support and generosity in allowing me time to work on revisions; Joan Veale for her unwavering encouragement; and Betty Richards, Lisa Morath and Adam Krasnopolski for stepping in when I needed it most.